ALSO BY BING WEST

The Village

Naval Forces and Western Security: Sea Plan 2000 *(Editor)*

Small Unit Action in Vietnam

THE PEPPERDOGS

A NOVEL

BING WEST

SIMON & SCHUSTER

New York   London   Toronto   Sydney   Singapore

SIMON & SCHUSTER
Rockefeller Center
1230 Avenue of the Americas
New York, NY 10020

SIMON & SCHUSTER and colophon are registered trademarks
of Simon & Schuster, Inc.

For information regarding special discounts for bulk purchases,
please contact Simon & Schuster Special Sales at
1-800-456-6798 or business@simonandschuster.com

Manufactured in the United States of America

1   3   5   7   9   10   8   6   4   2

Library of Congress Cataloging-in-Publication Data
West, Francis J.
The pepperdogs : a novel / Bing West.
p.   cm.
1. Marines—Fiction.   I. Title.
PS3623.E844 P4 2003
813'.6—dc21   2002040860

ISBN 0-7432-3589-4

TO GABRIELE

Whose courage while dying set the bar for any Marine,
And whose steadfast love was a precious gift.

ACKNOWLEDGMENTS

This is a work of fiction. The composition of some military units was changed, as were some geographic locations. The characters are not real persons, with one exception—and I sense I have her approval.

Drafts of the novel were critiqued by battlefield commanders and by senior policymakers. They provided the blend between the individual soldier under pressure and the statesman concerned with the larger consequences.

Concerning the Joint Task Force under naval command, I thank Admiral James Hogg, USN (ret.), for his comments. I am indebted to MajGen Ray Smith, USMC (ret.), and MajGen OK Steele, USMC (ret.), for reviewing the combat tactics. MajGen Don Gardner, USMC (ret.), and Capt. Owen West, USMC(R), provided a check on the sniper, recon and long-range patrolling. LtGen Mick Trainor, USMC (ret.), gave input on geopolitical themes and special operations. Col. Tony Wood, USMC (ret.), and Col. Jim Lasswell, USMC (ret.), made suggestions about emerging infantry technologies. Dr. Peter Saur, M.D., commented on the medical aspects.

I especially thank former Defense Secretaries James Schlesinger and Frank Carlucci for suggesting changes at the White House level.

Anne Joslin, William Turcotte, Arthur Murphy, Yusha Auchincloss, Fr. Tom West, OFM, Patrick West, Chris O'Connell, Katherine Seitz,

Orest Zaklynsky, Joyce Stabile and Colleen Smith provided valued advice in the development of the characters.

Kaki and Alexandra West graciously provided their photos for the KosoFinest website.

I thank Marysue Rucci for being an editor who can identify main themes and who supports the author while he is writing.

Finally, Dan Mandel is all an agent can and should be. He goes far beyond where his duties take him.

THE PEPPERDOGS

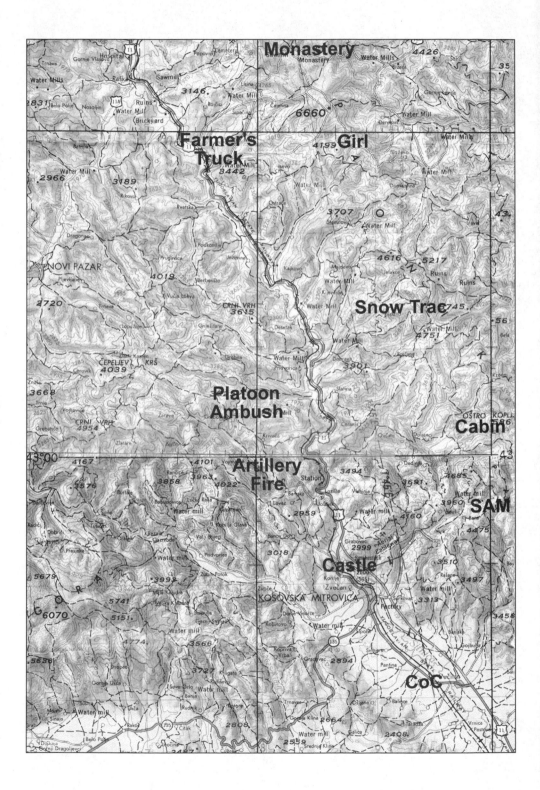

If one falls down, the others will lift him up.
—ECCLESIASTES 4:10

To the half-drunken Serb soldiers in the tan Toyota pickup, the farm looked inviting. Its orange slate roof, untouched by mortar blasts, glistened in the thin sunlight. No shells had burst against its whitewashed walls, and most windowpanes were intact, the few broken ones sealed neatly with white tape. A stocky woman in a blue mantilla was draping bright quilts over a rope strung to a nearby tree, taking advantage of the fickle winter sun to air out some bedding. The rich farm was war's joke, like a tornado that spares a single trailer home.

Holding their rifles carelessly, four soldiers hopped from the pickup, laughing back and forth like teenagers going to a party. Their leader had a full black beard and wore a shaggy black bear-fur coat with torn, floppy sleeves. His girth was so wide it looked like the bear was still inside. He didn't try the handle on the front door. Instead he raised back his foot and kicked, splintering the frame. Unhurried, he plodded up the stairs, trailed by his men.

The woman had scurried inside when the Toyota veered off the main road, but she found no place to hide. When they finished with her, she lurched out the kitchen door, stumbling through the mud toward the privy a stone's throw to the southeast, where the wind seldom blew the stench toward the house. Her skull had fractured at its base when they slammed her on the boards and threw her skirt over her head. The blood streaming from her nostrils was vivid red, and darker rivulets seeped from her ears. She lurched dizzily, everything whirling around and around her. Then she vomited and crumpled gracefully, settling down, folding her arms and hugging herself, as if she were very cold.

The soldiers paid no heed to the dying woman. They had wiped themselves, passing around a grayish towel, stiff as cardboard. Now they were wrestling onto the back of the pickup a Blutner piano with two broken ivories and several snapped strings. The woman knew several melodies that avoided the broken keys, including a little Liszt, but the men hadn't asked her to play.

Sergeant Saco Iliac, head bodyguard to the commanding general of the Tigriva division, picked up one end of the piano, smirking as his men struggled with the other end. He was thinking how he would arrive before the general's luncheon. The general would set the piano in the middle of the great room and pound Saco on the back of his thick fur coat.

Sometimes Saco intentionally lumbered like a bear to remind his men how he had won the coat. After they took Srebrenica, they had disposed of most of the vrags the first night, and blood caked their uniforms. No longer stupefied by drink, their heads splitting, the soldiers were anxious to get back home and wash up. There were fewer than a hundred to finish, but no one wanted to head back inside.

That was when the adjutant thought of the contest. Three officers held watches, and five finalists entered the barn where the last Muslims milled around like cattle. A Croat who had been a wrestler before the war did two more males than Saco. But so what? The small ones Saco went after wriggled like eels. His trick was to grab the ankles and swing their heads against the roof poles. Whack! and it was done. One girl bit his thumb, costing him several seconds. Still, the Croat did fifteen, while he, Saco, snapped eighteen necks to win the coat.

Saco sat next to the driver in the Toyota. The legs of the piano hung over the sides, and the soldiers sat at odd angles, their rifles swinging wildly as the pickup bounced down the hill toward the paved road at the far end of the pasture. The tarp thrown over the piano flapped and billowed, as though waving at the American Cobra gunships buzzing over the main road.

The Toyota was the muscle kind advertised in glossy car magazines, with high axles and four rear wheels, ideal for heavy farmwork or driving around a small town with the radio blasting. The left front tire soon caught in a pothole. They were five minutes in front of the general's convoy; it wouldn't do to arrive late at the castle. Four sets of shoulders set to rocking the overloaded pickup back and forth to push it loose.

Captain Tyler Cosgrove, U.S. Marine Corps Reserve—very reserved, he would say, laughing—handled the motorcycle with easy skill. It was his turn to be scout, and Sergeant Neff and the two corporals a quarter mile behind in the humvee would have to wait their turn. This was the first morning in a week without rain or sleet, but *Hey! I didn't make out the duty roster.* Cosgrove had the medium build and sharply handsome, slightly vulnerable face seen in advertisements for Prada and other upscale stores. Upbeat by nature, he felt his spirits lift to be on a fast bike on a Sunday morning. He tried not to think of his mother in the hospital. He would see her soon enough, his tour eight hours from ending. He would be at the airport by five. He swung the bike in short half-loops, enjoying the pull of gravity as his body leaned first one way and then the other. One final hour of playing Marine before coming to grips with his mother's mortality.

He had studied the overhead photos, the radio intercepts, the reports from locals. The route was secure. This close to Christmas, Cosgrove considered Fifth Avenue more dangerous. Wall Street commandos, flush with bonus money and guilt about missing their kids' soccer matches, would trample you on their way to FAO Schwarz. Here in Kosovo, NATO soldiers had pulled guard duty year after year. Nothing ever happened. That was why reserve units like Cosgrove's were sent over for three-month stints. The shooting war was in Afghanistan. Nobody worried about the reserves in the Balkans, an afterthought among the Pentagon planners.

So what if the confab with the Serb general was overprotected? For Cosgrove, riding a motorcycle was better than sitting around waiting for the evening flight to the States. This was the last U.S. sweep, and he was nearing his turnaround point, with the Serb convoy only a few miles to the north.

He glanced casually at the farm to his left. Smoke from a farm . . . that Toyota? "Arrow Five, this is Six," he said into the mike projecting from his helmet. "I have eyes on one pickup with a piano in back. It's Tesh on tour, the cows twitching their tails to the beat."

"Six, this is Five. Can you get us tickets?"

"SRO. First pasture around the bend. I'll save you a space near the stage."

"Roger. Three mikes behind you."

The bike was fast. One moment an open road. And now the bike was coming right at the Serbs in the truck. They barely had time to grab their weapons before the American stopped in front of them. He pushed back his goggles and said, "Arrow, this is definitely weird."

"Hey!" Saco smiled. "Is nothing. We help move."

Cosgrove was sitting back, his hands on the bike's crossbars, the 9mm pistol secured in his shoulder holster. Saco moved closer, eyes on the pistol. Cosgrove looked past him at the house, his gaze wandering until it came to rest on the fallen woman. He stiffened abruptly and reached for the pistol.

Saco didn't think. He rushed forward and knocked Cosgrove from the bike. He hit him once and then again, in the neck, on the side of the helmet, on the cheek. The great blows stunned Cosgrove, and he offered no resistance. Saco lifted the Marine's head, helmet and all, and slammed him against the ground. Cosgrove saw dazzling light, then black.

"Quick!" yelled Saco. "Throw him in back. And the bike. Move!"

The Marine hummer had started into the turn and taken the first path, twisting and bouncing toward the farm two pastures above. It took several minutes to reach the front step, where a farmer and his wife and a few children greeted them curiously. It was a few more minutes before Sergeant Neff realized he had turned off at the wrong farm. With slightly growing anxiety, he turned the vehicle around, bounced and lurched back to the highway and looked for the next cutoff. He soon found it and once again bobbed across rocks worn smooth by decades of wagon wheels.

When the hummer came around the curved face of the next tilled field, Neff saw the piano tilted forward in the rutted track, kneeling in cow dung as though awaiting execution, its keyboard legs broken and splintered. Another two minutes passed before the frustrated sergeant could bring himself to report that Captain Cosgrove was missing—plain missing, nowhere to be seen, no bike either, and farther upslope there was a dead woman and a farm on fire.

By then Saco's pickup was two kilometers south down the main road, with the Serb convoy coming into sight behind it.

Mitrovica Valley, Kosovo

Serbian Lieutenant General Ilian Kostica gave no particular heed to the tan Toyota pickup as it recklessly cut in front of his lead escort vehicle. That was Saco, showing off. Childish. The general's mind was on the meeting ahead, determined to impress the American, who also played childish games like arriving early for negotiations. *Only today, Mr. Ambassador,* Kostica thought, *I am the early one.*

The small castle was the town's strong sentinel, blocking entrance to the valley from the north. For centuries it had shielded the farmers from whatever raiding bands made their way south along the only road, which twisted for dozens of kilometers among the hillocks, narrow ravines and steep slopes of the mountain ranges on either side. Built in the seventeenth century, the castle was part fortress, part manor. Typical of the old Middle Europe style, it closely abutted the road, its massive stone facade indifferent to the occasional sideswipes of drunken farmers' tractors.

Tanks were another matter. When Kostica's armor—Soviet junk from World War II, shoddily reconditioned in the factory that manufactured the tinny Yugo auto—first clattered toward the town, the castle looked like a massive bunker, its minarets and cut-glass windows only minimally softening the thickness of stone walls that had withstood a half-dozen sieges over the last six hundred years. Kostica considered smashing it. Why take a chance?

The trembling proprietor persuaded him otherwise, running into the road in his hostler clothes, aware the tanks were taking aim, shaking but determined, offering the general an aperitif, a *petit déjeuner* for his staff. The meal was excellent, and Kostica had returned often. A good location for negotiations too, right in the middle of the neutral zone between Kosovo and Serbia.

When Kostica pulled up now, the security details of the two sides had already dismounted, the Americans robotlike in their oversize armored vests and helmets. He had told his guards to wear three sweaters under their jackets and not to shave for four days, so they, too, looked bulky and menacing. Saco had parked the Toyota around a corner. The other body-guards grinned and nodded to him, then stepped aside to let him approach the general.

"I had a piano for you," Saco said, "only an American came along, so I took him instead."

It had to be a stupid joke. The general heard the words, and his body reacted before his brain. For a moment he knew he was suffering a stroke. His heart stopped for a beat. He could feel his blood pressure drop to his toes, as if falling suddenly in an elevator. He said nothing, aware of those around him.

Images were clear in his mind—a cannibal offering to share his meal, a dog mouthing a putrid fox and expecting to be patted. And this, this dancing bear shitting in the village square and expecting a pail of berries. General Kostica was half convinced that Saco would raise his paws in the air and pant with his tongue hanging out, waiting to be scratched on his swollen stomach.

"Where is this American?"

"Right here." Saco grinned. "In the back of the Toyota. He's out. I hit him good."

Good? Good? The general pictured American helicopters taking off, tanks blocking road crossings, satellite cameras zooming in—all because of this *glummats,* this idiot.

"Get him out of here. Now. He's not to know you're part of this command. Get across the border and release him. Go away. Get out." The general turned away. He had weathered the Tito years, outlasted that lunatic Milosevic, outfoxed the Americans at Dayton. He was the first of his family to have a villa along the Amalfi, an apartment in Prague. He wasn't going to be brought down by this brute's stupidity. Was he responsible for the angry bull or for the weather in December? This wasn't his business.

The Watergate Condominiums, Washington, D.C.   Early Sunday morning

The secure phone to the White House rang with a discreet purr, a courtesy to the spouses of high-level officials who relished being summoned at any hour. Political power was more a narcotic than an aphrodisiac. The White House Chief of Staff, a large, balding man, glanced at the Caller ID and lifted the receiver while his wife fluffed her pillow and went back to sleep.

"Plane crash or terrorists?" He prided himself on his crisp manner, his voice abrupt even this early.

"Good morning to you, too," the Secretary of Defense said. "Don't be so grumpy."

"Okay, so how many did we lose?"

"Less serious. A Marine missing in Kosovo. May be kidnapped."

"We still have people there? And that's it—one missing?"

"Want me to add Armageddon?" the Secretary of Defense said. "I'm called when this stuff happens, and I call the White House. Now that you're awake, you can go to church. My good deed, like spotting you a couple of points."

"Don't let one lucky squash game go to your head," the Chief of Staff said. "Okay, at least it's not something with a press angle. I'll tell the President after he's up. When he was governor, I didn't wake him every time a cop had a bad day, and I'm not going to start unloading small stuff now. What's the next step?"

"We're searching. We don't know who has him."

"Damn, this is bad timing. We have to keep the decks clear for the health bill."

"Right, it's an HMO plot to shift votes," the SecDef said.

"All I'm saying is we have to stick to our game plan. It took a year to get back on track after the Twin Towers," the Chief of Staff said. "Every military incident can't end up at the Oval Office. We've agreed the domestic agenda is the focus for the next Congress. You'll keep this across the river?"

"It'll be managed from Brussels or Kosovo."

"Good. The farther away, the better. It's a distraction," the Chief of Staff said, "and we can't do anything to help from here."

25th Marine Regiment, Mitrovica Valley   **Noon Sunday**

The security patrols for the meeting were to the north, inside the two-kilometer red zone marking the Kosovo-Serb border. To the south the highway followed the river toward the open valley and the railhead at Pristina. There was a downward pitch to the road, as it paralleled the river rushing through ravines and gullies carved out of the limestone hills by centuries of spring snow thaws and heavy fall rains. Returning to the brigade compound, the road was deceptively steep, and most trucks shifted into a lower gear. So did the three Marines running uphill with rifles slung over their right shoulders. They ran along the shoulder of the road, taking short, choppy strides, faces down, concentrating on a steady, grinding pace, no wasted motion, their boots barely clearing the surface of the thin snow.

They wore soft covers, not the German-style helmets the U.S. adapted years ago, and none had on the flak jackets required of all U.S. troops outside base. The three ran as if connected by a giant elastic band, sometimes stretching apart, then snapping back into a tight triangle. On his back each wore a rucksack and a canvas water sack with a long straw-like tube. They were running, not jogging, up the grade, the strain showing on their faces and in their quick stutter-steps.

They had left the base after full light, not wanting to be hit in the early-morning gloom by some bleary-eyed truck driver hauling in CDs or Gucci knockoffs or BMW parts from some chop shop in Albania. NATO forbade training in the mountains—it was too politically dangerous to train like soldiers—so the recon team had to stay on the main highway to Pristina, racing down out of the foothills to a turnaround point at twenty kilometers, then facing the last ten uphill kilometers back to the base. A full twenty-six-mile marathon carrying thirty-pound packs, four hours the target time. Not likely they could achieve that, but hey, what else to do on a Sunday?

For three hours the captain—the twin bars prominent on the lapels of his camouflage jacket—had been running with the single-minded lope of the alpha wolf, sometimes allowing one of the others to slip into the lead for a mile or so. As long as the lead shifted, all three stayed energized, a pack confident that together they could not be stopped.

Mark Lang forced the pace even when he wasn't in the lead, pushing so that the pain in his lungs blocked out his thoughts, shut out the world. He'd first learned to do that in boarding school at thirteen, when he would sneak into the gym after study hours and lift weights until he couldn't feel his arms, then press his face against the cold metal of his locker and cry.

How did the son of the captain of an oil tanker, with a divorced mother who never wrote, fit in at a New England boarding school? Work was Lang's escape. A few classmates had snickered about his fanaticism. That subsided when, at fourteen, Lang was named starting linebacker and Cos decided to be his roommate. Mrs. Cosgrove swept him into her orbit as another son, and amid sports, studies and school breaks spent at her house, Lang learned how to smother loneliness. Even then, he punished his body to distract his mind. And now he didn't want to think.

"Six miles to go," Lang said, glancing at the GPS receiver held outside his breast pocket by a strip of velcro. "Eight mikes for the last split."

The other two said nothing, conserving oxygen. Eight minutes for a mile was excellent this late in the run, but could they hold that pace for six more miles?

Lang glanced at the sergeant clipping along feverishly at his side. Herbert Caulder was a head shorter than Lang and looked a bit cartoonish, with a face too small for a neck and shoulders absurdly thick from years of workouts with heavy weights. He had the coiled energy of a downed power line. For Caulder, patience was torment. In half the allotted time during the sniper championships at LeJeune, he put ten rounds into the black from the thousand-yard line, capturing first place and promotion below zone to Sergeant E-5. A most unlikely sniper, he always wanted to get on with it, whatever it was. Now he was pumping his legs furiously, trying to sprint past the others, get out in front, gain the lead, get inside Lang's mind and slow down the pace.

The upgrade worked against his strategy. He couldn't suck enough oxygen to open a lead. Each time he struggled ahead, Lang's long legs would pull even. It wasn't fair. God should give everyone the same size legs. Caulder's pulse was at max. After the third fruitless sprint, he eased off, gasping. *I'm a sniper,* he thought, *not an antelope.*

"I have a life after this death," Caulder said. "I'm reining it in."

His face was pasty gray, slick with sweat. Lang slowed, trotting beside Caulder for several seconds. "What do you think, Blade?" Lang asked the tall sergeant at his side. Like Caulder, he wore the three black chevrons of a sergeant on his lapels. Blade reached out and pulled Caulder to a halt.

"That's it. You're done," he said. "Two pitchers last night, dummy. Drinking's not your thing."

Caulder didn't reply. He leaned over and vomited as his companions jumped back.

"That's good. Solid test. I hope the monitors caught that," Blade said. "You should have seen him at Tun Tavern last night, sir. Standing on his head with a shot glass in his teeth, ass in the air. The troops were barking. The colonel was laughing. Totally embarrassing."

Caulder breathed deeply and stood erect. "Don't listen to him, sir. Last night was a glorious moment. We're the dogs. No one can run with the big dogs."

"Drinking upside down?" Lang said.

"My old man owned a bar," Caulder said. "Learned that trick when I was ten. Some Saturday nights I'd get twenty bucks in tips."

"Now you've learned not to drink and run," Lang said. "Sure you're old enough to drink?"

He flagged down a passing hummer, gesturing as though hailing a cab in New York City. After eleven weeks in Kosovo everyone in the regiment knew all the officers. The humvee driver agreed to drive Caulder back to base.

Lang and Blade resumed the run, matching each other stride for stride, agreeing to deduct a minute from their elapsed time for being so solicitous of Caulder.

"Caulder's crazy enough to take off after us, sir," Blade said. "He doesn't know he's nuts."

"Right," Lang said. "Let's pick it up. That way Caulder can't catch up and totally dehydrate."

In New York City the reserves trained on the Combat Decision Range—a computer program that played combat missions. Sergeant Paul

Enders made the right decisions so fast that throughout the regiment, he was called Blade. His honed body and relaxed manner—and family connections—had earned him an expanding clientele as a personal trainer to New Yorkers rich enough to be encouraged to sweat. Five hours a day of aerobics and weights gave Blade an advantage over the other recon reservists. And that was what he lived for—the weekend missions, the four-hundred-mile adventure races, the team against the elements.

His father, a banker, was forever urging him to stop wasting a first-class mind, chiding that five years ago he had wanted to be a ski instructor and now it was this "Marine Corps business"—another passing fad. Blade knew he was the classic spoiled only child from East Side wealth, everything coming too easily. Except this. Making the team hadn't been easy. Still, it wouldn't last. Doc Evans said the experiment would be over after the deployment. If the team broke up, maybe he'd apply in January—Williams, Columbia, possibly Lewis & Clark, the flower-child college. He smiled, thinking of his dad's face going red. But now he had a race to run.

Even for Blade the pace was harsh, and he looked sideways at Lang, trying to read his expression. The captain was a big man, larger than Blade, with a body shaped by decades of weights, runs and solitary weekends. His face was long, with the marathoner's anemic lack of flesh, cheekbones pulled taut like a bird of prey. His tight haircut exposed the back of his head, flat as the bottom of an iron, a gift from a mother who had never picked him up or shifted him in his crib.

Around another bend they went, giving each other room, neither hogging the spots where the footing was firmer. Blade was determined not to let Lang gain a step; if he fell back, the captain would pick up the pace, sap his confidence, break his will to win.

Worked the other way, too. Hell, the skipper was an old man, over thirty, and ten pounds heavier. That Lang won at long distance, as Blade saw it, was due to mental harassment. Lang distracted you, made some weird comment about a hot new actress or the Jets, took your head out of the game. Only not today. Sooner or later he could beat Lang, he was sure of it.

Blade knew he couldn't think too much about Lang, who had been acting strange all morning. He had to run his own race, force the captain to worry about him, not the other way around. He wondered when Lang would try to unnerve him. Uh-oh, he was doing it to himself, letting his mind drift. Concentrate.

"Let's do seven-thirties," Lang said.

"Let's not," Blade said. They were training, for God's sake, not trying to break their bodies. Seven and a half minutes for a mile, with a pack on? After twenty miles? Forget it. His lungs felt like a blast furnace. "We can't hold that pace. It'll take us a week to bounce back." He looked at Lang, who sped up without replying or turning his head. *He's in his own world,* Blade thought, *I don't exist.* He looked back to where the hummer was trailing them, three hundred meters behind. Caulder, plodding next to the vehicle, fluttered his hand, palm down, signaling Blade to fall back. Blade shook his head.

Lang unslung his heavy rifle and held it at port arms. It was an experimental design, ugly, with too much weight in the barrels. *This is it,* Blade thought, *Lang's latest psych trick.* Blade reached for his M16A3 with its bulky telescopic sight and imitated Lang, left hand under the barrel, right hand over the black stock aft of the trigger housing. Now they were even.

Lang didn't challenge Blade to exhaust himself, just lengthened his own stride, looked at the dull gray rock slabs bordering the road and set off to punish his body. Wherever his mind was, it wasn't on the road.

"Caulder's on the road, Skipper," Blade said. "I'm dropping back with him. I can't hold this. You got it today, but you're going to be whipped for a week."

Lang nodded without breaking stride or looking to the side. The run was a tunnel, and the light at the end was the base gate. Four miles. For thirty more minutes of fire in the lungs, he could run away from what was hurting him.

Blade dropped to a slow jog, letting Caulder catch up. They were professionals out for a workout. They could go the distance when they had to, and they knew when to back off.

Lang hit the main gate in under four hours and slowed to a jog, then a walk, circling near the guard gate, waiting for the others. The base looked like a high-rise complex set inside a maximum-security prison, with its perimeter of guard towers, berms and chain-link fences topped with curled rolls of razor wire.

"Did you do it?" Blade asked when he trotted up several minutes later.

"Yes." There was no enthusiasm in Lang's voice. The other two wanted to tell him they were impressed, but the captain held himself at a distance.

"Doc will want your time," Blade said, looking at his watch. "I'll send it to her."

"Three fifty-seven," Lang said, sounding flat. "See you in the mess hall."

Lang walked the few blocks to his brick-and-mortar BOQ room, opened the portable fridge and guzzled down a quart of Gatorade. There were two narrow beds in the room, one with a footlocker shoved at the end for Lang to rest his heels, and two scratched metal bureaus with too many books and pictures piled on top. One was a black-and-white photo of a striking woman in her mid-fifties, with long hair, high cheekbones, a bright smile and light eyes that shone with warmth and intelligence, leopard eyes. A gentle leopard.

Lang looked at the photo, at a stuffed duffel bag lying askew on the bed next to his, at the whitewashed cinder-block walls and back at the photo. For a moment his shoulders slumped. He didn't know why it was hitting him so hard. Seventeen years, that's why. He'd been going to the Cosgrove home for seventeen years. So maybe he should go home now with Cos. And leave the team behind? That was bright. Cos would keep him informed. She'd already fought it for a year; he'd see her next month. He didn't want to think about it.

He stripped off his sopping clothes, walked into the tiny bathroom and vomited. He felt his insides rush, voided himself, flushed, left the bathroom for a second bottle of Gatorade, returned and vomited a second time. Too weak to stand, he lay facedown on the cold tiles, weight on his chest and forehead, his overheated body glad for the cold.

When his body had cooled down, he showered, gulped a third quart of Gatorade and cleaned his ugly rifle. Then he walked slowly to the mess hall.

It was after eleven, and the cavernous room with its shatterproof glass windows and tables bolted to the floor was nearly empty. Caulder, Blade and Lang sat at a long table, a dozen glasses with different liquids spread out, trays heaped with sausages and eggs. Caulder had bounced back and was wolfing down the eggs. Blade and Lang were too exhausted to eat much.

"Staff Sergeant Roberts sleeping in again?" Lang asked. The Sunday runs were optional. Still, the absence of a team member two Sundays in a row was unusual.

"Maybe he sensed you were going to go wild, sir," Blade said.

The excuse was lame, but Lang didn't pursue it. They were enlisted, and he was the commanding officer, but that wasn't why they were holding back. You couldn't choose your parents or where you lived. And if you didn't go to college, forget about becoming an officer. But who chose to become a Marine, who went recon, who *liked* going thirty hours with no sleep on two canteens to reach a checkpoint eighty miles away while the wind cut like a whip—who became one of the dogs—that you decided for yourself.

They were a team. If the staff sergeant was off somewhere, that was like your older brother not showing up for dinner. When your father asked where he was, who'd ever answer that question?

Caulder changed the subject. "Me and Blade are hitting the souk, sir. Wrap up our Christmas shopping. You and Captain Cosgrove want to come along?"

"Meaning will our intelligence officer get a hummer for you?"

"That would help."

"Cosgrove's on security patrol," Lang said. "Then he's leaving on tonight's flight to Dover. His mother's been readmitted. So the souk's out."

The sergeants said nothing. The team, together for two years, had talked with Mrs. Cosgrove a dozen times, at parties, marathons, training exercises. They considered her good people, always interested in what they were doing. She never said it, but they sensed she gave them high marks. Especially nice from a professor, finely dressed, with a striking face and a direct gaze. She stared into their eyes when she asked questions in a clipped accent that made each word stand up straight. She really wanted to hear their answers, and as each man replied, he stood a little taller, like her words, his muscles swelling a bit under his trim uniform.

"Thought she was in remission," Blade said.

"Happened out of the blue," Lang said.

"We just sent her our pic," Caulder said, pursing his lips. Mrs. Cosgrove had always asked about his latest score on the range and congratulated him on concentrating so single-mindedly. Not many people appreciated the thousands of hours that went into the split second of squeezing the trigger. He thought of her wasting away, and his features puckered up like a little boy's, almost comical against the bulk of his shoulders.

"You going home, too, sir?" Blade asked Lang. "Knowing her and all."

"I'm not family."

"You almost are. The regs allow it."

"Captain Cosgrove will keep me up to speed."

"Well, you'll catch up with her after Christmas," Caulder said.

Lang kept his eyes on his tray.

"You will," Caulder repeated, holding a glass of orange juice close to his chest, as though he was cold.

"Who's filling in for Captain Cosgrove?" Blade asked. "They're not putting us under some squid, are they?"

Lang shrugged, and they resumed eating. The silence lasted until a corporal from Operations noticed them. He hesitated before slowly approaching their table. What if they already knew? Sergeant Caulder would chew on him. No, they wouldn't be just sitting there. Not the dogs. They'd be moving, doing something.

Blade looked up. "What's going on, Corporal?"

"I, I wasn't sure whether you all had heard—about Captain Cosgrove."

They looked up, and the corporal knew he had made the right choice.

"He's missing on patrol."

They were out the door in ten seconds, running toward the Operations Center.

To the uninitiated, the Combat Ops Center was a disorganized babble of noise. Two dozen intense, forceful men with close-cropped hair, looking like a 1950s Texas football team, were hunched over computer screens, yelling at one another for updates. On the walls, large electronic maps pulsated with military symbols in bright red, blue and yellow. Almost every officer had a field radio next to his chair, with the volume and squelch turned up. Even when they weren't shouting, a loud, annoying crackle and hiss of radio static sounded throughout the room.

The 25th Marine Regiment in Kosovo was a test bed for the digital battlefield, although no one knew quite what that meant. Four thousand bored Marines with no one to fight. A few years earlier, before computers became as common as coffee mugs, a Marine Trekkie said that the blinking screens in the Ops Center reminded him of the starship *Enterprise*. Two months later pieces from the set of the original *Star Trek*, purchased for $25,000, were shipped from a Hollywood back lot to Kosovo. With straight faces, Marines claimed that the pale gray gypsum boards muffled sound. In fact, the stark, polished walls, reflecting the glow from the computer screens, created a shimmering, cerebral atmosphere suggestive of a new form of warfare. To encourage that illusion, the radios were turned down whenever there were important visitors, who reciprocated by whispering in hushed tones, as if in a cathedral.

There was nothing hushed about the Ops Center when Lang and the sergeants entered. They walked to the message board and read the spot report.

```
1130 Zulu 1221

Arrow Six reported missing at 1126. Last seen on scout bike vicinity
of burning farmhouse at 623 510. Dead woman at same location.
Condition Red set at 1132 IAW Op Plan 70.2.
```

The watch officer on Sunday morning was a burly captain who compensated for his junior rank by bellowing. In his hand he held the spiral notebook labeled OP PLAN 70.2, DEPLOYMENT IN CASE OF ABDUCTION OR DISAPPEARANCE IN FIELD. Soon the place would be swarming with senior officers. The watch officer could wait for them or he could take the initiative. His voice left no doubt about his decision.

"I'm sending in three platoons. I want a tight cordon around that farmhouse where Cosgrove disappeared," he was yelling at his platoon commanders. "Nobody goes in or out of that area, nobody." With an electronic pen, he drew an orange square on the electronic wall map.

"Who puts out the fire?" asked Lang, standing behind the platoon commanders.

"What's your point, Lang?" the watch officer said. He was in charge, not a recon captain. He didn't have time for interruptions.

"With that fire, people will come and go regardless of what you order." Lang paused to let that sink in. "Insert my team as an overlook. We'll watch who leaves the area and report to you."

"The plan calls for aerial intell. Recon's not part of the plan."

"You know air sucks on a mission like this."

"I know the admiral doesn't change plans."

"This is about Cosgrove, not some stupid plan," Lang said. "He's the mission, and my roomie. Come on, man. I have to be out there."

In three months of working daily with Lang, the watch officer had never heard him ask for anything. Mr. Intensity needed something? But what he was saying made sense.

"Yeah, he's the mission. All right, go ahead, Lang," the watch officer said, "but don't screw me up. You're only to observe and report in."

Lang slapped him on the back and left at a trot, Blade and Caulder behind him. "Get gear and pull ammo," he said to them. "I'll get Roberts."

"With Cohen on leave," Blade said, "we need a communicator."

"Bring Cohen's gear," Lang said. "We'll find someone his size."

Once outside, Lang sprinted down the street, not caring that his leg muscles were screaming objections. He ducked into a square brick building, ran down a narrow corridor and into a wide room with several sofas, a Ping-Pong table and a large-screen TV. A few Marines in camouflage utilities were watching the rerun of a football game. One Marine was older, in his early thirties, with a compact build and the weathered, sharp features of a cop, someone ill at ease in a coat and tie.

For the past two years he had worn the same black tie to the biweekly inspection at Search and Rescue Company 143, where he was the senior lieutenant. Most firefighters worked split shifts, leaving enough time to earn a second income. John Roberts was no exception. Being a reservist brought in less than being a plumber, but how many plumbers were paid to parachute from ten thousand feet, or swim underwater to the beach using a rebreather, or visit scenic Kosovo at Christmas? At first Koso sucked. Not since Evette, though. Roberts sat on the couch, not paying attention to the television, his body feeling light and empty after last night's sex, amused that he still had a slight residual erection.

"All right!" Lang said. "Staff Sergeant Roberts!"

"Sir?" Roberts stood, followed by the others.

It didn't bother Roberts that in the real world he was a lieutenant, and here he was enlisted. Lang as captain gave the directions, and Roberts as the senior sergeant ran the team. He was the enforcer of discipline, the keeper of data for each patrol and telephone numbers of next of kin. Lang did the thinking; Roberts saw to the follow-through. It was the same as fighting a fire: Roberts went inside with the men while the battalion chief stayed outside to direct the action. The SEALs didn't get that. Their senior enlisted thought they could run things *and* think. They even called their officers by their first names. No way. That undercut the officer, screwed things up when chaos set in. When Roberts made battalion chief in a couple of years, he expected his men to call him chief or sir, nothing else.

"Cosgrove's missing from patrol." Lang's face looked strained, empty of color. "We're going out."

"Turn that fucker off!" Roberts shouted at the startled Marines. The TV went blank. He turned back to Lang, grabbed him by the elbow and walked to a corner. "Give me a quick fill, sir."

"Cos didn't report in from a security patrol. And his mother's been readmitted. He was flying back home tonight. Son of a bitch. Son . . . of . . . a . . . bitch."

Lang was glaring at the wall, back rigid. Caught off guard, Roberts was trying to make sense of it, not yet believing someone could just disappear from a routine patrol. "Could be a screwup. Hell, you know those intell weenies. Maybe he had a contact to meet or something."

"We're not waiting to find out. We snag a communicator type and launch. We're cleared through Ops."

They ran back to Ops, checked in with the watch officer and scanned the room. Word had already spread about the open comm slot. Officers and enlisted alike kept busy at their jobs, none wanting to appear pushy and spoil his chances. Most tried to make eye contact, many nodding their readiness, several pointing to themselves and giving thumbs-up. If every volunteer could be accepted, the Ops Center would be empty.

Caulder and Blade stood in the back with the packs piled next to them. They watched the silent competition and nudged each other, pointing out the front-runners. One contestant was half sitting, half crouching, waving his arms, his round face pleading for attention, almost panting.

"Harvell's pissing in his pants," Caulder whispered. "This time he's going out."

Blade shook his head. Corporal J. Kirwin Harvell had tried out twice for recon and failed. Harvell, who wore jungle boots to his programming job at a law firm, made no secret of his ambitions. He had even designed a recon website. Hero worship. Why should he pull a real op?

"No chance," Blade said.

"Blade, for all your smarts, you're still naive," Caulder insisted. "He has Roberts by the balls. Watch."

Roberts had walked down the narrow aisle lined with computers and was looking down at the slightly overweight corporal.

"I've been monitoring the net, Staff Sergeant. I'm up to speed," Harvell said. "I have the freqs and passwords plugged in. Good to go."

The sergeant rubbed the back of his head, his indecision obvious. *What the hell,* he thought, *an Observation Post is like standing a guard post. Even Harvell can do it.*

"We could use Harvell, sir," Roberts said to Lang, who had come up behind him. "He knows that computer gizmo, and he's the right size for the gear we have."

Lang hesitated. "If you say so, Staff Sergeant."

Watching from the rear of the room, Caulder rolled his eyes at Blade. When Harvell rushed over to them, Caulder gestured toward the extra pack, shaking his head in disapproval. Harvell didn't care. Sure, some mocked him for creating a home page for the Pepperdogs, the nickname for the recon team. But after all these months, he was going on an op. And he had his plan.

He fiddled with the borrowed pack until the other team members filed out. Then he darted into the admin section, sat down at an unclassified computer and opened his website. KosoFinest was the Web-based dating service Harvell ran during off-hours. Since the deployment began, fourteen hundred women had submitted pictures, with more signing up every week. That attracted eyeballs, two or three hundred a day. Hell, even Staff Sergeant Roberts had signed up. At the bottom of the page, Harvell added a line advertising that he was part of a recon mission.

Months ago Harvell had decided he was the only real entrepreneur in the regiment, the only one with a knack for e-marketing. Okay, there were thousands of dating services. Nothing new there, and he was clearing maybe three hundred a month. No future.

The recon site was different, though. Ever since Afghanistan, Special Ops were hot. *Hot.* He could sense when a property was about to take off. Sure, not many people had visited the recon page—eight in the past month, to be exact. That's because the site lacked zoom. Nothing was going on, and all the recon types did was run and lift and go to the field. Their idea of a promo was to climb a mountain at three in the morning. They were about as exciting as monks—well, except for Staff Sergeant Roberts.

He'd fix that. He'd write a few zingers while in the field, download when he got back and spam them. His ad on KosoFinest would provide

the initial buzz. There were thousands of programmers on the market, but how many had been on a recon op in the Balkans? If *Tetrabytes* or some other computer pub ran one blurb, he'd be set. Bye-bye to serf work at a law firm.

Harvell pulled up the recon website, Pepperdogs.com. He deleted Cohen's photo—since he was on leave—and inserted a space for comments by J. Kirwin Harvell, now with recon. It took only a few seconds. He looked at the page.

Harvell hesitated. Did his posting have enough sizzle? Maybe he should add—

"Harvell, what the hell? Get to the LZ—*now!*" Staff Sergeant Roberts burst through the door from the Ops Center and strode across the room. "Screw those damn computers. You're our comm relay. *Now!* You hear? A Marine is missing."

Harvell hit the quit key and scrambled to pick up his pack, trying to remember if he had made all the changes to the website. He spoke with-

The Pepperdogs

www.pepperdogs.com

"That Marine team runs like a dog with pepper up its arse."
Sgt. Ken Haight, British Commandos, during Exercise High Express in Norway.

Meet the World Champions from the 25th Marines Recon Company

Capt. Mark Lang, 31. Commodity trader, Pincus Warburg. New York City. Princeton University. Single. Winner, New York State Iron Man X	**SSgt John Roberts,** 32. Lieutenant, New York City Fire Dept. Married, two daughters. Winner, 9th Fireman's Fitness Challenge
Sgt. Paul 'Blade' Enders, 23. Manager, Toys Dept., Macy's. Single Winner, Combat Decision Range IV; Winner, Alpine Orienteering Course.	**Sgt. Herbert Caulder,** 22. Owner, Caulder's Auto Body Shop, Brooklyn. Married. LeJeune Trophy, XXIst USMC Sniper Championship

For comments by J. Kirwin: watch this space!!!

➤ Press Coverage   ➤ Contact Pepperdogs

➤ Recent Race Results   ➤ Contact KosoFinest

out thinking. "Just straightening up, Staff Sergeant. On my way. Captain Cosgrove's probably lost. He'll show up."

Roberts clenched his jaw. Harvell might be the smartest geek in the Ops Center, but he lived in la-la land. He clamped his hand on Harvell's shoulder, leaned over and spoke slowly. "That's what I mean. You think you know everything. We're staying out until they find him or it gets dark. For the next five hours you're a transmitter, not a person. You type or repeat what the captain says. Full stop. You don't think, you don't talk. No geek shit. And that computer better not fail."

On the table next to him Harvell had placed the compact End User Terminal. The EUT was an experimental computer and radio that carried voice-over data. You could type a message, connect to the classified Internet, pull up a map showing your location, send or receive a photo and talk as though on a telephone with no static. Harvell tucked it under his arm like an oversize book and stood up.

"Full charge, Staff Sergeant. We can reach anywhere," he said, relieved to show off what he knew. "Even KosoFinest—"

"Are you a slow learner or plain stupid?" Roberts squeezed Harvell's collarbone. "One word about KosoFinest and I'll plant my boot squarely up your rectum. I stuck my neck out for you. Get it through your head—this isn't an exercise. Captain Cosgrove's missing. You screw up one time, and I'll put your ass out your stomach."

"I'll chill, Staff Sergeant, I'll chill."

Harvell ducked around the glowering Roberts and, hearing the *whump! whump!* of a CH-53 Echo setting down, ran to join the waiting team. Lang and the two sergeants were adjusting their equipment. Harvell rushed up with the communications pack dangling from his shoulder. Blade roughly spun him around and began cinching up the straps. Lang watched the scene, running through a mental checklist as Roberts did the same with his notebook.

"Maybe we should bring a cell as backup," Lang said.

"Sir, I know this gear," Harvell said. "I—"

"Shut up, Harvell," Roberts said. "Caulder, zip back and get the captain's cell phone."

"I'm on it."

"Top drawer of my dresser," Lang said.

Caulder dropped his pack and left at a sprint. He was back before the last Marine had walked up the ramp. He boarded the helicopter, gave a thumbs-up to Lang and sat inboard of Roberts, who took the end seat as the chopper lifted off the cement pad, kicking up a swirl of snow dust.

The valley air was clear, with wispy mare's heads and chalk skies filling in over the mountains to the north, threatening an evening snowfall. Nothing for the pilots to be concerned about for several hours.

In a back corner of the Ops Center a navy corpsman, wearing his hair a bit too long for a Marine (despite his cammies), sat skimming an old *Playboy*, occasionally looking up at the five monitors mounted from the ceiling. One, labeled COHEN, was dark. The other four showed the heart rate and blood pressure of each member of the Pepperdogs. The corpsman had time-marked on the recording tape the plunge in pressure when Caulder threw up. Lang's tape had no markings. The corpsman knew the doctor would review the entire last fifteen minutes.

"Everything normal, Doc?" asked Gunnery Sergeant "Twigs" Twitchell, his shadow falling over the relaxed corpsman.

"Shit, no. Roberts is normal. The others are twenty points low, and Lang hit one-ninety, diastolic of one hundred. He can rip. I thought his implant had come loose."

"It's *Captain* Lang," Twitchell said. "Now translate what you said into English."

"The monitors show *Sergeant* Enders and *Sergeant* Caulder with low pressures. They'll be okay tomorrow. *Captain* Lang almost ran himself to death. He has to be hurting. The doc's going to be pissed."

"Better," Gunnery Sergeant Twitchell said. "There's hope for you."

Reserve Marines, the corpsman thought, *just as tight-ass as the regulars.*

The Castle Restaurant, Mitrovica Valley   **12:30 P.M. Sunday**

With flags flapping on both fenders, the Mercedes jounced along, wrapped in the dust of a tank to the front. As the armored luxury car bounced over the potholes, its springs sagging under too much steel plating, the ambassador's head occasionally hit the car roof. Ambrose Briggs tolerated the annoyance. He intended to arrive at the Castle Restaurant like Patton, with two tanks in the lead and five armored personnel carriers, all flying pennants, battalion and regimental banners with eagles swooping from the sky, American flags, the UN flag and a heraldic symbol of the province in its medieval glory, a knight slaying a red dragon. A touch of theater never hurt.

What was he doing, returning to this backwater? Why had he accepted the assignment? He had money, position, prestige. He didn't need this special-emissary bullshit. Around the globe, America was pulling back its troops, in no mood to leave them dangling in places where hatreds festered. How had his previous White House masters allowed the Joint Chiefs to send reserve units to Kosovo year after year? So clever of the unclever Chiefs. Five thousand soldiers from Texas one year, four thousand from Kansas and Iowa, then four thousand from California—ninety-nine electoral votes, for Christ's sake—and now thousands of New Yorkers deployed over the Christmas holidays.

And in Kosovo what did these American voters do for their country? Drove around in armored vehicles, wearing stinky flak jackets and clunky helmets, peering out at jocular schoolchildren and their surly parents who complained the Americans were too afraid to do anything. Commanding officers acted like bureaucrats in the Department of Health and Human Services, keeping tabs on who was pregnant, who was behind on credit payments, which employers in the States needed letters thanking them for giving twelve weeks' leave to valued employees, ensuring there were enough computers, on and on. The average reservist sent and received a total of twenty-seven e-mails a day. Some soldiers spent two hours on-line each evening with the kids' homework; others watched sports via live feeds. As fast as fiber optic was laid, there was a demand for more.

Every year the boredom and complaints increased, ratcheting up the political pressure to pull out, and protecting Kosovar Muslims was not a priority in Washington. Briggs wanted a deal before Congress cut funding and put a bad end to a decade of American military occupation in the Balkans.

The Serbs were at the castle when he arrived. The military staffs were exchanging stiff pleasantries in a large stone foyer draped with heavy tapestries of knights on horseback firing arrows into large-racked stags and thrusting spears into red-eyed boars with enormous curved tusks. Briggs rubbed a corner of the rough cloth between his finger and thumb, appraising its authenticity, although he wouldn't have known whether the weave had been stitched ten days or ten centuries ago. Lieutenant General Kostica stood at his elbow, the genial host.

"Our young men still lance boars," Kostica said.

"We have hunters, too, Charlton Hestons, trying to prove manhood."

"But ours do so—how do you say?—more directly."

Briggs didn't reply. *Meaning we're too soft to stand up to you man to man,* he thought. *Macho bullshit. Let's get this over with.*

They entered the great hall of the castle, oversized chandeliers that held a hundred candles, rough plank banquet tables and huge, heavy chairs in which a drunken noble could pass out and not hit his head on the stone floor. At the far end was a fireplace large enough to stand in. Its blaze looked like a small house on fire. In a corner, away from the searing heat, was a small table for two, covered with a white cloth and set with fine china, in contrast to the haphazard settings on the larger tables.

Kostica led the way. He was heavyset, with jowls and a full stomach, miscast in his rumpled army uniform, too paunchy, too soft. Briggs wore a dark blue suit with a tasteful tie and walked with his shoulders back. He, too, was heavy in middle age, his girth concealed by a good tailor, his jowls touching his neck when he leaned forward. Both wore their hair long and swept back, like the manes of aging lions. The general gestured, and Briggs sat down, casting a quick glance at his aides and the NATO generals, who accepted their exclusion with ill grace.

"Usually we include our top staff at the head table," Briggs said. "They produce better when they think they are included."

Kostica shrugged. Some on his staff were from Belgrade. He intended none to hear. The plates were large and faded with age, with gold detailing and a crest of arms in the center, a black eagle with outstretched wings and talons wide, eager to seize whatever food was placed upon it. The embossed sterling-silver plates, heavy in the hand, reminded Briggs of the generations of nobility now gone. He wondered what had become of the owners and, for a fleeting instant, had an image that he was dining with the Wehrmacht in the south of occupied France, where he had recently bought a villa complete with silver plates. A waiter poured red wine into crystal goblets.

"Salut." The general held up his glass, aware from *People* magazine that Briggs routinely paid two hundred dollars for a bottle of dinner wine. "This is a Gasstad, our cabernet. Our growing season is short, but I find it satisfactory."

Briggs sipped cautiously, anticipating the acrid tingle of shriveled grapes ruined by an early frost on some forsaken hillside plowed by mortars and artillery. Instead the wine tasted smooth, with no hint of acid. A pleasant aftertaste of fruit and wood smoke lingered in his throat.

"You should make wine, not war."

The general smiled. He would remember to refill the bottle with another Pomerol from France.

"A secret formula." He laughed, then turned serious. "The formula for peace is not so secret. The rebels leave the valley or I attack."

"NATO is doing its best."

"Its best?" Kostica waved a hand. "That bandit—Baba—burns Serb farms and butchers the families, and NATO refuses to patrol beyond the highway. That's doing one's best? No. The fact is, NATO won't risk one soldier, not one."

"Don't even think of moving your troops in," Briggs said. In his briefcase he had the satellite photos and heat-sensor imagery. Two hundred vehicles on the roads, some already forward of the border, high up along the ridges.

"You allowed Israel to drive the PLO out of Beirut. That wasn't even their country. This is our province. We're the ones facing terrorists. You know it."

"We won't tolerate an invasion."

"Invasion? I drain a swamp, as you said about Afghanistan. We are not hillbillies like those Taliban. We respect your air force, but it will be more dangerous for you than the last time."

"Our air force chief of staff is trembling," Briggs said, not looking up from his food.

Kostica cut into the blackened meat and dipped it in the cream sauce. "Try the boar," he said, "no lead in it."

They ate in silence, the general satisfied that Briggs understood Russian surface-to-air missiles would accompany his move. A SAM could cost the Americans a hundred-million-dollar aircraft. Was that worth a few Muslim rebels?

"Russia has applied for another loan, sixteen billion," Briggs said, chewing cautiously. "If their SAMs go in, that loan stays home."

So that was it. Only a few SAMs so far had moved across the border; the rest were waiting inside Serbia. Without them, the Americans would destroy Kostica's force at no risk.

"Home? You Americans are the ones who can't go home," Kostica said. "Without our help, your army has to stay here forever, like the Turks on Cyprus. Know why? You're on the wrong side. Albanians? Pfft. The thieves of Europe. We both know it."

"Do you want to cry or deal?" Briggs said.

A tall American soldier was approaching their table, his camouflage utilities starched and his pant legs tucked inside his black boots. On his lapels were two large black stars. With no attempt at manners, he leaned and whispered in Briggs's ear. The ambassador grimaced.

"A recall has been issued. An American soldier is missing," Briggs said, hastily folding up his napkin. "We don't need this, General, neither of us."

"This is Kosovo, Mr. Ambassador. Thieves and terrorists. You helped the Muslims, and they repaid you in New York. Now they're doing it again. You're on the wrong side," Kostica said. "Want to find your man? Arrest that rebel Baba and his damn *imams*. My *tigrivas* will help search."

"We don't need help, especially from your *tigrivas*." Briggs rose and extended his hand. "I hope we understand each other."

"It's Baba who doesn't understand yet."

"No, you don't understand. I propose a mutual withdrawal. If instead you push forward, General, you lose," Briggs said. "If you back off, well, we don't want to stay forever. Give us, shall we say, a decent interval?"

"So much time since Dayton. You Americans are as stubborn as the Turks."

Briggs ignored the remark. "An IMF loan of, say, a billion is reasonable"—he tilted his chin—"if you pull back your armor, say, fifty kilometers."

"And Baba?"

"We can isolate him politically"—Briggs brushed the air with his hand—"as long as you don't stir things up. This is a generous offer, General. I'm flying out in two days, and after that, well, the president won't send someone every day, will he?"

Exaggerating didn't perturb Briggs. A billion-dollar loan wasn't in his instructions—a simple warning was all the Secretary of State wanted him to deliver. But if Kostica showed interest in a larger deal, the details could be ironed out. Momentum, movement—that was what Briggs wanted. Once success shimmered, minor excesses would be overlooked.

After the Americans left, Kostica lingered over his coffee. A decent interval, wasn't that what North Vietnam had given Kissinger? The north had waited two years before taking over the south. Perhaps at last the Americans understood these Muslims, these *vrags*. What was another year? If he delivered IMF funds to Belgrade and finished Baba later, why couldn't he, like Eisenhower, become a president? As for the missing American, that changed nothing. By now Saco had released him.

Mitrovica Valley border area   **1:00 P.M. Sunday**

Captain Mark Lang crouched behind the pilots as the helicopter circled the valley. The smoke from the dead woman's farmhouse provided a clear beacon. Beside him Blade knelt studying a map and looking out over the instrument panel, trying to select a ridge from where they could watch that farmhouse.

"You pick it, Blade," Lang said.

Off to the left Blade noted the smoke from the burning farm, while in front the land lifted sharply in a series of steep foothills and granite cliffs. To the north, the hills merged into a giant mountain chain, the farthest peaks hidden in snow clouds. The early afternoon sunlight was beginning to streak with thin clouds, Kosovo's usual bad weather returning. Lang seemed distracted, so Blade reached around him and handed his map to the copilot, pointing to the spot where he wanted to land.

"Ten mikes," the pilot yelled.

The pilot was pointing to a green knoll at the top of a sheer rock slab half a kilometer to the west. Blade nodded and settled back to wait. The slick arced and sideslipped gracefully, no need for a bumpy tactical approach. The nose flared up and the chopper settled down. They were out and clear in seconds.

The heavy beat of the departing blades hung in the air as the team trotted toward the cliff side. To the east lay wide pastures and thin tree lines, tilting up toward the thick brush sides of the mountain. Scattered

among the open fields were several farms, their orange slate roofs paint-
ing a pleasant scene from a distance too far to reveal the scars of shells
and fire.

Lang was indifferent to the high pastureland, his attention focused on
the valley below. The cliff was bare of trees, and as they approached its
edge, their view to the west was unobstructed for several kilometers. The
countryside reminded him of Switzerland. The broad, square plots of
open land, bordered by neat rows of hedge, resembled a giant chess-
board, and the farms were the chess pieces, set one to a square. The dirt
roads leading to each farm seemed as lazily twisting and harmless as
summer streams. A good place for a picnic.

"Scope around that farm with the smoke, Caulder," Lang said. No
need to whisper. Caulder was carrying a .308 bolt-action rifle with a long
barrel, its sleek lines ruined by a telescopic sight, like setting the pilot-
house of a tugboat on the deck of a graceful sailing sloop. The rifle
matched Caulder, bulked up for power but lacking in proportion.

Caulder snapped a portable bipod to the rifle stock, lay down and
looked at the valley through the scope. The apertures of the 3-18X
Leupold variable scope were wider than a man's fist. On its left side were
a night-battery switch and separate dials for magnification, bullet-drop
compensation and focus. The adjustable lens kept targets in focus a kilometer away, without undue parallax. Caulder complained that technology took away the art of sniping. He neglected to add that he spent over a
thousand dollars a year of his own money on technical upgrades.

Through the scope Caulder could see each individual near the burning farm. After several slow sweeps, he turned toward Lang and shook
his head. "Nothing, only Marines and civilians milling around," he said.
"I could piss more water than they're throwing against that fire. That
farm is going, going, gone."

"Have the men put up the tarp, Staff Sergeant." Lang enunciated
clearly. Even on patrol, he refused to use slang or change how he spoke.
Some company commanders occasionally slurred—"Staff Sarn't"—or
chewed tobacco and spat every few seconds, affectations the grunts accepted from their own. Lang didn't spit or slur. Instead he passed the
word through the regiment—name your game, a run, push-ups, pull-ups,
whatever—every Friday noon at the gym. Beat the captain. Bring it on.

And for eleven weeks, bring it on they did. The troops loved it. The challenger would show up with his buddies, and the contest would begin. Some would wait until Lang was midway through his end-of-the-week workout before issuing a challenge, others would practice on a new technique and then surprise him. His body and mind became tougher and more flexible, while in every company there were two or three Marines who had a bit of a swagger because they had beaten him.

With the tarp over their heads, the team glassed the valley while Harvell guarded the rear. They watched the civilian and military vehicles converge on the smoking farm, saw the smoke darken as water hit the flames, roiling clouds of steam curling off to the southeast and thinning quickly. Vehicles were racing across the fields to other farms, while all traffic on the main road halted at roadblocks. Cosgrove had to be down there somewhere.

Harvell had their End User Terminal set to voice. With the twist of a knob, the compact computer could transmit voice or text or probe information from any military database in the world. Every ten minutes the EUT sent back their position. The heavy radios of Vietnam and Desert Storm were stored in warehouses in Barstow, California. The units in Kosovo carried only small computers, five times better than the radios.

"Ops wants us to move west, sir," Harvell said. "We're too close to the red zone."

"Our next step west will be five hundred feet vertical," Roberts said, looking out over the cliff. "I swear, ever since we went to computers, Marines have forgotten how to read contour lines on a map."

"Tell them we'll try to move west," Lang said to Harvell. "Make sure you use the word 'try.' "

"I'm not as smooth as you, sir," Roberts said.

"Costs nothing to keep people on your side," Lang said.

"It does when they give dumb-ass orders like that."

For a while they monitored the voice traffic of the house-by-house search in the valley. After twenty minutes Lang told them to saddle up. "Harvell, bring over the Translator."

From a pouch strapped on his chest, Harvell pulled out a thin, square black box with a large CRT screen and keyboard. Lang poked at small buttons, scrolled through a few command prompts and spoke evenly into the black box. "American forces operating here. You are being watched. Leave at once."

Lang hit a button, the machine buzzed like a fax machine and the message, typed in Cyrillic, inched out on waterproof paper through a narrow slot. He scrolled through the language selection, highlighted "Albanian" and repeated the procedure. Lang taped the two messages to the tarp. Harvell looked puzzled.

"You didn't really think recon camped out, did you?" Lang said.

With Blade at point, they traversed down the cliff for several feet and moved laterally across the steep face. The granite rock offered safe footholds, and they made good progress. When they were a few hundred meters away from the tarp, Blade led them back up to the lip of the cliff, which was covered with scrub growth. There they settled in.

The observation site was well chosen, perched five hundred feet above the farmland. Through their binoculars, the valley floor to the west stood out with the clarity of a foldout photo page in *National Geographic* magazine. To the south was nothing but a cliff wall and a steep vertical drop-off. To the east and north were pastures and narrow tree lines, open land that got steeper as it sloped upward to form the shoulders of the mountain. Anyone approaching across the pastures would be visible for a kilometer or more.

Through his scope, Caulder had been watching a farmhouse on a far knoll to the northeast. Now he slid down to where Lang and Roberts were sitting. "Incoming traffic. A jeep and a truck."

They scrambled up and peered through the shrubbery at the two vehicles bouncing across the fields.

"All right, gents, we have a fish on the line. Looks like local guerrillas," Lang said. "Harvell, grab the Translator and come with me. Staff Sergeant, organize target sectors. Caulder, take any close-contact shot. If I drop to the ground, you fire."

"Stay out of my line of fire, geek," Caulder said as Harvell brushed by him, hurrying after the captain.

Harvell and Lang began climbing back toward the tarp. Lang was leading, edging along the scree, his thighs threatening to cramp after the morning's run. He moved slowly, stretching each leg. Conscious that

Harvell was watching, he spoke to distract him, not wanting to leave the impression of a leader too stiff to move.

"Sergeant Caulder's bad-tempered, Harvell. Moody. Snipers get like that. You have any questions this afternoon, ask Blade. He's the easy-going one. And remember, if I drop, you drop. Caulder sometimes misses."

Harvell almost slipped. He glanced at the captain to make sure he was joking, but Lang was crabbing sideways, not looking back. Harvell followed, grabbing for handholds.

"What are we doing, sir?" Harvell was totally confused.

"Who would know about Captain Cosgrove?"

It didn't sound like a trick question; Harvell turned it over in his mind. "The locals who are in charge? They'd hear what was going on."

"Very good, Corporal, and they want to meet us. So let's meet them."

At slow speed, the vehicles jounced and rattled through the ruts and dips and stopped when they were almost at the tarp. A half-dozen soldiers got out, wearing camouflage utilities with individual idiosyncrasies—bandanas and Air Jordans and sunglasses and other trinkets that gave them a rakish air and relieved the Marines watching them over gun sights. The less disciplined a unit, the easier to destroy.

Their leader wore the tight-fitting gray uniform favored by German nobility in early World War II. An old-fashioned Sam Brown leather belt ran diagonally across his trim chest and attached to a wide belt and holster. His matching gray cap had a small black brim, and his trousers were tucked inside brown leather riding boots. He carried black leather gloves that he slapped against his palm as he bent to read the paper taped to the tarp. He laughed, ripped the paper off and turned in a slow circle, waving it above his head.

"Come out, Americans," he called in English.

"That's Baba, the main man for the guerrillas," Lang whispered. "Let's find out if he knows something."

They climbed the few feet to the lip of the cliff and walked forward, rifle muzzles down, while the guerrillas watched them curiously. Lang stopped several feet from the leader, leaving space for covering fire.

"No need for that." The German pretender pointed to the Translator strapped to Harvell's chest. "You know who I am?"

"No," Lang lied.

"I am Baba. This is my territory." He spread his arms wide. "You should have asked my permission."

"We decide where we go."

Baba hissed. Harvell started. Hissing was a local custom, a way of showing irritation. In the souk, when an American bid absurdly low, the merchants hissed. Part of the bargaining. This sounded more like a snake.

"You look for Marine. We help," Baba said.

"You know where he is?"

"No. I hear the Serbs took him. We search together. Come, in my jeep."

"Go ask them." Lang jerked his head slightly toward the valley floor. "We don't need help up here."

Baba looked at the ground. He nodded as if agreeing. "I am to go down there, where you are meeting with the Serbs? What do I do? Surrender?" He rubbed his face. "Why are you difficult? We're not your enemy. The Slav is your enemy. You want to see Slav?"

Baba gestured, and two soldiers reached into the back of the truck and dragged out a small youth in a dark, disheveled uniform with his arms bound behind him. He was hatless, and his hair was sticky and matted down. His right eye was black and swollen shut, and his nose and lips were smeared with caked blood. Dazed, he tottered a few steps before stopping with feet spread wide, afraid of what would happen if he fell.

"Take him," Baba said. "Perhaps he knows something. Maybe you trade him for your missing man."

Lang looked at the dried blood on the prisoner's face. "You've had him for days. He knows nothing."

Baba blew out through his cheeks, as if tired of explaining over and over. "During war, we fight together. After war, peaceniks win elections. Know why? America gives money to peaceniks. Now we fight together again—okay?" He looked at the double bars on Lang's lapels. "Out here alone, a captain, you're recon." He shrugged to show he was not impressed.

Lang looked at him without replying. He didn't have time for this sideshow. He wanted it over with. Nothing here but the usual Serb-Muslim savagery. Baba had nothing to offer. He was a distraction.

"I am a colonel," Baba continued. He was perhaps five years older than Lang. "Call your colonel. I talk with him."

Baba nodded toward Harvell and his communications equipment. Lang slowly shook his head at the colonel who commanded a jeep and a truck. He didn't care whether Baba was a farm burner or a patriot or both. This matter was staying here. One call and he'd be stuck jawing for hours with the Ops staff.

"I offer to help. You don't report my generosity." Baba hissed again. "No respect."

Harvell shifted nervously. *This wacko was seriously pissed,* he thought. But his soldiers hadn't reacted yet. Their muzzles were still down. *Seriously, how good is Caulder? Is it time to drop?*

Baba tried another tack. "You are a hunter," he said. "There is nothing here. You come with me. We hunt together."

Lang looked detached. He again shook his head.

"I have no time for nothings," Baba said to keep face. He gestured toward the terrified prisoner. "You don't want this thing? Me, too. I don't want it, neither."

He signaled his men back into the vehicles. An older Muslim guerrilla with a peaked cap and a limp approached and spoke with Baba briefly. The guerrilla limped to the Serb prisoner and cinched a heavy rope under his shoulders. Then the guerrilla climbed into the cab, and the vehicles turned away. The prisoner stood with his head up, his eyes bulging, twisting his head from side to side, looking for a miracle. With no more warning, the truck started forward. The rope jerked tight, and the man half flew a few feet before crashing onto his shoulder, bouncing and jerking crazily in the dust as the truck accelerated.

"Jesus, sir," Harvell whispered, "shouldn't we do something?"

"Not our business," Lang replied.

Suddenly Harvell was shoved sprawling to the ground. It was so quick, so hard, he couldn't get his breath. He thought he heard a shot but couldn't get his head up, didn't know which way to look.

"Nooo!" The scream came from almost on top of him, so loud he flinched, shutting his eyes. Some training, deep inside, took over. He knelt, looking for his rifle. Bang, bang, bang . . . the sharp pounding of a 5.56 mm next to his ear. He winced, fell back down, saw his rifle, grabbed it, knelt again, looking wildly around. Lang was next to him on one knee, his heavy gun pointed at the truck, right elbow raised high in classic rifle-range fashion. Outside the truck the Muslim soldiers stood frozen in different poses, none injured by the burst over their heads, none inclined to raise a weapon.

The prisoner lay on the ground, not moving. The rebel leader was shaking his head and waving his gloves back and forth, as if shooing flies. Harvell's head was clearing. Behind Baba, he saw the Muslim driver with the limp slumped out the door of the cab, half his head blown off, blood running out like someone pouring out a large cup of coffee.

"He's with me five years." Baba was gesturing at the dead man. "What I do now, huh? Why you kill him? You pay his wife? Ha! Where I get money to pay her?"

"Cut him loose, Harvell," Lang said without shifting his glance, "and stay out of my line of fire."

Harvell half walked, half crabbed to the prisoner and cut the ropes. Both scrambled back to where Lang knelt, still aimed in.

"You crazy, you know that, crazy!" Baba yelled as he pushed his soldiers back into the truck. The body of the old soldier was loaded into the back, and a new driver hastily shifted the truck into gear. Soon the truck and jeep were several pastures away.

The Serb youth stood in his soiled uniform with his head down, haggard and numb-looking. Lang gestured down the fields toward the valley. The youth looked and hesitated. Lang waved his hand impatiently. The youth turned and started to run. A few times he looked back, expecting to be shot.

"What a screwup," Lang said, more to himself than to Harvell.

"You did the right thing, sir," Harvell said.

"I didn't do a thing. Caulder took that shot. Let's head back."

The Serb soldier was several pastures away, running awkwardly, his limbs still constricted after being tied up, his heels kicking up puffs of light snow. He looked like a boy let out of school early, running with exuberance as the snowflakes swirled lightly around him. He disappeared from view over the crest of a hillock as the Marines turned away. The sharp stutter of a light machine gun from some distant ravine echoed and rolled over the hillside. Lang stopped and cocked his head, listening. After a few seconds he heard the flat, dull *pop!* of a pistol.

"I didn't think they'd driven too far," he said.

"You mean they just killed that boy?" Harvell asked. Lang didn't answer.

They returned to their lookout by the same roundabout route. No one said anything as they approached. Roberts and Caulder, both on one knee, were glaring at each other.

"I didn't drop," Lang said, looking down at Caulder. "You had no green light."

"Rules of engagement say to prevent murder," Caulder said, standing to face the captain.

"If the Corps wanted us to stop murders, we'd patrol Manhattan," Lang said. "You jeopardized our mission. That shot could get us recalled. Then we're no help in finding Cosgrove. Care to explain that to his mother?"

Caulder started to come back. He'd lined up his arguments and had his plastic rules of engagement card clenched in his hand. He hadn't backed off when Roberts jumped him right after he took the shot. He'd been sure he was in the right—up until the captain mentioned being re-called. Of course that's what the Op Center would do—pull back the team, insist on a written report, followed by an investigation, followed by a review higher up the chain of command. The process would take weeks, and it had nothing to do with finding Cosgrove. The team would be grounded. Caulder knew he hadn't thought it through.

"Aye-aye, sir," he said. "Fault on me."

Lang let it go. "Very well. Good shot anyway."

"Good?" Caulder tried to recover his pride. "Moving head shot at four hundred meters? Fucking world-class. Quals for FBI SWAT. Righteous kill, sir."

"Righteous isn't smart. In the FBI, that qualified for hard time," Lang said. "They're not our people. Muslim, Serb, whatever. They've been going at each other ever since prophets discovered swords. They're not ours and we're not theirs. Keep your focus on Cosgrove. That's all that counts."

Caulder looked away. Contentious but not unobservant, he knew

Lang was right. Still—at last he'd had the chance to pop someone. And the fucker deserved to die, too. Awesome shot, even from the prone.

"They snuffed him as soon as he was out of our sight," Lang added.

Caulder frowned and stroked the stock of his rifle.

"Who was that German?" Blade asked. "Someone who doesn't know Hitler's dead?"

"That was Baba, head Muslim guerrilla, with an ego problem," Lang said. "This valley would've erupted if we lit him up."

"What'd he want?"

"Oh, the usual—join forces, torture a few Serbs, torch a village, call an air strike on Belgrade," Lang said. "He doesn't have a clue about Cosgrove."

"Who were they dragging?" Roberts asked.

"A Serb," Lang said. "Probably killed someone's grandmother and slaughtered the children."

"Sir, stop breaking my balls," Caulder said. "I know I fucked up."

"All right, Caulder. You tried to prevent a murder," Lang said. "Your mother would be proud. Connie would think you're an idiot."

Caulder smiled. Over the past two years, the family members of the team had met a dozen times at the end of exercises and races or at parties and dinners. When the captain mentioned Caulder's wife, that signaled the ass chewing was over.

"So who reports this to the Ops Center—Caulder?" Roberts asked, determined that the sergeant would pay a price.

"Report what?" Lang said.

"The whack job by our own Have Gun, Will Travel," Roberts said.

"I don't see anybody," Lang said.

"Shit, sir, I tore that driver's head off," Caulder said. "I . . . oh, right. Could've missed. Yeah, that's possible."

"Or they could be taking him to a hospital," Lang said. "Ops has a lot on its mind. We don't want to distract them. Maybe later. Now let's get back on station."

Meaning, Roberts thought, *don't prompt anyone to recall us.*

"Sir, that man I snuffed—what'd he look like?" Caulder said. He wanted some satisfaction out of this.

"Gentle, dignified. Nine children, all girls."

"Thanks, I knew you'd let me off easy. Who's signing my card?"

"You giving autographs?" Roberts said.

"I need a second to get credit for the kill. Usually it's the spotter. How about it, Staff Sergeant?"

"Go ahead," Lang said, "what's a manslaughter sentence between friends?"

"Seriously, I need the chit signed," Caulder said. "Three years in and this is my first confirmed. All we do is bomb people. Real kills aren't easy to come by."

"You need DNA. It's a new NATO regulation," Lang said. "Better take an ear."

"Sir," Roberts said, "don't encourage him."

They settled in among the rocks and scrub, within easy talking distance of one another. Blade and Harvell watched the flanks. Caulder lay prone behind his rifle scope, focused on the burning farm. A few feet away Roberts sat down next to Lang, and both began to glass the valley, which they divided into quadrants. They rested their elbows on their knees and slowly swept back and forth. Once settled into the routine, Roberts spoke up again.

"What were you going to do, sir? That is, before Psycho here popped the driver."

Caulder bit his lip and kept his mouth shut. He hadn't asked the staff sergeant before he took the shot, and he knew Roberts was still seething.

"Not one single thing," Lang said.

Neither lowered his binoculars. They might have been two Marines at Khe Sanh in 1968, or two sailors in the Far Pacific in 1944, or two Confederate soldiers on picket duty, or two Cheyenne braves guarding their horse herd, or two Roman legionnaires on a stone wall in Gaul. They were comfortable with silences and with one another.

"You and Captain Cosgrove are tight," Roberts said.

"Since high school. Seventeen years."

"That long? Thought you were from Alaska."

"My father sent me to school in New England. Cold enough to be Alaska. Cos was my roommate."

"He cracks me up when he gets on a roll," Roberts said. "He must have been a handful for Mrs. C."

"She took that single-mom stuff seriously. We didn't get away with much."

"You, too?"

"Her house was a lot closer than Juneau," Lang said. "Same rules applied to me."

"We didn't know she was this sick," Roberts said.

Lang looked down at his rifle.

"She's tough. She'll beat it," Roberts said. "Captain Cosgrove's the one who's got worries. You'll never let him hear the end of this."

"He wouldn't surrender."

"Hell no, sir," Roberts said. "He's hard. I saw his one-handed pull-up stunt. No give in him."

A pause.

"Oh." A longer pause as Roberts thought of alternatives. "Could be only wounded. A flak jacket can stop a Kalashnikov."

"No it can't."

"Well, depends on the angle."

"So exactly what am I looking for?" Caulder said, scanning with his scope. "Even if he's still alive, they're not going to parade him around down there."

Lang looked at him. "They might. In Vietnam the gooners ran a stake through the cheeks of our people, tied a cord to it and pulled them through the villages. In Somalia the skinnies dragged bodies through the market. The Iraqis paraded our pilots around in trucks. Sure, they might show him off. We're trophies."

"Well, the Corps won't let them keep Captain Cosgrove," Roberts said. "I guarantee that."

Lang put down his binoculars and looked up the slope where the Muslim guerrillas had driven away. He rubbed his eyes, rolled his shoulders as if relieving a small cramp in his neck and clasped his hands on his knees, rocking slightly. He sat that way, looking at nothing as the seconds ticked by and the others tried to think of something to say.

"Anyone hear of the *Mayaguez*?" Lang finally said. He often did that, tossed a question out for anyone to answer. Sometimes that annoyed the sense of good order in Staff Sergeant Roberts, but not now. He was pleased Lang had backed him and put Caulder down.

"An American tramp steamer. We rescued the crew," Blade said, quick as usual. "Snatched them out of Cambodia after Saigon fell. President Ford himself congratulated the Corps for that one."

"You should go on some goddamn quiz show," Caulder said. "How can you remember that stuff?"

"Taught it to us in boot camp," Blade said. "You heard it, too, only you weren't paying attention."

"I didn't sign up for history," Caulder said.

"Did they teach you that three Marines were left on the beach by the task force?" Lang said. "That the Khmer Rouge beat them to death with pick handles after the President declared the *Mayaguez* a great victory?"

"Had to be a mistake, sir," Roberts said. "Had to be some royal fuckup."

"I believe it, Staff Sergeant. Hell, look at us, we're working for an admiral. The Corps doesn't run the world," Caulder said. "Know what I think? Surer than shit, some patrol will find Captain Cosgrove and the rear-echelon pogues will slap each other on the back and forget about us, and we'll freeze our bojangles off until they pick us up in the morning."

"Caulder, if I hadn't seen your cert, I'd never believe you're a sergeant E-Five," Roberts said. "You make the Blues Brothers sound intelligent."

For an hour they continued to glass the valley, now in deep afternoon shadow. Wherever they looked, they saw a helicopter, those in the distance buzzing black smudges, those nearer hovering like birds of prey about to snatch up a farmhouse. The air was filled with the staccato, machine-gun-like chatter of the turning blades. None flew near the cliff where they sat hidden. On the map they were inside the red hash marks marking the border zone, off limits to helicopters or small patrols.

"Maybe they'll release him," Roberts said, "like they did those two army guys in Bosnia."

Lang shook his head. "The Serbs held them three weeks until a senator begged for them. Cos doesn't have three weeks to get home. Besides, we knew who had those soldiers. That was a Kabuki dance; this is a black hole."

"A weasel couldn't hide down there," Caulder said. "No way he's still there."

"So where do you think he is?" Lang asked.

"If I had him, I'd move his ass out of this province, head for safe terrain." Caulder pointed at the dark peaks to the north. "Find a safe house, definitely not stay around here."

"He might talk his way out of it," Blade said. "Like he did with the colonel after he sent us into that swamp in Colombia."

"Worst three days of my life. I'm still digging chiggers out of my ass," Caulder said.

"You have to admire a man who screws up that bad and gets a letter of commendation while we had to beg for an extract," Blade said. "He's always putting you in it, sir. Captain Cosgrove has a golden tongue. He'll beat this."

"What is this—a 'We Shall Overcome' karaoke?" Lang said. "We all know how it works. The best chance for escape is in the first few hours. Time's working against him."

The team lapsed into silence, frustrated that they could do nothing, sensing a tragedy in the making, picturing an anonymous e-mail giving the location of the body, or a tip in a month or two from some informer about a decomposed corpse. Cosgrove wouldn't be on a flight home that evening.

"Skipper, maybe you should call the hospital," Blade said, connecting the dots, picking out the one action they could take.

"You know the rules in the field," Lang said. "The cell phone is emergency backup only."

"Shit, sir, what's one call? We're not exactly fighting for our asses out here," Caulder said, piling on, anxious to amend his earlier mistake. "If I was snatched, I'd hope you'd call Connie before some headquarters pogue did. Here's your cell." He reached inside his jacket and pulled out a bright metal cell phone about the size of a VCR tape, with a thin telescoping antenna and a large display window.

"Damn," said Lang, "that's Cosgrove's Quotron."

"A what?"

"A computer, like a high-powered digital pager. Tracks the market via satellite. Cosgrove uses it to contact his floor trader. It doesn't have voice, only digital."

"Looked like a cell. I didn't know which drawer was which."

"My fault, not yours. I can still reach the Web with it." Lang glanced at his watch. "Eight A.M. Newport time."

Lang drummed his fingers on his thighs. Staff Sergeant Roberts sat next to him, eyes firmly on the valley. There were reasons for regulations. He couldn't see how breaking this one jeopardized anything, but that wasn't the Marine way. And in front of the men. Harvell wasn't even one of them, and this would only encourage Caulder, who had to be kept on a short leash. Still, it would suck for Mrs. Cosgrove to hear the wrong way.

He looked at Lang, who was waiting for him. The captain had to be hurting, but he wasn't going to do anything until he had a read from his staff sergeant. Caulder had it right for once. One little message, what could it hurt?

"Send it, sir," Roberts said. "It won't affect the mission."

Lang turned on the Quotron.

"Slide over here, Harvell," he said. "I'll show you how to use this. Add to your comm skills."

III

Newport, R.I.

The pain had smothered her at three in the morning, a vise suddenly squeezing her chest. She flailed her arms, frail, panicky blows like the flutter of a sparrow's wings across his face. It took Bart Easton a few seconds to realize she was gasping for breath. He carried her to the car, raced down the empty streets, skidding around corners, and in minutes was at the emergency entrance. An emergency crew and a few nurses were standing on the ramp, bundled up, having a smoke. He grabbed a wheelchair, lifted her into it and rolled it up the ramp past them.

He pushed the wheelchair down the corridor and around a few corners to the emergency-room door. On the wall was the large metal button controlling entrance and he slammed it with his fist.

"Hey, you can't go in that way! You're not authorized," said an attendant who had followed him inside.

Easton ignored him and backed the wheelchair through the doors. The emergency room was small, four or five cubicles on each side of a wide corridor. In front of the main desk a man in a tan camel-hair overcoat sat slumped in a chair, hands handcuffed behind him, a policeman on either side. A young doctor in a white jacket and fashionable eyeglasses was shining a light in his eyes. Easton pushed the wheelchair up to them.

"She's in pain," Easton said.

"Put her over there." The doctor gestured toward the desk, not glancing up.

"I said she's in serious pain."

"And the doc said to wait, buddy," the larger policeman said.

"She doesn't have the time to wait," Easton said. He was a large man with a weathered face and a pronounced jaw, his eyes wide and bright. His words came out as a command, husky with authority and strain. He was giving an order, not a request.

The attendant and the policemen stared at Easton. The doctor straightened and peered at the woman, whose head was bent toward her chest, face gray, breathing shallow and fast. Without a word, he turned away from the drunk and took the wheelchair. Within a minute he had injected two needles of Demerol and had her breathing through an oxygen mask, the pain subsiding. The attendant angrily took back the wheelchair, looking over his shoulder at Easton, and the doctor began to fill out a form for the policemen. Without a word Easton left to move the car.

"Wonder what he's like when he really wants something," the doctor said.

Had the doctor asked those who knew Easton, the answer would have differed. His platoon sergeant from Quang Tri would have said his skipper exhibited newfound restraint with advanced age. Why, the old Cupcake—Easton's call sign in recon—would have leaped the desk and searched for painkilling drugs before talking to anyone. Those who worked for him recently would have thought he'd be more reasonable, like calling the head of the hospital at three A.M.

The nurse had found the record for readmittance and the doctor read it slowly, shaking his head.

"Sylvia Cosgrove, fifty-five," he said. "What a shame, still young."

Throughout the night they stabilized her in the intensive-care unit. Before dawn they wheeled her into a single at the end of the fifth floor, away from the noise of other patients. The room held a hospital bed in a facade frame of mahogany, lumpy ten-year-old chairs and a television recessed in a heavy wooden cabinet. Flowers were everywhere, yellow roses, blue hydrangeas, red chrysanthemums and Brazilian white orchids with thin purple lines, each as delicate as the vein that held the tube in her right arm.

She lay propped up in bed so she could hack up the mucus from her chest. The suction tube hissed insistently in its sheath next to her right arm. She had swiftly become proficient at probing her own throat to suck out the yellow pus from the dying lung. The radiation had stripped her throat raw, and she hadn't eaten in weeks. The loss of weight and fluid had tightened her face into the mask of starvation. Her high cheekbones seemed about to puncture her skin. Her soft hazel eyes were too bright. Her long brown hair had lost its luster and hung wanly around her shriveled face. Death hovered in a dark corner. She was sure of it, and whenever she dozed, she wanted to wake to see Bart Easton there.

"You keep the ogre from the door," she said.

Easton sat on the right side of her bed, legs braced and elbows tucked close to his sides so that he wouldn't jiggle any of the tubes. Face set and hard, he had been sitting that way for hours, ignoring the breakfast a nurse had brought. He felt like punching the wall or crying or both. He was determined that she would not see him tearing up, because then she would cry. They had counted on a reprieve for three months. That's why she had gone through that hellish chemo and radiation. She had well concealed her suffering until last night. Now here she was, admitted for the third time, and he knew it was the final watch, death dismissing the plans they had nurtured for the holidays. His Vietnam experience did him no good on this duty, nor did the finances of his software company. The best doctors had offered scant hope weeks ago. He could only stand grim sentinel as the ogre ate her lung.

"Tell me again when Tyler arrives." Her voice was a whisper.

"He'll be here tomorrow," he said. "He leaves tonight at seven, arriving Dover at . . ."

A transparent plastic oxygen mask covered her nose and mouth. She pulled the mask outward. "Stop. You sound like an airport announcement," she said. "May I see the picture again?"

Last night Bart had printed out Ty's latest e-mail picture, labeled "The Front." She held it with trembling fingers. Captain Tyler Cosgrove was pointing at a map, surrounded by four ferocious-looking Marines clasping weapons, faces striped white and black, hanging on Tyler's every word. Looking closer, you could see they were biting their lips to keep straight faces.

"Tyler is sending Mark's team on a mission," she said. "He's the intelligent."

"No, dear, Ty's the *intelligence* officer, and he's sending them to the bar for beer."

"I don't care," she wheezed, "I like it." She lay back and her eyes drooped.

"You've had a terrible night," Bart said. "Doze off. I'll get the paper and be right back."

He walked to the corner store to buy the Sunday papers. When he came back, Sylvia was trying to write a note, but the intravenous needle was inserted between her knuckles, and she kept dropping the pen on the sheets. Bart removed the pen and smiled.

"All right, Miss Stubborn, what are you doing?"

"Changing my will. The ships over the mantel are perfect for Mark. You know, the Gratins, early nineteenth century."

"Aren't they too placid?" He laughed. "Why not Homer's *Gulf Stream*? Sailor on broken boat, sharks circling, that's his style."

"My Gratins are authentic, not prints. And don't criticize Mark for trying so hard."

"Hard? No, no—normal people try hard. Mark is *driven*," Bart said. "And I'm teasing. You know I like him."

"I forgot about him until I saw the picture."

She was speaking through the oxygen mask, on the verge of tears. She couldn't understand how she had done that. Mark had always listened to everything she said, so bewildered all those years ago by her interest in what he was doing, so intent on achieving, so grateful for her praise. He had never forgotten her birthday or any other important date, sometimes reminding Tyler. Yet now she had forgotten him. How could she?

"That's understandable." Bart patted her hand. "You're in pain, and Mark's not your flesh and blood."

"You don't know what you're talking about," she said, eyes glistening. "He'll miss me. He needs me."

"What's to miss? You're not going anywhere. We'll all have dinner together when he gets back. Mark pays."

"Stop it. You sound childish talking like that."

Stung, Bart didn't reply. Sylvia watched him, feeling more empty than
sad. She couldn't find the right words to say good-bye to him. It was easier to talk about the boys. She reached for his hand. "Will Mark come
back with Tyler?"

Easton glanced at his watch. He, too, had forgotten Mark. Only five
hours ago he had called the regiment, insisting Ty return immediately.
"Why don't we give it a day or two and see how things develop. I, ah,
pushed them a little hard a while ago."

"You do that too often," she said. "I'll ask Tyler to arrange it tomorrow. He knows how to do those things. I want Mark here. He's been so
good, the perfect roommate. Tyler was better at talking his way out of
things. The beer smell in the closet, the bra . . ."

"I haven't heard that one."

She smiled. "It was their first year at Princeton. I found the bra behind
a chair in their dorm room. Mark apologized, but I knew it was Tyler. I insisted he return it. So Tyler put it on and marched over to the girl's
dorm."

Bart laughed and she giggled, a burp behind the mask.

"They're friends for life," she said, "like you and me."

She was feeling better, playing along again, shutting out reality.

"Humph. When we're married, you'll have to submit like a good
wife." His fear of a second divorce, of eventual rejection or nagging, had
led to "dating" her for five years. Yes, he had said, he was committed.
Committed to what? To his own fears. Now she was dying and all he
could do was play make-believe.

"You're just after my fortune," Sylvia said. "Now tell me again when
Tyler arrives."

Bart groaned. "All right, but first let me check e-mail."

The hospital room had two phone jacks but no phone to upset her
with unwanted calls. A line ran from one outlet to a laptop perched on a
hospital tray, the sort wheeled up to a bed and cranked up or down. Bart
drew up a chair and scrolled through his messages. He looked at the list
of incoming mail. There it was, one of the last entries.

From: #@V+   2:00 P.M. Sun., Dec. 21
To: <beaston@eastoninc.com>

T missing on patrol. All looking. Using T's Quotron. Woody at
Warburg has password. Contact me emergency only. USMC pissed if I
communicate from field.
Mark

He read the message twice. Ty and Mark had been traders at Warburg
for six years, and during their visits to Newport, Easton often saw them
use the Quotron to check their positions. To avoid tipping off competi-
tors, Woody, Warburg's floor trader, would feed any large orders from the
Quotron a little at a time into the frenetic bidding pit. Once Easton had
the password, he could communicate with Mark.

Easton knew the Marine routines, the emergency-action drills, the
list of next of kin. Some official right now was trying to contact her, and
Easton had to cushion that shock. He looked up from the laptop, keeping
his expression neutral.

"What is it?" she asked.

"I forgot. I should swing by your house and pick up yesterday's mail.
I'll be back in twenty minutes."

He kissed her on the forehead, smelling the decay through the oxygen
mask. In the car he listened to the news. Nothing. Once inside her house,
he checked the answering machine; a lieutenant colonel had called half
an hour ago. Easton called him back.

"National Military Command Center. Lieutenant Colonel Swinford
speaking."

"My name is Bart Easton, calling for Mrs. Cosgrove. She's in critical
condition at the hospital."

"Understood, sir. I'll cut to the bottom line—Captain Cosgrove
was reported missing at noon Kosovo time, six A.M. here. All we know
is that he was on patrol. His commanding officer will call as soon as
he can."

"I spoke with him earlier about emergency leave for Captain Cosgrove. I have his number."

"Ah, he's real busy right now, coordinating the search . . ."

"I understand. Don't call him, he'll call us. Ask him to speak to me first."

Bart gave him the telephone number for the nurses' station on Sylvia's floor, and the colonel said a polite good-bye. Bart immediately called Woody.

"Woody speaking." The voice sounded like a truckload of gravel. Easton held the phone away from his ear. Floor traders could be heard miles away.

"Woody, this is Bart Easton. I'm a close friend of—"

"Sure, Mark and Ty talk about you," Woody's booming voice cut him off. "You're Old Corps, right? Some of those stories are pretty wild."

Bart explained what had happened, and Woody gave him the company password to reach Ty's Quotron.

"It's a wireless e-mail system that only accepts our order forms. I'll send you a form for a natural-gas trade," Woody said. "Sounds like that's what Mark sent to you. Use the comments section. It's limited in word space, but it works. I'll send Mark a—"

"No. We have to limit this to one channel, Woody—me. Mark broke regulations when he contacted me."

"Hmm. Then make your message sound like a trade so it won't stand out. As long as you don't hit the confirm icon, it'll look like an order that was never placed. Mind if I log on and read along?"

"As long as it stays between us. I don't want Ty's mother hit with bad news, and Mark can alert me. But the Marines could come down hard on him for this."

"I'm not a snitch. This stays with me on this end. And if something ever did leak, Warburg will back Mark. Our trading group is up seventy mil this year. The partners aren't going to piss us off. I guarantee Mark is covered."

On the ten-minute drive back to the hospital, Bart tried to sort out what he should say to Sylvia. He walked in quietly. Her eyes were closed. When he moved a chair, she woke with a start.

"I thought you were Tyler," Sylvia said. "He likes to surprise me."

He glanced down. Somehow he gave it away. She looked at him with that quick intelligence. "What's the matter?"

He walked to the bedside, where thin tubes were dripping glucose, morphine, blood thinners and anti-nausea liquids. He sat gingerly and placed his fingers on top of hers, careful not to disturb the needle inserts.

"Tyler's on patrol," he said. "He hasn't called back to his unit. The Pentagon will let us know when they find him."

That was enough. He would tell her the rest a little at a time. She said nothing. Her eyes half closed and her breathing slowed—in and out, pause, in and out.

Mitrovica Valley border area   3 P.M. Sunday

The recon team was perched on top of a sheer rock crag, the houses, roads and trails in the valley clear and distinct in their binoculars. They could zoom in on every cow, every dog, every person. They watched, straining to pick out anything unusual, scanning in the dimming light the same patches of farmland being crisscrossed by hundreds of other Marines. The wind had freshened from the north, and motes of snow danced and jerked and swirled in the updrafts.

Staff Sergeant Roberts looked at his watch. "Fifteen hundred, gents. Time to pop the pills."

The skipper might assume the team knew what to do; Roberts didn't make assumptions. There was a reason for order, a reason for checking gear, a reason for schedules, even in the field. Young Marines were like the young firefighters back at his firehouse. They thought they were organized, but sometimes they weren't. They'd forget something if he didn't impose the rules. Blade might remember without being told. Caulder, though, went too much on his own instincts.

"I hate the EMM," Caulder said, holding a large beige pill. "Gives me a sore throat."

"Cut it in two," Blade said, "like the doc suggested when you bitched to her last week."

"I'm a sniper, not a pharmacist," Caulder said.

"You're an auto mechanic who works on cars that don't have computers," Blade said.

"Stick it. I could ding every one of those mothers upslope if I wanted to."

Lang turned around. On the shoulder of the mountain behind them, he could barely make out a vehicle and a few black dots on the twisting road. He brought up his binoculars. The figures were plodding forward, their frames angled toward the ground as if they were hauling on unseen ropes a tan pickup that inched along behind them.

"Nine hundred meters," Lang said, clicking the laser range finder on his binoculars. "What's that all about?"

"Mine clearing?" Blade said.

"Doesn't make sense," Lang said. "The locals know their own roads."

"They're out of our operating area, Skipper," Roberts said. Every so often the captain had to be reminded of the rules, too.

Lang took the Marine computer from Harvell and unclipped the radio talk piece.

"Six Zulu, this is Pepperdog Six actual. Unusual activity involving small group one click north of our pos. Oscar Mike to check it out. Out."

The Pepperdogs were going deeper inside the red hash marks marked out-of-bounds to NATO personnel. The team was ignoring the standing order to stay well back from the Serb border. Yet no one in the Ops Center objected. More than forty patrols were involved in the search for Cosgrove, and frustration had mounted.

In a loose diamond formation, the patrol struck out across the snow-patched fields, their strides long and fast. Blade was point man and he moved fast. At the barbed-wire fences, the lead man used the barrel of his weapon to hold up one strand while he stepped on the next, and the others slipped through easily, with scant time wasted. Within fifteen minutes they had closed on the group and could distinguish individual figures. The activity of the group picked up as the Marines approached.

Before they were within hailing distance, there was a puff of black smoke, a bit taller than a man, in front of the bumper of the tan pickup. The dull *crump* reached them seconds later. The figures scurried around, stumbling, as the pickup gained speed up the road toward the mountain.

When the patrol reached the road, the people were clustered around a girl lying on the ground. A fat woman in a thick brown sweater and black skirt was on her knees, holding her hands to her face, rocking back and forth, shrieking like a boiling kettle. The wounded girl's face was the color of sand, her eyelids drooping, boots twisted, heels and toes both flat on the ground. Roberts pushed past the trembling father, ignored the distraught mother and ran his hands along the torn skirt, stained dark brown-red below the knees. One boot flopped over. He placed his finger and thumb on the carotid vein in the neck and looked into her eyes. He shook his head. "She's failing fast. We need a medevac ASAP."

"Can she make it?" Lang said.

"She's lost both legs. I don't give her a chance. But what do I know? I'm a firefighter, not a doctor. I've been called out to only one or two accidents this bad," Roberts said. "Where's my medevac?"

Again Lang ignored the question.

This was the first civilian casualty the Marines had seen. The cordite still lingered, and the blood was pooling. They weren't shocked or even mildly upset. Somehow the scene seemed less graphic than those that Hollywood created for the Cinemax screens. They stood outside the tragedy, unaffected onlookers, anxious to get away, to give chase, though each would later remember her waxy stillness, how she lay there, deep in shock far beyond pain, ebbing away. Lang turned away from the dying girl. Staff Sergeant Roberts still knelt beside her, not wanting to appear callous, knowing Lang was calling in no medevac.

"Get out the Translator, Harvell," Lang said. "Set it for the local dialect."

Harvell fumbled inside his jacket and pulled out a flat military-green panel with two embedded speakers, about the size of a book. He entered a few keystrokes on the screen, powered by a four-gigahertz CPU and two digital signal processor chips, and handed it to Lang, who had pulled a teenage boy away from the stunned family. The boy was in shock, trembling before the fierce-looking Americans with their slashed-paint faces.

Lang gestured at him to watch the panel. "Speak at the box," he said. "Who was in the pickup?"

After a few seconds the panel repeated Lang's words in the local dialect.

"*Doggo kleina,*" came the boy's tentative reply. "Slav bastards."

"How many?"

"Four, maybe five."

"Did you see an American prisoner?"

"No."

"Could a man be hidden in the truck?"

"No, yes, I guess. I don't know. They said to walk in front and point out the mines. Olga was frightened. She forgot where to step."

"Are there more mines?" Lang pointed up the mountain track.

The boy shook his head. "These are the last. Too dangerous up there."

Harvell was wide-eyed. "These people set the mines, sir?"

"The rebels call the shots," Lang said. "Did these people help? Sure."

"Girl's dead," Roberts shouted over. "Call it in?"

Lang took the End User Terminal from Harvell and switched to voice. "Zulu Six, this is Pepperdog Six actual. Tan pickup with four armed Serbs heading up switchback at six two three four seven nine. One civilian fatality here from a mine. Request heliborne intercept of pickup. Over."

They waited several minutes for the reply. "Pepperdog, this is Zulu Six. Joint Task Force sends a negative on intercept. That area is hot, repeat hot, with Serb military movement. Intense diplomacy under way. We are not to jeopardize by military action. It was a good idea, though. Out."

"That's that," Roberts said. "Regiment sounds pissed, but they have their orders."

"You mean they're going to let that pickup go?" Harvell said.

"Shut up, Harvell," Roberts said.

Lang didn't reply. He walked several steps away, studying his map. The team slowly followed, ignoring the wailing and crying behind them. The snow had picked up and swirled around them like a mist, stinging their faces. The mountain loomed large, blocking out the skyline, the afternoon shadows sliding toward them. Lang looked at the track leading up into the mountain range. The Serb border ran along the ridgeline at the top of the six-thousand-foot mountain.

"Our observation post is useless now that the light's fading," he said. "That pickup's running from something, risking mines."

"Then let's move ass. They know something," Caulder said. "Fuck, they're Serbs. They'll be drinking before the sun sets. Maybe they'll stop or skid off the road. We can be up there and back before daylight."

Roberts had cut Caulder slack the last time, but not now. He'd shut this down before it got out of hand. "This is the red zone, Caulder," he said. "We're to stay two clicks away from the Serb border. We've violated that order already. We call in before we push."

"Regiment wanted to send a chopper, Staff Sergeant," Caulder said. "They were overruled. If we mother-may-I, we'll be overruled, too."

"The Nez Perce walked from Wyoming to Canada. The army never caught them," Blade said. "We turn off the EUT, and who knows where we went? We leave no tracks, like the Nez Perce."

"Blade, stow your Indian stories," Roberts said. "We're not psyching ourselves up for some adventure race. This is serious shit. We turn off that EUT and the colonel will take our stripes."

"Not if we have a comm failure," Caulder said.

"And I won't tell," Harvell said.

"Shut up, Harvell," Roberts said. "Sir, regiment will know we're screwing with them."

The skipper should have spoken up, Roberts thought. Caulder and Blade had only three, four years in, weekend drills and summer exercises that for them were the extreme races. They didn't know how serious procedures could be. And Harvell was clueless. Okay, he, Roberts, hadn't much active-duty time, either. He was a lieutenant in the NYFD, not a full-time recon-team sergeant. But Lang had five years in the Fleet Marine Force, two tours to Southeast Asia. He knew the drill better than any of them. What was he thinking?

"Do you think regiment wanted to follow up?" Lang said.

"Yes, sir," Roberts said, "but that's not the point."

"Maybe the point is taking initiative, not asking others to decide for us," Lang said.

There was no bite to the words, but they hung there, waiting for Roberts. The others didn't say anything; they just looked at the staff sergeant. For two years the team had pulled together. The captain had led the way, picking the men, training for the races, volunteering them for the hardest missions. Now his best friend was missing. Ah, what the hell, who was Roberts to keep objecting after what he did last night, when he hadn't been out there with them for the morning run? If they wanted to hump all night without sleep, it was no biggie. And that's what this would be, another hump with a royal ass chewing when they got back.

"Roger that," Roberts said. "Comm failures happen, right?"

"Definitely!" Caulder said. "Magnetic interference from that mountain. Or better yet, we say Harvell crashed the computer. They'd believe that."

It had been four hours and ten quarts of liquid since their morning marathon. Caulder was running in place like a sprinter warming up, trying to loosen up his sore legs. Blade was looking at his GPS and his map, already plotting their route. Roberts shook his head and adjusted his shoulder harness.

"Harvell, send a text message, no voice," Lang said. "Say Pepperdogs in hot pursuit of a suspect vehicle. Will report in later. Then switch off the computer."

Harvell was still sweating lightly from the jog across the fields, yet his stomach and chest felt cold. The captain was telling the Ops Center nothing. Harvell had seen recon do that before. But this team had watched a soldier almost dragged to death, and Caulder had killed a man. Now there was a dead girl, and they were going up that thing, that black mass with no top, rising up and up. He sensed the captain watching him.

"What's your best hump, Corporal?" Lang asked.

"Three hours, thirty-one minutes in the marathon, sir," Harvell said.

"Shit." Caulder shook his head. Roberts spat and looked away. Blade checked his rifle and didn't look up.

"Split Harvell's pack. Dump all extra gear," Lang said. "Harvell, you carry only your weapon and the comm gear. Everyone fill up with water from that farm. We leave in five mikes."

They walked to the farm well, drank until their stomachs were distended and filled plastic bottles to drink and discard later. They took the pack from Harvell, dividing the ammo and food. Last, they crisscrossed on Lang's pack two fiberglass wings with rounded ends that looked like short skis.

"We're only going eight hours," Lang said. "Carry ammo and some rations. Cache the rest."

"We'll bring one sleeping bag for Captain Cosgrove," Roberts said.

I should have thought of that, Lang thought. *A bag means we expect to bring Cos back. Solid Roberts.*

Selecting a thicket off the road, they stowed their clothes, climbing ropes, a few books, goggles, knives, all manner of survival gear each Marine loved to carry. When they were done, each man's pack felt empty,

only sixty pounds. Light by infantry standards—160 rounds of ammuni-
tion each, fragmentation grenades, Claymore mines, smoke grenades,
GPS receivers, handheld radios, packets of Meals Ready to Eat, quarts
and quarts of water.

They compared waypoints on their GPS receivers and twitched
and shrugged their shoulders to settle their loads. Each had his FM radio
secured by a Velcro strap on the collar of his jacket. They checked the
channel setting and switched them off to save battery life. Caulder
snorted and pawed at the dirt like a horse. The others laughed. Lang nodded, and Roberts gave a casual hand signal, and they trudged off in a
loose triangle.

Lang remained behind. Harvell looked at the captain bent forward
under the pack. With the black mountain looming behind him, Lang
looked enormous, the wings of the model-scale plane with its tiny
video camera protruding from his shoulders, a prehensile creature from
a childhood comic book. Harvell was embarrassed to be carrying only a
few pounds. Lang sensed this and squatted, then abruptly sat on his
ass, leaning back against his gigantic pack, his legs stuck straight out in
front as if he were pinned by the weight. He looked less threatening,
almost like a turtle on its back, and Harvell smiled when the captain
gestured for him to sit in the dirt near where the girl had died. With no
pack, Harvell sat and crossed his legs Indian-style, as if at a Boy Scout
campfire.

"Harvell, this will be hard," Lang said. "At first it will seem easy. Then
it will grind on you. Remember, no matter how you feel, it will end.
There's only one rule. Don't stop."

Lang reached out a hand, and Harvell pulled him to his feet.

That was it? Harvell had expected a speech, an exhortation, something more than "Don't stop." Of course he wouldn't stop. Now that he
was in the field, feeling how it really was, he was confident. He wasn't
tagging along; they were all sharing this together. After this morning's
run, Lang should watch out for himself. Harvell might outlast him, and
that smart-ass Caulder, too.

Together they struck out, Lang holding to a steady pace, not rushing,
the Marine computer turned off. The map contour lines were so close together that the team could be halfway to the top of the mountain before

Ops asked what they were doing. Harvell wasn't sure he could answer that. One thing he did know—this team didn't sit around and wait for something to happen.

Once they struck out, the pace seemed easy, and Harvell had time to daydream. How many programmers had humped with recon? Only one, J. Kirwin Harvell. He had the Quotron. He didn't have to wait until they got back before filing. What could the Corps do—issue him a letter of reprimand? He was a reservist. What was that compared to job offers? He hadn't started whatever this was becoming. He wasn't Lang. He was simply the reporter on-scene. Hell, his PR would help the team. So what if he sent a few messages?

In single file they followed a twisting route upward. Twilight was brief, but the snow cover reflected enough light in the dark for them to see where they were climbing. They stayed off the road, close enough to glimpse it through the bare trees. Eventually Lang signaled a halt while he and Roberts discussed something. Farther up, Caulder and Blade were checking for signs on the road.

Harvell looked at his watch. Five P.M. For over an hour he had been composing his posting, short, punchy sentences. He took out the Quotron, typed quickly and hit send. His career was about to take off.

Koplje foothills   **5:00 P.M. Sunday**

Four kilometers and three thousand steep feet above the team, the tan Toyota pickup steadily churned up the switchbacks, headed north for the border, a crust of frost providing solid traction on the dirt road. The Americans rarely ventured away from the flatlands, where their armored vehicles swiftly surrounded and quelled any disturbance. On the mountainside, the tracks of armor ground away the porous slates of gravel and clay. Only light, wheeled vehicles could negotiate the sharp turns without disturbing the soft bedrock, and NATO didn't like moving without armor.

There was no sense risking casualties to patrol an area too wild to be controlled. Let the half-drunk soldiers of whatever side skulk for the winter in backcountry wood shacks, breathing the fumes of tiny kerosene stoves while the northern winds sliced though the mud mortar between the cabin boards and the snowdrifts mounted with each storm, isolating the soldiers as firmly as any cell block.

Over his right shoulder Saco could see the valley floor. He watched the dozens of pairs of yellow lights scurrying about, like an overlarge family of foxes bounding around a field at twilight, stirring up the mice to eat with a snap of their sharp teeth. The Americans hadn't snapped him up, though the general had turned him away like a stray dog. Get rid of the American. Go! Go where? NATO checkpoints dotted the valley, while Baba's *protivs* hid off the main roads, hoping to ambush some stray Serb family. He'd done well, no thanks to the general. Driven straight through Baba's territory, gambling that the Muslim fanatics would stay hidden while the conference was going on. The Toyota looked like a farmer's. It should; its owner that morning had been a farmer. The rest of the drive up the mountain had proved easy after that *dete* girl found the mine for him.

Saco knew the general had small units scouting up here, looking for a route so a larger force could get behind Baba and pin him down. Saco felt safe up here. He could dump the American and it would take him hours to stumble back down. Saco would be over the border by then. Who else had ever captured an American? No one. And now he had to let him go. Balls. Well, at least he had the Toyota and the motorcycle, not bad for a day's work.

"So, have you decided what we do, Saco?" asked the driver, a sallow, thin man in his early forties.

Three soldiers sat in the back, swaying and bouncing at every turn, paying no attention to Cosgrove, whose head occasionally banged against the side of the truck bed. Lost in his broodings, Saco didn't answer. "You have the American's things?" he asked.

"Yes, one hundred American dollars in his wallet, some identification and a cell phone."

The driver gestured at a sack on the floor. Saco rummaged through it, shoving the money into his tunic. Over a week's salary. The bike would bring a thousand Euros, maybe more. He took a long pull on the bottle of cheap apple brandy. He was feeling better.

He fiddled with the cell phone. Such simple things, so handy. The only problem was every time his men stole one, it was good for only a day or two before the phone company cut it off. Should he call his uncle in Turkey or his cousin in Chicago? No, he didn't have the numbers. He'd have to wait until they got back to the mill. He poked at the speed-dial numbers and smiled. Why not have a little fun?

"Pull over," he said. He lumbered out and stretched. The reception up this high would be good. He held up the phone and pressed a number. "Let's see who answers."

New York City   **11 A.M. Sunday**

A year after the terrorist attacks, Manhattan had regained that special air it wears at Christmastime. Pedestrians walked briskly, a few even dressed in fashionable overcoats and carefully chosen hats. The cold revitalized the air, each breath sharp, alive. The whistles of the traffic police, shrill and demanding, signaled that the city's habitual bustle had increased. Thousands of strings of white lights danced in the chill winds, and the restaurants filled early.

For Katharine Bennington, Sunday morning was the chance to finish her shopping before the stores became jammed. She was small, almost wispy, with the angular features of the dedicated runner. Her laugh was infectious, and when she and Tyler Cosgrove, with his enthusiasms, got on a tear, they pulled everyone along with them. Katharine looked forward to her happy life. She and Tyler would live in Larchmont or Harrison, summer in Newport, raise one boy and one girl, collect oddball friends and take long walks with a chocolate Lab that would grow fat. They would stay trim, nurture their children and enjoy the rhythms of a long and prosperous life, which shouldn't be too trying with intelligence, good looks and a healthy trust fund.

The problem at hand was selecting a scarf for Tyler's mother, something with subtle colors and a clever pattern. She had been to two specialty stores and was now down to Macy's, in the back of the third floor, hoping against her sense of fine taste that among the Hermès she might find something fitting.

When the phone rang in her purse, at first she didn't recognize it as hers, since she had accidentally left it on. She started to turn it off when she saw the Caller ID number. "Hello! Wait, wait, darling. I'll be right with you," she said, rushing to an open space next to the escalators. "Okay, I can talk now. I'm out shopping for your mother. You're calling early. How are you, darling? I miss you frightfully."

"Dawling, I miss you." The voice was harsh, mocking, playful.

Katharine froze. What was this? Tyler's friends fooling around? Didn't sound like it. The voice wasn't friendly. She felt a trace of fear.

"Who is this?" With her tone of voice, she let the caller know she didn't think this was humorous.

"I ask same. Who are you? Where are you?"

Saco was enjoying himself. He stood a few feet from the pickup, bellowing into the cell phone, the others clustered around.

"Put Tyler on," Katharine said, sounding more firm than she felt.

"Is name of husband? Ty-ler Cos-grove," Saco said, thumbing through Cosgrove's wallet.

"Put him on the phone," Katharine said in a loud voice. A few shoppers glanced at her, annoyed. A saleswoman, arranging a pile of scarves, looked up.

Saco pulled back the oily canvas in the bed of the Toyota. Cosgrove lay facedown, arms bound, a thin icicle of blood hanging from his left ear. "He don't talk. I talk. You got money? Americans have plenty money. You give a little to me and you get Ty-ler. You get money ready, okay? I call back."

The thought had popped out. He didn't know where it came from. He was just breaking American balls. The Americans had everything. The asses, riding around on their tanks, fat and scared in their armor, looking down on everyone, thinking they owned the world. Sure, this one had money. They all had money. Call her back? No, he'd give her time to scream and cry or do whatever rich American women did. Okay, so he'd hung up because he didn't know what to say next. So what? He'd figure it out. He grinned at his soldiers, who were grinning along with him, handing the apple brandy back and forth.

Katharine gripped the cell phone and took a deep breath. More shoppers were staring at her, and one or two had hesitated, ready to offer assistance. This couldn't be happening. Here she was, surrounded by the sights and sounds of Christmas, shopping. With trembling hands, she dialed the number on the screen.

"Hello? Is pretty lady calling back," Saco said, looking at the phone number. "That was fast. You got the money? Where we meet?"

Katharine hung up without speaking, dropped the phone into her purse and buried her face in her hands. The saleslady looked across at her. "Are you all right? Do you want to sit down or something?"

Katharine shook her head and stumbled down the escalator. She needed fresh air. She had to think. Who to call? Ty's unit? The number was back at her apartment. Mark? Yes. She brought up his number and hit send. No luck. His voice mail answered. Who else? She tried Sylvia and got an answering machine. Sylvia must be with Bart, she thought. She dialed Bart's number. Someone had to have a phone turned on.

"Katharine?" Bart answered, after glancing at the Caller ID.

"Bart? Thank God, I've finally reached someone. This sounds absurd, but some man with a thick accent called me claiming he has Tyler. He was laughing, asking for money. It has to be some sort of sick joke or something, doesn't it?"

Katharine was standing at the corner of Thirty-fourth Street and Seventh Avenue, the wind biting into her hands. She didn't know how she had gotten outside. She didn't notice the cold, but it was becoming difficult to hold the cell phone. She was biting her lip, trying not to break down.

Bart had walked outside Sylvia's room. There was a pause while he drew a breath. He spoke slowly, trying to calm her. "It's not a joke, Katharine. Tyler is missing as of a few hours ago. I'm sorry, I should have called you right away. But I was hoping for good news before I did. Sometimes someone on patrol will get separated and turn up a few hours later."

"Oh God, what do we do? Call the FBI? The CIA? What?"

"His unit is doing everything possible. This is the first news anyone has had, so let's go over this. What phone? How did this person choose to call you?"

"Ty has a company sat phone. Warburg agreed he could call me every day. What does this have to do with—"

"It could help us find Ty. Let me look into it. You reached me at the hospital. I had to rush Sylvia here last night."

"Oh God, this gets worse and worse." Her voice was breaking.

"Katharine, we'll work through this." He spoke in the same command voice the policemen and the doctor had heard in the emergency room. "Your job is to keep that cell phone on and agree to anything the caller tells you to do. Take a cab to your apartment and call me from there."

She put the phone back in her purse, shaking in the cold.

An ordinary person would have called the FBI or the Pentagon. Bart Easton never considered that. The moment he heard Katharine's news, his mind switched into survival mode, sorting through options, determined to act before the clock ran out. He understood bureaucracies, each with a Sunday duty section and a procedure to follow once he had called, confirming who he was, whether someone was missing in Kosovo, what was known at the Department of Defense, at NATO headquarters in Brussels, at the subheadquarters in Naples, Italy, at the Joint Task Force afloat in the Adriatic and, finally, at the regimental Ops Center. By dinnertime, the coordination and vetting would be complete and the recall list activated. By Monday morning actions would be under way, eighteen hours after Katharine received the call.

Any help, any lead he could generate had to be delivered in minutes, hours at the most. Bart knew only the regiment could rescue Tyler, not police in New York, not investigators in Washington, not military staffs in windowless rooms at the Pentagon. The Warburg satellite phone was the key. He called Woody and explained what had happened.

"How's Katharine taking it?" Woody asked.

"You know her?"

"Sure. We all get together after work sometimes. She used to say Ty was playing at being a Marine. Playing, for Christ's sake. She's nice enough, but not cut out for this hard stuff."

"This sat phone Ty has," Bart said, "can you track where the call was made?"

"All our sat phones have GPS chips inside. We're charged point-to-point for each call. Once you make a connection, your location is recorded. It shows up on the bill at the end of the month," Woody said. "We run a big account with that tel company. I'll get our security people on it right away."

"No officials, Woody. There's no way the government will authorize ransom."

"Ransom? Who's talking ransom? Those Marines must be rip-shit. They'll take care of this."

"They're my first choice," Bart said.

"Like there's a second choice?"

Silence while Easton thought of what to say next. He hadn't figured Woody as a rules player, but the Enron collapse had made all traders pay attention to rules.

"Companies pay off every week, in the Philippines, Colombia," Easton said. "Know why? Governments can't get their employees back. Ty's mother's dying, Woody. So, yes, I'll pay to gct him back."

"How many laws am I breaking?" Woody asked.

"None that I know of. I'll pay all legal fees. I'm not asking you to—"

"I got nothing about breaking the law. There's a difference between what's legal and what's right," Woody said. "But ransom is bullshit. If you're using the Marines, I'm in. That's our deal, right?"

"Agreed. Whatever you turn up goes straight to Ty's unit, and to Mark," Bart said. "But Woody, if that doesn't work, I'll pay. I want Ty back."

"Pay? They'll pay, all right. Once Lang gets on their ass, the jaws of life won't pry him off," Woody said. "I need the ID on that phone. Where's Katharine?"

Katharine was barely back at her walk-up apartment in SoHo when Alexandra Bove rang. She buzzed her up. Katharine was by nature relaxed and fun-seeking; Alexandra was organized and thoughtful. Full-figured and athletic, Alex had been dating Mark for two years and ran with him on weekends or picked him up at the end of his two-day hikes. While Mark had been avoiding commitment, it had seemed so easy for Katharine, one year with Ty and her future was secure, predictable. Not that Alexandra wanted someone else to provide her security. Quite the opposite. But it would help if Mark relaxed and let their relationship flow naturally.

They hugged, Katharine burst out crying and Alex, ever the lawyer, asked a dozen questions, going over certain facts a second time.

"Let's be sure I have this straight—Woody is coming over to pick up the cell phone because Bart Easton told him to. No one else is coming, not the NYPD, not the FBI—just Woody?"

"Why are you saying it like it's strange? You know Woody as well as I do. We've all been out together."

"Katharine, that's what strange. Woody's a trader. Why is he involved? What's Bart doing?"

The front-entrance buzzer rang. "You can ask him yourself," Katharine said. "But please, no courtroom cross-examinations. I want this nightmare to end. I don't care how as long as I have Tyler back."

She buzzed him up. A huge young man in a Yankees jacket with a round face, long brown hair and a cowlick that hung over his forehead, Woody looked like an out-of-shape rugby player, and his eyes held a hint of natural belligerence. Katharine opened the door with the sat phone clutched in her hands, knuckles white, face raw from rubbing at tears.

"Hey," Woody said, no hugs or cheek kisses. He looked over her shoulder. "Hi, Alex."

Katharine gave him the cell phone, grabbing his large forearm at the same time.

"Can you find him? Can you call him? Can you—"

"Katharine," he said, taking her hand. "I'll try to help. Easton filled me in. Now, what I need—"

"We should go to the FBI," Alex interrupted. "They're—"

"Wait," Woody said. "Mark and Ty are high on Easton. You both know him, right? He's a been-there, done-that type. He says we get any info ASAP to Ty's unit. First I need the ID from this sat phone to confirm a connection. I'll call from outside."

After Woody left with the phone, Katharine and Alexandra sat on the couch, clutching each other's hands. "I have bad news," Katharine said. "Sylvia's relapsed. I have to go to Newport and I don't know how to handle it. What do I say to her? She's the one who's terminal and here I'm the one falling apart. Ty's missing and I can't think. My mind's a blank."

Alex hugged her, pushing aside the shock in her own mind. This was not the time for emotion. Work out a plan. Concentrate on the practical, on the logistics.

"I'll go with you," Alex said. "We'll talk to Woody and then leave."

It seemed only a few minutes until the buzzer rang again.

"Got it," Woody said, entering and handing Katharine a business card with two rows of numbers written on the back. "It took a little talking, but Warburg's a big account. I gave them the usual emergency bullshit, blah, blah."

"I still think we should give these numbers to the FBI," Alex said.

"One more time," Woody said, "I call Bart right this minute. He gives it to Ty's unit. We cut out the middlemen. Police don't add value."

"That's how a trader thinks," Alex said. "As a lawyer, I have an obligation. You and Bart Easton are out of your league. This should go to police professionals, right now."

"This isn't a law case, Alex," Woody said. "So please hold off with the advice."

"Mark's involved. So I have more right to be involved than either you or Bart Easton."

"Stop the bickering! You both sound so self-centered. I can't take this," Katharine sobbed. "What if Ty's tortured or shot or something? He's all alone. What if he doesn't come back? What if, if . . ."

"Katharine, don't think that way. His buddies will get him back," Woody said. "Besides, Ty's a natural talker. You know that. He'll figure his way out of this."

"No, no, he won't. That, that creep wouldn't let me talk to him. He's hurt. I know it, I can feel it."

The tears that had started as trickles were splashing onto the coffee table. Her shoulders were shaking, and Alex sensed they were seconds away from catastrophe, a real bawler with Katharine incoherent, all semblance of control gone. Alex put an arm around her and looked up sharply at Woody, who sat with his mouth agape, anxious to flee.

"Go on, Woody. We can continue this later," Alex said. "And tell Bart what I said. I'm going to drive Katharine to Newport, and I'll talk to him then."

"Remember, if there's another call, ring me," Woody said, retreating from the apartment. "And don't talk to any police. They'll screw it up. His unit will take care of it from here."

Alex slid around the table and walked to the door with Woody. "Sorry if I came across like an obnoxious trial lawyer. I really do understand why

Bart wants to get this to Ty's unit," she said. "But why keep Mark involved?"

She hadn't intended to say it; it slipped out. She immediately felt disloyal to Katharine, guilty of trying to shield Mark, to cut him off from whatever this was becoming. She knew Mark Lang. If he had information, he would act. If he didn't . . . well, what could he do then?

Woody seemed surprised by her question. "Mark would want to know what's going on. Seemed a no-brainer to Easton."

"It still seems strange to me. I mean, shouldn't the unit be the link to Mark, not Bart?" Alex said. "But that's beside the point for now. Let's hope this gets Ty back and ends it."

IV

Bart was becoming increasingly worried about Sylvia. She hadn't spoken since he told her about Tyler. Her eyes were closed, and she would stop breathing for long seconds before taking in another breath. Where was that specialist? There was a light tap at the open door. The lung specialist was middle-aged, rumpled, with sad, knowing eyes.

"Hello," he said softly, waving his hand.

Bart noticed the large yellow envelope under his arm, the results of last night's CAT scan. The doctor was looking at Sylvia, who had not awakened. Her right arm was rail-thin and already punctured by three tubes. Her left arm looked like an overstuffed sausage that would burst at the slightest prick. The doctor didn't bother examining her. He slowly shook his head and walked out the door, Bart following.

"We're losing her, aren't we," Bart said. "How long?"

"The CAT shows two embolisms in the left lung. Best guess . . . hours, a few days at most." There was nothing more to say. The doctor patted his arm and went down the hall, and Bart reentered the room.

Sylvia looked at him, her eyes clear. "I couldn't stand more prodding, I know what's happening. It's so hard to breathe," she said. "Why isn't Tyler here? He always came home when I needed cheering up."

"We're trying. Everybody's trying."

"We had such fun, boarding school especially. Mark would score goals, and we would all cheer and Tyler would hug me. It was always cold and windy. We'd go out to dinner afterward."

She was fighting, her body wanting to shut down, the disease sucking greedily at her lung while her mind clung to the vision that her son would soon walk through the door. She jerked away the mask with sudden strength. The prayer welled up and spilled out. "Mark," she said. "Tell Mark to bring him home."

She sank back into the pillows and gradually closed her eyes.

The low beep of Bart's phone startled him. When he saw Woody's number, he rushed out into the hall to answer it. Good news! God, that was needed! He took down the location, hurriedly called the regiment in Kosovo and demanded to speak to Colonel Davis.

"Hello? Davis here."

"Colonel, this is Bart Easton. I'll be brief on this open line. We had a sat-phone call from a man who gave Ty's license number, date of birth, stuff from his wallet. We have the lat-lon of the call from the telephone company, two hours old."

He gave the coordinates, not mentioning that he planned to e-mail them to Lang. Davis said he'd be back in touch, hung up and ran back inside the Operations Center to organize the rescue.

The White House   **2 P.M. Sunday**

It wasn't an ordinary game. This was end-of-the-season stuff, the Redskins and Cowboys squared off, the winner moving on to the playoffs. Traffic on the parkways was light. The cold drizzle offered the perfect excuse for thousands of males to avoid the malls and huddle before their TV sets. The First Male set the example. Patrick Cahill was an informal man with Ronald Reagan's genial obduracy. As governor, he focused on improving education and lowering taxes. As president, he focused on improving education and lowering taxes. Cahill left foreign policy and other complicated subjects to his advisers. His mantric style, too simplistic for the press, was effective with the voters, who liked his no-frills approach.

The layout for the football game was typical of his presidency. Some senior White House staff, a few close political advisers and the off-duty Secret Service detail clustered around. He, the Press Secretary, the Chief of Staff, plus a few non–White House friends clustered around the large set in the comfortable sitting room, potato chips, sodas and beers at the ready. They made no pretense at talking shop. This was a serious tribal ritual. All remarks revolved around the players, the matchups, the coaches.

The call from Secretary of Defense Luke Nettles came at the end of a scoreless first quarter.

"What do you have for me?" Cahill said. "Nothing for a couple of hours, I hope."

"I'm tuned in, too, Mr. President. I'll keep it short," Nettles said. "That soldier missing in Kosovo? We have a location. They're mounting a rescue op as we speak."

"That's great. Anything we can do?"

"No, sir. It's being handled through NATO channels. The Pentagon Command Center is monitoring it."

Luke Nettles spoke with his usual crisp confidence. The Secretary had flown F-4s in Vietnam and been elected governor of Illinois twice. His defeated opponents said he smiled as he broke arms. The press feared Nettles because he challenged them to intellectual hand-to-hand combat. He specialized in syllogisms, first framing a contentious issue, then advancing selected facts and concluding that they confirmed his point of view. Under this Secretary, the President wouldn't propose thousand-dollar toilet seats or mixed-gender "hot bunking" aboard submarines. Military business stayed inside the department, especially if it looked messy.

"With everything else we had going on, I'd forgotten we were still in Kosovo, for God's sake, and now this," the President said. "Hold on, hold on—did you see that? Dallas just scored. Anything else?"

"No, sir. I'll keep you informed," the Secretary of Defense said. "We'll get it back on the kickoff."

"Which side are you on?" Cahill asked.

"I'm from Washington, Mr. President."

Koplje Mountain, near the Serb border   **8 P.M. Sunday**

"Don't go so fast," Saco muttered as the Toyota slipped slightly. With the high beams on, the driver could see several yards ahead through the thin,

swirling snow. The dirt track was a labyrinth of switchbacks, dips and
long straightaways, a gradual ascent etched into the mountainside by
centuries of mules, horses, carts, wagons and peasants carrying their
loads on their backs. At the higher altitude the snow was heavier, laden
with moisture, melting when it hit the windshield, sticking sodden on
the ground. The tires squashed it flat and found good purchase on the
hard ground beneath.

The driver didn't protest, though Saco usually yelled at him to hurry.
It had been several hours since Saco spoke to the American woman. He'd
been laughing then but had barely spoken since. The driver was used to
that. Saco had been moody ever since that raid last month. British soldiers had come at night to the colonel's big house on the hill, the one you
could see from any place in town. They drove away with the colonel, right
through town, and no one fired a shot, the bodyguards drunk or asleep,
the colonel now in jail in The Hague. That's what happens when you
lose, the driver thought. Did NATO say anything about Baba blowing up
that bus last month? Nooo. But us, we're the bad boys. No wonder Saco
sulks, after what he did at Srebrenica. Everyone knows how he got that
filthy coat of his. Hell, the government gave up Milosevic. Saco? He'll be
gone one day, too, and he knows it.

The driver reached into his sack for the half-empty brandy bottle,
took a swallow and held it toward Saco, who shook his head. The driver
shrugged, rolled down his window and passed it to the soldiers half sitting, half crouching in the truck bed, their faces turned away from the
snow.

"Make sure the American stays covered," Saco yelled.

A soldier idly kicked at the rumpled canvas under his feet. The other
two laughed and passed the bottle. A rock clanged off the hood of the
cab, barely missing them. The driver jammed on the brakes, the pickup
swerving as it abruptly stopped. The soldiers in back looked stupidly
around as Saco fumbled to open his door.

"*Dras strano!*" A loud Serb yell, close, from the trees on the upslope
side of the Toyota. "Out. Arms up."

Saco got out. "We're Serbs. Tigriva."

Three soldiers emerged from the woods, skidded down the embankment and casually walked up, their weapons pointed away. The one in the

lead wore a long overcoat, not large enough to hide his potbelly. He looked pregnant.

"By yourselves?"

"Yeah," Saco said. "We were down at the general's meeting, part of security. Now we're going back to Kraljevo."

"You were crazy to cut through here. Baba holds this area. You should have gone back out the valley."

Saco shrugged. "Baba's an asshole."

The fat man appraised him, impressed by his size and the offhand attitude. Still, he was in charge here. "We're moving something. When we're finished, you can go on up."

His attitude annoyed Saco. The fat one was a technician, not a real soldier. "You're the one who should get out of here. Baba will scrape you off his boot heel."

A voice came from the top of the embankment. "*Combien pour un coup au coeur?*"

Saco looked up. The speaker was only a few meters away yet hard to make out. He wore hunter's clothes, pale gray with thick brown diagonal stripes. His face was painted American-style with dark slash marks, and in the crook of his arm he carried a long-barreled rifle that bulged in the middle.

Saco broke into a huge grin. "Like before. Cognac and first search of each kill. Someday when you kill enough, you'll be rich like me."

"Merde," the slashed-faced one said, admiring the shining paint and wide body of the Toyota. "Great truck."

"A present from a *vrag* farmer this morning." Saco laughed, continuing in French. "So, Luc, why you not in Paris?"

The man called Luc slid down the bank, ignoring the fat soldier, and walked up to Saco. He was of medium build, and the rifle seemed too large and heavy for him, but he held it lightly as he looked up at Saco. His eyes were oval like a cat's, and they seemed to catch and hold the light. Saco beamed and clasped him on both shoulders. Luc smiled or grimaced and didn't return the embrace.

"Didn't think you had the balls to leave Serbia, Saco. They'll pick you up in Kosovo."

"Who will? You think a few pussy soldiers capture me? Three years in the trenches. I know war," Saco said. "NATO forgets about me soon. But you—you're back. No other place to hide, huh? You're big game."

"A mistake. All I did was set them up, rent a house, change car plates, get a few cell phones, check border points, stuff like that. Easy to get into the States from Toronto. They didn't speak French. Quick money. How did I know?"

"Shit, you knew. You had to know. They were fucking *vrags*."

"Not what they did, not that. I didn't know they were pilots. They weren't hard, not soldiers, not mujahideen. Okay, so I think maybe they blow up an electric plant or something. What do I care? Jesus! What maniacs."

"They were *hadjuks*. Muslim scum. Dirt. You shoot them over here. What you help them over there for, huh?"

"Know what they paid? Ten thousand. I was finished in a week. Their Euros spend the same as yours, my friend. I'm a professional."

"Ha! You run for the rest of your life. The Americans have you on their list."

"I'm not staying here. I know where to go."

"Sure, sure. So what you doing freezing your ass off on this mountain?"

"Guard, for thirty Euros a day. Crumbs."

"So what happened to Luc the great sniper, the man with a hundred kills? A guard? A guard?"

"Be careful, Saco. I haven't changed. I picked you up a kilometer out, right?"

Luc looked directly at the fat soldier, who nodded and grinned back, bobbing, anxious to please. Saco laughed, a snort that sounded like a horse. Luc looked at him for several seconds, not smiling.

If he starts to step away from me with that rifle of his, Saco thought, *I'll rush him.* Instead of moving away to a safe firing distance, Luc turned a dial on his rifle's huge scope and peered up the slope, slowly turning the rifle until he saw something. Then he adjusted another dial and held out the weapon for Saco, pointing toward the black woods. Saco looked through the scope. At first all he saw was a washed-out field of green and black. Luc guided the barrel up slightly, and suddenly Saco could see three men, all whitish green with black faces.

They were so clear, so obvious, that he grunted in surprise and lowered the scope, still looking at the same spot. Nothing was there. Luc twisted a knob and gestured for Saco to look again. The men reappeared, only now their faces glowed white against the greenish background. He handed the rifle back.

"Good trick, eh? No one can hide from my new scope. Their heat appears as black or white, I have my choice. Four thousand Euros for this," Luc said, patting the rifle. "Only a dead man has no heat."

"I'm the one with no heat," Saco said. "My face is freezing off. When we can go?"

"When we're finished," the fat soldier said.

The clanking and grinding of gears from higher up on the road was distinct.

"We'll wait down the road," Saco said.

The Toyota backed down to a small square of flat ground, Saco looking for a turnoff where they would be hidden from the eyes of curious sentries. The driver shifted into four-wheel drive and squeezed between a few scraggly scrub pines. The soldiers huddled around the cab with the driver, passing the brandy back and forth. Saco stood under the trees, hands jammed into his long coat, his chin sunk to his chest. The wind had freshened from the north as night fell, and the new snow felt light under his feet. He scuffed at it, remembering the sawdust at the lumber mill. That had been good work. He liked hauling in the big trees.

He glanced toward the tarp where he had wrapped the American in two wool blankets and shoved a pack under his head, making sure the gloves were on his hands. Valuable property. He sensed he was close to money now, if only he could find a way. Luc came down the road, walking *crunch, crunch, crunch* in the center of the track lest he startle some drunken soldier with his Kalashnikov off safe.

"Figured out what we're doing here, Saco?"

"Sure. Moving in SAMs for the general's raid. You forget I am bodyguard? Of course I know."

"This is merde." Luc gestured down the mountain, dismissing the Balkans with a wave of his hand. "I'm a sniper, not a guard for Russian machinery."

Saco's foot pawed at the snow. "So where you go from here?"

"Philippines, Indonesia. Warm weather. Not freeze my balls off. Warm women, too," Luc said. "They got ten thousand islands, you know that? The Americans can't search them all. I get some cash and I'm off."

"Muslims. Filth. That what you want?"

"I want to be warm, drink wine, lie on the beach. Muslims don't lie on the beach, so what do I care? You know what I want, Saco? Money, plenty of money."

He knows, Saco thought, *the bastard wants a split.*

"Four." Luc tapped the thermal scope. "I see four hot spots in the back of your truck. But only three soldiers. Know what I think? You got a woman under there. I'm cold. Why not share?" Before Saco could move, Luc flipped the tarp back with the barrel of his rifle. He said nothing for several seconds, then he laughed.

"Saco, you're as crazy as they say. The Americans will come after your ass now. You're in deep shit."

"Someone will pay me for him."

Luc hesitated, then pulled Saco back into the trees, where the others could not hear them. Saco took the sat phone from his pocket and told his story. When he finished, Luc shook his head.

"How you get the money? They're no help." He pointed to the soldiers. "Look, we work together, you and I."

Saco shook his head. Luc started talking. He talked and talked. Round and round they went. Luc would offer a thought. Saco would shake his head. Luc would make the same point another way. Saco would mutter no, then propose Luc's first idea. Luc would agree. Saco would say it wasn't a good idea. Luc was patient. Arguing with Saco was like training a bear; it took time.

"We should ask for more," Saco repeated for the fifth time. "You said they get millions in the Philippines."

"You've got one, maybe two days before your general's all over your ass. Belgrade will fire him if the American is kept. You have to dump him fast. That means low price. Not like the Philippines. There they keep hostages for months, send back one or two heads. Eventually they get their price."

Luc watched Saco to see how he was taking it. Good, he was nodding, buying the Indonesia bullshit. That's what he'd tell others when Luc left for Colombia, where they paid by the hit. Get this over with quickly. Then he was on his way.

"Let me think some more," Saco said.

Luc tried not to laugh. Saco couldn't think. He survived by sensing his environment. He was the bear, sensing danger, feeling when he was safe. Now he felt at ease, up high near the Serb border, far from the NATO troops in the valley. Luc had to hurry him along before he guzzled down a bottle and decided to sleep before pressing on in the snow.

"No more thinking," Luc said. "The key is speed. One, two days, that's it. We pick a bank and open an account. Next day we bring the American. The bank says he's there, over the phone. Three hundred thousand—his company sends that without thinking."

"What if the bank don't have that much cash?"

"We take what they have," Luc said. "And a draft for the rest. Sure, it might be useless to us, but we'll have something."

Enough to get me out of this country, Luc thought.

"They could arrest us," Saco said for the fourth time.

"Pfft. In Belgrade they piss on Americans. They remember the bombs."

"They are afraid of the Americans."

"Sure, that, too. That's why we get the money quick. Don't fool around. No one will arrest us if we're fast."

"The general will shoot me." For the sixth time.

"Not if you give him one hundred thousand Euros."

"We have to hide the American."

"You said you had a place. Now, let's go. That SAM's off the road. The American rides in the cab. I don't want him freezing. Put your idiots in the rear."

Luc walked over and pulled back the tarp. Cosgrove lay huddled on his side, shivering. Luc reached into a pocket, took out a ski mask and put it on.

"Hey, I should do that, too," Saco said.

"Go ahead," Luc said to feed him hope, knowing Saco was finished. He was too big, easily identified once the kidnapped American was returned. Saco had no mask and, after rummaging through his pockets, shrugged and forgot about the idea.

"Give me your knife," Luc said.

Saco handed him a long, thin blade.

"Ho!" Luc balanced it lightly. "I heard you liked to cut. How many you do with this?"

"Five, six, who knows? I don't do no more. See, if you stick wrong, blood spurts. Poof! Sometimes it squirts three, four feet. You know how hard it is to get that shit off? Twisting is better. No blood."

Luc cut the ropes and gently rocked Cosgrove's head. "You hit him hard," he said. "Help me get him inside. He better not die on us." He handed the thin knife back to Saco, who inserted it into a scabbard inside his sleeve. Saco squeezed behind the steering wheel, shifted into the wrong gear and stalled out. The soldiers in the back tumbled against the cab and sorted themselves out. Not one yelled at Saco as the pickup stuttered forward. The fat corporal had succeeded in wedging the Russian surface-to-air missile carrier between two tall fir trees on a narrow ledge overlooking the valley. The soldiers were shoveling snow on top to conceal it from any American heat-seeking thermal imagery. The steel vehicle looked as big as a tractor trailer, and Saco squeezed carefully by, admiring the skill of another driver as good as he.

Koplje foothills   **8 P.M. Sunday**

After leaving the farmhouse and the dead girl, Lang kept the team moving, stopping for ten minutes each hour. The country was open, and they made good time in the dark without going near spots easily mined. The upper pastures sat on a bedrock of limestone; the spavined grasses and stunted trees sustained few livestock and fewer habitats. As they climbed, they left the last farms behind.

It would be hours before they reached the ridgeline. Blade had increased the pace, and Harvell was lagging, Lang falling back to urge him on. Roberts was tempted to slow down and help him. When the skipper screwed down, nothing distracted him. That's how they won the internationals, pushing through a blizzard on the glacier while the other teams hunkered down. Roberts knew the skipper would carry Harvell if he had to.

But Roberts didn't want to leave the two sergeants alone at point.

Caulder was anxious for another target, and Blade might use that over-grown brain of his to launch them on a Great Adventure, complete with Indians. Already the team had overstepped its bounds by climbing this mountain. They'd spot Serbs eventually, and Roberts wanted to be up front, keep Caulder from tapping another soldier. This wasn't the time to be thinking about last night, what he'd promised, how he'd screwed up his personal life. Roberts looked down the slope to where the skipper and Harvell were huddled in the middle of a field. He signaled Blade to halt.

Harvell had stopped in the open to give the Quotron a direct line of sight to the satellites twenty thousand miles overhead. He was breathing hard. All right, so running only an hour a day had brought him up short for this team. But when it came to the Internet, he was on top of it. And who was the skipper hanging with now? Not those ball-breakers Caulder and Roberts. The skipper was right here beside him.

"Message for our screen name, sir," he said, holding up the Quotron. "I don't understand it, but it refers to Colonel Davis."

By the Quotron's back light, Lang read the message, just one among thousands of trades read by a half-dozen sources as it flowed across the satellite and Internet channels.

```
From: <%x^v                              2:00 P.M. Sun., Dec. 21
To: #@V+

At 1130 received phone bid at 20.45 and 43.15 wanting cash for wet
product. Sylvia desperate for your help in obtaining product.
Profoundly regret her offer will terminate in days. Am passing to
Davis for his bid too. Semper Fi, Bart
```

Lang faced upslope and spoke into his handheld radio. Within minutes the five of them were standing inside a thin tree line. Lang explained the message as the Quotron was passed around, then said, "I'm calling it in to make sure."

Harvell handed the EUT headset to Lang, who said, "Six, this is Pepper-dog. We have a report that Cosgrove's sat phone has been located at . . , Oh, we must have hit the off switch . . . No, the report was sent to me . . . I understand you're busy . . . Roger. Go get 'em, man. Kick ass. Out."

Lang turned to his team. "They're on it. We're to hold in place. Where are those coordinates, Blade?"

"Five clicks north, cross-corridor. Three hours maybe."

"Don't say we humped halfway up to sit on our asses, sir," Caulder said. "Mrs. C. wants the captain. Let's go get him."

Roberts spat; addicted to chew, he spat even when he had no tobacco. Caulder was so predictable.

"Something to say, Staff Sergeant?" Lang asked.

"We're already pushing our luck with regiment, sir. It sucks to say it, but we should wait here. It'll be over before we get there."

"Regiment works for Joint Task Force, which works for NATO, which will dick around all night, Staff Sergeant," Caulder said. "We can get to Cosgrove first. Then the captain would owe us, cut us slack, like no more dumb-ass road patrols."

"Regiment's on it," Roberts said. "We work for regiment."

"What's another five clicks?" Caulder said.

"You're looking for an excuse to whack someone," Roberts said.

"So it's better to sit around and put in twenty for a pension?"

Roberts stood not moving while, unseen by the others, the blood drained from his face. Caulder sensed he had gone too far and went into a crouch to protect his treasured scope when Roberts charged. But Lang took a quick step forward to stand in front of Caulder. "As you were, Sergeant!" he said.

There was silence while he let Caulder think it over.

"I didn't mean that, Staff Sergeant," Caulder said. "I was thinking about your advanced age."

"And I didn't mean you were Al Capone," Roberts said. "He was taller."

"Brotherly love is a wonderful thing," Lang said. "Now, back to business. Blade, do you want to sound off, too? You have an input to this."

"Regiment doesn't care what we do as long as we don't interfere," Blade said. "Lots of trails up there. Captain Cosgrove could be anywhere. The more people looking, the better, is the way I see it."

Lang kept his gaze level, looking at the dark trees without seeing them, knowing he had to make a decision now, not falter, not hesitate, not show uncertainty. To inform the Ops Center was to invite an automatic refusal. The FI—friendly identification—chips clipped to their hoods like giant dry-cleaning tags would alert any prowling Cobras and prevent friendly fire. That was enough in the way of support. Higher headquarters was an impediment, not an aid.

"That's it, then," Lang said. "We continue up and position ourselves to help if called on. We climb until we're one click from the coordinates, then reappraise."

"What do I tell Ops?" Harvell asked.

"Same as last time. We're continuing hot pursuit," Lang said. "Send the message digital, not voice. Be sure to include our route. Blade will provide it."

Blade looked out at the gathering gloom, the skyline erased by fog and snow. He clicked on a penlight, looked at his map and pressed some numbers into his GPS receiver. The others looked over his shoulder and copied the numbers onto their GPS screens.

"Hot pursuit of what, sir? Ops will come back on the Net," Harvell said. "What'll I say?"

Caulder groaned. "Harvell, when you're in the shower and the phone rings, do you splash water everywhere or pick up the message later?"

"You mean don't reply?"

"Any other questions?" Lang said.

"This Bart guy on the Quotron, sir," Harvell said, "he's our own Combat Ops Center? He's giving us our heading?"

Harvell expected someone to snicker. No one did. They all waited for Lang to answer.

"Affirmative, he's our Ops Center," Lang said. "Let's get up there."

25th Marines Combat Operations Center   **8 P.M. Sunday**

In the Ops Center, Gunnery Sergeant "Twigs" Twitchell had checked and rechecked the air tasking order. He was a midlevel accountant in civilian life, and his reserve duty gave him a certain cachet at his firm, a few stories at lunch, a few hints so a partner or two knew he worked on programs they weren't to know about. Twitchell was content being cautious. As the ops chief, he liked things neat and nailed down.

He hated these naval air tasking orders. The grunts were always making last-minute changes that screwed up his spreadsheets. Well, okay, the Ground Combat Element had so many moving parts, he sympathized with their delays. The amphib ships were worse. To reposition a ship threw the plan hours off schedule. And carrier air was the biggest headache. He'd program an F-14 at angels ten, and an F-18 at angels fifteen would come up on the voice net. Twitchell knew no task sheet was ever complete while a carrier was launching strikes.

Naval fixed-wing wasn't causing the delay tonight, though; the CH-46 chopper was. A stick of one CH-53E and one CH-46E had priority one for the rescue operation, with two Cobras and two Black Hawks flying cover. Command and Control was in a third Cobra. Two F-18Es were in high cover, monitored by an AWACS. All good to go, except for the 46, one sick old bird, forty years old. Shoot it, don't send it up a mountain in snow showers.

Not his call, though. He stretched and walked into the admin section to check on the rest of his watch standers. Nothing going on. He was about to leave when he decided to take a peek at KosoFinest. He had arranged the credit-card payments for the website. No programming had been done on Marine computers, and no porn, dating only. Trivial cash flow. He took 20 percent on three hundred or so a month. Fun to set up, though, and helped pass the time. Twitchell sat down at a computer. He'd run a quick check on payments month-to-date.

Twitchell felt his stomach turn over. Harvell wouldn't do that—would he? He couldn't. Impossible. The EUT had a firewall so it couldn't connect to the unclassified world. Slowly, one finger at a time, Twitchell pecked in www.pepperdogs.com. He didn't want to see. And there, directly below the team bios, was a posting from J. Kirwin Harvell.

---

www.pepperdogs.com   1700, Dec. 21

We are on the hunt for Captain C., a kidnapped Marine! Our recon team was challenged by Baba, head guerrilla. We had to snuff one mean mother and we freed a Serb. Break. Saw a girl killed by a mine. Break. Now on heavy hump up mountain after four gunmen in pickup. Check Pepperdogs.com for update.
Posted by: J. Kirwin

Gunnery Sergeant Twitchell, mediocre accountant and excellent ops chief, felt the pangs of panic. What would he say to the colonel? Harvell was posting total bull on the Pepperdogs.com site, spammed to KosoFinest. Who was Baba? And shooting someone? Harvell was fantasizing again. Nothing like this had come through the Ops Center. So that's what Harvell had been doing before he left. Of course! He couldn't send an unclass message from the field. This bull had been posted before he went out. Such wild stuff, who'd pay any attention? Harvell would be mocked forever, sending crap like this. He'd face office hours, too.

The coffee had gone cold. Twitchell poured out his cup. Let someone else find this mess and turn Harvell in. He had his own problems. He walked back into the Ops Center. By now the air officer had removed the 46 helicopter from the op. Time to update his spreadsheets.

TRAP—tactical recovery of aircraft or personnel—was a basic Marine mission, like tackling in football. Recovering personnel was obvious. The Marines brought back every crashed aircraft, too, even charred hulks that no one else would salvage. The real Marine slogan, Twitchell liked to joke, was "The Few, the Proud, the Impoverished." Only Marines engaged in firefights to drag home a twisted pile of metal. Mean as junkyard dogs, and as rich.

Twitchell looked at the electronic board. The CH-46 was still fragged, still on the board. A chopper older than Colonel Davis, held together by bubble gum and stubborn maintenance crews. No one wore Alphas or whites on a 46. Hell, no one wanted to wear clothes on a 46. There was always a hydraulic leak somewhere. Twitchell didn't believe the 46 had not been scrubbed. Neither did the air officer working the phones. "One-oh-six Aviation can have a Black Hawk here in fifty mikes," the air officer was telling the colonel. "The navy can give us two CH-fifty-three Echoes in ninety mikes."

Everyone wanted to help, but each change took additional time and additional crew briefings. Colonel Esting Davis rubbed the bald spot on the back of his head. At his brokerage house, his salesmen knew that meant he was worried about the direction of the market. In the Ops Center, the staff knew he was worried about the direction of an operation.

To him they were the same—forces of nature. He wasn't an operator; he was a raconteur with a quick wit, a friendly manner and a knack for organizing without ruffling feathers. His private-client bond division handled $2 billion for coupon cutters from Palm Beach to Kennebunkport. For the Marines, he built the Christmas Toys for Tots from a $10 million mom-and-pop charity to $100 million, with Harvey Keitel and Robert De Niro at the annual ball. The Commandant loved it.

Like their career colleagues, civilian Marines—an oxymoron for the reserves—were a mixed lot. The first-term enlistees tended to be quite bright, many signing up to pay for school tuition. Those who stayed in for twenty years of weekend drills ran the gamut of skills and motivations. Some looked for challenge, others for the retirement money and a few, like Davis, enjoyed the feeling of success as they climbed the organizational ladder.

Davis wasn't all schmooze. He simplified the logistics of the reserves, turning sleepy depots into profit-and-loss centers. Okay, for a logistics officer, maybe command of the Kosovo brigade was a political reward. What wasn't? He performed well by not interfering with his Air Combat Element—a beefed-up helicopter squadron—or his Ground Combat Element, a reinforced infantry battalion. Still, he didn't like it when they shoved their expertise in his face, like halitosis. Here he was with a lost Marine, his senior aviator reluctant to launch a CH-46, his battalion commander clamoring to go. "We put max effort into the search during the day," the aviator said. "We exhausted our best assets. We need to wait for a replacement, not fly up a six-thousand-foot mountain at night in snow and fog with a crappy bird."

It had been like this for two hours, one delay after another. First his own staff had complained: A call from a guy who has cell-phone coordinates where Captain Cosgrove may be? Sir, that's not intelligence. It's rumor, unconfirmed, no corroboration or reliability, pure and simple rumor. Well, yes, the coordinates do match this area. No, sir, we don't have any other leads. Well, yes, intercepts of radio transmissions and thermal imagery do confirm unusual activity in that area. Um, maybe it's worth a look. Then from Zines, the National Guard major general serving as Joint Task Force Deputy: Has anyone confirmed this? That spot is in the red area, off limits to NATO. His staff better look it over. Then from the UN deputy overseeing the Joint Task Force: Would the American force be authorized to initiate fire? Ah, then please wait a day. Must discuss with both sides to avoid misunderstandings. Back and forth, back and forth, a colossal waste of time. In the end they had to let him launch. What if they ignored the phone call and Cosgrove was there?

"This is a recon mission, sir, not a raid. A quick snatch, if we're lucky," the battalion commander, Lieutenant Colonel Tom Bullard, had finally argued. "I'm putting only thirty trigger-pullers on the ground. Let me launch the Fifty-three and the Forty-six. I have enough margin."

Bullard was right, Davis knew. His mistake was calling it a rescue mission in the first place. That had ricocheted through the commands. Wouldn't be surprised if it got back to Washington. Should have labeled it a reconnaissance, then nobody would have noticed.

"If a bird goes down," Davis asked Bullard, "do you have backup?"

"We will in fifty mikes," the commander of the Air Combat Element answered, miffed that the question had been misdirected to the battalion commander.

"Where're the nearest friendlies?" Davis said.

"Pepperdogs're on the mountain," the Ops Center watch officer said, "checking something out. I told him not to clog the net and we'll get back to him."

Davis nodded. Recon was the only small tactical unit that reported directly to him. Lang had been pretty much on his own during the eleven weeks of the deployment, and that had worked out well. He shouldn't be wandering around now, though. Well, not enough choppers to extract him. He'd get back to Lang later.

Bullard shifted his weight, and the floor panels, which could be lifted to reset the cable wires, squeaked and sagged. The recon symbol on the large electronic map was several kilometers from his landing zone. Not part of his plan, a distraction.

Davis got the message and turned back to his commanders. "What's the latest?"

A captain from intelligence had rehearsed his lines. "We have cuts on a few radio emissions, none of interest. Thermal imagery indicates the coordinates for that phone call are cold. There are some hot spots higher up, a few scattered vehicles."

"Sir, I recommend we alter the plan to land near those spots. Work our way down from there," Bullard said.

"I'm afraid not, Tom," Davis said. "If we submit a change now, we'll wait all night."

"Then I'm ready to launch, sir. We shake the tree, something may fall out."

Davis hesitated. Launching with a Forty-six, for God's sake, older than he was.

Bullard, who had played guard at Michigan before taking a job in the athletic department at Villanova University, was standing uncomfortably close. Davis took a step back. Bullard sensed he had been too aggressive and switched to leatherneck jock talk.

"Sir, I need Cosgrove to keep my rabble informed. They could have grabbed one of my ugly company commanders and I'd still have a few more to kick around. But he's my only intell weenie. Without him, chaos."

Davis smiled. He, too, liked Captain Cosgrove, who had a light touch, brains, the right background, doing well on The Street. Reminded him of himself. Still, all these uncertainties—the snow, dark, an antique helo . . . Davis's civilian life selling bonds revolved around evaluating risks of one-eighth of a percent. The risks here were what, 60 or 70 percent against finding Cosgrove? Odds were Bullard would return empty-handed, no matter how pumped he was.

"No one's bigger than the market," Davis murmured.

"Sir?"

"Nothing. You're authorized to launch. No more than two hours on the deck up there, unless you're on to something," Davis said. "And Colonel Bullard, under no circumstances are you to cross the border into Serbia. Is that clear?"

"Aye-aye, sir."

Davis turned to the commander of the Air Combat Element. "Bring up that backup as soon as possible."

Bullard bolted from the Ops Center, followed by the senior aviator, who seemed just as delighted. Davis realized both had intended to go in the first place; he could have given his order earlier. Both were willing to take the risk. The aviator had been making a case for future resources. Davis should have seen that sooner.

After two hours of waiting, rehearsing and bitching, the troops boarded the choppers, and the birds were airborne in six minutes. Davis remained in the Ops Center, looking at an electronic map that told him nothing, waiting for Major General Zines, who wanted to monitor the action with him. The troops would be on the ground inside half an hour.

Serb high border   10 P.M. Sunday

Near the unmarked border at the top of the ridgeline, Saco and Luc stopped the Toyota and got out. A clear sight line to the satellites for the cell phone.

"Remember," Luc said, "keep it short. We have to make one or two more calls before this is over, and if the battery dies, we're fucked."

Saco nodded in irritation. Luc kept repeating and repeating. Did he think he was deaf? The connection went through right away.

"Hello, hello? Pretty woman? Okay, you listen. Get three hundred thousand dollars in bank ready for wire to Europe. I call back in a day. You be ready. Good-bye."

"Good." Luc nodded. They stood saying nothing. Saco's soldiers were stomping and flapping their arms to beat off the cold, showing how they suffered in the rear. Then they heard it—the deep *whup! whup!* of chopper blades, not rising to them, not coming on, holding somewhere. Luc reached into the truck bed, took his rifle from its covering and trotted to the edge of the cliff. He flicked on his thermal sight and peered into the darkness.

There they were, pulsing black spots standing clear against the dull gray background in the scope, one, two, three of them circling two hundred meters down the mountain, off to the south. Luc hastily sat down in the thin snow, worked the bolt back, took off his gloves, inserted a cartridge and shoved the bolt home. Next he drooped his elbows over his knees and searched until he had a sight picture. One chopper was in hover, scarcely moving. Two thick black hot spots in the scope. Two engines. Perfect. He aimed between them and squeezed. The rifle bucked, and the sharp, deep *crack!* startled the soldiers, who hadn't bothered to look at what he was doing. Bolt back, forward. *Crack!* Two seconds. Back, forward. *Crack!* Two seconds. Back, forward. *Crack!* Two seconds.

The chopper was falling off, out of the sight picture. The pitch of the engines changed. Cobras and Black Hawks were out there somewhere, scouring back and forth along the ridgeline, looking for their own hot spots, rockets and miniguns aligned. Luc ran back to the Toyota.

"Let's go!" he shouted. "I think I got a chopper. I know I hit it!"

He ignored Cosgrove lolling between them and slapped Saco on the knee. Saco paid no attention. He was concentrating on getting off the ridge, down the track and into the nearest patch of thick trees, or behind a boulder, anything to hide their heat in case a Cobra popped up above the ridgeline, ignored the border and searched the northern slope inside Serbia proper.

"You're insane!" Saco yelled. "We need money and you go shooting. Insane!"

"I'm a sniper. You snap necks, I shoot." Luc was laughing in delight. "A helicopter! How many snipers have shot down a helicopter?"

"Now the Cobras come after us!"

"They don't know where to look. They won't cross the border. Don't worry."

"Fucking crazy Frenchman!"

"Of course, why else would I be here? Now, find a place out of this snow."

On TRAP 3, the CH-46 bird at the rear of the formation, Corporal Myles Ansom sat next to the crew chief, nearest to the pilots. The company gunny would lead them out the rear ramp, and he would be the last out, making sure all the others were clear. All right! Inbound, maybe into a hot LZ. He went over the brief one last time. No shooting unless there was incoming, and even then it had to be aimed incoming, not a few stray shots. Captain Cosgrove could be anywhere. They didn't want to waste him. He could feel the 46 slowing down, starting to hover. The stern would hit first. Rear panel dropping now. He looked down to make sure he could pull loose of his safety belt. His neck felt wet. He reached back and felt a stream of oil dripping on him. Damn 46s. He heard a *whang! Shit, what was that?* Had they hit a tree branch or something? More oil, all over him. *What the hell?*

"Incoming! Incoming!" the crew chief yelled into his intercom. "Abort! Abort!"

Ansom looked frantically around. He was thrown back, the cockpit suddenly tilting. The crew chief fell into him, still yelling. Were they going in? Another lurch and he was jerked forward. The crew chief was on his knees, scrambling to stand, slipping in the oil pouring out above Ansom's head. The chopper seemed on a level course now, only the nose was down. The crew chief yelling at them all.

"We're going in! We're setting down hard! Head between your knees!"

Fourteen Marines needed no further urging, all bending forward, a moment of terror looking like prayer. Ansom felt the bird rise at the nose. That was good, how it was supposed to be. They hit hard and bounced, the rear panel down, and the gunny was yelling, "Out! Out!" and then Ansom was in the snow, putting distance between himself and the chopper, looking back, seeing no fire, slowing down, finally stopping.

In under a minute the gunny had them spread out and tactical. Ansom heard the chopper blades whine to a halt and looked back to watch the crew walk down the ramp and shine flashlights along the fuselage, inspecting for damage. There were shouts and giggles and nervous laughter among the troops.

"I ain't never riding a Forty-six again!" someone yelled.

"Shut up on the line!" the gunny screamed. "Shut the fuck up!"

The team was over two hours into the climb when Lang heard the choppers pass by, close and unseen, rattling in and chugging away, their echoes dampened by the snow, lingering somewhere up above them. That meant they were settling into a landing zone. He stopped climbing and looked at Caulder, who was nearest him. Caulder shrugged. Who knew what they'd find? They stopped to listen, and after a few minutes the sound increased, then fell away. Silence, save for the wind blowing steadily.

"Harvell, put us on the voice net," Lang said.

Harvell punched numbers into the keypad on the End User Terminal, and they heard angry, strained voices. A bird was down, Bullard arguing with the Ops Center that he continue on, let the downed helo take care of itself. Negative. Hot LZ. Mission aborted. Secure a perimeter around the downed helo.

"Turn it off," Lang said. "Staff Sergeant, what do you make of it?"

"We didn't hear any firing. May have been a lucky shot, not a hot zone," Roberts said.

"Now we know someone's home," Caulder said. "Knock, knock."

"Harvell, tell Ops Center we're investigating shots fired at choppers," Lang said. "Send it by digital text, no voice. We're going up fast. You won't be able to keep up. Follow the waypoints in your GPS. Call on the intrasquad radio if you have to."

Harvell's eyes popped wide. Unsure whether he was being put on, he peered closely at Lang. The captain placed his glove on Harvell's shoulder.

"We won't leave you. We'll be out in front. Take your time. If we don't link up in an hour, meet us at this rally point. Wait another thirty mikes. If we don't show, go back down by another route."

Lang took Harvell's GPS and entered the digits for a spot a thousand feet above them. He labeled it "RP" and handed back the GPS. Harvell was still in shock.

"Set to go?" Lang said.

Harvell nodded, not knowing what to say. It was all happening so fast. The others disappeared up the slope. Harvell listened until he could no longer hear them cracking through the bush. He typed the message in the Marine computer and sent it to the Ops Center. Then he pulled out the Quotron. What should he say? Not too much, enough to keep people interested.

---

www.pepperdogs.com   2130, Dec. 21

```
Choppers went by us close. Shots fired. Choppers pulled off.
We're going up fast. Pepperdogs on the move! We may be closing
on Captain C. All right!
Posted by: J. Kirwin
```

He had considered several signature endings: *Harvell sends*. No punch. *Cpl. Harvell sends*. That had snap, but if Staff Sergeant Roberts saw it, he was in trouble. *Posted by J. Kirwin*. That had style. People would ask—who's J. Kirwin? They'd find out when they read *People* magazine.

That done, he began to climb. He was sweating freely, and the sting of the snow felt almost pleasant. Occasionally he sipped from the five-quart water pack on his back as he trudged upward. The brush hadn't thickened. Stunted pines clung by exposed roots to rocky outcroppings. With no pack and only a rifle, he could grab roots and branches to scramble up a few feet before crabbing sideways and reaching for the next handhold. He felt no fear. The team would clear the way, of that he was certain. He was content knowing his body was moving well after four hours of climbing. In four layers of Gore-Tex and poly, he was warm enough, and he shuffled along, the rifle now slung over his back, using both hands to pull from snowy branch to snowy branch, zigzagging his way slowly up, glancing every few yards at his GPS screen. He paused frequently, thankful Caulder wasn't there to mock him.

The White House 4 P.M. Sunday

The Redskins and Cowboys were tied, the game about to go into overtime, when the call from the Pentagon came in.

"The rescue mission in Kosovo failed, Mr. President. One helicopter was shot down," the Secretary of Defense said. "Luckily, there aren't any casualties. I don't have any details yet."

"Anything on the missing serviceman?"

"Not a word, sir. The Task Force commander out there—an admiral—is handling the press release, keeping details to a minimum, in case we have a chance to mount another rescue op. I'll keep you informed."

The President returned to the game, but his enthusiasm had diminished.

"It's a Pentagon problem, Mr. President," the White House Chief of Staff said. "It should stay on the other side of the Potomac or, better yet, in Europe."

"Don't worry, I'm not going to pull an Irangate. It's frustrating, that's all, frustrating."

Alexandra Bove drove up Third Avenue, three changes of lights to move one block, scarcely noticing the holiday crowds that snarled the midafternoon traffic. Katharine sat next to her, clutching the sat phone.

"When do you think we'll get there?" Katharine asked.

"Um, two days by car. One day if we walk."

"I shouldn't be going up there. Tyler was going to tell her we were engaged, a Christmas present. What if she won't see me?"

The words tumbled out. Katharine had been doing this ever since the phone call, blurting out contradictory sentences then lapsing into silence, running her fingers through her hair, messing it up, then combing it out, squeezing the sat phone between her hands as if praying.

"You're upset, and you have every right to be," Alexandra said in a calm courtroom manner. "But you're doing the right thing. Trust me, she'll be happy to see you. You two need each other."

"Not just me. She'll be glad to see you, too," Katharine said. "You've known her longer."

"You're the engaged one," Alex said, staring through the windshield for a green light. "Me, I'm still waiting for Mark to find himself, or whatever he's doing. She will love seeing you."

"She treats Mark like family. I think she sees in Mark things she wants in Tyler," Katharine said. "She approves of Mark's derring-do."

"What's wrong with that?" Alex said. "Who told Mark he was terrific when he was in boarding school? Not his classmates. That was not cool. And not his ship-bound father. Sylvia was the only one. You know what that's called, don't you?"

"Oh God, I never stopped to think," Katharine said, putting her hand on Alex's shoulder. "Tyler was coming home, and Mark has to be hurting just as much. Oh, Alex, I'm so sorry."

"It's okay, Katharine, it's taken me two years to figure out," Alex said. "Mark keeps everything to himself because he's afraid if he tries and fails, he'll be rejected. I'm scared he'll go through life from success to success, thinking he's a failure, afraid to commit. If there's one woman I resent, it's his mother."

"I never heard about her," Katharine said.

"She left when Mark was five," Alex said. "He's been out there setting records and slaying dragons ever since. 'Look what I did, Mommy, now won't you come home?' Know what she did? Sent him a card from France on his graduation. Selfish bitch. I hope she drowns in her vodka. That's why Sylvia's such a blessing. She constantly encouraged him."

They both cried a little and felt better for it, and talked about what they would say to Sylvia. The hours passed quickly, and they were approaching the Essex exit on Interstate 95 when the next call came in. Alex pulled onto the shoulder, and Katharine scribbled with an unsteady hand as trailer trucks roared past, their side winds buffeting the Acura. Alex took the notes and immediately called Woody, then Bart.

"He wants three hundred thousand dollars, Bart, ready to be wired tomorrow."

"Good. I'll have the money," Bart said. "Right now let's hope Woody gets another fix on that phone."

"How did he call back? I thought the Marines were going to rescue Tyler," Alex said. "And how can this possibly sound good?"

"Obviously something went wrong with the rescue," Bart said. "Alex—I know it sounds absurd, but this is encouraging. It means the kidnappers are under pressure to get this over with. Usually they drag it out and haggle about much higher ransoms."

"Will they . . ." Her voice was so soft Bart had to strain to hear, but he understood.

"No, absolutely not. Reassure Katharine about that. They're not sui-

cidal fanatics. They want money, and they won't get it until they've released him. Come straight up when you get into town."

U.S.S. _Bon Homme Richard_, 60 miles off the Adriatic coast   11 P.M. Sunday

Vice Admiral William E. Faxon III had a mind as precise and rigid as
the crease in his khaki trousers. First in his class at Annapolis, Ph.D. in
nuclear physics, three command tours in nuclear submarines, every
decision by the manual, every decision thought through in advance.
Throughout the fleet, he was called "the Razor." He could not, _could not_,
understand how any mature commander could make this many mistakes
In one operation. Accepting unconfirmed intelligence from some civilian,
slapping together a rescue effort into the red zone without coordination—_the UN deputy had protested, the little twerp_—employing a decrepit
helo, flying up a mountain at night in a snowstorm, trying to land under
fire . . . where did Marines find such incompetents? Marines belonged in
the mizzenmasts, not in the captain's cabin.

Thank God for the new simultaneous-communications suite on
board the _Richard_. At least he'd heard everything and ordered his deputy
to step in and cancel the op. Luckily no one was killed. What a mess. The
timing couldn't have been worse. The special ambassador was about to
land. _Imagine what he's thinking!_ Faxon put on his brown leather jacket
with the black fur collar and the gold dolphin wings of the submariner—
aviators weren't the only distinguished group—and walked out on the
flight deck. He strode across the undulating deck as the CH-53 Sea Stallion landed.

They didn't try to talk until they were out of the wind and chopper
noise, alone in Faxon's austere office. Ambassador Briggs wasted no time
on pleasantries. "What a royal balls-up, Bill," he said, sipping his coffee
and shaking his head.

"The man responsible has been relieved, Ambrose," Faxon said.

Briggs cocked an eyebrow over his coffee cup, more surprised by the
use of his first name than by the end of a man's career. Faxon was confident, he'd give him that. Perhaps they could do business.

"Perspective's important," Briggs began, "we can't be too, ah, ram-
bunctious about one missing serviceman."

"Rescue isn't a frivolous game," Faxon replied. "I'm sure you recall a pilot named O'Grady. It took considerable coordination to bring him back."

"That pilot was shot down and you knew where he was," Briggs said. "In this case, we don't know if the man's missing, drunk or enjoying a piece of ass. The Marines have turned this into *The Blair Witch Project,* chasing coordinates concocted by some mystic six thousand miles away."

"What do you want, Mr. Ambassador?"

"Time. A few days of diplomacy to get him back without mayhem. I need the Marines kept on a tight leash. No more escapades."

Faxon agreed the mission had been haphazard, but he said nothing.

"Look what happened in Somalia," Briggs continued. "We went after some tribal illiterate and left with our tail between our legs. The Balkans are the same—lighter color, same tribal mentality. If we embarrass the Serbs they'll strike back."

"Their loss if they do." In thirty-two years of impeccable service, Faxon had never been in combat. Assigned to the NATO staff in Brussels, he had had no role in the strikes against Afghanistan. Now, as a Joint Task Force commander, he looked forward to the day when he would approve an op plan after making incisive changes and overseeing air and cruise missile strikes from Flag Plot. The submarine community would be proud as he applied power precisely.

"You and I are here to play chess, not checkers," Briggs said, shaking his head in mild disapproval of Faxon's attitude. "We're not characters out of Conrad, bombarding the African bush. When our spy plane crash-landed in China, diplomacy, not force, brought back the crew."

He leaned forward and lowered his voice as though others—under the desk, perhaps—were straining to hear. "There are larger equities involved than one detained serviceman. I am this close"—he held his index finger next to his thumb—"to a deal. The President needs an honorable withdrawal from this miserable backwater, not another War of Jacob's Ear."

Faxon smiled slightly. Briggs sensed it was time to close the deal.

"Would it violate naval tradition to ask for a port? This coffee tastes like coffee."

Faxon buzzed a steward, and soon both were sipping port from crystal goblets.

"What do you think of the Turkish currency?" Briggs asked, apropos of nothing.

Surprised, Faxon observed that it was slipping as overseas remittances fell.

"How do you think Cyprus could be settled?"

So it went for half an hour, Briggs playing mental hopscotch around southern Europe.

"Joe Pfizer's tour as CinC South is up in June," Briggs concluded.

For six months Vice Admiral Faxon had kept meticulous records to show how his Joint Task Force was resolving centuries of hostility in Kosovo. Thirteen houses burned in May, nine in June. Two markets opened during the summer. Four border attacks in September, two in November. He saw the triviality in those figures. The diplomats expected him to enforce the de facto partition between the Serbs and Albanians and control the sectarian violence, nothing more. He knew this peacekeeping command was a trial run. If he performed with a subtlety that won European approval, a fourth star was likely.

Now here was a special ambassador, hinting at that prize—Commander-in-Chief for NATO's Southern Region. Faxon didn't respond, bothered by Briggs's manner. The ambassador was too unctuous, too smooth. Eel-like. Where was Briggs slithering to? What did he want?

Briggs read the silence and filled it with promise. "Look, Bill, the Secretary of Defense will defer to us diplomats in deciding who's the next CinC South. Naples, fine food, magnificent palazzo. Interesting command, the sensual Levant, the obdurate Turks, the tragic Kurds, to say nothing of the exasperating Balkans. A challenge. You'd have your hands full. Not all black-tie dinners and operas, though there's that, too."

"Right now, Mr. Ambassador, I have a missing American."

"Of course, of course. I've taken much too much of your time." Briggs looked at his watch. "Can I trouble you for a lift to land—and a day of negotiations to retrieve your lost man? I don't mean to lecture, Admiral, but you almost upset the apple cart tonight. Not you personally, you understand these things. But others, well, suffice to say we don't need Marines running amok, do we? I'll persuade General Kostica to stay away from the search area, if that's what you want. But no more charging off without giving us in striped pants a chance to work this out on the tea-and-biscuits circuit. That's what diplomacy is for—working things out. Do try not to have a war for a few days, will you, Admiral? Are we agreed?"

Faxon did not like being lectured. Still, the admiral admitted to himself that the rescue effort had been slapdash. Anyway, it would take his Joint Task Force several hours to come up with a solid plan. "We won't be precipitate, Mr. Ambassador," he said.

Together they walked out to the flight deck. Briggs put on the canvas cranial with its oversize ear protectors, smiled at Faxon and backed toward the Sea Stallion, holding up both arms, waving politician-style at a hidden crowd. His large body was silhouetted by the helicopter's revolving blue lights, arms akimbo, ear shells sticking out. Faxon was reminded of a giant praying mantis.

Faxon returned to his stateroom and thumbed through the CRITIC traffic that had accumulated during his talk with Briggs. His tour as aide to the Secretary of the Navy had taught him the importance of symbols. That was why he had set up shop here on the newest amphibious ship, the *Bon Homme Richard*. It suggested the Joint Task Force in Kosovo was temporary, and the White House and the Pentagon appreciated that.

Faxon loved command at sea. Unlike the land, with erratic civilians scurrying around, there was a predictability to operations on the oceans. Faxon sensed the Marines onboard felt a bit displaced. After all, the *Richard* was the queen of the amphibious fleet, and amphibious ships carried the Marines to their battlefields. Well, that was the nature of command. He had his choice, he preferred the sea to land, and his staff needed room. The Marines would have to make do.

The red light on the secure phone was blinking. Briggs hit the return key on his computer and read the name. Most contact with his staff was done electronically. It saved time. This was Zines. Owned a large meatpacking company. Unimaginative but careful, not a cowboy. A solid deputy, even if a reservist. Brought political clout, too. Faxon had assigned him to the land headquarters ninety miles inland to deal with the daily minutiae of dyspeptic UN officials, petulant Serbs and conniving Albanians.

Faxon picked up the secure phone.

"Sir, the rescue mission is back," Zines said, "except for a party guarding the downed bird. They'll lift it out in the morning."

"They should trash it."

"Davis is putting together another effort. Launch in fifteen mikes. A rifle company will link up with the recon team."

"What?"

"A recon team is on the mountain."

"We have people on the ground still? How'd that happen?"

"Unclear, Admiral. Anyway, Davis has decided to send another unit up there."

"Unacceptable. We're not going off half cocked again. You're my deputy for land operations. All ops will be checked by you personally."

"We don't have time for a review, sir. There's this unexpected—"

"Tom, I had command of one attack and two missile boats. Thirty-two months at-sea command. Not once did I encounter the 'unexpected.' And I only had to relieve three officers. Well, make that four."

"Sir?" Zines said.

"Relieve Davis, Tom, on my orders. The man lacks judgment."

"Sir, it's a commander's prerogative to—"

"General, it's not his prerogative to lose unit integrity. To be willing to split his force after that chopper went down was a fundamental error in judgment."

"Continuing the mission was a judgment call, sir, his to make as the commander. He ran into some bad luck."

"Bad judgment should not be called bad luck, Tom. The reason we have these new communications is to enable the senior chain of command to get involved," Faxon said. "I intervened because I lost confidence in Davis. If I hadn't, who knows how many casualties we'd have had. Now, who's the next senior Marine?"

"Executive officer's on leave. So it's the Ground Combat Element commander, Lieutenant Colonel Bullard."

"Give him the helm. Put Davis on the first lift out here. I'll find a job for him."

"Sir, I—"

"The subject is closed, General. Pull out that recon team. No more wandering around in the dark. By zero-eight I want a comprehensive plan. Ambassador Briggs just left, and he wasn't here for crumpets. The Marines almost started a war this evening."

The Razor's mind functioned like a nuclear power plant, and in nuclear safety, bad luck happened only to the unprepared. Zines could offer no further arguments. "We'll get on it, sir," he said.

Faxon put down the phone and turned to his keyboard.

```
Personal  From: CJTF 34.5                      2230 Zulu Dec. 21
            cc: CINCSOUTH
                CINCEUR
                Chairman, Joint Chiefs of Staff
                Commandant of Marine Corps
                Chief of Naval Operations
                J-3, The Joint Staff

Due to lapses in operational judgment by Commanding Officer of 25th
Marines, rescue operation canceled and tragedy narrowly avoided.
Details follow. I have relieved Col. Davis. Next senior Marine has
taken command temporarily.

However, Col. Davis did an outstanding job unscrambling a tumultuous
logistics problem. I request he be assigned as G-4 of this task force
when the current G-4 finishes his tour.

We are doing all we can to find missing Marine. Updates will be
provided by this command.
Very respectfully, Bill
```

Before hitting send, he reread the message. Davis did what in civilian life? Shuffled bonds in New York. His own offers of employment were on the West Coast—a think tank, a university, a Defense corporation. No backlash there. Too bad the Chairman of the Joint Chiefs was a Marine. He and the Commandant would be miffed. Those Marines stuck together like some persecuted minority, but that op had been on the brink of disaster. The G-4 job offer was window dressing, of course. There would be no more freelancing by that brigade of reservists. He hit send and gave the destruction of Davis's career no more thought.

25th Marines Combat Operations Center

Lieutenant Colonel Bullard took control without delay or pretense. He walked into the Ops Center, announced he was in command with orders from the Commander, Joint Task Force, to deliver a plan by eight in the morning. There was more than enough for the staff to do.

As the planning cells were formed, the corpsman in the rear looking at his four monitors thought he would be ignored as usual. Instead the op chief paid him a visit.

"How are the dogs doing?" Gunnery Sergeant Twitchell asked.

"Pressures are low," the corpsman said. "They haven't recovered from that insane run this morning. Plus, they've been on the move for the past five or six hours. I thought they were sitting on an observation post."

"You know the dogs aren't sitters," Twitchell said. "Anything for me to tell the new commanding officer?"

"They're cold and tired," the corpsman said, "normal stuff."

Koplje Mountain, upper slope

Harvell had been on his own for over an hour. The snow was falling a bit thicker, but the wind had lessened. His sudden surge of energy upon hearing the helicopters had long since passed. He was numb, stumbling, not taking care. It was the cold and the dark. He was shaking slightly, chilled despite the protective layers of clothing, stung by the cold that clung to his face like a mask of ice. He wanted to feel warm, to recover the feeling in his face. Above all, he was lonely.

He continued to plod upward, wondering how he would ever catch up. He couldn't see more than a few meters. He knew the training drill. Never, ever doubt the GPS and the compass. Check the direction on both. If they agree, don't double-guess them. Still, it was so dark. He knew he should check his six, look around, look behind, but he didn't have the strength of mind to be cautious. The GPS receiver showed him where to go and where the rally points were in case something went wrong. The radio was working, and he had extra batteries. So why did he feel nervous? No, not nervous; he was afraid.

Afraid of what? Of being out in the middle of nowhere, absolutely nowhere, seven thousand miles from Manhattan, on the side of a pitch-black mountain, abandoned to freeze to death. Or maybe he was left behind to be the bait so the Serbs would come looking for him while the team escaped. Why had he come out here? This was insane.

He heard a branch crack, probably overladen with snow. He took a few more steps. There was a soft, heavy thump. It seemed to come from above him, close, within grenade range. Probably a tree shedding snow. Sounded, though, like a man flopping down, getting into the prone firing position. He took another step. His foot slipped on an icy rock and he was flailing in midair, reaching out to grab something, anything, missing, sliding facedown through the brush, closing his eyes, feeling the sticks and twigs scraping his cheeks, tumbling over once, twice, before smashing into a tree trunk. He lay still, the breath knocked out of him, scared to move, sure he had broken something. Slowly, tentatively, he rolled over and knelt, scrabbling away from the branches, then stood erect, digging some snow out of his collar, breathing deeply.

"Screw this," he said.

He reached for the handheld FM intrateam radio. What if Roberts or Caulder answered? What would he say—"I'm scared"? They'd laugh at him. He stumbled and slid back downslope until he reached the road. Humans used roads. A road was safety, man-made, no brush, no trees. You could jump up and down on it, imagine cars going by, wave at people. Normal. By staying on the road, he couldn't follow the waypoints on his GPS, but there was no way he was going back into those woods. He'd stay out here in the open. If he walked up the road, sooner or later he would bump into the team. They wouldn't leave him. They wouldn't, would they?

He'd walk up the road for a bit, then check again. It was their fault for leaving him; they'd be sorry if he froze to death or was captured. Maybe the Serbs would shoot him. If this was the end, someone had to know about this. He dug out the Quotron and pecked another message. He didn't care how it read.

---

www.pepperdogs.com   2230, Dec. 21

may be being tracked   really dark   snow everywhere
cold, very cold   too far behind the others   am taking road
to catch up   if I don't make it, remember I tried
Posted by: J. Kirwin

When they left Harvell, Caulder took point. They rotated the lead every fifteen minutes to keep alert as they climbed. Roberts was in fine shape, but the other three were slowing. They forced themselves to drink constantly to avoid dehydration, despite the bitter iodine taste that seeped through the thickest mixture of powdered lemonade. They ate their peanuts and trail mix and M&M's and tried not to think of their aches or fatigue. Their thighs burned from climbing straight up and it was tempting to take the road, which they often crossed as it wound back and forth following the curves of the mountain toward the ridgeline. They knew, though, that sooner or later there would be a sentinel.

When they reached the coordinates of the phone call, there was only an empty road. Without a word, they went on. The snow was falling steadily, and they were unwilling to slow the pace to use their night vision goggles or thermal sights. The wind had lessened, and their ears were their sensors for danger. They were confident they would hear anyone else first.

They did. At first the sounds were dull scrapes and thumps, accompanied by the revving of an engine, as though a teenager were learning by the bumper-car method how to park in the family garage. As they approached, they could hear the high whine of a diesel engine and the clanking of gears. Soon they could hear voices and distinguish guttural Slavic phrases. Caulder and Blade adjusted their thermal sights while Roberts and Lang used their night vision goggles.

They were close enough to the Serbs to hit them with snowballs, which would have been a gesture of camaraderie, a sign of the universal brotherhood among soldiers in arms. The thought never entered their minds. They looked at the soldiers as prey.

A fat soldier in a long coat was in charge, yelling at a few confused soldiers who were trying to guide a Russian armored personnel carrier around a sharp curve. The tracks were grinding away at the soft dirt, and it was a near thing whether the armored hulk would make the turn or pitch off the side. Lang recognized the slender tubes and round dish on the chassis. Lashed on top of the vehicle were a half-dozen fuel barrels, packed in mounds of snow.

"It's that new SAM model," he whispered. "Mark it."

Roberts took out a digital camera, screwed on a night vision lens and clicked a picture. "What's it doing up here? Definite violation," he whispered. "Those fools will be lucky if it doesn't tip over."

"They're not yet tactical," Lang whispered. "Look at that fuel. They're setting up a SAM trap."

A few meters down the road from the vehicle carrying the surface-to-air missiles, a jeep with a mounted machine gun idled in neutral. The dogs stood back in the trees for another minute, admiring the pretty targets, before Lang shook his head and gestured upward. They were turning to resume climbing when Caulder grabbed Lang by the shoulder and pointed down the road. Lang looked through Caulder's rifle with its heavy thermal scope. A figure was trudging around the bend, head bright white in the scope. The face was downcast, the back bent over, all effort concentrated on plodding along, not looking up, not seeing the jeep, not hearing it, stumbling blindly forward in exhaustion.

"It's Harvell," Lang whispered. He turned on the thermal sight on his over-and-under rifle. The jeep headlights suddenly went on and pinned Harvell. A soldier opened the passenger door and stepped out, slowly raising his rifle. Lang had no time to think, no time to reflect on what he was doing. Harvell could be dead in a few seconds.

"Shit," Lang said. "Caulder, Blade, take him!"

The noise for the next six seconds was deafening. Caulder's first shot knocked down the soldier aiming at Harvell, as Blade slapped a burst through the windshield of the jeep. Lang had selected the lower barrel of his rifle and squeezed off twenty-millimeter armor-piercing rounds, thick as cigars. He was aiming at the top of the Russian APC, trying to pin down the two soldiers sitting atop the hatches. The third or fourth round struck the fuel barrels, and there was a *wuff!*, a flash of glaring white light for less than a second, as though the steel box had been hit by lightning, then a burst of red, as if the embers from a huge bonfire had suddenly kicked into the air. The red ball sucked the air toward it like a sudden wind, and the Marines were scarcely conscious of the sound, a sharp crack like lightning hitting directly overhead. They watched in disbelief as two or three soldiers, or parts of them, shot into the sky, tossed higher than the trees, vivid and puny in the fireball, looking like black paper dolls pinned to a picture of an explosion.

Caught off guard, camera still in hand, Roberts clicked the shutter as the APC exploded and the bodies blew apart, the scene lit up by the brilliant flash from the exploding fuel. It was over in seconds, the Serbs dead or dying before they knew they were under attack. Lang and Blade ventured out onto the road and walked to the blazing SAM vehicle, with Caulder set to provide covering fire.

There was no need. Seven or eight bodies were strewn about. Two soldiers were still moving, neither groaning, both bleeding out. Lang turned and walked toward the jeep, stepping over the soldier crumpled next to the bumper. He checked the driver. Shards of glass had lacerated his face, and the rounds had pounded through his chest. It looked like he had been beaten to death with hammers. It was the first ambush by the team, and they hadn't controlled their firing. Both soldiers had been hit, and hit again, and again.

A figure lay huddled on the ground several feet farther on.

"Harvell," Lang yelled. "Get up here."

Harvell was shaking on the ground, mewing softly. He scrambled up, pawing at his clothes, looking for holes or leaks. He stumbled forward, grinning, giddy, patting his teammates.

"Dumb-ass, ditty-bopping up the road," Roberts snapped at him.

Harvell brought his emotions under control, took the camera from Roberts, looked at the burning SAM vehicle and backed off several meters to frame it in the viewfinder. The others collected grenades from the dead Serbs, walked back to the jeep and blew it. The gasoline ignited in a soft, bright *woosh!*

The men were not reflective types, but as they stood by that fire, they sensed a power. The oldest of Marine lines—*Yea, though I walk through the Valley of Death, I will fear no evil, 'cause I'm the toughest mother in the valley*—rang true. They felt no fear, no remorse. They were prepared, fast, disciplined. The killing was a matter of technique, not right or wrong.

They were uneasy about what would follow, not on the mountain but when they returned to base. None had dreamed they could or would inflict such devastation in a matter of seconds. A few minutes ago, they were just another recon patrol that had exceeded its terrain boundaries. Now they had crossed over a gigantic barrier and were sure to be the subject of discussions between the Joint Chiefs of Staff and the Secretary of Defense. They would be on the front page of newspapers, perhaps on the evening news. They were in the deepest trouble of their lives, and they had no one to turn to, no one to give them advice, no one to suggest what to do next.

"That lit up some AWACS scopes. Bet the Ops Center is hopping now," Blade said. "Riding into battle on fuel tanks, dumb as Custer."

"They didn't know they were in battle," Lang said.

"Shit," Roberts said, "this is going to take some explaining. Regiment will have a kitten."

"They would have smoked Harvell. They showed hostile intent, definite hostile intent," Caulder said. "Besides, that SAM was inside the red zone. That's a clear violation. And we didn't know it was going to blow."

"That's it—we didn't know how powerful our weapons were," Blade said. "I fear it's the outlaw life for us now. The Wild, Wild West."

"Caulder, give us cover in case someone else comes down the road," Lang said. "Harvell, check for messages. We're out of here in three mikes."

Harvell sat down near the fire and opened the End User Terminal. He read before saying anything.

"Something's up at regiment, sir. Lieutenant Colonel Bullard has taken command," he said. "We're to report in for extraction."

"They think we're three clicks to the south," Roberts said. "We have to clarify our current pos."

"Give me a second to think, Staff Sergeant. That order was sent from the Op Center before we hit the SAM," Lang said. "Harvell, any word from Easton?"

Harvell turned on the Quotron and typed Tyler Cosgrove's password for trades on the Warburg channel.

"Incoming for you, sir," Harvell said, pulling up Bart's message. "It's a little old."

From: <%x^v   5:00 P.M. Sun., Dec. 21
To: #@V+

New bid 20.46 43.16 received 4 P.M. Expect exchange within 24 hours
for $300,000. Have not informed Davis group. Uncle will not agree to
these terms. S/F, Bart

Each Marine looked at his map and GPS screen.

"Those coordinates are on the ridgeline above us, four clicks away," Blade said. "What's the rest of the message about?"

"They want three hundred K for Cosgrove," Lang said. "The government won't agree to ransom, so Easton didn't pass this to regiment. Left it to us."

"The ridge marks the border," Roberts said. "That clinches it. Ops will extract us for sure."

"You know," Lang said, "when that air force pilot was shot down in Serbia, a four-star admiral wanted to take a chopper in after him."

"No admiral's coming out this time," Roberts said.

Blade picked up on Lang's suggestion. "If an admiral could go across the border, so could we," he said. "How long did the Serbs keep those army dudes they captured?"

"Four weeks," Lang said.

"We're wasting time. Let's slap a hat," Blade said. "Mrs. Cosgrove has days, right?"

Blade hadn't forgotten. He filed facts away and pulled them out days, months later, connecting the threads. His focus remained intact. To him, the SAM was unfortunate, the fortunes of war, like an avalanche or a hurricane, something that happened, not often, but it happened. When it did, you rode it out and continued on.

"Each of you has to think this over," Lang said. "I'm not making the decision for anyone else on this one."

"I'm for following the field manual," Blade said. "Every mission includes the intent of the higher commander. The intent is to get Captain Cosgrove. That's my defense and I'm sticking to it. How's that sound?"

"You think too much, Blade," Roberts said. "The Corps is the hammer, and you're a little bitty nail. Let's not dream up excuses."

Lang had expected that. Roberts had the most time in, the most to lose by pushing on—a wife, two kids, a pension. He could step on a mine, or be shot, or survive to wear his dress blues to his court-martial.

"Staff Sergeant's right," Lang said. "We cross the border, you all could be out of the reserves or in front of a judge."

"No, sir, I meant let's not hang out with two burning vehicles. This is target city," Roberts said. "Let's di-di, not bullshit. We have one mother of a hump getting up there."

That stopped Lang. He fumbled for something to say. "You're my law-and-order provider."

"I've gone over to the dark side. All we ever do is train. The Special Forces got Afghanistan, and we got this hillbilly country. We go back now, there's still an Article Thirty-one investigation. We're screwed already, ever since we didn't report that girl."

"Fault on me," Lang said. "Up to now you've all followed orders."

"Come on, sir, we can read you six-by. You're not turning back while you've got that guy Easton feeding you," Roberts said. "There's no way we're letting you push on by yourself and grab all the glory. No, no, when CNN interviews you from Belgrade, we want face time, too. Now, let's get out of here."

Lang didn't know how to react. In his mind he had seen this as the turnaround point, where he sent the team back under Roberts. He didn't know how to express what he was feeling. Going on alone was foolish, but he had planned to do it. Having the team with him gave him a real edge. He let his breath out slowly, nodding. Maybe he'd think of something to say later.

"Caulder?" Lang asked.

"I have to think this over," Caulder said.

Even Staff Sergeant Roberts laughed.

"All right, thanks," Lang said. "Harvell, send a sitrep. Upload a pic from the camera. Tell Ops we're in pursuit and will destroy the EUT. We're not taking it across the border."

Harvell quickly typed the message and hit send.

```
From: Pepperdogs                          0030, Dec. 22
To: Combat Ops Center Via Admin

Firefight at this pos. SAM-14 and crew destroyed. They showed
hostile intent. No prisoners or friendly cas. In accord with
commander's intent, in hot pursuit of one vehicle four kms due
north. Will destroy our terminal so no sensitive equipment is
compromised. Will report via civilian computer.
```

"This is definitely cool," Harvell said.

The Pepperdogs looked at one another. Lang waited for Roberts to deliver the blow. Roberts waited for Lang.

"Not across the border, Harvell," Lang said. "We'll arrange a pickup for you here. It'll be too tough over there."

Harvell had prepared for this and had his line rehearsed. "Blade navigates, Caulder shoots, the staff sergeant organizes and you lead, sir," he said. "Me, I communicate, like Cohen."

"You're not Cohen," Roberts said. "He's team, and royally pissed somewhere that he missed this. You, you're . . ."

"I know what you think of me. I know what everybody says," Harvell said. "I screwed up one time because you left me. I'm okay when I'm with you. The captain's going because he has to. The rest of you are going because you want to. Well, I have to. So what if you walk faster? You won't come back anyway. I'm the only way anyone will know what you did. I can communicate and you can't."

Harvell was almost screeching, and tears of rage started to run down his cheeks, glistening in the light of the burning SAM. Roberts, mouth open in disbelief, could think of nothing to say.

"Good guilt, Harvell," Lang said. "Righteous complaint."

"White Man makes sense," Blade said. "Someone has to fat-finger Captain Cosgrove's computer."

"I won't let you down again, sir," Harvell went on. "I clutched after you left me. That's over. I can stay up on the road. I'm all right when, when there's the rest of you around."

"Know how to count, Harvell?" Caulder asked. "Can you sign your name to a chit next time I shoot?"

"I suppose he could carry some ammo, like a gun bearer in those old flicks," Roberts said. "But Harvell, you fuck up again, I swear I'll leave your bones over there."

They all grinned and shuffled a bit, waiting for Lang to decide, not wanting to stand around any longer and cool down.

"All right, Harvell, you stay," Lang said. "Don't know how we'd get you out of here anyway."

Harvell looked at each of them. He said nothing, shivering and trying not to smile while the tears still ran down his cheeks, trying to look tough, failing miserably.

"You look like shit, Harvell," Roberts said. Harvell grinned.

"All right, I'm ordering the team to cross the border in hot pursuit," Lang said. "If we don't make contact, we come back while it's dark."

"Why's this on you? This is that initiative thing the Corps talks about," Roberts said. "We've trained years to do this. We come back heroes, all will be forgiven."

Lang and Blade took out their GPS receivers and held a map between them, deciding on the route. Blade looked up at the sheer wall of rock above them and shook his head.

"We'll have to follow the road to the top. We stay here any longer, we're going to be in another firefight."

They moved out tactically, two bounding forward while two scanned with thermals for heat sources. Harvell scarcely slowed them down, lagging only a little. They reached the high pass in half an hour and saw nothing, just the faintest track in the snow. They stood on the ridgeline that marked the border, shown clearly on their GPS screens. Blade bent over his map.

"It's a vertical mile downhill to Route Eleven," Blade said. "This snow is slick. My bet is that pickup pulled in someplace."

"What's special about Route Eleven?" Caulder asked. "They could stash Cosgrove anyplace."

"No. They need a town, a bank, some way to get the money," Lang said. "They're not going to hibernate for the winter."

"What'll we do?" Roberts asked.

"We own the night," Lang said. "We recon forward and leave enough time to get back here before it's light. We have seven hours."

While the team huddled to update GPS waypoints and rally points, Harvell hastily typed into the Quotron. It never occurred to him not to. It was like writing in a secret diary, locked away where no one could see. No one else had reached for the computer. This was his third posting, but he sensed it wasn't time yet to tell the team. He'd wait until they were over the border, where no one could send him back. He took out the digital camera and fitted the port cable to the slot on the Quotron, scrolled through the pictures Roberts had taken, selected one and pasted it into the message.

www.pepperdogs.com   0035, Dec. 22

Whacked a SAM. I was decoy. When they shot at me, the team lit
them up. Skipper hit fuel tank. Bodies flew everywhere. Cool.
On to Serbia to find Capt C.!
Posted by: J. Kirwin

VI

Those on the mess deck were the first to know that the Pepperdogs had crossed into Serbia. As the midnight change of the watch neared, sailors and Marines crowded in for a fortifying meal of hot dogs, burritos or warmed-over lasagna. They grabbed the indestructible plastic serving trays and stood in line, shifting from foot to foot, with nothing to talk about. Petty Officer Second Class Claire Bott, Combat Information Center Information Integration Division, age nineteen, one semester Fresno State, one genome away from insanity by boredom, changed that. She had glanced at Pepperdogs.com before going off-duty. Well, more than glanced. Harvell was kind of cute, not mega-macho like most Marines. She'd taken a computer security class with him at the start of the deployment and had heard he was out with recon.

Sure enough, three postings, the last a truly gross pic of a guy sailing through the air, an arm and both legs blown off. She printed out Harvell's message and the picture, enlarged it and adjusted the hues so there was no mistaking that this Serb soldier was going for his last ride. When she picked up her tray in the mess hall, she brought the printout and taped it on the bottom of the PLACE TRAYS HERE sign. That way everyone leaving the mess deck could get a good long look. When her shipmates saw that pic, there'd be no more macho jerk-off talk about Info Section dweebs like Harvell or herself. She used a triple stitch of Scotch tape and printed DO NOT REMOVE! above the message. Marines would obey before they thought to disobey. Odds were, when no Marine was looking, a sailor would eventually pull down the message to hang in his duty compartment.

The picture and Harvell's three postings to Pepperdogs.com lasted unsnatched for thirty minutes, read by over four hundred sailors and Marines. All right—something's happening at last! Who's J. Kirwin? Who're these Pepperdogs? They iced some Serbs, maybe Russians, too. Cool. And they're going into Serbia alone. Big brass ones. What's the name of that website again?

After leaving the mess deck, each sailor or Marine e-mailed or mentioned the pic to one or two others who, in turn, sent an e-mail on to a close friend or two or three. Within two hours almost every American ship and shore base had someone logged on to Pepperdogs.com; within three hours the AOL home page was featuring it as an HTML link, right below a link to Madonna's site on hip religions. J. Kirwin was achieving his ten minutes of national fame before he could cash in.

In the Combat Information Center, all operational computers operated on a secure net, with elaborate firewalls separating them from the open, unclassified Internet. The staff on duty had received the team's final report via the EUT, so they knew the dogs were headed toward Serbia; they didn't know, however, that Harvell had informed thousands of others as well.

When Vice Admiral Faxon read that the Pepperdogs were crossing the border, he ordered an immediate video conference, all aides excluded. By the time Lieutenant Colonel Bullard and Major General Zines appeared on the screen, the Razor had scribbled out his agenda.

"Bullard, enlighten me later on how this happened," Faxon said. "Right now, as I understand it, there are five Marines on a six-thousand-foot mountain in a snowstorm, a forecast of single-digit temperatures. By morning they'll turn themselves in to keep from freezing. What a balls-up. Americans captured."

"Ah, I don't think so, sir," Bullard said. "They're used to the elements, and they're in that special BuMed program."

Faxon was not thrown off stride. "I'll look into that. Are you saying they could be out there several days, like pilots in our escape and evasion courses?"

"They're not evading, sir. They're hunting for Captain Cosgrove."

"Hunting? Five against five million Serbs? What do they have to go on?"

"I don't know," Bullard said, "maybe updates from that civilian who gave us the coordinates."

"This isn't Ouija, Colonel. We don't use dowsing rods or mystic civilians to locate kidnappers. First a chopper goes down, and now you have not one but six Marines missing. This, this ad hocery in your command multiplies like loaves and fishes."

Zines listened to the cadenced phrases, the right words with no clear orders. The Razor was covering his ass, playing to another audience. When the tape of the teleconference was reviewed—and it would be if this operation went south—Bullard would be the one who looked incompetent. Bullard accepted the rebuke in silence, knowing better than to say a word.

"They nailed a SAM, Admiral," Zines said. "Kostica can't squirm out of that."

"And how many Russians did they kill with that SAM? Two? Three? What in God's name are they doing?" the Razor asked. "What's this civilian computer they mentioned?"

"We don't know," Zines said. "We're hoping they contact us via unclass e-mail. What are your orders, sir?"

"First, low-key this with the press. Second, tell both the Serbs and the Albanian guerrillas not to screw with our people." He paused for effect. He meant it, and if it leaked, well, it would make a good quote in the *Times*. "Third, I want a comprehensive, coordinated search plan on my desk by zero-eight in the morning."

He's clever, Zines thought. *He comes across as in charge and offers no suggestion on how to get the team back or find Cosgrove. We're sitting on our hands.*

Faxon next visited the Combat Information Center on the third deck of the amphib. He was in a foul mood, tired and frustrated. He wanted information he didn't have. His chief of staff shook his head slightly when he entered. There was no news.

Faxon wandered idly from station to station, saying a few words, pausing before the large electronic map that showed a tangle of blue and orange symbols, including the blue triangle of the recon team, alone on the Serbian border. The contour lines reminded him of the ovals he had drawn in fourth-grade penmanship, trying to make each one almost touch the other. "Tough terrain," he said. He had no idea whether it was or it wasn't. He never went hiking. "How do they train for it?" he asked. "What's this medical program they're in?"

A thin woman in khaki walked to the map and looked up at him. "Commander Gail Evans, sir. The recon team is part of my medical program."

Faxon detested set briefings. He immediately asked the pertinent question. "How long can they go in this weather, Commander?"

"A week or longer."

"This is a reserve unit from New York City, not a bunch of mountain men like Jeremiah Johnson."

"Admiral," Commander Evans said, "as I recall, Johnson was chased by Indians and ran one hundred miles in two days in the Yellowstone. This team can do better, much better."

"How?" Technicalities interested Faxon.

"With training, water in the bloodstream increases, cooling down body temperature. The heart ventricle expands to pump more blood. The Pepperdogs are like Energizer Bunnies."

"But they deplete their oxygen," the admiral said. "They can't recover right away. That's why people can't run marathons every day. Even I know that."

"In the British Columbia Race, sir, this team traversed two hundred and forty miles in five days. They have some, ah, experimental supplements."

The Flag Plot was crowded, a dozen and a half figures in khaki draped over screens and tables. None was talking. All strained to hear. Faxon considered clearing the room, but that might implicate him in whatever she said next.

"Experiments that I didn't know about?" he asked.

The doctor was short, almost tiny compared to the admiral and his aides. Her dark blond hair was tied back in a tight bow, and her eyes were too wide to be handsome. She attracted universal admiration when she replied without missing a beat.

"The medical chain of command, sir, and the team's parent unit were involved at every step."

He sidestepped the rebuke. "What pills are they taking?"

"Blood thinners and capillary-enlargement pills to store more oxygen. Plus darbepoetin to produce red blood cells, which carry more oxygen to the muscles."

"Didn't the French police raid the Tour de France to seize that stuff?"

"That was EPO. Darb lingers longer in the bloodstream. We don't exceed the Olympic standard of fifty percent red blood cells. Of course, that's almost twice what you or I have."

"So the East Germans are running the Olympic drug tests," Faxon said, "and this stuff is your secret weapon?"

"Uh, no. There's creatine to produce amino acid, plus antioxidants to detox the free radicals that collect in the diaphragm." She waited a beat before continuing. "We're also experimenting with EMM to increase enzyme molecules in the metabolic pathway. That shows potential."

"Nothing to leap tall buildings?"

"No, sir. The rest is the usual mix—anti-drowse, anti-nausea, anti-diarrhea, iodine and the like."

"That team wouldn't pass a Chinese drug test. You have a reason for this?"

"Human muscles are fast-twitch fibers. Even professional athletes don't work out hard for more than four hours a day. We humans can't keep moving like wolves or wild hunting dogs," Dr. Evans said. "In Kosovo the Pepperdogs average five hours a day of weights and aerobics and an eighteen-hour run on Friday. We're increasing their load every week."

"Why?"

"To consume more oxygen, what we call mitochondria. My VO2 is sixty; theirs is over ninety. I don't mean to tell you your business, Admiral, but in battle, sleeping in the mud, cold and scared, the need is for endurance, twenty hours a day, day after day, without becoming a zombie. If we can do this, when we get on a terrorist band, we can stay on them for thirty-six, forty-eight hours without rest."

The Razor was silent. He had never been in battle.

"We wanted them to grow new muscle cells," Dr. Evans said.

"You were *altering* them?"

"Not permanently. If they stopped extreme workouts, they'd revert into couch potatoes. They haven't raced professionally since the tests started, of course."

"Of course," Faxon echoed. "And why these particular men?"

"When we found the dogs, they were already champions, and in the city we had access to the finest clinics. They were a stable test group. In fact, they're, well, probably monophyletic."

"Meaning . . ."

"They've come together because each was driven to excel physically. I mean, why did they join the Marines? These men didn't have to prove their manhood. No one was kicking sand in their faces. It's like they were warriors, seeking each other out."

"Nothing unusual there," Faxon said. "Annapolis, West Point, we've been turning out professionals for centuries."

"Professionals, yes, in the sense that the military is a career. The majority, though, don't seek to fight. I'm talking about a warrior instinct, Admiral, men who join to fight and then get out. They don't readily admit that. But in questioning, it comes out."

"Uebermensch or right-wing Montana freedom fighters? Commander, this is ridiculous."

"Politics isn't a factor, sir. We've studied this. Approximately one one-hundredth of one percent of our population joins the infantry, and most get out after several years."

"I feel like I'm getting a briefing on an alien force. My concern is with the here and now. What can you tell me about this team, in practical terms, in one sentence or less."

"I know these men, Admiral. They're the hunters, not the hunted."

"Meaning they won't turn back?"

"I don't think so."

"And these superstars, how good are they?"

"The enzyme activity in their muscle cells is four times ours."

"Four times," the admiral said. "Great, you've created biologic Robo-Cops who are out of control."

"Actually, Admiral, we've only seen a five percent increase due to the chemicals. The rest they do on their own."

The Razor looked around and beckoned to a tall, chiseled young man in camouflage utilities to join them. "Commander Evans is impressed with this recon team, Lieutenant. If your SEALs were inserted at their last coordinates, could you find them?"

The SEAL platoon commander looked startled. Lieutenant Colonel Bullard would ream him for talking ground tactics with the commander of the Joint Task Force.

"I'd have to know where he was headed, sir," he said, "not where he'd been."

"You don't sound confident," the admiral said. "You know this Lang?"

"I've raced against him, sir, and pulled an op with him. He's wound tight."

"In English?"

"He's not rah-rah. He kids around, but it's an act. Once he makes up his mind, he won't let go. He'd be hard to take down. He's a pit bull with a smile."

"I didn't suggest force," Faxon said loudly for the record. "Or that you go into Serbia. I am pursuing information, not opinions."

"We couldn't walk them down, sir. Of course," the SEAL officer added, "I didn't know what the doc was doing."

"Excuses aren't required." Faxon thought. "Could you give the SEALs the same pills, Doctor?"

She shook her head. "A placebo, Admiral. The pills have to be taken for thirty days, and they make only a small change. Those Marines push each other. That's what makes them. There aren't five teams in the world who can stay with the dogs."

"Let's skip the nicknames, Commander," Faxon said. "This is a military unit, not a football team or a kennel. They're subject to the military code of justice, as they're going to find out."

"They're polite, Admiral, even withdrawn. They're not loud or demanding."

"I'm not interested in their manners. You've administered to them, or whatever you're doing, for how long?"

"This is my second year."

"And which pill makes them disposed toward insubordination?"

"They're close to the battalion's intelligence officer, Captain Cosgrove. He oversaw their missions," Evans said. "Admiral, this team is like a family. They work out together every week. Afterward, the wives and girlfriends meet them at the armory and they all go out for dinner. I've never known one of them to quit. They're very close, even insular."

"Under the circumstances, that's not encouraging," the admiral said. "We don't even know where they are."

"Well, at least I know when they're under stress, or running, or hurting . . ."

"You monitor them?"

"Yes, sir, via radio emissions from their implants," Evans said. "Regiment has three microwave relays on mountaintops. This is our fifth week of monitoring."

"Can we track their position?" Faxon asked.

"I'm afraid not, sir," the SEAL officer said. "There are only two receiver stations, too close together to get a resection."

"Set up another repeater, farther away," Faxon said. "I want a fix on that team."

"Aye-aye, sir," the SEAL lieutenant said. "It'll take a few days."

"I want it done tomorrow. In the meantime, Commander Evans, I want you back at the Ops Center," Faxon said. "Report any changes to me immediately."

Dr. Evans had seen this before. Faxon was like the frantic parent rushing in after the accident, ranting at the medical staff, unable to control anything, desperate to be informed. The Razor was concerned rather than querulous. She felt no warmth but some understanding for this aloof man commanding—well, possibly commanding—a lost patrol a hundred miles away. The admiral wouldn't act without data, and he had none.

"Aye-aye, sir," she said and left for a flight to the Ops Center.

When Dr. Evans arrived, the corpsmen had moved the four monitors next to the main screens at the front of the room. She got cold just running in from the landing pad, and she imagined how bone-cutting deep it was thousands of feet higher in a snowstorm on the northern side of the mountain range. Lieutenant Colonel Bullard stood beside her looking at the screens, his bulk casting her in shadow. She liked that. He stood there as her companion, unable to assist, every body signal flashing that if she could give him the slightest information where the team was, his regiment would be on its way in minutes.

The monitors were standard in any American hospital. The same technology monitoring Sylvia Cosgrove's failing signs in Newport, Rhode Island, showed the vigorous health of Mark Lang in Cajetna, Serbia. Dr. Evans watched the data signals from the team and interpreted for Bullard.

"All body temps are a little above normal, pulses ranging between fifty and sixty, pressures lower than normal," she said. "I can read every individual, Tom. Each has a medical fingerprint. Lang has the lowest pressure, the result of that run this morning."

"Gail, would you keep an official log?" Bullard asked. "How long they're on the move, when they sleep, any reports of what they're doing. You're the trained observer here."

"We do that anyway. What's your interest?"

"It's going to be important when this is over, either for awards or for courts-martial."

"That's a joke, right? Barracks humor?"

"Lang's no longer the Marine poster boy for a Super Bowl ad," Bullard said. "The admiral wants me to prepare charges."

"They go to get Cosgrove and they're the bad guys? Only in America," Evans said. "My payback service is up, did you know that? I can resign anytime. Don't expect my reports to help your court. That team is special."

"So's every sailor and Marine."

"Bull," she said. "I treat too many patients screwed up because of self-neglect, not caring for their own bodies. That team deserves more care because they try harder."

"So they can disobey because they work out?"

"I think they had a good reason for what they did, and you think so, too."

"I don't know them that well," Bullard said. "Colonel Davis liked to brag how little direction they needed." He shook his head at the colonel's mistake in judgment.

"You don't need much direction when you have trust," Evans said.

"What?"

"Trust in the system. It's what's lacking here. Remember Brigadier General Cutto last year, when the trailer went off the dock and he jumped in with the dive team to salvage parts worth, what, two hundred bucks? He was nuts," she said. "When your rescue mission came apart a few hours ago, you needed Cutto to back you. Instead you're stuck with a reserve army general politician and a submariner who talks like a physics book."

"Come on, Gail, don't make a service thing out of this. We all do what we're told, period. Makes no difference who tells you if he's your superior. That team disobeyed, clear and simple."

"When did they go over? After you turned back, right?"

"I was ordered back."

"I rest my case, thank you. You were ordered back, and Tyler Cosgrove's still out there. That's why the dogs went over. You know that. So now the Joint Task Force is bitching because they disobeyed some stupid order? Loyalty up but not down."

"Be careful, Gail, you're getting close to the line. You stick to being a doctor and I'll stick to being a commander," Bullard said. "We'll let legal sort out the other matters, okay?"

"Tom, that team is so driven, even fellow New Yorkers can't comprehend what universe they're from," Evans said. "We tell them their buddy is kidnapped, then mutter about a court-martial when a flag officer they don't know aborts the rescue mission?"

Bullard rolled his eyes. "This is the military, not the Lions Club. And I won't listen to any implied criticism of our common superior."

"Which military?" she said. "What does that team care about orders from some staff they've never met on some ship a hundred miles away? What's a bad fitness report to them? They're not in the military for a career. They're reserves from New York City, not martinets from Prussia."

"This discussion is over," he said. "Back home I may be an athletic director, but over here I'm a commanding officer in a chain of command, and that's it."

"And I'm a doctor, back home or over here. I'll stand watch in this Ops Center, *Lieutenant Colonel*. If anything goes wrong, you'll hear my chirp," she said. "I'll be your canary for medical advice. But if this comes to a court, remember which side I'm on."

Bullard walked away, knowing he had strained a two-year friendship. What she said nagged at him. He wondered if the Pepperdogs' disobedience would affect what the Joint Task Force would do to help them.

VII

It was Sunday, the lightest news day of the week, and even the most nar-cissistic politicians were Christmas shopping or watching football rather than shaping news releases. It took Harvell's accidental genius to pro-voke a news flood.

Around noon a few American cable news outlets had briefly men-tioned the missing American, a story without legs. That's how it may have played out, a story about as prominent as a mugging, had it not been for the Pepperdogs home page. It started with a few people contacting a few others, an e-mail from a sailor on the *Bon Homme* to a girlfriend back home, a secure phone call from one Ops Center to another in Brussels and so on. It wasn't long before dozens, then hundreds, clicked on the home page and read J. Kirwin's blurbs. *Hey, check this out.*

After meeting with Katharine, Woody had some traders over to watch the Jets game. He kept running into the bedroom to watch CNN, and soon everyone knew the missing Marine was Cosgrove and that Woody was somehow helping, Woody telling them to keep it to themselves and being hooted down. *It's on the news, for God's sakes, Woody, and on the Web. Cell phones out at each commercial. Call Hank, he should see this. Katy, too, what's her number?*

When Harvell's message popped up about a helicopter being shot down, Woody rushed to call Bart, who had heard nothing from Lang. More cell phones buzzing. The game ended and the guests remained, gathered around the computer screen. Then J. Kirwin's third message— he was scared, alone on a cold, dark mountain, the Serbs closing in. Had the team abandoned him? *I'm calling my mom in L.A., she's always on the Web. It's been an hour since the last message, maybe Harvell's dead. Wait, wait, he's back on the Net. Ah, he's saved. They were setting a trap. He was putting us on. What's a SAM? And that pic, are those really bodies flying in the air? Damn, my father in Chicago was in the army. He loved* Black Hawk Down. *He has to see this. What's the address of that website again?*

What news outfit could resist the story? Human drama, an international setting, violence, a story line, a home page with photos and bios and links to in-depth materials, fresh Web postings every couple of hours, the Pentagon refusing comment but not denying. Sunday-evening news at the click of a mouse, packaged and ready to go, a definite ratings boost.

Provided such a gift, the broadcast companies in New York eagerly prepared their evening shows. At seven P.M. nine million viewers on four major television networks learned of Sylvia Cosgrove's plight, her kidnapped son, the team's pursuit and the informative Pepperdogs.com home page. Five of New York's own against the world—a fair match. Most stations gave a full minute to each biography, complete with pictures, schools, jobs and families. Assistants to producers called the families and friends of the team members, asking for quotes, deciding who had enough to say to be booked for live interviews the next morning. The trickle of press coverage became a flood.

The White House   **7 P.M. Sunday**

The President was looking forward to a simple dinner, as demands on his time usually slackened a bit before Christmas. Even his kids home were hanging out. Patrick Cahill had encouraged his staff to take time off, insisted his national security adviser leave early for a backcountry trek west of Vail, seven days' skiing in deep powder. Nothing happened at Christmas. People and leaders were abnormally nice for a week.

Shortly before seven Secretary of Defense Nettles called in his brusque manner.

"Mr. President, about that missing Marine? Bad news. A recon team has disobeyed orders and gone into Serbia on their own hook, looking for him. Now, are you sitting down for the next part? They're sending reports, via the Internet, to the whole damn world."

"Say that again."

"They shot the bejeezus out of a Russian SAM site and crossed into Serbia. They're going to be splashed all over the evening news. They're posting to their own website, called Pepperdogs.com. I'll pepper their dog when they get back."

"You mean they're on their own?" Cahill asked.

"Totally. My staff says these recon guys are out of control. Wild stuff."

"What are they saying? What are they up to?"

"We've sent you a copy of what they're posting. Their e-mails read like a Bonnie and Clyde travelogue. Saw someone, killed someone—low-key, fun stuff like that. Near as I can tell, they're going to shoot up the country until their buddy is released. Brilliant plan."

"How do we get them back?"

"We've asked the Serbs to cooperate, whatever good that'll do," Nettles said. "They deny knowing anything. And these guys, these Pepperdogs, are shooting first, not introducing themselves. It's a mess."

The President thumbed through the papers the Secretary had sent over. "I'm impressed with their bios," he said. "I thought our reservists were support troops, like the ones at the airports."

"Marines treat their reservists the same as their active forces. That's the problem. They know what they're doing," Nettles said. "I feel like I'm watching a rerun of *The Wild Bunch*. If Congress gets pissed, this could cost us the supplemental."

"Try not to be too sympathetic."

"The way my luck's running, tomorrow they'll pop up on *The Tonight Show*. How about shifting me to some nice, quiet Cabinet post like Agriculture?"

"I need the farm vote, so you stay where you are. How do we handle the press?"

"Public affairs is on top of it. The basic line is that a few soldiers willfully disobeyed and acted irresponsibly, and that the press should think twice before they repeat what's posted on the Web with no confirmation.

Five rational men do not invade a country of five million. I'll keep you informed, but I won't drag you into this. I don't think this'll have a happy ending."

"I'm here if I can help."

"Everyone appreciates that, sir, but there's nothing you can do."

The President's wife, Rachel, had a firm rule barring televisions from family meals. But fourteen-year-old Timmy had been in the basement ready room again with the Marine helicopter crews—he had become their mascot—and was bursting with news about the Pepperdogs. Their seventeen-year-old daughter, Emily, had seen a picture of Mark Lang on the six o'clock news and wanted to see it again. The President wanted to see how the networks pitched the story, and Rachel Cahill felt bad for Mrs. Cosgrove. So, well, all right, this once. They had a TV wheeled in.

The Pepperdog home page was a treasure trove for the Sunday-night anchors, the second-stringers filling in on the lightest news night, four days before Christmas. The networks had an action-adventure and mystery unfolding as they spoke, complete with pictures, graphic action shots, biographies and the latest updates. Freed from having to rely on tongue-tied local reporters, the anchors made the most of their twenty minutes of prime-time fame. This story was theirs to mold and speculate about.

As Cahill flipped among channels, he saw that the networks were using the same format. Each anchor began with the team in Serbia, then filled in their backgrounds. It had taken the news departments only a few clicks on the Net to confirm that these were the genuine articles, well known in their small, hard world. Given biographies and pictures to work with, the men—not the ambiguous Pentagon snippets about what they may or may not have done—became the breaking story.

There was more than a bit of hometown pride in the way the anchors introduced five reservists from Manhattan, Brooklyn and Queens. Lang, the Ivy League athlete; Roberts, the firefighter with two cute daughters; Blade, the department-store employee with an IQ of 150; Caulder, the auto mechanic turned sniper; J. Kirwin, the computer whiz; and, at the center, the handsome missing Captain Cosgrove and his dying mother.

Would the kidnapped Marine see his mother in time? Would they succeed or be captured or worse? Even for New Yorkers, this was over the top; five of their own challenging a whole country.

The First Family ate a simple chicken dinner, the President continuing to click around the stations. They said little until the news was over.

"I feel like I know them," Rachel said. "Will they find him?"

The President was rubbing his forehead. She didn't like him doing that; it brought out lines and wrinkles that made him seem too old, too soon.

"I don't know," Cahill said, "they sure have the Pentagon upset. Those TV stories slid right over the fact that they disobeyed and went off on their own. Typical of the press, not taking the time to get it straight."

Rachel put down her fork and looked at him with concern. When he began to criticize, it was a sure sign he was worried. At such times he was apt to say the wrong thing, to blurt out what he was thinking, a good characteristic in a husband but not so good in a politician, especially if the press was the target.

"The generals may be angry," she said, "but I understand why those reporters sound sympathetic. Those soldiers seem like good men, the kind you would like. In New York City I think the people are cheering for them."

"I know, and that concerns me. This could end badly. Another blow if it does."

"Is there anything you can do to get them back safely, or is that a silly question?" The President's wife had long ago learned how to phrase what she wanted as a question for her husband to solve. Patrick Cahill liked taking action.

"If the Serbs get them, you bet I'll get involved. Right now we don't know where they are. I can't rush into something I know nothing about. This is a matter for the command in Kosovo."

Their two children had been listening in polite silence, both keenly interested.

"Gunny Melton knows Blade," Timmy said, relaying the latest news from the ready room. "He says he's a horse."

"Timothy," his mother said, "try saying he's in excellent condition. And use his real name. 'Blade' is a terrible name."

"I like Lang," said Emily, who was anxious for the freedoms of college. "He has bedroom eyes."

The parents looked at each other but didn't bite.

"Blade's tougher," Tim said.

"Lang's the leader," Emily said, "like Dad."

"Oh, that's clever." The President laughed. "So naturally I have to side with Lang?"

Both children looked seriously at him, appraising.

"You're a Lang type, Dad," Tim said, "when you squint your eyes like that."

Emily nodded. Rachel shook her head. Since the election, her husband frequently squinted when the cameras were on him. Her daughter was right; he did it to look stern, to show he was in command, but it made him look unattractive. The children had given her an opening. Later she would remind him not to squint like a Marine. He hated imitating anyone.

"All right," Rachel said, "let's say a prayer for Mrs. Cosgrove and hit the books. Only two school days this week."

As Cahill bowed his head, he thought about how quickly America was identifying with the team. His wife was praying for a dying woman, his son admired Blade and his daughter had a crush on Lang. Each member of his family had a favorite character and, he admitted, so did he.

John Mumford called immediately after the news. Before becoming Chief of Staff at the White House, Mumford had been the President's senior legislative aide in the governor's office for twelve years. If Mumford had any interest or life outside politics, the President was unaware of it.

"Mr. President, did you catch that?" Mumford asked. "The networks make those Marines sound like the Sopranos on winter vacation. Nice, everyday guys who kill for a living. So much for the SecDef's spin about disobedient misfits. This story has legs, I can feel it."

"I agree, but it's a military matter, John," Cahill said. "It doesn't affect us."

"With the exposure they're getting? Your policy advisers are terrific, but listen to old John for a minute, Mr. President," Mumford said. "If this unravels, you'll have a hostage situation or worse. We need to focus the press on who's accountable from the start, and that's not you. Remember when those army guys died in Somalia? The President fired the Secretary of Defense. I mean, the military created this mess."

"You're always looking at the downside."

"This could be a paper bag full of crap, Mr. President. Someone drops it on your doorstep and lights a match. If you put out the fire, you have to scrape off your shoes."

"John, for once we're ahead of you. This one's staying in Kosovo until it's over. And we're not, I repeat, not pointing any fingers at anyone across the river."

U.S.S. *Bon Homme Richard*   1 A.M. **Monday**

After questioning Dr. Evans, Vice Admiral Faxon returned to his state-room for a short nap. He was fully asleep when the call came in. Over thirteen years of duty at sea, he had honed his mind to snap awake. Three minutes later he entered Flag Plot fully alert. He saw his chief of staff looking flustered, unusual for a man who had commanded two missile-carrying submarines.

"Televideo conference in five minutes, Admiral, called by the chairman."

"Agenda?"

"The Sunday-evening news, sir. We were about to call you after we made copies. I—"

The Razor cut him off. "Someone leaked? My orders were no further press releases until after our morning staff update."

"It's the team, sir, posting to the Internet. Not to our admin section but to the goddamn unclass, everyday, wide-open, worldwide Internet. They have their own website. They've sent three postings so far. It's like they planned this from the start."

The chief of staff gargled each word as though he wanted to spit, so it took a moment for Faxon to grasp what he was hearing. He grabbed the printouts and, with increasing horror, read J. Kirwin's literary master-pieces. In a few minutes he would be talking live on the worldwide video command net, and he didn't know what to say. He had zero data about this. Zero. He would look like a fool. This could not happen in sub-marines, he thought, could not.

"Have they lost their minds?" he asked. "How are they getting this stuff out?"

"We think that civilian computer of theirs is hooked to a satellite feed," his chief said. "I'd like to hook them to a satellite. This violates every op-sec rule known to man and beast."

Shuffling the messages, Faxon sat down in a large blue swivel chair facing a video camera, feeling as comfortable as a condemned man, his staff perched like birds behind him.

The Chairman of the Joint Chiefs of Staff was a large man in his late fifties who ran five days a week to avoid the hint of a paunch. General Ray Scott had his gray hair cropped weekly for five dollars by an on-post barber who overcharged for his skills. His ears stuck out and lent a hint of comic relief to a deeply wrinkled face with a pockmarked shrapnel scar across the left cheekbone. His light eyes seemed to change with his moods, and his aides called them the Twin Blues.

Right now they were flashing disbelief as he watched a press briefing from NATO headquarters in Brussels. At one in the morning only a few reporters had made it to the unscheduled NATO briefing, prompted by the American news broadcasts. The briefer was a lieutenant colonel from the British Royal Air Force with the proper good looks and upper-class accent. Neither helped.

"Ladies and gentlemen, as we told you earlier, a United States Marine is missing since eleven hundred Kosovo time, and an intensive search is under way," he began.

"Is this recon team in Serbia?" a reporter interrupted.

"I can't comment on an ongoing operation."

"Is this an allied operation or Americans going off on their own?"

"As you know, Kosovo is a NATO command."

"We've checked LexisNexis. The soldiers listed on Pepperdogs.com are real. You can confirm that, can't you?" a large male reporter yelled from the third row.

"We're not going into details."

"Well, can we use J. Kirwin's details?" a female reporter asked amid general laughter.

"Have you lost this team as well as that captain?" The large male reporter was hectoring again.

"I didn't say the rank of the missing NATO serviceman." The British colonel kept cool. "This is a kidnapping, a criminal offense, not a military action."

"The Serbs say these Americans are criminals," a Russian reporter shouted. "And they destroyed a Russian military vehicle. Were any Russian citizens killed?"

"I won't comment on ongoing operations."

"Why are we here in the middle of the night if you won't answer the simplest question?" The large male reporter wouldn't be put off.

It went on like that, the NATO spokesman refusing to provide information, the press doggedly asking stupid questions, hoping he might slip up. General Scott shook his head, turned off the TV and prepared for the televideo call, which he detested. You couldn't make direct eye contact through the camera, so everyone looked shifty. No one could read the other person's body signals. Everyone sat stiff, defensive, buttoned up, aware that every word was recorded. Scott thought video calls were worse than useless. Still, the Pentagon had paid so damn much for the equipment, it had to be used.

The J. Kirwin stuff caused Scott to chuckle. He could picture some twitchy kid, a communicator type, scared to death, typing whatever came into his mind, the grunts probably encouraging him, thinking it amusing. Well, in a way, it was. *We always found something to laugh about.* He remembered how, when he was little, the navy anti-submarine blimps flew over the beach, dropping notes to his baby-sitter; and later, the time he was calling in a fire mission and this North Viet was harassing him over the frequency and he yelled at the Viet to get the hell off the Net, that he had an important mission. And for a few minutes the Viet had obeyed him! The troops always put a twist on the newest tech gadget. Why not the Internet? J. Kirwin aside, though, that team sounded like a tough unit.

From his perch in the National Military Command Center, Scott, dressed in a sweater and corduroys, looked at the other principals on the screen. In Brussels there was General Hank Stevens, commander of all NATO forces, wearing camouflage utilities. The actions a year earlier against the terrorists had taken place outside his theater, and Scott knew

Stevens had wanted to be involved. *I hope he's not planning to fly down there,* Scott thought. *This situation doesn't need any more brass.* In Naples Admiral Joe Pfizer sat erect in starched whites, the four stars on his gold-colored shoulder boards glistening. Joe had come straight from some reception, Scott chuckled to himself. On board the *Bon Homme,* Vice Admiral Faxon sat in starched khakis per usual, lips tightly pursed. In the Marine Ops Center, Lieutenant Colonel Bullard, the newly appointed commander, wore rumpled cammies and a rumpled expression. Behind each principal perched a dozen staff officers. *Ridiculous,* Scott thought, *hundreds of people around the world sitting at attention to hear a few old farts who have nothing to say.*

A young-looking colonel announced that all stations were up, and General Scott began speaking without preamble.

"Watching that young fella in Brussels get chewed up by the press, gentlemen," he said, leaning back in his high swivel chair, "reminded me of those new aquariums. You know, the big glass tanks where the fish swim round and round and the people peep in from every side? Well, that's us. We're the fish."

He paused. That should keep this short and controlled. Only a fool would say what was on his mind.

"We have a Marine missing and a recon team that crossed into Serbia. We've all read the reports. No need for a brief. Let's get to it. Are there any issues to discuss? Do we have the right channels open?"

General Hank Stevens had expected the question. He was SACEUR, Supreme Allied Commander Europe, commanding forces from NATO's assorted nations, and he was also the commander in chief of U.S. forces in Europe.

"The task force is a NATO command, Ray," Stevens said. "They're mostly U.S. assets involved in the search, but I expect everyone to go the extra mile to keep our allies in the loop."

"Is NATO setting the ground rules for this, or is the U.S.?" Admiral Pfizer asked.

So much for keeping control, Scott thought. *Pfizer's right, though. Might as well have this out now.*

"Kosovo's a NATO operation," Stevens said. "I've informed the Secretary General. The military committee here in Brussels will make the operational decisions."

That meant Scott was in the spectator stands, watching this game, not a coach on the sidelines. The Chairman of the U.S. Joint Chiefs of Staff was to be an observer while NATO made the decisions. Problem was, it would take the NATO military committee a week to decide what day to meet.

"Last year, when our choppers went in to get a downed pilot, they asked to take out a SAM, and NATO refused," Pfizer said. "We were lucky not to lose an aircraft."

"Let's not look for trouble," Stevens said, shutting down Pfizer. "Each of us wears two hats. We're all American commanders here, and we're working in a NATO chain of command. Practically speaking, it shouldn't make any difference. We all apply common sense."

Scott looked down at his hands. No sense pointing out that so many nations might differ on common sense. "So who's the belly button?" he asked. "Who makes things happen?"

"Bill Faxon will run things," Stevens said.

Vice Admiral Faxon was the commander, Joint Task Force. He held a U.S. Navy command as well, but it was as a NATO commander that he oversaw the 25th Marine Regiment in Kosovo.

Faxon could now speak, after the four stars. "We have under way a co-ordinated search—electronic intelligence, satellite coverage, agents, multispectral imagery, mounted patrols, the works."

"All right, this is a NATO operation, run by Americans. I'm glad that's clear," Scott said. Everyone chuckled, glad they had avoided an open spat. "This recon team sending us—hell, sending everybody—these reports, can't we contact them?"

"No, we don't have their address," Faxon said. "It's strictly unauthorized one-way communication."

"Umm. Does the regiment with the lost Marines have anything to add?" Scott asked, his tone encouraging. "Bullard?"

"No, sir." The lieutenant colonel knew better than to speak.

"This team, good men? Reliable?" Scott was not letting go.

"First-rate, sir. The team leader and the missing Marine, our intell officer, are tight."

"So this team leader wandered off because he had a buddy in trouble? Or was he on to something?"

"On to something, sir."

"I've asked the Naval Criminal Investigative Service," Faxon cut in, trying not to show anger that his subordinate was being directly questioned, "to interrogate the civilian who provided the coordinates that started this thing."

"I heard he was a former Marine," Scott said, his neutral voice not a vote of confidence.

"Then he should cooperate all the more, sir," Faxon said, irritated by these Marines with their secret handshake. Bullard shouldn't be part of this meeting in the first place.

A moment of silence. Scott mused on how TV shaped their agenda. Here they all were, on a Sunday evening, without much to say to one another. Faxon should be on top of this, moving heaven and hell to get his people back, and the rest of them should be having dinner, not holding hands around an electronic campfire.

"General," Faxon said, taking a new tack, "Ambassador Briggs thinks he can reach a deal for Cosgrove's return, provided there aren't any unnecessary actions."

"Meaning no more rescue attempts, I assume," Scott said. "We'll look at that on a case-by-case basis. If you feel you're on to something, launch."

"Some here in Brussels think the team exceeded NATO rules in destroying that SAM," Stevens said. "There are many other nations involved in this."

The televideo blocked out the tension between the men. If they had been in the same room, the hair on the back of their necks would have been standing up. *The President shouldn't have sent Stevens, with his Oxford Ph.D., to Brussels,* Scott thought, *not with that McMansion palace and all the fawning and ass kissing. Now he thinks he's Caesar. Happens too often. Has to be the water over there.*

"Europe doesn't decide U.S. disciplinary matters," he said. "We shouldn't second-guess a firefight we know nothing about. Maybe the SAM crew gave them no choice."

There was silence, neither general willing to be conciliatory.

"At least let's shut down their damn website," Stevens said. "That's public insubordination."

"How do we know what's going on or what they need if we pull the plug?" Scott said. "The secretary and I discussed this. It's better to let them communicate."

No one said anything. Stevens was seething at the public put-down. *No manners,* he thought, *Scott lacks manners; no wonder the Europeans avoid him.*

J. Kirwin Harvell lacked the temperament of a Marine rifleman, but he was careful at his craft. When he designed Pepperdogs.com, he registered the site with AllNet, a top Internet service provider. AllNet charged him a hundred dollars a month and guaranteed service and security against hackers and graffiti artists. AllNet confidently claimed there was no upper limit to the number of eyeballs that could visit a site. Obscure Pepperdogs.com tested that claim in the hour following the Sunday-evening news.

In the Ops Center of the 25th Marines, messages from Pepperdogs.com replaced the map on the center screen, and there was much cheering, groaning and laughter at each of J. Kirwin's descriptions. In the Combat Information Center onboard the *Bon Homme Richard,* the verbal outbursts were restrained, more like the reaction to a loud fart at a cocktail party. All NATO bases, of course, brought up the site despite the late hour, as did American bases worldwide. The military interest was to be expected.

The extent of the public reaction, however, was unexpected. A hundred million homes in the U.S. alone had access to the Internet. After the TV broadcasts, many dropped in to see what was posted. Soon the Pepperdog site was overwhelmed, but the nimble entrepreneurs at AllNet recognized they had a golden marketing opportunity and quickly set up a series of mirror sites, duplicating anything J. Kirwin sent to the home site. AllNet kept up with the demand, and Pepperdogs.com set the new record for eyeballs. The previous record stood since the day the Starr Report was released, detailing sex in the Oval Office. Pepperdogs.com recorded two million hits on its first day, and no one would say J. Kirwin's descriptions of sex were a threat to Philip Roth.

No, J. Kirwin had his own technique. He took the reader onto a live battlefield, where no one knew who was going to win and who was going to die.

VIII

Koplje Mountain, lower slope, Serbia   **2 A.M. Monday**

The road from the ridge down into the valley wasn't steep but Saco was a poor driver. There wasn't room for the regular driver, and Saco refused to ride in the open back. He kept the Toyota in second gear and rode the brake, tap-tap-tapping, the pickup jerking and bucking, the soldiers in the back pinned against the cab, cursing his clumsiness. He peered through the windshield as if he were nearsighted or expected a deer or a tank to appear in the headlights. The windshield wipers swung back and forth, clearing away the light film of snow. On the driver's side, a small arc ignored the repeated swipes of the wiper, much to Saco's annoyance.

"Damn snow," he muttered for the tenth time, "hard to see a thing."

"I see fine," Luc said. The wiper on his side was working smoothly.

"Too long." Saco banged his fist against the steering wheel. "Too long a drive in this shit."

The pickup bounced and shuddered along, Luc occasionally thrusting out his left arm to prevent Cosgrove's head from hitting the dashboard. Cosgrove seemed half conscious. He hadn't spoken, but his eyes were slightly open, heavy-lidded.

Saco felt like a band was tightening around his head. His eyes ached from trying to see around the snow clinging stubbornly to the windshield. He thought he saw a log ahead, lying in the middle of the road. He hit the brake hard, and the Toyota skidded to the right. Panicked, he swung the wheel the other way, and they almost rolled over. When they stopped, the pickup was facing uphill.

Luc looked at Cosgrove. There was wet blood on his ear, whether it was fresh or frozen blood now thawing he didn't know, but he was concerned. This was his airfare to Colombia, where one or two kills a week were all that was needed, where it was always warm, with cold beer and weekend flights to Rio.

"Saco, my friend," he said, "you've convinced me. It's time to stop. We need a rest." He spread the map on his knee. "Let's get down lower and look for a little farm to the west."

"West? That's *hadjuk* land, filthy Muslims. Know why our great president, a schoolteacher, allows them to remain with us inside Serbia?" Saco lowered his voice so the snow wouldn't hear him. "The Americans have paid him off. You watch, NATO will give him a villa in Italy."

The shooting has dried up, Luc thought, *and I'm left making deals with crazies.*

They resumed crawling and jerking down the mountain, veering west. Luc insisted they stop several times while he went on foot up a side path or turnoff. Each time he returned shaking his head, and they crept on downward. After half a dozen such stops, he walked around to the driver's side. "I've found a place," he told Saco.

"Muslim?" Saco asked.

Luc shrugged. How could he know? What difference?

They left Cosgrove slumped in the cab. The three soldiers climbed down stiffly and hopped up and down and hawked and spat and cursed the cold until Saco hit one hard across his back, driving him to his knees. "Shut up."

They walked up a trail marked only by Luc's tracks. The snow was over their ankles and they made little noise, the soldiers especially quiet, afraid Saco would break a nose or loosen some teeth. They saw the grotty cabin set at the base of a steep hill that broke the wind and acted as a shelter against the wintry blasts from the north. The building looked like three or four sheds nailed together, one floor, a few windows stuffed with clothes to lessen the drafts, a single pipe for a chimney. Between the outhouse and the shack was a boxlike car, so small its roof was below Saco's chest. Behind the tiny car was a barn, and they could hear the occasional stamping and shuffling of a few large animals.

Luc signaled two soldiers to go around to the rear, which annoyed Saco, who considered himself in charge. Inside the cabin a dog began barking. Saco gestured for the third soldier to bang on the door. Luc hung back, letting the soldier take the chance of a stray shot. The door opened slowly. The soldier spoke a few staccato sentences, then turned back to Saco. "*Vrags.* Two."

Saco barged forward and the others followed. Inside it was dark, the only light coming from the woodstove against one wall. A large man stood in the center of the small room, and behind him cowered a thin woman. Both were fully clothed. That was how they slept. In a corner by the stove, a small boy had his arms around the neck of a small dog that was barking shrilly. Luc fumbled to light an oil lamp, then poked his head briefly into a tiny bedroom where the blankets were thrown back. A corner of the main room held a hand pump and a sink but no stove. They cooked over the tiny fireplace.

"Where's your gun?" Saco asked the Muslim.

The man said he didn't have one. Saco hit him across the face with the barrel of the AK-47. The man fell to one knee, then looked up with blood pouring from his right cheek and forehead. "All right," he said, and stumbled over to a loose floorboard near the stove, one hand slowly pulling out a bolt-action rifle.

"You should have had the balls to use it," Saco said.

The Albanian stood wobbling, dazed by the blow.

"Let's bring the American here," Luc said, "and take these outside."

The four Serbs stood, shuffling uneasily.

"What's wrong? Let's get this over."

"It's Baba," one of the soldiers said. "We kill them, he kills two Serb families."

"All right. I'll take him to help," Luc said. "I'll move the truck up and bring the American inside." He gestured for the man to put on his boots and follow him. He even smiled a little while waiting. They walked back the few meters to the road in almost comradely fashion. Luc, ever fastidious, considered using a club. No blood would spatter. But the man was big, and if he had the head of an ox, he would have to shoot. So instead he used the knife, letting the man walk in front and then shoving the knife up to its hilt in the small of the man's back. The man tripped over his own feet and crashed into a ditch. No shout, no cry. Good. There was no way Luc was going to retrieve the knife, though. If the man wasn't quite dead, he could do damage. Luc would get another knife later.

He drove the pickup to the door and helped the American into the cabin and into the bed. The woman was sitting with her arm around her son, and both were shushing the dog, who growled and whimpered. The Serbs stood around acting like uninvited guests, unsure what to do. It was too cold inside to take off their jackets just yet, and they breathed out thin strands of vapor. Still, they were out of the cutting wind.

"Where's the Muslim?" Saco asked.

"Tried to run away," Luc said with a shrug.

"You cause big trouble, Frenchman," Saco said. "This is not your country. Someone may get hurt because you kill that *vrag*."

The four Serbs glared at him. *Amazing,* Luc thought, *they kill Muslims like cows in a slaughterhouse and then get upset if a Serb family or two gets hurt.*

The soldiers were too cold and tired to pay attention to the woman, although she was rather pretty. She had a smooth face, thin lips and large, round dark eyes, the kind that promised to sparkle if she laughed. No hint of womanly figure showed through the layers of clothes, but she wasn't large or thick or fat. She didn't ask why her husband hadn't come back. She said nothing, just crouched down shielding her son. In the way she tensed her shoulders and lowered her head, there was a hint that she would fling herself at any soldier who approached the boy.

They helped themselves to hot coffee and a few pieces of bread, then settled down to doze in corners away from the drafts. No watch was set. Who would be out in the freezing snow at three in the morning? One soldier started to snore loudly and another kicked him. Saco sprawled out, his head and neck propped against a wall, his lower lip blubbering with each expulsion of air. No one kicked him.

Only Luc's eyes showed a flicker of movement. He watched the woman go quietly into the room where the American was. In a few minutes she came out, poured some hot water into a bowl, gathered some cloths and went back in. Luc didn't stir. Any help for the American was help for him. Soon he was lightly dozing.

Koplje Mountain, upper slope, Serbia   2 A.M. Monday

As the team walked down the road from the top of the mountain, the snow tapered off and the temperature fell. The snow crystallized, soft as powder, and squeaked under their boots, to the annoyance of Blade and Caulder, ranging ahead at point. After an hour, Lang called a halt and had Harvell check the Internet for the latest weather forecast. Intermittent snow.

"We might launch Dragon Eye now, before it snows again," Lang said.

"We destroyed our computer, so we can't mark what we see," Blade said.

"We can estimate by flight speed, heading and time."

"What are we looking for?" Roberts asked.

"Hot spots, a vehicle with a big black spot under the hood, parked near a house or some sort of shelter. Blade, you fly. The rest of us write down the time and size of what he calls out."

From Lang's pack they unstrapped the plastic wings. Soon they had assembled the small airplane with its tiny camera.

"Set the drone to run north-south sweeps until it runs out of gas," Lang said.

Blade studied the map and entered his calculations in the handled remote-control panel, which contained a GPS chip the size of a fingernail. He readied the tiny plane by connecting a wire to the spark plug, adjusting the carburetor until the engine was running smoothly, then pulling back on a long bungee cord, which, like a slingshot, launched the over-sized model airplane. It swooped off into the black.

Blade walked into the middle of the road so no trees stood between him and the plane. In his hand he held a square box with a long antenna and two dials that controlled the flight. He slipped over his head what looked like a thick monocle attached to a plastic headband. The monocle for the head-mounted display was less than an inch before his left eye, and he tweaked it for several seconds, then said, "Good image. Stand by to mark. Last two digits of each pos." After a few minutes he said, "Nine two, seven six. Large spot." Several minutes later he said something similar. So it went until the plane ran out of fuel and crashed after thirty minutes of low-level flying.

The team backed off the road into a stand of fir trees, where they huddled together and went over the notes.

"The drone swept fourteen square kilometers," Blade said. "We have six probables spread out over eight clicks and no moving vehicles."

"We split into two teams, search four kilometers each," Roberts said, "no big deal."

Lang said nothing. His head was down, and he had the thumb of his glove against his lips, a sign his men didn't like.

Blade tried to head off what was coming. "Captain Cosgrove would come for us, sir," he said. "Of course, he wouldn't walk. He'd talk the American ambassador out of that armored Mercedes, hold a rally and persuade the farmers to search. Then he'd drive us home."

"It's not going to work," Lang said. "We can't get back by daylight."

"What's the difference if we're over here one night or two? We go into the bush during the day, then retrograde tomorrow night," Caulder said. "Tell you what, sir. You're rich, right? Okay, set us up with trust funds. That way you got no more guilt if we get the boot. Now, let's go."

"That's practical," Blade said.

Caulder nodded vigorously, proud of himself.

"No one would dare court-martial us," Harvell said. This was his chance to make a contribution. "We have too large a following."

"Shut up, Harvell. You don't know what you're talking about," Roberts said. He thought. Something was not right here. "You mean your stupid recon website? It gets one hit a month."

Stung, Harvell pulled out the Quotron, typed in www.pepperdogs.com and checked the hits. "Over one mil," he said without thinking. The others looked quizzical. He waited, then rehit the count. "One million, one hundred thou."

Roberts spoke first. "Harvell, what the fuck have you done?"

Harvell had expected praise. He froze, not knowing what to say, not wanting to admit what he had been doing since they started up the mountain. He had meant to tell them, but the timing never seemed right.

"Harvell, you've been sending out messages, haven't you?" Lang's tone sounded amused, at least not hostile. Harvell felt hope. "Show us."

Harvell knelt and pulled up each message he had sent, holding the Quotron's backlit screen above his head so the team, clustered behind him, could read each line. There were only a few scattered flakes of snow in the air, and it had turned sharply colder. They could feel it in their lungs as they breathed deeply and tried to comprehend what they were reading. Roberts and Caulder cursed. Blade and Lang laughed. Like the participants in a *Survivor* show, they were all alone on their mountain, only the five of them and millions of viewers.

"You sneaky, miserable, slimy turd," Roberts said. "You had to brag, didn't you? You shouldn't be allowed near real people, Harvell, you live in la-la land. We should leave you here by yourself."

No one else spoke, each trying to grasp what the postings did to their mission.

"Wonderful invention, the Net," Lang said after a while. "We can reach out and touch anyone."

Harvell, one knee in the snow, stayed very still, hoping they wouldn't notice he was there. No such luck. Roberts turned on him again.

"We're a world-class laughingstock. Dumb-ass, how could you tell people you suckered that SAM? You? This ends any talk about going back. I'll jump off a cliff before I quit on this."

He swatted Harvell across the back of his head. Harvell saw a few stars but held on to the Quotron. He hunched over and didn't move.

"This isn't an Article Thirty-one or a court-martial anymore," Lang said. "We're a full-fledged congressional hearing—five Ollie Norths."

"Do we turn it off?" Roberts asked.

Lang thought. The military prosecutors would come after him as the team leader and officer. The others might not face charges if they got their story out and built support. "And disappoint our worldwide audience?" he said. "We're better off keeping our own record. J. Kirwin here has already seen to that. Harvell, send an update."

"To the Ops Center?"

"No, to Pepperdogs. Somehow I think the Ops Center is among our readers."

Harvell kept his head down as he typed what Lang dictated.

---

www.pepperdogs.com   0300, Dec. 22

Dragon Eye has given us solid leads. Several hot spots. Captain
C. may be close! We're following up.
Posted by: J. Kirwin

"We split the team and move?" Blade asked.

"Affirm," Lang said. "We each take three hot spots."

"We knock on doors," Caulder said, "and ask if they have a stray American?"

"At each spot look for fresh tire tracks," Lang said. "If you find any, check out the vehicle and report in. Watch out for sentries."

Roberts and Blade broke to the east, Lang and Caulder to the west, while Harvell stayed at the rally point. Each man's GPS held all the hot spots. They would use their thermals and night vision goggles for the recons when close to the farms. Dogs would be a problem, so they would approach each farm upwind.

The cabin   4 A.M. Monday

In the middle of the night Luc came fully awake to look in on Cosgrove, who had a thick bandage around his head and bedcovers up to his chin. An hour later a series of soft scraping sounds awakened Luc. He gripped his rifle and listened. The sounds were coming from the tiny bedroom. Quietly he got to his feet, crossed the room and looked in through the open door. Cosgrove was standing at the small window, opening it a few inches at a time.

Luc raised the butt of his rifle to hit him in the small of the back. *No, can't risk killing him.* He lowered the rifle, walked in and stood beside the American in the freezing-cold room.

"Hot," the American said, *"j'ai très chaud . . . Ouv . . . rez . . . cette . . . fen . . . être, s'il . . . vous plaît."*

Luc had to smile. The American was quick, a good sign. His brain was working, maybe he'd stay alive. The window looked too small to wiggle through, and even if he had, how far would he have gotten? A few hundred meters. Luc shook his head, slammed the window shut and pushed Cosgrove, not too hard, back onto the bed.

Before dawn Luc shook Saco awake, and they spoke in French in low tones.

"Time to get going to your sawmill. If we can finish this today, we should. The American, I don't know how long he lives. As long as he doesn't vomit. That's the bad sign," Luc said. "We can't have three soldiers in the back when we leave. Nothing to attract attention. They can take the car and follow. Whatever. They come out of your share."

"Okay," Saco said. "They've been with me three years. They're all right."

He has these strange loyalties, Luc thought.

"Maybe I can buy the sawmill," Saco said.

"You can buy a mountain. We leave now—you, me, the American. No one else."

"What do I tell them?"

"Whatever you want. Only they can't come with us."

"What about her? You killed one *vrag*. What about the other two?"

"It's your country," Luc said. "Tell your soldiers to finish it. Only later."

Saco considered that. Luc had no idea what he was thinking. Suddenly Saco roared at his soldiers. While they were listening to him and collecting themselves, Luc gently pulled Cosgrove to his feet and zipped up his jacket. He took out a wool cap but decided not to touch the American's head. He helped him into the cab. Saco got in, started the engine and turned on the headlights in the full dark. A soldier stood in the doorway watching them, then angrily slammed the door before the pickup was in gear.

"What'd you tell them?" Luc asked, hoping he would never see the soldiers again.

"I said to finish things up, take the car when it's light and meet me at the mill."

"Do they know what we're going to do?"

"No. They know something's up. They asked when we release the American."

"How far to the mill?"

"Once we're off this damn mountain, not far. Maybe twenty, thirty kilometers. Two, three hours, depending on this snow. I took some gas from the *vrags*."

Lang was almost down to the valley floor, checking out the last farm on his list, when he found something. That is, he heard something, the faint whine of a low-powered engine in low gear slowly going downhill, the sound distinct in the cold, still air.

After the car engine receded, Lang picked up his pace. Within several minutes he and Caulder came to a cutoff and saw the faint tire treads leading in and the fresh tracks out. Caulder found the body in the culvert, knife frozen in the back. They looked at each other in frustration. Lang used his radio to call in the others, and he and Caulder slowly circled the dark cabin. The walls were so flimsy, Caulder's thermal picked up the heat from five heads.

"Five hot spots inside," Caulder said, "and there's a dump next to the front door. That's not where the owner would take a crap."

After Caulder went down to the road to guide the others in, Lang swept away some snow and sat back against a thick tree trunk with a clear view of the cabin. How far could he go? The Marines burst in, some guy jerks awake, scared out of his wits, and reaches for a weapon. Lights out, sleep tight. Was it a legal kill? Who was he? A farmer? A kidnapper? Farmer, ha! What was the frozen guy with the knife, fertilizer for next spring?

Fifteen minutes later the five Marines were huddled near the cutoff, and Lang gave them the facts.

"Are they enemy, sir?" Harvell asked.

"No, Harvell, it's an orphanage," Caulder said.

"Harvell has a point. The two in this corner"—Lang drew a sketch in the snow—"one's a small skull. Good chance it's a kid. So be careful. Door opens to the right. I'm in first—"

"Oh good, sir," Roberts cut in, "we begin with our leader, straight out of the Lang textbook. Then something happens to you and we don't accomplish the mission. No, no, no. This ain't going to happen."

"The door has to go down fast," Lang said. "I'm the largest."

"Could be booby-trapped," Roberts said.

"No. They don't even have a sentry," Lang said. "Okay, I knock down the door, Blade in left, Caulder right, Roberts at the window. Harvell, take the rear. Stay off at an angle. Rounds will go through those walls like paper."

"Shoot to kill, sir?" Harvell asked simple, impossible questions.

"Use your judgment. You'll know what to do when it happens," Lang said. *No he won't,* he thought. *But no one's coming out that rear. No one.*

They were seventeen hours into the hunt now, and a twenty-six-mile run before that. Not long by their standards. Lang was tired, but the cold cut too deep for him to feel sleepy or sluggish. He was sure his mind was sharp. He knew exactly what he was doing. Why was he hesitating? Some recon teams practiced rescuing hostages. His team had been on those exercises as the watchers and backup marksmen. His men were the deep patrollers, specialists in calling air or artillery, survivalists. They weren't police. They weren't trained to rescue hostages. They had no stun grenades, no flash blinders, no armored vests, no coordinated signals, no practice, no techniques. The Marines had taught them how to kill, full-stop, nothing else. He either ordered death in that cabin, or he quit the search for Tyler Cosgrove and walked back to the border.

"Caulder, can you get a pic of the dead man with the knife sticking out?" Lang asked.

"Easy do," Caulder replied.

"Harvell, send this message along with the photo," Lang said.

---

www.pepperdogs.com   0415, Dec. 22

Encountered killing shown in pic. Tracks and human feces at
door of cabin. Murderers inside. Believe they know about
missing Marine. Will take action before they kill again.
Posted by: J. Kirwin

Harvell asked to sign the message. Lang didn't think it made any difference; he was setting up a defense for the whole team. *Would it hold up in a court-martial? Who knows?* The American legal system was wondrously inventive.

"It'll be dark in there. If you can take someone alive, great," Lang said. "Go with your instincts. If you're gut-shot, we'll pack you in snow and pick you up on our way back."

"That makes the choices clear," Blade said.

"Be careful of the kid near the fire," Lang added. "Get around back, Harvell. We go in three mikes."

Roberts slowly sidled up to the window at the left of the door. Caulder carefully put in his rubber earplugs. Lang half emptied his pack, adjusted it as a pad over his right shoulder, nodded at Caulder and Blade, took a ten-meter running start and hit the door so hard it shattered in two. He flew several feet across the room, not trying to keep his balance, falling on his pack, not waiting to draw a weapon, scrambling up with the pack in his hands, looking for someone to throw it at.

None of the Serbs was asleep, dozing perhaps but not asleep, not with Saco gone. They had been at war for years. It was as normal for them to reach for a rifle as for a morning cup of coffee. Two had good reflexes. Their hands had clasped their weapons seconds after Lang burst through the door and sprawled across the floor.

Caulder and Blade shot them without thinking. The noise was like a dozen hammers banging on tin pots, deafening, overwhelming. Lang was stumbling forward with his pack, a woman and boy sitting bolt upright in terror a few steps in front of him, when the third Serb tried to get to his feet before reaching for his rifle. Lang continued his rush, shoving the pack into the man's chest, knocking him back against the wall, jamming the pack into his face, once, twice. The man turned his face to the side, and Lang pulled the pack back and whacked him across the head. The man slumped to the floor.

In seconds they had tied the hands of the dazed Serb survivor. The other two were hit in the chest and would soon die. The woman clutched her son and appeared too petrified to speak.

Blade turned up the oil lamp. "They're bleeding like pigs," he said. "Can we dump them outside? It'll be a mess in here soon."

"Go ahead," Lang said. "Search them, too."

"Wish I had rubber gloves," Caulder said. "They might have AIDS or gangrene or something."

"Gangrene?" Blade asked.

"Yeah, something scuzzy like that," Caulder said as he dragged a body out the back door.

"Send Harvell in with the Translator," Lang said, picking up the pieces of the front door.

"*Vlah!*" screamed the woman, striking at the Serb lying near her feet.

"Shit!" Lang dropped the splintered door and leaped at her, Roberts rushing in behind him. Too late. She had shoved a thin hunting knife into the side of the Serb's neck. Lang grabbed her arms and easily lifted her back. She seemed to have no weight. His fingers wrapped around her arms, and he held her in the air as she twisted and screamed at the Serb. Roberts found a piece of rope, and they tied her wrists behind her back.

That wasn't enough. She kept trying to kick the man. Lang pushed her back and she fell over the bed. The boy, who had soft brown eyes with long lashes and didn't come up to Lang's hip, rushed forward, kicking at the captain, slapping at his leg, tears streaming down his face, not saying a word. Lang ignored the boy and bent over the Serb. The boy, confused, ran back to his mother, who was trying to kneel. Lang bent over the Serb, shielding him from another rush.

"Don't pull that knife out, sir, or he'll spout like a fountain," Roberts said. "Damn, we needed one alive."

"On me," Lang said. "I thought she was catatonic."

"Good word. Let's use it on Caulder."

"I screwed up big-time, Staff Sergeant," Lang said.

"No," Roberts said, "she must have been ready to use that for hours. Bet it's her old man we found outside. Took guts, though. Most people can't stick another person."

"Will he live?"

"Missed the main artery." Roberts peered at the wound. "Knife's not buried that deep. We dump him outside, he'll freeze quick. We leave him here, maybe his buddies come along. He might make it, might not."

"Leave him here. Throw some covers over him," Lang said.

Using the Translator, they told the woman they would untie her if she left the wounded Serb alone. She agreed and immediately put on her boots and coat. Caulder took her out to the body of her husband. When they had left, Lang snapped a piece off the frozen chocolate bar he kept next to a grenade in his outer vest and walked over to the boy, who wouldn't look up. Lang knelt, opened the tiny hand and placed the chocolate in the boy's palm. The boy hurled the chocolate to the floor, rushed into the bedroom and threw himself on the bed, facedown.

Outside in the snow, the woman sat patting the cold, stiff shoulder of the dead man. Caulder stood off to one side, scanning the dark woods. Then she returned to the cabin, bundled up her son and together they revisited the dead man in the freezing cold. The Marines stoked the fire and set about cooking a large, very hot meal. When she returned, Lang questioned her using the Translator.

Her name was Litjie, and yes, she had seen the American. She had bandaged his head. A large Serb and a Frenchman—yes, he spoke French and bad Serb—had taken him away. Could she describe them? She tried, vaguely. No, she had not seen their vehicle, but it sounded small, not a truck. The others were planning to meet them. Where? A sawmill in the Dadjak region, thirty to forty kilometers up the valley.

She was not good with a military map, but she picked out Route 11, the only paved road through the valley, and pointed to Dadjak. Her finger zigzagged across ten kilometers of ridges, ravines and steep slopes, with a few pastures and tiny black squares of houses snuggled next to the twisting black line of the road. Did she know where there was a sawmill? She shrugged. There were several.

"Tough terrain," Blade said. "Good concealment for us."

"How do we find Cosgrove?" Caulder asked.

"We don't," Lang said. "We get close and wait for their next call to the States. Then we get the coordinates. Twenty minutes' sleep. I'll take the watch. Harvell, notify Easton. Tell him we'll be close in about twelve hours. Then sleep until we wake you."

Harvell took out the Quotron, typed a message and showed it to Lang.

```
From: #@V+                              5:00 A.M., Mon., Dec. 22
To: <%x^v
Package held by large local and a Frenchman, driving to region 40 km
north of last pos. Our ETA there 6 P.M.
```

"Not exactly hidden as a trading offer," Lang said.

"You think it'll be intercepted?" Harvell asked.

"With the money there is in trading? Sure. A dozen firms will scan it. This doesn't tell much, though." Lang handed the Quotron back to Harvell, who didn't put it away. He looked at Lang, who smiled.

"All right, Harvell, continue with your masterpiece. Don't disappoint the Ops Center."

Harvell crawled into the sleeping bag, typed quickly and fell asleep immediately after hitting the return key.

---

www.pepperdogs.com   0500, Dec. 22

Three murderers snuffed. We saved two. I covered the rear. It was over fast. We are in hot pursuit.
Posted by: J. Kirwin

In the Combat Operations Center, the message popped up on the screen. Dr. Evans read it and returned to the medical monitors. The heart rates were in the sixties, then fifties, then high forties. She called Bullard over to share the news with him, a peace offering.

"Their rates are down, except for Lang."

"Meaning?"

"They're asleep and he's on watch."

"That's what they need."

"If I know my team, this isn't a real REM sleep. It's a catnap, fifteen, twenty minutes, and they're off again. A refresher. I'm concerned about Lang. He's not dozing, not recuperating. If he goes squirrelly on us . . ."

Bullard phrased his response carefully. The idea that Lang might prove to be the team's weak link had never occurred to him. Lang, the most experienced captain in the reserve battalion, with two active-duty overseas deployments, the calm Wall Street trader rumored to be worth millions. This didn't make sense.

"Perhaps you're too concerned," he said. "I mean, maybe you see the littlest signs, which don't affect the outcome. Everyone loses sleep."

"You might be right. But I've seen other team leaders go down. They take on too much, and when their bodies run out, they push through on willpower. That's when they make mistakes."

IX

It was approaching midnight, and Bart was dozing in a chair when Sylvia began to cough. In seconds she was out of breath, gasping, waving her hand feebly. Bart quickly handed her the suction tube, which gurgled like an underpowered vacuum cleaner. She shoved it roughly down her throat to clear her lung, stopped coughing and lay back, breathing hard. It took her several minutes to recover.

"I was dreaming Mark was in trouble," she wheezed. She sank into her pillows. Bart walked around to the window side of the bed to avoid jiggling the tubes in her right arm. He sat and stroked her hair.

"It's going to be all right," he said, "it's going to be all right."

"No, no, it's not," she said, tears in her eyes. "I don't want to lose them both . . ."

He continued to stroke her hair, hoping she would fall back asleep. But she kept her eyes on his face, and he found it hard to concentrate. He didn't know what to do. They sat in silence for ten minutes.

"Stop this, Bart Easton, stop what you're doing," she was trying to speak strongly, but her voice was a weak rasp. "It's my time to go, not theirs."

Bart was startled by the outburst. Sylvia seemed to be drifting in and out of a coma, yet her mind had suddenly snapped back, clear and sharp as a trap, repeating back to him his own fears. If one of the Pepperdogs went down, the team would be pinned and the Serbs would ship the bodies back in plain pine boxes.

"They're coming home, together," Bart tried to sound encouraging. "They'll look out for each other. They . . ."

"Oh, hush. You don't know that. That worries me. You and Mark— you both try to make things right when you can't. I'm leaving now. Don't you see, my love? It's too late. Stop it."

She fell back and her eyes half closed. Bart didn't know what to do. He clenched his hands and looked at the floor. He didn't remember dozing but he jumped when he heard the soft buzzer and the nurse's voice asking if Katharine and Alex could come up from the lobby.

He reached for his laptop. It had all seemed so direct, so clear at first. Everything falling into place—the phone call from the kidnapper, Woody getting the coordinates, Marines to the rescue, end of story. Now it was unraveling. He was going into a second night without sleep, and his mind felt the strain—Sylvia's deterioration, the helicopter rescue failing, Mark going into Serbia, now a second firefight, more killings. At least he knew something about the kidnappers, but it was too unclear. This hadn't turned out right. Time to end it.

He finished typing and sent his message. He didn't bother with the simplest concealment code. He wanted to be clear: Mark was to come home.

He met Katharine outside the room. He spoke calmly, eyes averted, on the verge of losing it. "She wants to speak with you," he said. "The doctor doesn't think she'll last another day."

They didn't know what to say, unprepared to hear the definition of finality—a day. He turned away and walked down the corridor, shoulders back, leaving the women to look at each other through glistening eyes.

They knocked and tiptoed in. Only one light was on, and in its gloom Sylvia was a frightening apparition, a dim, shrunken face with bulging eyes, lurking in the shadows, the oxygen mask amplifying each gasp and exhalation. Aware that she looked fearful and pitiful, she gestured to turn on the lights. In the sudden glare, she blinked and cried, ashamed of her body, of her face. They rushed to her, lightly touching her good arm and patting her legs, and wept.

. . .

Bart came back into the room as Sylvia fell into a half doze. She seemed on the verge of lapsing into a coma, and nurses came and went on various pretexts, changing the IV bag and checking on the morphine drip. Alexandra and Katharine went to the lounge to watch the cable news while Bart sat next to the bed, huddled over his laptop. When the women returned, their faces were strained, Alex plainly angry, Katharine trying to restrain her.

"Bart, can we see you outside, please," Alex whispered.

Once in the corridor by the window, Alex turned on him. "Mark is in Serbia, on his own. CNN reports he's been in two firefights. What's going on?"

Bart explained, then added, "I thought the Marines would close the net around the kidnappers. It wasn't supposed to be Mark's team out there alone. I've sent him an e-mail that Sylvia wants him to come back."

"You left the choice up to him?" Alex whispered. "You know how fixated he gets. If you insisted, he'd turn around."

"He's over thirty, Alex," Bart said. "I can't tell him what to do."

"No, you don't want to tell him. You're hoping he makes a rescue all by himself. You only care about one of them. Damn you." Alex gestured toward Sylvia's room. "Why don't you tell her what you've done?"

In tears, she rushed back to the lounge. Katharine looked at him, wanting to believe in him.

"Tyler would do the same for Mark, wouldn't he?" she asked.

"Of course. He wouldn't hesitate a minute."

Satisfied, Katharine went to comfort Alexandra. Bart drew a deep breath. *If Mark had been taken,* he asked himself, *would I have urged Ty to go after him?* He didn't know how to answer that question.

The cabin   6 A.M. **Monday**

After his body had relaxed for a few minutes, Staff Sergeant Roberts snapped awake. It was quiet in the cabin, the only sound the heavy breathing of the Marines and the crackling of the wood in the stove. He put on his boots and jacket, picked up his rifle and walked outside to the tree where Lang sat, watching the empty trail.

"I'm taking the watch, Skipper," Roberts said. "You're getting Z's for the next twenty mikes. No arguments."

Lang smiled. "Thanks, Staff Sergeant."

He went into the cabin and closed his eyes. It felt so good not to think. No thoughts at all, not cold, either. Soon he was standing on the bank of a wide river lined with large trees alive with the vivid greens of late spring. On the far bank he could see laughing boys at the top of a granite cliff, peering down nervously at the waters, waiting for someone to work up the nerve. Then silence as all watched the first try. It was Lang's son, leaping out, plummeting down. Only the leap wasn't far enough, and in a split second the boy smacked on the rocks. Lang heard the splat. Instantly he was whisked across the river and was holding his son, who lay shattered, a thighbone driven into his pelvis. The boy died without saying a word, the soft brown eyes with long lashes disbelieving. All Lang could do was hold him.

Trapped in the web of a dream too frightening to shake off, he couldn't move. He lay rigid, determined to get rid of the dream. He had heard the sound of the body hitting, and he never wanted to hear another sound like it. There was a loud stamp and he jerked awake.

"Sorry, sir, I just reacted. Never saw a roach the size of a mouse before," Caulder said, scraping the goo from his boot. "He was trying to haul off that piece of chocolate you left on the floor. Want it?"

Lang glanced at his watch. He'd been out almost twenty minutes. He felt sluggish, disoriented. He looked at Caulder, who stood staring blankly at the squashed cockroach. *That run yesterday took something out of both of us,* Lang thought. The others were on their feet, collecting their gear.

"Take the car outside?" Caulder asked.

"Won't hold us all," Lang said, "and won't get through the snow."

The woman asked through the Translator if they would bury her husband.

"I'm a killer, not an undertaker," Caulder replied.

The others said nothing. The woman spoke briefly to the boy, who sat listlessly on his cot next to the stove. She put on her coat, walked out, took a shovel from the barn and started down the path toward the body, ignoring Roberts, who sat watching the road.

"Ah, hell," Blade said, "all this sitting around. I need some exercise."
He put on his jacket and picked up his weapon.

"Ground's not frozen," Caulder said. "Two of us will get it done
quicker. If you'll keep the chow hot, sir, I'll help our saint here."

Lang said nothing and turned back to the stove. He had a large pot
boiling, filled with potatoes that he jabbed repeatedly with his knife. He
had swirled in some sugar and salt and what seemed to be fat and some
sort of pepper.

The boy was still sitting on his cot, looking at Lang, when his mother
and the others stomped back in. The Marines sat down and began to
slurp the soup. The woman had prepared a large bundle and was wrapping her son in layers of clothes.

"Ask her where she'll go," Roberts said, though he wasn't particularly
interested.

The Translator was fast, clever software. There was no hesitation
from the machine when the sentences were short and direct. People
quickly learned to adapt to its style. She answered in childlike sentences,
unanswerable in her demand: "The Serbs will come and kill my son. We
go with you."

The Marines stopped eating. Roberts stared at the Translator as if the
English didn't make sense. Caulder laughed in approval or derision.

"No. Go to friends," Lang said.

"No." Litjie shook her head. "The Serbs will kill them, too. No killing
here for two years. Then you come and my Majstck is killed. Please, we
go with you. The border is not so far."

They looked away and said nothing, avoiding the grief and the plea in
her round, deep eyes. No weeping or ululating for her, no soft moaning in
the corner or keening at the cold grave. Her man was gone and her son
would be next. She was accusing them.

Like her neighbors, she had cheered years ago when Americans had
rumbled into Kosovo, the long convoys of tanks and amtracs, the soldiers
sitting on top, impossibly large in their armor and helmets, the women
throwing flowers and smiling, the children giggling and waving, a parade, a holiday.

Now everyone complained about the Americans, how they still rode
in their tanks after all those years, afraid of the people, returning to their

forts every night. They didn't help anybody. What good were they? Her mountain had always been mixed Serb-Muslim, and it was not so bad once Milosevic was sent to The Hague. The Serbs left them alone on the ridge where the soil was poor. The Americans had never crossed the mountain range to these farms and cabins, but it was still a comfort to know they were several miles away. America was the country everyone ranted and cursed against and conspired to send their children to.

Here they were in her cabin, the Americans whom her Majstck watched on video whenever the single hijacked strand of electric wire to their cabin worked. Her husband cheered and laughed and reran scenes from war movies for Litjie and Marik to enjoy with him. Now Majstck was dead, and these real Americans had, like servants, mopped up the blood on the floor and dug his grave, as if that made a difference. Conquerors, huh! These weren't conquerors like in the other wars. Those Serbs would have raped her and smashed in her head. Russians? Raped her and moved on. Germans? Shot her. Austrians? Burned her cabin. These Americans? They ignored her.

Her fear was to be left behind by these men who shrugged off the cold, who snuffed out Serb soldiers like ants, who hunted only to get back one of their own and leave. They were not good and not bad. To them she was like a chair or bed, something useless, outside their world. Somehow she knew that to insist on what was right was the only way with these men. Would it be enough? They cared only for their own, not for her or little Marik.

She continued to bundle him in layers of her old clothes, so that he looked like a small mummy and walked stiff-legged. She wore two sweaters and a *dimije*, billowy pants tied at the ankles. She stuffed herself into a bright blue overcoat and carried a large rucksack to the door. She held Marik's hand and stood there, waiting for the Americans to say something.

"That blue would make a great target on the thousand-yard range," Caulder said to Blade.

"You're too sensitive for your line of work," Blade replied.

They ignored the woman as they slurped up the potato porridge and complimented Lang on his cooking—"It's hot." They then repacked their gear and looked to their weapons.

"I'll take an AK and smash my Sixteen. We redistribute my ammo," Roberts said to Lang.

"Take the boy," Litjie said to Lang through the Translator.

It was as if she had not spoken.

"How many AK rounds you taking?" Caulder asked.

"Four hundred."

"Heavvvy. We get in that serious, we're not going home."

"We'll go home, all right, even if we have to send some more to Allah," Roberts said.

"Wrong side," Caulder said.

"I'll send them to whatever hell they want."

She tried again. "The Serbs will kill my boy."

The Translator spoke the words in perfect English. Lang seemed busy eating. Caulder and Roberts continued to ignore her.

Blade jerked his head toward the bodies outside in the snow. "Think those Serbs were going to kill her?"

"No doubt in my mind," Roberts replied.

"So, ah, she and the kid are dead meat once we leave?" Blade said.

"Maybe they can make it over the mountain," Roberts said.

"Right, and maybe Cosgrove's lying in white sheets surrounded by pretty nurses in Belgrade," Caulder said. "Humping uphill in the snow with a kid? Say she makes it to the summit, which I doubt. Then she walks by that SAM we smoked. The Serbs will love that. She's walking dead."

Litjie did not speak again. Lang took his rifle, walked around her and went outside to where Harvell stood watch, looking at the Quotron.

"You moving all right, Harvell?"

"Stiff, sir, but that sleep felt terrific." He handed Lang the Quotron. "You have a message."

```
From: <%x^v                          12:00 A.M. Mon., Dec. 22
To: #@v+

Sylvia needs you. Wants you home. I will pay ransom instead. We are
proud of all of you. You are national news. Come back. Nothing more
you can do.
S/F, Bart
```

The others came out and read the message.

"All Ops Centers are the same," Caulder said, "thinking they know more than we do in the field."

"I monitor the Quotron once an hour, sir," Harvell said. "With the Tricup battery, it'll last several more hours. Will we be out long?"

"Not more than ten days."

Harvell looked at Lang, but there wasn't enough light to reveal his features. The Marines returned to their chores, and when they were done, they walked outside and stood quietly in the predawn, ignoring the woman and the boy. The air was crisp and heavy, and soon snow would be falling again.

"I've got a good route," Blade said. "We stay east of the highway in the scrub above the high pastures. I figure ten or twelve hours to that district."

Lang said nothing, merely gestured to the northeast. The woman and the boy had stayed inside, and Lang was glad of it. He wanted to forget them. Without a word, they fell into their places and walked away from the cabin, not looking back. Caulder and Blade set a slow pace, apparently mindful of Harvell tagging at the rear. Lang followed in trace behind Blade, not concentrating on tactics. He was rethinking Bart's message. With less than an hour's sleep, he knew he had to be careful and go over it twice. *If Bart pays ransom, will the kidnappers release Ty? And Bart's line about the team being in the news, what difference does that make?*

His mind was tired, thinking in slow motion. He would make a connection, put the pieces together, then forget and have to go back and start over again. What was bothering him? Mrs. C. She was in that hospital bed but was also here, watching him, disappointed, talking to him.

Mark, you left them to die.

Mrs. C., they're not the mission.

This was his imagination, the mental deterioration they met on all long treks, thoughts that tricked them, evil-spirited, oozing through the mind, changing shapes. Lang called it Grendel. In Morocco Blade had almost fallen off a cliff because Grendel told him Indians walked on clouds. In Thailand Grendel whispered to Caulder to stroke a puff adder, and in British Columbia Grendel urged Roberts to slide down a glacier. Mrs. C.

didn't seem to be Grendel, though; her spirit was gentle. It meant no harm. *Let it go. Focus on the mission. Focus on Cos.*

They hadn't walked a kilometer before he gave in, raised his hand above his head and twirled his arm around in a circle. The others gathered around.

"Bad move, leaving them there," Lang said. "Fault on me. Suggestions?"

"We can't take them with us," Roberts said. "She's not our problem. Women have to be treated the same as men."

"Deeply philosophic, Staff Sergeant," Lang said.

"You wouldn't do a thing if her husband was alive, sir," Roberts said.

"No, I probably wouldn't," Lang said. "And he's not."

"How much money do we have?" Blade asked.

Between them they had two hundred and eighty dollars, thanks to Harvell bringing his wallet, credit cards and two hundred in cash.

"Harvell, you plan on buying a farm while you're out here?" Caulder asked.

"If we give her money, she can bribe a ride across the border," Blade said. "We're fifteen mikes out. At most we lose an hour."

"That's a solid plan," Lang said.

They turned around and set out for the cabin, moving through the underbrush at a brisk pace. The low snow clouds cast a gloom over the valley, more twilight than morning. They heard the cabin before they saw it, the squawking and cawing of ravens summoning their progeny from mountains near and far to partake in the feast, a winter's carnival of carrion, a jamboree of large black birds with iron beaks that stabbed like chisels through the crusted blood and layers of clothes and frozen skin of the Serbs dumped outside the cabin. The birds flew in a tight spiral over the cabin, a black finger pointing to the scene of the killings. The Serb with the neck wound was one of the three corpses.

"She cleaned house before she left, practically sawed his head off," Caulder said. "Her Serb neighbors are going to be highly pissed when they find this."

"Stuff them in the cabin," Lang said. "With luck, they won't be discovered for days."

The birds hovered above their heads, complaining shrilly.

"Tracks lead to the highway," Blade said. "She's trying to get out on her own."

The snow was above their ankles, and no vehicle had come down the mountain.

"Double-time up the road," Lang said. "We can hear any engine coming."

"What if somebody's out for a morning walk?" Blade asked.

"Say good morning," Lang replied.

In twenty minutes they ran down the woman. Her blue overcoat shone like a beacon against the bleak background of the dark clouds and darker trees. She was holding her son's hand and carrying the overstuffed rucksack on her back. The snow was deep enough that the boy had to lift his feet to clear it, and the steep slope of the mountain added to his exertions. The brown mongrel dog, scarcely older than a puppy, was trotting ahead but turned back to bark sharply as the Marines ran up.

Litjie was startled, fearful. She had given up on the Americans, but now they were back. Were they being chased? No, they didn't seem afraid. The hawk-faced one with the telescope on his rifle walked by, looking alert and suspicious, but he patted Marik on the head and nodded to her. The others seemed glad to see her, gathering around her, smiling slightly. The big redheaded one knelt to calm the dog, which barked more furiously. The captain—everyone knew the American ranks— gestured that they should get off the road. The ditch was filled with snow, and she reached for Marik's hand. But the older sergeant—easily over thirty—picked the boy up under his arm and strode across the ditch. Litjie followed, slipping under the weight of her pack.

In the shelter of some trees, the soft-faced Marine drew out the black box. Litjie was relieved. Now she could talk.

"You left us," she said.

She didn't know why she blurted it out. Majstck was always chiding her for speaking out. But the captain had an intelligent face. What was intelligence for if you didn't know when you did wrong?

"You won't make it up the mountain," Lang said. "It's going to snow again. Go to a neighbor."

The Translator spoke clearly.

"I told you. They would be killed. Me, too. And Marik."

The captain looked at the snow in the trees, at the sky, at the boy, finally at her.

"Some farmers must cross the mountain—for food, clothes, tools. We saw many trails."

"Yes, there is a farm with a tractor. They go all the time. But they won't take us. We have no money."

"How much does it cost?"

"Fifty Euros a person."

"Here's one hundred fifty."

She took the folded American bills, stuffed them in the deep pocket of her overcoat and began to cry. It was all too sudden. The filthy Serbs killing her Majstck, then these Americans bursting in. Now they were handing her more money than they seemed to understand, enough for two months. She tried to stop the tears. She didn't want to worry Marik. The Americans looked embarrassed. The one who looked like an American Indian with those black and white stripes across his face rolled his eyes at Marik, as if to say *What can we do?* Marik giggled, and she laughed as she cried.

"You go for the American with the injured head?" she asked, drying her eyes. When Lang nodded, she continued speaking into the Translator. "The Serb? He is very big and wears a brown bear coat. He looks like a bear. His name is Saco. The Frenchman is little. He wears camouflage, and he has a rifle with a big scope like yours."

She took her son's hand and started up the road, explaining that she would cut over to a farm in the west. They watched her go.

"That was nice of her," Harvell said.

"Shut up, Harvell," Roberts said absently. He was grinning, and when he looked around, he saw the others smiling back.

"The milk of human kindness," Blade said. "I'm a believer."

"All right!" Caulder said. "A description to go with a location. We're, what, forty clicks from that district? Holy shit, Cosgrove, here we come."

"Whoa, whoa. There are three mills on the map," Lang said. "And maybe they're at one that's not marked."

"How many man-bears and snipers with telescopic sights are there at sawmills?" Caulder said.

The others nodded, the two young sergeants caught up in mutual enthusiasm. Too many sawmills was a detail to leave to the skipper. He'd figure it out.

"A sawmill needs trees, right?" Blade said. "So it's out of town. We're looking for a few guys in a pickup, maybe a few more at the mill. We scope out the mill, take them down, grab the good captain and extract."

Lang sensed that their mission was like the trading pit. The market would sometimes turn against you and then swing back in your favor. Now that the search was swinging in their favor, Bart's timing was off. He was acting on emotion and old news. Lang was twenty-four hours into exhaustion, but he knew one thing: *When you have momentum, press on.*

"All right, we can do this," Lang said. "We're going on. Harvell, send this message."

From: #@V+   6:00 A.M. Mon., Dec. 22
To: <%x^v

A big negative on going back. No more downers from the Old Fart
Corps. You are supporting, we are supported. The main man is Saco.
Need his address.
S/F, Mark

X

Alexandra and Katharine had left to get a few hours of fitful sleep. Bart sat dozing in the darkened hospital room, semi-listening to Sylvia's deep, ragged breaths, which occasionally faltered, leaving several seconds of silence that constricted his heart, before resuming the battle for life. It was after one in the morning when the computer alarm—a soft *beep-beep*—alerted him to Harvell's latest message. He read it and called Woody.

"We now have a name, descriptions and the district they're in," Bart said. "Now how do we locate them?"

"In this city the NYPD would nail that big bastard in an hour," Woody said. "He'd have no place to hide. Over there the Serbs will cover for them."

Bart thought for a moment. "No, the government doesn't want to get bombed. These are some local hoods."

"We still don't know where they are," Woody said. "We give this to the feds, they'll get them and Cos."

"Eventually, maybe. Or they'll get rid of Ty because he's the evidence against them. His odds are better if we can get to them fast."

Easton was remembering a car trip he and Sylvia had taken in Eastern Europe a few years before. She was brushing up on nineteenth-century portraiture, and as they drove leisurely from city to city, he had been impressed with the number of Internet cafés in even the smallest villages. Computer links seemed to be part of every bistro, like cigarette or condom machines.

"We could offer a reward on the Net," Easton said.

"Hell yes. Warburg'll come in for a good pop."

"No, we need to post this now, so when people go on-line over there in a few hours, there it is. I'll guarantee the money."

"Who'll believe you?" Woody said. "You'd sound like another crazy. No, you need a good front man, you know, a defeated senator or something. A Jimmy Carter type."

"I listened to a former Serbian ambassador at a World Affairs Council meeting a few months ago," Bart said. "He lectures at Columbia. I have the invitation and name on my laptop. I'll send it over."

"Good, a professor. Then he doesn't earn spit," Woody said. "What are you willing to throw at this?"

"Fifty, a hundred K. I'd go higher, but I have to keep several hundred liquid for the ransom."

"There we go again with the R word."

"Woody, I just want Ty back," Bart said. "This may be a dry hole."

"I don't think so. A giant at a sawmill? It's like looking for the basketball team with the midget. We'll get hits when we post this," Woody said. "Look, what do you say to ten K for the starving Serb diplomat and fifty more for the right info? I've got the troops. Every trader on the floor wants to help. I have to beat them off with a stick. We'll organize this for you."

"It's after one in the morning," Easton said. "We have to research the most popular Serb sites, find out how to post to them, how to offer a credible conduit so people can contact us in confidence. This may be too hard."

"Stop for a moment, stop. What's hard about this? You're talking about setting up a petty fifty-thou trade, cash for information, with a cutout to keep the seller anonymous. Hey, let us traders handle this, okay? On the floor we'd give this to an intern to handle. I told you—my phone's ringing off the hook. We'll be on ten Serb websites inside four hours, I guarantee it."

"All right," Easton said. "I'll try to call the Serb professor and—"

"No, Bart, no. You sound upset, maybe a bit unglued. You stick to your line of work," Woody said. "We're New Yorkers, let us handle our city. That Serb professor probably lives in some walk-up on West One-twenty-fifth Street, freezing his ass off because he can't pay the gas bill. I call at two in the morning offering ten K for a couple of hours' work and he says he doesn't work nights? I don't think so."

Northern Koplje Range   **Monday morning**

They held to a fast pace until they were deep in the scrub above the pastures. After an hour Lang called a halt. Harvell pulled up the latest message and read it aloud.

```
From: <%x^v                          2:00 A.M. Mon., Dec. 22
To: #@V+
```

OK, you get any info I get. Am posting on Serb websites the reward page shown below. But I'll still pay ransom if that works. Sylvia and Alexandra expect you back, asshole.
S/F, Old Fart Bart

<Attachment>

MISSING AMERICAN IN KOPLJE:

$50,000 REWARD. MAY BE HELD BY HUGE SERGEANT NAMED SACO, OR BY FRENCHMAN. MR. TILIAC, FORMER PRIME MINISTER OF SERBIA, IN CHARGE OF FUNDS. ALL NAMES KEPT CONFIDENTIAL. REPLY TO: tiliac@easton.com.

"Easton's been busy," Roberts said. "But would a Serb turn in another Serb?"

"Ever watch *America's Most Wanted*?" Lang laughed. "Fifty K is fifteen years' salary in Serbia."

"I can post the reward on KosoFinest," Harvell offered.

"Have at it," Lang said. "And all of you—brag to your families about your paid holiday."

"Okay, Harvell, send this," Caulder said. " 'Connie, snowboarding is terrific. I love you. Skipper promises to have us home for Christmas.' "

"Copy," Harvell replied. "Staff Sergeant Roberts?"

" 'Toni, love to the girls,' " Roberts said.

"Don't get carried away with the Christmas spirit," Lang said.

Lang was feeling optimistic about the information Litjie had given them. As soon as Harvell had sent the messages, they would leave. Blade walked up to deliver his message, and Roberts sat down beside Lang, away from the others.

"What was that about that woman back at the cabin shifting for herself, Staff Sergeant?" Lang said.

"A woman doesn't have to have a man."

"Reading *Cosmo* again?"

"Maybe I'll get a divorce," Roberts said.

"And maybe I'll get a DVD player. My VCR is getting old."

Roberts spat into the snow. The captain could be a pain in the ass when he got into his smart-mouth act. He'd better clear this up now in case Harvell fell out later.

"I'm serious," Roberts said. "Toni has her teaching and the girls. I do my shift at the firehouse, then team workouts on weekends. We have separate lives. If we split, she'd have her job and child support."

Lang paused, then said, "Why do I have the feeling there's more?"

"That KosoFinest dating service?" Roberts said. "I tried it, for laughs. I don't know. I figured I'd bring Harvell out with us one time. You know what a pest he is."

"That's where you've been the past two weekends, enjoying Kosovo's finest? You bring Harvell out as payback and now you're pissed at yourself, so you chew his ass all the time?" Lang said. "Tell me how this relates to Toni, in case I'm guessing wrong."

"There's this girl, I mean, she's a woman, only younger—Evette—I mean, she listens to me. Christ, she adores me. She's what I really need," Roberts said. "Growing up in Brooklyn, my brother and I shared a bedroom. I went away for a while. No women where I went. Then I married Toni. I've never had anything like Evette."

"Umm. Evette, that common Kosovo name, like Kitty or Lolita." Lang paused, then added, "Great sex?"

"Getting personal, aren't we, sir? There's more to life than making trades or winning races."

"Don't shift this on me, Roberts," Lang said. "Harvell's here because of you, and that affects the mission. What happens if this girl wants you as a ticket out? Or if she's the same as Toni, only desperate, and ten years from now you have four daughters and two unhappy women who think you're a class-A jerk?"

"You think I'm pussy-whipped, don't you?"

"Did I say that or did you?" Lang said. "It afflicts most of us males at one time or another. You know the saying, 'God gave man enough blood to use his head or his dick but not both at the same time'? You'll recover after your balls freeze off out here."

Lang had pierced Roberts's defense and the staff sergeant couldn't argue. "I feel like an asshole, sir."

"You are," Lang said. "That's not love, it's sex, and there won't be an Evette after this op. We'll be on the next plane home, maybe in orange jumpsuits."

"You make it sound like I'm in a no-win situation."

"I can bring you up on charges of adultery, if that would help. We could have adjoining courts-martial."

"All heart, sir, all heart."

"I'm glad we had this Dear Abby chat, in case Oprah calls," Lang replied. "Now, e-mail something cute to your daughters. Your little fling is terminated. And cut Harvell some slack. Stop acting like Ivan the Terrible. He's scared to death of you, and today's hump will be a mother. If he falls out, we're in trouble. We're here for only one thing, to bring Cosgrove back."

Roberts walked over to Harvell to send a new greeting. Lang sat alone, watching him, and momentarily felt smug, content with himself for dispensing wise advice, counseling men older than he. Then he felt uneasy, restive, and he knew why. *I'm risking Roberts, all of them,* he thought, *to get back Cos.* He got up and walked downhill, almost tripping over Blade, who sat on the military crest, glassing the way ahead.

"Better get your message in, Blade."

"I'm your scout, sir. I'll talk to my parents when it's over."

"Do I hear a bit of jealousy, Sergeant?"

"Women don't come on war parties. It distracts."

Lang paused. He hadn't thought of Alexandra, not once, since they boarded the slick. "Same in every war."

"No, sir. Some guys at regiment send home four e-mails a day. That's ridiculous. The front's too tied to home. If Roberts and Caulder start worrying about their wives, we're screwed. When we go to war, we should leave our families behind."

After the break, the team made good progress. They walked along the high edge of the shrub growth, where the pastures faded into fir trees and low bushes. The fences on the upper mountainside were flimsy and easily passed. Cows and sheep ignored the scrabbly bush where they couldn't graze. Stripped of leaves, the undergrowth wasn't hard to penetrate. The point man twisted and turned, avoiding the thorn patches and thickets of juniper and holly bushes, while the others followed fifty meters to the rear.

The footing was tricky, though. The wind had pushed the snow up the open pastures to settle in mounds along the edge of the scrub. The midday sun melted the top covering, which would freeze again at night. The men tried to walk where the glaze of ice seemed thickest, but every tenth step or so they would crash through and have to pull a leg out of knee-deep snow. It was like slipping in loose mud, and it took a toll on their endurance. It didn't slow them down, but it sapped energy.

Lang had a destination, not a plan. If Bart paid to get Cos back, the team would climb some backcountry ridge and call for an evac. If the team found the sawmill, then he would need a plan, but it was another eight hours to the district. No sense thinking about it. It was up to Bart to find an address.

The weather was strange. They were walking into a slight, steady breeze from the northwest, and new snow fell intermittently, like showers in the spring. The clouds seemed low enough to reach up and touch, gray, heavy billows as much fog as cloud, the snow lurking higher above, ready to fall as steadily as rain. Blade, no matter where he was placed in the formation, kept running up the heels of the man in front, anxious to cover distance before the weather slowed them down.

The land rolled like waves, an endless series of cleared fields, each eventually sloping down into a rocky gully. Up and down they trudged, skipping across small streams where the rocks were encased in ice, and they splashed through frigid waters that sometimes reached above the tops of their waterproof boots. Any man could call a halt at any time to change socks or wring the water out of undergarments, and every fifty minutes they holed up for a short rest.

The team held to a steady, almost relaxed pace to preserve Harvell. He was fourth in line, where the snow was broken down, and either Roberts or Lang stayed behind him, constantly encouraging: "Ten minutes to the next break. You can do it," or "Looks like flat terrain ahead. You're looking good."

The praise worked. Harvell wasn't alert, and he slouched as he walked, but he kept moving forward, hour after hour. It was ten in the morning, after almost a full day on the move with twenty minutes' sleep, before he vomited. Even Roberts gave him credit.

"Most beginners barf after the first twelve hours," he said, patting Harvell on the back.

Harvell's body had hit the wall. He had consumed the last of his glucose hours ago, and his body had gone to work breaking down its fat reserves. Now they, too, were gone, and he was out of fuel but continuing to exert, straining the liver and generating an excess of bile that drained into the stomach cavity, creating spontaneous gagging and vomiting. Once the body's liquids were voided, the body would overheat even in the cold, the muscles would lock and cramp and Harvell would collapse into a twitching bundle of screams as leg cramps locked up his calves and the backs of his thighs. If they were in range of a medevac, it would bring him to a hospital, where a glucose-rich IV would be inserted in each arm and corpsmen would grab the back of each ankle and push his legs straight up until they squeezed out the cramps. They would strap down each leg so it couldn't curl and cramp again, and they would give him as much orange juice and ginger ale as he could drink, and ice cream and chocolate, any sugars he wanted, and after a day it would seem a bad nightmare never to be repeated.

For Harvell there was no medevac, only Roberts or Lang comforting him, insisting he swallow the foul-tasting iodine water each time he heaved, insisting he stand straight on his feet, allowing no slack for a cramp to reach up like a spring trap and slam the muscles shut. There were no wisecracks from Caulder and Blade. Their bodies were a day away from the vomit stage, and they knew the sudden, hard, thumping rushes of the next firefight, rushes repeated again and again in the loose snow, five yards, ten, five again, would have them throwing up alongside Harvell. So they remained silent and hoped Lang and Roberts would baby him, coax him to keep up. Carrying him would be a bitch.

The cold was tolerable. They had the best equipment, compliments of commercial companies seeking endorsements from the winners of so many extreme endurance races. Their deep-treaded boots kept out the water and the cold, yet allowed their feet to breathe. They wore Gore-Tex socks and SmartWool socks, and when water came in over the tops of the boots, they would empty them, change socks and be ready to go in a few minutes. Next to their skin they wore breathable Capilene body socks that absorbed sweat and wicked it out to the next layer, which passed it through their woolen outer garments.

All wore wool hoods to retain the heat of their neck and head, and wool caps and fleece gloves. Each had a wool face mask. As long as the temperature and wind chill stayed above zero degrees Fahrenheit, the cold and the snow wouldn't stop them.

To each generation, a different challenge. The Pepperdogs weren't marching out of the frozen Chosin against thousands of Chinese. They weren't drinking their urine while pinned down under a white searing sun along the DMZ in Nam. Their crucible was exhaustion, being alone in a harsh land with no support. Hour after hour after hour of walking, minds drained, bodies empty, no crusty old Marine colonel limping along beside them, encouraging them, telling them what to do. Their own commanders wanted them to quit. America wouldn't care. Who joined the Marines anymore? And reserves, who were they?

They didn't think of that. They weren't thinking much at all. Dimly, they knew that others before them hadn't quit. They drank frequently, refilling their collapsible water sacks from the streams, adding iodine tablets. They had eaten close to seventeen hundred calories in the potato soup at the cabin, and it wasn't until noon that Lang signaled a halt for a meal. Caulder led them in a wide circle, ending at a small cliff that overlooked the tracks they had made ten minutes earlier. From their perch they could place grazing fire on anyone who stumbled over their path. They unrolled their ground cloths, loosened their boots and ate.

The meals were precooked, high in fat and calories. They poured water around the small iron and magnesium sacks, inserted the cold-weather ration sacks and waited as the water bubbled and warmed noodles and chicken and gorp. They needed the warmth and the calories; Lang accepted the risk that someone might smell the food a hundred meters away. Roberts cut a chunk of C-4 explosive to boil water, and each Marine poured coffee or chocolate powder into his cup as the steaming water was passed around. They ate slowly, savoring the break. The food was hot, heavy and nourishing, tasting like porridge mixed with sawdust.

"Sir, you should be the chef for one of these food companies," Caulder said. "Your potato soup would fit right in."

"Definitely," Blade agreed. "You have the talent."

"Very good, Blade," Lang said. "Very good."

"We're down to one more meal and it's still morning," Roberts said. "After that, it's on to Harvell. That's why we brought him."

"Harvell, ignore the Donner party. You're too skinny," Lang said. "What's the traffic?"

Harvell, burrowed into the bag brought for Cosgrove, lay propped up against a tree, only his wan face showing. He fumbled to unzip the bag and drag out the Quotron. Lang walked over and took the computer from his shaking hand.

"I'll do this for a while," Lang said. He'd give Harvell's stomach a half hour to settle. "Doze off if you want."

The others looked at him sharply. They were anxious to be off, the sawmill district eight or ten hours away, no mountains to cross, long ridgelines to follow. They did not want to tarry. They could feel the finish to this. Time to be off. Only they were saddled with Harvell. Well, what could they do at this point?

Harvell jerked in and out of dream world, trying to show he wasn't folding on them. Lang called up the home page and pressed for messages. The screen held only a half dozen at a time, so he began to scroll down but then stopped. *Have to include them all, make a game of this,* he thought. *Give their minds a rest.* "Where's the counter?" he asked.

"Hold down the tab and press five, sir," Harvell said.

Lang entered the command and studied the screen for fully five seconds. He looked at the others with a bemused smile, as if he had either won the lottery or contracted AIDS.

"Gentlemen, we have underestimated the talents of our resident writer, Mr. J. Kirwin. The number of site hits is, da, da, two million . . . No, no, it's two point seven mil."

"Read us some?" Blade asked.

Lang scrolled down the latest list.

" 'We hope you find your friend. Bucharest Public School Seventeen.'

" 'Kick ass, Marines. Singapore behind you.'

" 'American aggressors, leave Serb people in peace. Moscow.' "

"The admiral will love that one," Caulder said.

" 'You should be jailed for murder. Berkeley Free Press.' "

"Told you not to take that shot, Caulder," Lang added.

" 'Go Marines Go, New Zealand.'

" 'You're so hot! Tau Theta Sigma, University of Georgia.' "

"Keep that address, sir," Blade said.

" 'Cooz, don't slide down any greased poles. Station Forty-two.' "

"That's Staten Island South," Roberts said with a grin.

"Cooz?" Caulder said. "Staff Sergeant Cooz?"

" 'Big pool here who gets hit first. Please advise. Belfast.' "

"They're used to this stuff," Blade said.

"Can I have the rights, sir?" Harvell said. "We're hot."

Roberts swung around. Even before he spoke, Harvell was shrinking back.

"Blade gets Europe, Caulder Asia, the skipper and I split America," Roberts said. "You, Harvell, get Serbia."

Harvell joined in the laughter, and Roberts winked at Lang.

"Lot of people rooting for us," Blade said.

"And against us," Caulder said.

"Harvell, you are a marvel," Lang said.

"Then I continue to work the Quotron, Skipper?" Harvell asked.

"Wouldn't have it any other way."

The sawmill   **Midmorning Monday**

It had been a bad drive for Saco. Nursing did not come naturally to him. Since they had left that Muslim cabin, Luc had nagged. "Give the American room, watch out you don't knock him when you shift gears, be care-

ful, your shoulder is bumping his head, stop, let's give him some water."
Saco had inched forward in first gear, sometimes in second. The snow
wasn't deep, but they were the only vehicle on the road before dawn, and
he didn't want to end up in a ditch.

When the sun came up, they shared the road with a few others, a tractor or two, a horse pulling a heavy wooden sled, a truck. Around eight
they reached the turnoff to the sawmill. They were on each other's
nerves by then. To Saco it made no sense, treating the American like a
baby. And Luc was a pain in the ass, thinking he had all the answers.

"He's not going to die," Saco said. "They die when they vomit, or
when they get the glass eye. The American, he's fine."

"The swelling's worse since he's been sitting up," Luc replied. "He's
bleeding inside his face. Not good."

"What do we care? We ask for the money anyway."

"No, he has to say something into the phone when he's at the bank."

"What if they hold us?"

"Who? A bank manager? Why? For the American?" Luc laughed.
"Would you try to hold us? If the American is alive, this'll work."

"I hate Americans, bombing, no honor," Saco said. "They didn't
dare fight us in Kosovo. We would have done to them what the Vietnamese did."

"Milosevic was an asshole," Luc said.

"He was right about Greater Serbia. The *vrags* had to go. You fought
for us."

Luc shrugged. "I go where the fighting is."

"You're a mercenary. Me, I fight for my country."

Luc laughed again. "We're both selling an American. What's the difference?"

"No, it's not the same. I will share, build back the sawmill."

To him, Luc thought, *that sawmill is Paris.*

He glanced around at Saco's promised land. The dull morning light was
as strong as it would be all day, and the black stumps of large trees stood
clearly etched against the white background. Not even the snow could
soften the desolation of the hillside. It reminded Luc of a vast cemetery.

Saco parked the pickup, saying it could not make it up the steep grade
in slick snow, and trudged up the path. Luc sat in the cab with the engine

running and smoked and patted the American's knee, encouraging him to remain alive. After a while an old tractor with enormous rear tires wheezed down the road. The driver turned the tractor around, and Saco attached a thick rope to the pickup's bumper and squeezed back behind the wheel. The tractor slowly climbed back up the road, pulling the Toyota up to a level pasture.

At the north end, next to a fast-flowing stream, was the sawmill, sagging at an alarming angle, a large, rickety structure with huge doors and a crude stone chimney with no smoke. It looked like one good shove would topple it to the ground. They stopped slightly uphill at a sturdy wooden house, smoke hanging thick from its chimney in the cold, humid air. As they lifted the American down, a half-dozen men and women stepped out onto the cluttered porch and stood looking, not offering to help, not smiling. They reminded Luc of backwoods characters from the American movie *Deliverance*.

All ignored the American, but the men came alive when they saw the motorcycle in the back of the Toyota. They rushed off the porch and quickly started the bike, roaring, slipping and skidding in the snow, taking turns going nowhere. Saco and Luc carried the semiconscious American into a back bedroom, where they placed a blanket over him and told the women to feed him soup. They then ate bacon and bread and sipped coffee at the long table in the main room. Gradually the men and boys tumbled back inside, laughing and gushing at Saco, who beamed and uttered guttural sounds of approval, like some monstrous, bearded Buddha. The clan leader had come home bearing gifts.

No wonder they kiss his ass, Luc thought, *that bike cost more than they all make in a year. We better get some money for that American.*

Saco said something, and a woman brought over a large white bowl. He reached into his bear coat and pulled out handfuls of coins and paper money and earrings and bracelets and odds and ends of jewelry. The women and children exclaimed and spread out the loot, pawing through it while Saco basked in their glee and thanks. Luc thought back. He dimly remembered Saco poking around the Muslim cabin, taking a few things. All this didn't come from there.

The man's a first-rate robber, Luc thought, *he must have hit three or four homes when he was escorting the general to that restaurant.*

"So, Saco," he called out, "you were busy before you captured the American?"

"Only *hadjuks*. Muslims aren't people." Saco laughed. "I never take from people."

In the mountain passes, the radio in the Toyota had picked up only static. The house by the sawmill had a long antenna wired to the chimney, and they listened attentively to the news. An American officer was missing near Kosovska Mitrovica. The BBC suggested Serbian military elements might have taken him. Lieutenant General Kostica insisted Islamic terrorist Baba had seized the American. There had been a clash in the mountains between Serb forces and an American team that was searching for their missing man.

"The general will expect the American to show up today," Saco said.

"Don't worry," replied Luc. "We release him tomorrow. The general becomes rich. What difference one day?"

They lolled around most of the morning. Luc dozed and occasionally checked on the American, who seemed half asleep, half delirious. To Luc's astonishment, Saco foozled with the children, padding around the floor on all fours while a half-dozen boys and girls sat on his back and whooped and dug their heels into his fat sides, urging him to go faster. The men went back outside in the fitful snow showers to take turns on the bike, revving it constantly, the sudden high, whining noise intermittently jerking Luc out of his light sleep. When Saco strode down to the mill, like the grand landlord returned to inspect his holdings, the men trailed behind.

Luc looked at the enormous Saco and thought of the American expression "hillbilly." He was detached enough to smile at the idea that he was jealous, not of someone living on the side of a muddy ravine surrounded by sniffling, curious dimwits, but of being able to relax among one's own. It would be several years before Luc could return to France without fearing a trial. Time to get some money and get out of this backward country.

XI

Once they had eaten and read the e-mails, the team pushed on in high spirits; the next stop would be a sawmill. But Blade set a hard pace and soon Harvell began to wobble. Roberts took away his rifle and handed him a walking stick. Harvell quickly learned how to lean on the stick whenever he plunged a leg through the snow crust, and for the next hour he kept up. Then, crossing a small stream, he slipped on the ice-covered rocks and thrust out wildly with his stick, which caught between two rocks. He leaned on it too heavily, and it broke; he lurched forward, his foot caught between the rocks. He fell hard, bruising his hip and cutting his lip. When he tried to stand, his right knee buckled and he collapsed.

Roberts and Lang dragged him up the bank and set him back on his feet. He took a few wobbly steps, holding his knee, and fell again, panting.

"Are you hurting?" Lang asked.

"Not bad, sir. It's more like a rubber band snapped in there."

Roberts lifted Harvell's right foot and pressed against the knee. Even through the white cammie coveralls, the wobble could be seen.

"Inside ligament or MCL," Roberts said. "He can walk straight ahead, but each time he tries to turn, he'll fall down."

"We passed a shack half a click back," Caulder said. "I'll scrounge there for something to carry him."

Caulder and Blade doubled back while the others waited in a copse of mulberry and fir trees. The two sergeants soon returned, dragging a piece of rusted tin that looked like a bathtub. "Engine hood off an old truck," Caulder said.

They strapped Harvell in, forcing him to lie on his side so his heels wouldn't drag, and cinched up short lengths of line for two to pull. They would trade off every ten minutes. They headed out again, the two on the ropes sinking through the crust at every step, the hood scraping a reddish furrow in the snow. Anyone would notice where they had passed, but they didn't care. No one was behind them. What counted was where they were going, not where they had come from.

The Pentagon   **7 A.M. Monday**

Ordinarily, the Chairman left operational matters to the CinCs, the Commander in Chiefs of each geographical theater. On paper each CinC, like General Stevens in Europe, reported to the Secretary of Defense; in practice, the theater CinCs informed and worked with the Chairman. General Scott intended to stay abreast of the rescue op in Kosovo. He and the rest of America had awakened on Monday to find the editorial pages divided about the recon team. Not since the Florida presidential vote had a story been so ready-made for controversy. Scott read the papers on the way to his office.

The Wall Street Daily had turned to a retired general to write its editorial. In his final paragraph, he wrote: "An American was kidnapped and his buddies have set out to bring him home. Though the odds are long, the team is to be commended."

That wasn't how the *Times* saw the team. Its Monday-morning editorial had taken the staff six hours to compose, each sentence carefully phrased: "Serb authorities must find the kidnapped American. On the other hand, a senior official has confirmed the Marine team disobeyed orders by entering Serbia. The Pentagon must restore chain-of-command authority and halt this misadventure. The rule of law applies equally to us and to others. How this episode is managed will tell much about the character of the administration."

As the car pulled into the Pentagon garage, the Chairman put aside the editorials, muttering to himself. Who was the "senior official" leaking to the *Times*? This was no time for finger-pointing.

Within a minute he was in his ground-floor office, conveniently located below the Secretary of Defense's office and of modest size. He sat at the mahogany table with officers from the Joint Staff and read the update from the Commander of the Joint Task Force. Vice Admiral Faxon had a stylish way of saying nothing; no word from the team since they reported killing three murderers eight hours ago. Scott looked at the files of the team. Under "Person to Notify in Case of Emergency," Mark Lang had entered "Sylvia Cosgrove." *Uh-oh*, Scott thought, *who let you loose, Lang? You're not coming out without Captain Cosgrove, are you?* He turned to his staff.

"Judging from the files, this isn't a pickup team. These are first-round draft picks. Any ideas where they might be, Marty?" he asked the J-3, a stocky Air Force lieutenant general.

"They're into their second day since they were inserted, sir. Our Special Ops people think they could be seventy kilometers inside Serbia by now. Our best hope of finding them is the guy who sent the coordinates, a Bart Easton. FBI's on it."

Scott looked down the table at a trim middle-aged man in a gray suit and nodded.

"No one around Mrs. Cosgrove will talk to us. Ordinarily that means they're in touch with the kidnappers about paying ransom," the FBI agent said. "Early this morning Easton posted a reward on websites all over Serbia. He's the key. We've sent a team to Newport to interview him. We could seek an injunction against that website—"

"Stop. Let me get this straight," Scott said. "This team's trying to rescue an American and the FBI goes to court to seize their communications link? Why not commit hara-kiri on the Capitol steps? Let's hear a more practical step."

"Well, the kidnappers used one of Cosgrove's speed-dial numbers. No such call shows on his personal phone records," the FBI agent said. "So we're checking his firm next."

"Good, but remember these are our people, fellow citizens—not criminals. Let's not be heavy-handed."

"We'll be unobtrusive," the FBI agent said.

At a quarter to eight Dr. Orest Sikorsky knocked briefly and walked into Sylvia's room. He was wearing a cashmere sports jacket with a subdued herringbone pattern and dark leather buttons. His blue shirt was lightly starched and his yellow silk tie knotted with precision. As chief surgeon, Sikorsky projected confidence and authority. The nurses were deferential, impressed with the attention he paid to his dying friend.

Sylvia brightened. She looked forward to his visits and had developed a schoolgirl crush. She liked how he held her hand and spoke in soft, cadenced tones. His solicitude and offhanded inquiries about art distracted her from the finality of her condition. Now he stroked her hand, chitchatted for a while about Chagall and left the room, beckoning Bart to follow.

In the corridor he shook his head. "The breathing's more labored. Another embolism. I won't discomfort her with further tests. She hasn't long." He paused. "I think you'll know when to page me. I mean it, day or night, you page me."

He started to pat Bart's arm, then withdrew his hand and fumbled about, looking for the pipe he no longer carried. They looked at each other. Bart felt his heart tearing.

"This sucks," Bart said.

"Yes, yes it does." Both ached, and neither tried or wanted to say anything further.

"Well, time to be about my rounds." The surgeon walked away, back erect, concealing his frustration that his renowned skill could not excise this disease. This was his hospital. The proper example was professionalism. He did not look back.

Bart stared out the window without seeing until a nurse came up to him to say, "Those two government agents are still in the lounge. I told them you wouldn't speak to them, but they said they were staying until you do. They're polite but very insistent."

Bart walked the short distance to the lounge, trying not to feel or think anything. Kenshaw was FBI, short, grim, in his mid-forties. The Naval Criminal Investigative Service had sent Cummings—tall, young and earnest. Kenshaw had the maturity to be direct.

"Yesterday you reported a location of the kidnappers, Mr. Easton.

Since then you've communicated with the team. I need to know your sources and how you're communicating."

"I'm sorry you made the drive from Boston for nothing," Bart replied. "I can't tell you that yet."

"It would help those missing Marines," Cummings said.

"They're not missing."

She hesitated, then said, "Your security clearances . . . this is a security matter."

Bart turned his tired face toward her and shook his head as if he hadn't heard correctly. Kenshaw intervened. The nice-cop routine. "We're not threatening, Mr. Easton. Our bosses are concerned. Any reason you're holding back? Any, ah, trade we can make?"

"They're going for Cosgrove. I have a line on him."

Kenshaw liked this wrinkled man with the sagging eyes who looked so directly at him. Trying to work interrogation tricks was the wrong approach. Threatening him was as useful as yelling at a tree stump. Easton was already out the door mentally, not paying attention, not interested in any games they were playing. Still, it would help if Kenshaw could report what the man's plan was. "Five soldiers can't rescue a kidnap victim. They'll be killed or captured," he said.

"Really? Then you and I are looking at two different maps. I see a porous border and long ridgelines at high elevation, same as Stingray. Now, if you'll excuse me," Easton said, leaving for Sylvia's room.

The agents took the elevator down.

"Four hours for nothing," Cummings said.

"Easton believes Cosgrove is being held in the country, not in a town," Kenshaw said. "He thinks that recon team can get Cosgrove back."

"He said all that?"

"Yep. Stingray was the Marine recon op in Vietnam. The North Viets never could stop them from getting behind their lines and back out again," he said. "Easton was part of that. He thinks that team can do the same."

Once in the car Kenshaw opened his laptop and typed his report. Within thirty minutes Vice Admiral Faxon had read it and called Easton.

"Mr. Easton, I'm not an unreasonable man," he began after the introductions. "What can I do to help you in your dilemma?"

"Would you launch a rescue fifty kilometers into Serbia, cleared hot to fire at any opposition, if you had Cosgrove's location?" Bart asked.

"I'd have to secure NATO permission, and we both know that's unlikely. But we'd demand his release and get it."

"How long?"

"A week or two, I'd guess."

"That's not soon enough, Admiral."

"Mr. Easton, you're being unreasonable. The Serbs are cooperating. But you're not. We have no idea if what you're saying is true. You're jeopardizing lives instead of helping."

"You don't save any life, you only extend it." Bart's mind was turbulent with grief. "Remember BAT Twenty-one?"

"Vaguely. Before my time."

"That was the op where the Air Force put six aircraft into the dirt to bring out one pilot. Cost them more dead than they brought out alive."

"What's your point?"

"The Air Force was making the point, Admiral. If saving lives was all that counted, they wouldn't have gone after the first pilot. You did the opposite. You pulled out after the first helo went down."

"I'm the commanding officer, charged with the responsibility. You're meddling, and you face a series of federal charges."

"Does that mean more to you than a kidnapped American?"

"That's why you haven't been arrested so far, Mr. Easton. But I worry about your emotional stability. You're saying you won't help us get that team out of there?"

"I'm not pulling strings on puppets. That team is committed," Bart said. "And so am I."

"You're leaving us no choice in what we do next."

"Good-bye, Admiral."

XII

After strapping in Harvell, the team walked less than an hour before they came to the end of the tree-lined ridge and looked out at a valley that ran northeast for several miles. It was over a kilometer wide, bisected by a ridge stripped bare by centuries of cattle grazing.

"The map showed a tree line," Blade said, "but there's no concealment out there. If we cut around, we'll lose a couple of hours."

They appraised the steepness of the bare ridge, none deceived by the soft covering of snow that made the ascent look smooth and easy.

"An hour to the crest, a half hour down the other side," Lang said. "Let's get to it. Single haul will go faster. We'll trade off."

In single file they trudged quickly up the white slope, the terrain too open for any meaningful tactical formation. Blade took point, with Caulder right behind. Roberts was in front of Lang, carrying the captain's heavy rifle, which fired bullets and twenty-millimeter explosive shells. Lang was in the rear pulling Harvell, who lay uncomplaining in his tin sled. Lang placed first one and then the other foot in the shin-deep snowpack, stepping where the others had broken trail.

They were close to the crest and breathing heavily when the snow trac popped over the top of the hill. The moisture in the air had deadened the sound of the vehicle, and in their fatigue, they were caught off guard. The

trac skidded sideways in a flurry of white mist as the driver saw the figures directly below him. There might have been hope for him had he
twisted the throttle and hurtled down, bowling into the Americans like a
crazed taxi driver. Instead he stopped to let three soldiers climb clumsily
out of the back and seek cover behind a large boulder to organize a plan
to kill the four men strung out below them.

Blade fired as the soldiers reached the rock. They crouched behind it,
unnerved by the high, keening shriek of the ricochets, hesitant to poke
their heads around the rock and return the fire.

Lang had no such indecision. "Pin them, pin them!" he shouted at
Blade.

Blade went on instinct, throwing short bursts against the rock, pre-
venting return fire, not caring whether he hit anyone, freezing the soldiers behind the boulder.

"Trac! Take the trac!" Lang yelled at Roberts.

Roberts went down on one knee in the snow, selected the trigger for
the lower barrel of Lang's weapon and sighted in on the trac. Three heavy
slugs destroyed the cab and killed the driver.

The boulder took a few seconds longer. Roberts's first twenty-
millimeter shell was long and coughed with a burp several yards behind
the rock, kicking up snow and doing no damage. He quickly corrected,
and his second shot struck the rock and exploded in a beehive of splin-
ters. Roberts then sprinted in slow motion to his right and caught sight
of the men, stunned by the blast. One was down. A second was on his
knees, wiping at his eyes. Scarcely bothering to aim, Roberts stitched
him with a short burst from the upper barrel.

The third soldier ran. The Marines watched him stumble crazily
across the snow, Blade still snapping shots at the rock. Caulder had his
rifle at port arms, his head swiveling around. He glanced at the lonely figure slipping and sliding toward nowhere. No threat, no attention. He
squeezed a quick shot out of instinct and focused back on the rock. The
single round struck the fear-crazed soldier in the leg, and he pitched forward, dropping his rifle and tumbling several yards down the slope.

Roberts, who had the best view, signaled to cease firing. They all stood
up slowly, searching for targets. There were none. Lang had dropped the
lines to the sled and was untangling the AK-47 from his back.

Without Lang as an anchor, the toboggan slid back downhill, Harvell's face jerking up to look in numb bewilderment as snow rushed by on both sides of him. He twisted at the straps binding his chest and legs, horrified to realize that he was loose, gaining speed for a half-mile toboggan ride amid rocks and logs and cliffs and drifts too deep to avoid and too thick to breathe.

"Whoa! Whoa!" Harvell screamed. "Lang! Roberts! Skipper! Skipper!"

Lang reacted in an instant, churning downhill to catch the sled before it gained too much speed. He lifted his long legs high above the snow-pack, almost bounding downhill, throwing aside the AK after a few strides, realizing he was in a sprint he would win or lose in a few seconds, in a few meters. He gained on the rope dangling behind the sled and launched his body forward, grabbing and holding on and rolling on it, wrapping the line around him and bringing the sled to a jerking halt.

Harvell was clawing at the shoulder strap, making hoarse whining noises. Lang placed his glove on his chest and pushed him back. "It's under control, Harvell," he said. "Give it a sec."

In the Combat Operations Center, Dr. Evans read the signs.

"High stress, high stress!" she shouted, and the Ops Center went quiet. "Every systolic's up, over a hundred. Lang's really pumping, heart rate's over ninety. They're into something heavy!"

The staff clustered around, watching the four monitors, waiting for Evans to tell them what they were looking at.

"Lang's rate is dropping," she said after a minute. "He's stopped running or climbing or whatever he was doing. He was going all out there." She looked at Bullard to interpret the medical signs.

"They all went high before Lang's monitor went crazy?" he asked. "Then the team bumped into somebody. Firefight."

"Look at that, Lang down from ninety to fifty in forty seconds. Those are my boys," she said. "They're all back down to normal now."

"Somebody else isn't coming back to normal," Bullard said.

Lang undid the strap around Harvell's chest and helped him sit up. They sat for a moment, breathing hard, looking down the white slope.

"Sorry I yelled, sir. I thought I was gone."

"Yell? Hell, our shooting woke the dead long before you yelled."

Another look down the silent slopes.

"Are we going to die, sir?"

"Only if we give up," Lang said. "Want to give up?"

"I'm having a hard time breathing, sir."

"That's adrenaline," Lang said. "Knee still hurting?"

"Knee? Oh. I'd forgotten. Too scared." Harvell struggled to get up.

Lang smiled. "Welcome to the zone." He gripped Harvell's shoulder and held him down. "You can do five times what you think you can. Any hard thing, cut it into chunks. One step after another. Separate your mind from your body."

"Want me to walk, sir?"

"Stay there. It's downhill from here. I'll slide you first. That way, if there are any mines, you'll find them first."

Harvell laughed, and Lang grinned as he took the rope and pulled the corporal back up to the others, who had searched the soldiers at the rock.

"Let's get off this slope," Lang said. "Two mikes to take anything we can use."

They walked over to the crumpled trac, its small rear hatch ripped open.

"Wonder where they stole it," Caulder said. "Who were these guys?"

Roberts pulled out blankets, which he tossed in the snow, followed by some bags, which he dumped out. Cans, bottles, flashlights, magazines, a loaf of bread, cheese, gloves, scarves, a pair of boots, loose bullets and a few grenades tumbled out. They all jumped back.

"Great, we get killed robbing the dead," Caulder said.

"They have the pins in them," Roberts said.

"This rabble," Caulder said, "probably put the pins in backward."

Cautiously they resumed their search.

"No water," Roberts said. "Four wine bottles, rotgut brandy and sody-pop. These aren't soldiers. They're alcoholics."

"Split the soda, cheese and bread," Lang said. "We're out of here."

"What about him?" Blade gestured at the figure huddled fetal-like several yards away in the snow. The boy's head and shoulders were bobbing gently, as if he were rocking himself to sleep. His weapon lay several yards away in the snow, where Caulder had thrown it after a quick, rough search of the soldier. Lang and Roberts walked over and looked down. Where the bullet had entered, above the back of the right knee, the pant leg was dark. At the bullet's exit there was no cloth, just a gaping hole as large as a baseball. As they watched, the blood spurted out in gasps, as if it had to gather itself for the next effort.

"Caulder's seven-millimeter is purely nasty," Roberts said. "Hit the femur and drove a chunk of bone clean out of him."

The boy groaned and turned his face up when he heard the voice. He was fourteen, possibly fifteen. His thin features accented the size of his eyes, and he looked at them as a dying deer looks at a hunter, softly, uncomprehending.

"Tourniquet?" Lang asked.

Roberts turned his head away and spat. "Wouldn't do him any favors. He'd take longer freezing to death."

The boy looked at Lang like a doctor at his bedside. Lang shook his head. The shivering boy held his gaze. Roberts hastily searched the boy's pockets, throwing into the snow some papers, chewing gum, a mitten and a small wooden crucifix.

"At least we didn't kill the good guys," Roberts said, turning back toward the burned-out trac. "Let's di-di, sir."

Lang had the feeling that she was there again. There might be some life in the body back in Newport, but no one, no one, could convince him her spirit was not here with him, somehow connected to the bright red snow. *God, that blood is bright.* It was supposed to darken when it sopped through to the earth. *Oh, it's red because he's still bleeding out, more like a garden hose trickling.*

Do something for him.

What? What would you have me do?

Lang reached around the grenade in his vest pocket and broke off a piece of his frozen chocolate bar. He placed it in the boy's mouth. The light in his eyes was dimming. Lang patted him on the shoulder, picked up the crucifix, showed it to him and put it on his chest. He left the boy to die and, in the growing dusk, went down the long slope at a fast pace. Caulder jogged beside him. He had watched what Lang had done.

"Strange, isn't it, Skipper? These guys rape, burn, kill," Caulder said. "When they're dying, they get religion."

"Better than the whack jobs who believe killing gets them into heaven. Besides, we don't know what that kid did, if anything."

"Think there's something on the other side?"

"I don't know. Maybe. Probably."

"Think God buys that deathbed whining stuff?" Caulder asked. "Redemption?"

"Could be some get a last chance to even things up," Lang said. "Don't ask me. I'm not God."

Caulder giggled, wondering who, then, had brought them on this crazy mission. He started to open his mouth.

Roberts sensed what was coming. "Stow it, Caulder."

"Staff Sergeant, blow the trac," Lang said over his shoulder. "Harvell, report it. Keep the bullshit out."

Lang waited while Roberts taped some C-4 to the Serb grenades and placed it next to the fuel tank. Lying on the sled, Harvell took the Quotron out of his breast pocket, tugged off his gloves with his teeth, shoved them in his pocket and typed.

---

www.pepperdogs.com   1430, Dec. 22

Firefight with a snow trac. Four killed. No friendly cas. I
almost went over a cliff but managed to recover. Continuing msn
in accord with cdr's intent. Good fix on where we're going.
Snowing and cold. We will prevail.
Posted by: J. Kirwin

"Done, sir," Harvell said, "no bullshit in this one."

Roberts pointed his arm down the slope, and they picked up the pace.

Lang thought back over things as he walked. It was automatic in him to review the firefight for tactical flaws. He could find none. It seemed ordinary, routine. They had developed a rhythm, like a professional basketball team, dodging and weaving and converging at speed, passing the ball back and forth, closing on the basket and feeding the ball to the open man, scoring and turning away, with no words spoken. He had not fired.

There had been no need, seeing the end from the beginning. They had put down four men in half a minute and a dying boy had prayed to God and it was over and they were on their way. Nothing to remember, nothing to critique.

On the downhill they were loping more than walking, and Lang thought of the wild hunting dogs of Africa, padding silently across the vast plains, afraid of no beast, watched in fear by antelope and lion alike. Like those dogs, this team was on the hunt, and all others were prey. They were up, on top. *After a pilot shoots down an enemy plane,* Lang thought, *he paints its emblem on his aircraft, and the press takes his picture. We should paint skull and bones on our helmets.* Lang felt alive, into it, sure it would end well and that Cosgrove would be back with them soon.

"When I was in infantry officer's course," Lang shouted, hopping through the snow like a giant jackrabbit.

"That's a good beginning, sir," Roberts shouted back, "now we're all officers."

"We were told about Captain Barrow attacking Hill Ten-eighty-one in Korea. Chinks on every side, thousands of them."

"Not PC, sir," Harvell joined in from his sled. Lang had the holding rope wrapped around his hand, the tin sled out in front, tugging him downhill.

"This is sixty years ago, pre-PC," Lang said. "So Barrow calls out, 'Look at all those targets!' And up his company went, all one hundred Marines."

There was a moment of silence.

"We'd better check ammo," Blade said.

"I hate stories with bad endings," Caulder said.

"That Old Corps got home for Christmas," Roberts yelled. "You getting us home for Christmas?"

"Ingrates," Lang yelled back, picking up the pace and letting Harvell, eyes alert, slide down faster. "Christmas is when, three days? We have all this."

Lang let his hand go free of the sled rope, and Harvell's eyes widened. Lang gestured at the darkening skylight, the white snow and the black, bare trees limned along the far ridge toward which they were running, an

Ansel Adams photo. "You want to go home? When we have miles to go and promises to keep?"

"As your scribe," Harvell said in a loud voice, "that's awful, sir. Let me send the postings."

Even Roberts joined in the laughter.

When they hit the short flat at the bottom, they kept to a jog and soon were on the slope toward the thin scrub higher up the ridgeline, anxious to gain the shelter of the next tree line, confident no man could stop them.

The White House   8 A.M. **Monday**

The President was having breakfast with his family, and all had agreed to watch the news for the latest on their favorite characters. To introduce the lead story, *The Morning Show* flashed a picture of the knifed man outside the cabin, an update the President had already seen but his daughter hadn't. "Oh, gross!" she said.

The camera zoomed in on a frozen hand clutching at the snow, poignant and final. The peppy everywoman anchor narrated a cautious but sympathetic story line, referring to Captain Cosgrove and his gravely ill mother and how the team was trying to bring him back. She was reading a list of the team's accomplishments when the screen shifted to the e-mail that showed the exploding snow trac.

"This is surreal, even for television," the anchor said. "Here I am talking, and we receive fresh updates from the combatants themselves. For years the Pentagon has been giving us video of bombs hitting their targets. This now seems to be the ultimate step in reporting. Who can get closer to the action than those instigating it?"

The story ended on speculation. Would the team be captured or would they rescue Captain Cosgrove? Cahill walked to the Oval Office, feeling restive. The press was shaping the story. The *Times* editorial stressed control of the military—the President wondered about the source—and *The Morning Show* centered on the human-interest angle. Leaving this to NATO wasn't working out. The story was getting out in front of the administration.

The Chief of Staff was waiting for him in the outer office, and he gestured him in.

"What's your take, John?" the President asked.

"Images of Marines running amok is not something we need. Let's head this off now," Mumford said, rubbing his bald spot. "Nettles should issue a short statement placing this squarely in NATO's court."

"So we insinuate they're not Americans?" Cahill said. "I mean, this thing is bizarre, but we can't throw them out of the lifeboat claiming they belong to some country called NATO. We'd look like schlemiels. Try again."

"We refer everything to the Pentagon. The White House does not manage military tactics," the Chief of Staff said. "We don't comment on ongoing operations."

"That's safe enough for now," the President said. "Ah, out of curiosity, who do you think is tougher, Lang or Blade?"

XIII

Saco ate a large lunch and told the women to feed the American some more soup, not coffee or liquor, and keep the children away from him. Luc warned that the man might be tricky, though he seemed to be only semiconscious. Then he and Saco drove the twenty kilometers to the town of Prestovic, in a high valley to the west between two mountain ranges. They had put chains on the rear wheels and kept a low speed, seeing few other vehicles. The snow was falling persistently, and most potential travelers stayed at home. The AM radio reception was poor, and the two had little to say to each other. Luc closed his eyes and dozed most of the time.

The town served a scattered population of several thousand. It was cozy, with the warm feel of the villages in the Etruscan region outside Florence. The steep valley sides squeezed the houses, with their bright orange tile roofs, toward the bottom of a natural bowl, and the competition for flat space resulted in twisting, narrow passageways and neighbors who knew all the gossip. The main thoroughfare ran straight for two blocks, populated by stores and bars that eked out a living. The meager supply of electric power and telephony was adequate because exorbitant prices kept demand low.

Saco and Luc locked their weapons in the cab and looked in several

small shops for a power cord to recharge the cell-phone battery. They had
chosen a town Saco rarely visited, yet both he and Luc had the feeling
that several people stopped and gawked as they walked past, as if recog-
nizing them. Luc decided it was Saco's size.

They entered the bank, a simple concrete building with bright posters of
sunny beaches and cities alight at night, like one would see in a travel
agency. There were two teller windows and, behind them, an iron safe
the size of a small closet. The bank manager sat at a worn desk behind a
low wooden railing meant to show that he couldn't be approached without permission. Almost half his desk was annexed by an ugly computer
monitor the size of a small television, the sort that took two grown men
to lift and had been replaced years ago by thin LCD screens. The manager
was in his mid-forties, with thin-rimmed glasses and a sour look. He
wore a rumpled gray suit and white shirt without a tie.

Saco laboriously filled out the application papers. He and Luc had
agreed he would open the account by depositing forty Euros, compliments of Cosgrove's wallet. Together they approached the manager,
identified by a nameplate as Mr. Dobvrik. Saco introduced Luc as a friend.
That was all, no name. Dobvrik rose to greet them but did not offer to
shake hands. The two men sat like supplicants before his desk, the chair
too small for Saco.

"I'm expecting money from Germany," Saco said. "Can I receive it immediately after it is wired?"

Dobvrik seemed surprised. He started to speak, stopped, stammered,
began again. "N-no, not right away. We would have to verify with the
other bank. Perhaps a day or two later."

"What if it's a wire from your own bank?" Luc asked. "I'd get it the
same day, or I could drive to another branch?"

"Yes, of course."

"How many banks do you have?" Saco asked.

"I personally have none," Dobvrik said with a quivering smile.
"Stassa Banks has nine branches."

Why is this man so nervous? Luc wondered. *Saco must frighten him.* He
held up a bank brochure. "These are the telephone numbers of the other
branches?"

"Yes." Dobvrik was studying Saco's application. "Gustadd Slkbka, Route Eleven. I'm not familiar with that address. Where is it?"

"A sawmill," Saco said. "Near the Celluc monastery, in Dovad."

Dobvrik got up and walked to a wall map, four large aerial topographical sheets, taped together and glued to a poster board.

"Show me. I get so confused. I like to know where my customers live."

Luc's chin went up, but Saco had already stood up and was pointing with pride. "There. You see the monastery. That's us, below them, there."

"That looks very nice," Dobvrik replied. "Your unit is near there? Which unit is that?"

A strange question. Luc stood up. "We are late," he said, "could we finish, please?"

As soon as they had an account number, Luc hastened Saco out of the bank and walked hurriedly down the street to the pickup. He was certain now. Something was wrong. Saco grumbled but followed. The light was dimming fast and Luc was glad of it. Were people looking at them? Yes, Luc was sure of it, a few he had seen earlier. Now they were back, hanging around, looking sideways at him or Saco. They drove east out of town, down the long, gradual slope toward Route 11. Luc kept looking back.

"That banker asked about our unit," Luc said.

"So?"

"So maybe General Kostica wants to know what happened to the American. Maybe he's looking for you."

"It's only been a day," Saco said. "What could happen in a day?"

"Call that American woman now. Tell her she puts the money in Stassa Bank in Belgrade today." Luc handed him the bank brochure. "We bring in the American tomorrow and pick up our money here. Don't tell her this address."

They pulled over and Saco called. As before, the woman listened without interrupting, then repeated the bank numbers. She promised the money would be wired as soon as possible, perhaps in an hour. Could they wait right there for it? Could she talk to— Saco cut her off and hung up.

They resumed driving, the downgrade a series of twists and turns. Saco drove cautiously. After a few kilometers a truck fell in behind them. It was too dangerous to pass. Soon there was another truck behind it. Luc was uneasy. True, Saco's clumsy driving created a moving roadblock, and he wasn't going to pull over to accommodate others. Still, people had looked at them too long in town.

"When we get down to the highway," he said, "go north. Drive in the wrong direction for a while. Let's make sure no one is following."

Mr. Stanislaw Dobvrik, obscure manager for the lowest branch of Stassa Banks, Inc., proud father of three sons and one daughter, husband to a woman who never complained, salaried at two thousand Euros a year, put his hand over his chest. *Thump, thump, thump,* his heart was knocking on his ribs. Fifty thousand U.S. dollars or Euros, the same amount either way. Twenty-five years of salary. Belgrade. A fine house. Good schools. A used Volvo. A vacation. Italy!

That had been Saco in here, and Dobvrik had his address. Could the American be trusted to pay him? Why not? He had posted his company's name and given Prime Minister Tiliac as a reference. Would he refuse to pay for the information after advertising on the Web? No, Americans paid. Dobvrik needed to set up an alias so Saco's friends wouldn't discover him, and a place to receive the money. That was easy. His brother in Italy would open an account for him.

Dobvrik walked to the map and meticulously copied down the latitude and longitude of the sawmill. He was not a dullard. He understood, given Saco's size, that others would also quickly identify him. He sat at his computer and sent an e-note to his brother, who replied immediately. Next, he composed his message to Bart's company, sent it to his brother to readdress, printed out a hard copy and deleted the message from the hard disk. As was his custom, he was the last to leave the bank. He folded the hard copy, placed it in his wallet and hurried home to his cramped apartment, in his excitement not feeling the cold, anxious to share the good fortune with his wife.

Newport, R.I.   **Monday morning**

When Bart came back to the hospital room after his talk with the FBI agent, Katharine was serving Sylvia a late breakfast. Alex had promised she would come later. Katharine flicked the tip of a spoon into a bowl of oatmeal, sprinkled on a dash of brown sugar and placed the morsel in

Sylvia's blistered mouth. Sylvia closed her eyes, trying to swallow quickly without irritating her burned throat or upsetting her radiated stomach. In half an hour she swallowed almost a teaspoonful, an exceptionally large breakfast.

Katharine put down the spoon and stepped into the corridor to answer the ringing of the sat phone. Saco was brusque. Was the money ready for transfer? Okay, send the money to Stassa Bank, Belgrade. He would call tomorrow. If money was transferred, boyfriend would be released. Yes, Katharine could speak to boyfriend and banker before transferring money.

Bart wrote down the instructions and called Woody, reaching only his voice mail. Woody was on the trading floor.

"When will the FBI know we're using Ty's phone?" Katharine asked.

"They'll have a record of all calls by this afternoon," Bart said, "tomorrow at the latest."

"Then what?"

"Then they'll meet. There'll be meetings at the State Department, at the Pentagon, at Justice, at the White House, calls to our theater commanders, discussions with the Serbs. Within a week whoever has Ty will be feeling real heat."

"A week?" Katharine looked toward Sylvia's room and put her hands to her cheeks. "That creature wants the money tomorrow."

"Our government won't do that. No ransom."

"But you'll pay him, won't you?" Katharine asked.

"I'd pay right now to have them all back."

"You sent them in."

Katharine didn't know why she was accusing him, like Alex had done. Bart was trying his best, but everything seemed so enormous now, so involved.

"I took a risk," he said. "Things spun out of control. You have to believe me, Katharine, I'm doing my best to get them both back, to get that whole team back."

New York Mercantile Exchange, New York City   **Monday morning**

Bart underestimated the speed of the FBI investigation by half a day. Three agents had arrived at Warburg's when the first clerks were straggling in. By the opening bell, they had confirmed Cosgrove's sat-phone number and sent it to the telephone company. By ten in the morning they had records of two previous calls from Serbia and a tap in place. When Saco called the third time, the FBI recorded every word and soon had the coordinates, an obscure highway leading to obscure Prestovic, thirty kilometers west of the sawmill.

But who was calling the phone company and sending the coordinates on to the team? Only someone in Warburg's could do that. Who was closest to Cosgrove? Who covered for him when he was overseas? the agents asked.

Woody. His floor trader. Woodberg. Double Zero, that's his trade name, what he marks on his confirm chit after a trade. Two 0's, easy to remember. He's on the floor. Can't miss him, a big guy in a madras jacket. Colors make you puke. He works the oil pit. Joey, take these G-men over there. Yeah, I said G-men.

A few years earlier the FBI had gone undercover in the Chicago pits and snared several midlevel cheaters, traders who chiseled five or ten cents per lot. Most floor traders were glad to see them jailed. Still, G-men who pretended to be traders to rat somebody out were not good form. New York wasn't Chicago.

The New York Mercantile Exchange saw itself as the little engine that could. The Chicago Exchange was older, bigger, louder. NYMEX, after a growth spurt in the nineties, had constructed a plush building south of Houston Street with a knockout view of the Statue of Liberty, a chromium gym and an absurdly priced restaurant nobody used. The crown jewel was the trading floor, a football field in length, with eight pits to accommodate hundreds of screaming, sweating traders dealing in commodities as diverse as gold, oil, cotton, natural gas and coffee. The noise was like talking in a coffee shop while ten bikers roared by on Harley-Davidsons.

The walls surrounding this amphitheater, the gladiator pit of the modern economic man, featured a twelve-foot-high band of sockets embedded with millions of tiny lights, white, green, red, yellow, that monitored the health of the developed world, the prices of energy, food and capital exchange, the basic commodities of life. These hieroglyphics were interpreted at a glance by the cognoscenti, the traders who spent every working day yelling and shoving. On the north wall, the centerpiece visible from anywhere in this raucous mass of men not asking or giving any quarter, flashed an enormous electric sign: COS AND LANG, WE'RE WITH YOU!

The two FBI agents walked into this den of economic Darwinists, following the young clerk who bellowed, "Make way for the G-men!"

"Why do I think we've been set up?" the younger agent asked.

"Good thing there aren't any trees and ropes in here," Hunter Mitchell, the older agent, replied. Agent Mitchell was a fast riser in the fraud division; he had scored twenty-eight white-collar arrests and nineteen convictions in two years. The cost of living in the city was impossible, but he'd make senior executive service within a year, or bolt to Stern, Weber CPA for twice the salary. He preferred the challenge of the bureau, if Congress would just raise the pay a little. He liked going after rich bad guys who stole big-time.

He had liked stepping onto the trading floor, hearing the roaring, seeing papers strewn over the floor, feeling the press of jostling bodies, nearly all male, young, vigorous, in-your-face types. He had enough ego and self-respect to see himself as the intrepid agent ignoring the tumult, focused, cool, moving inexorably forward, separating out his quarry from the herd.

Only the scene wasn't made for Clint Eastwood, and these men weren't the good and the bad. They were four hundred traders who knew one of their own was kidnapped and another of their own was trying to save him. And here came the fed, the fucking fed, not to help. Hunter Mitchell didn't get it. So they helped him understand. Word spread in seconds. Then it was only a matter of voicing the resentment. Later, Cotton claimed to have begun first, although most agreed Oil had the edge by a few seconds. Whatever, it didn't take them long to find their rhythm.

Oil. "Give me an F!" Fifteen male voices, throaty, raspy bellows. "Give me an E!" Thirty voices. "Give me a D!" Sixty voices. "Whattaya got? Asshole!" One hundred voices.

Cotton. "Give me an F!" Thirty voices. "Give me an E!" Ninety. "Give me a D!" Two hundred. "Whattaya got? Asshole!" Four hundred voices.

The chairman of the board was in the natural-gas pit, at first shaking his head tolerantly. He was a mature forty-something, $20 million tucked away in bonds, chuckling at the high spirits of the younger crowd, his constituency. Then he saw the television crews, not one, not two, but three cameras on the floor, darting about, looking for the best angle. "What? Who let them in? Guys, the language, clean it up! We've worked hard on our image. Don't blow it. Come on, guys, give it a rest!"

"One, two, three, four, we don't want you on our fucking floor! One, two—"

"No, no, look, cameras, cameras, for Christ's sake, use your heads!"

Gradually, controlled bedlam prevailed, and MSNBC, CNN and FOX News captured the anger without the profanity. Perfect for reruns throughout the day.

As for the scene seen around the world, Woody improvised it on the spot with no coaching, despite the later claims of a dozen other traders. Bart had insisted that under no circumstances was Woody to lie or withhold information from the feds. So when Woody saw taut-jawed Agent Hunter Mitchell approaching, he rolled with the punch.

"Okay, Officer, you got me," Woody screamed, thrusting his huge arms high in the air. "I'm guilty. I was helping my kidnapped buddy. It's over for me, boys!"

That was how they left the floor, Woody's hands up high, the traders booing the feds, packed in so tight the cameras couldn't glimpse the two agents trailing behind, no weapons, grimacing in frustration. The government against the traders, the feds against the Pepperdogs.

The agents brought Woody into the NYMEX boardroom, a tasteful, modern setting with a spectacular view of the Hudson River. Woody kept silent until his lawyer and three lawyers for NYMEX arrived, shortly before noon. Their advice was the same as Bart's. Be direct. Answer all questions. Don't fool around.

Woody pulled the Quotron from a pocket of his garish trading jacket. "I sent Bart Easton a trade order form," he said. "He fills in the comments section and sends it to Mark."

"The form isn't entered in Warburg's records?" Mitchell asked.

"It's for after-hours trading," Woody said. "I marked the form they used yesterday as canceled, voided out. We record only confirmed trades."

"Do we need a Quotron to reach the team?" Mitchell asked.

"No, use any computer," a NYMEX technician answered, writing down the passwords. "You need the form. I'll give you one."

"And the phone calls?"

"The kidnappers have Warburg's sat cell," Woody said. "When they call Katharine, she's—"

"Cosgrove's fiancée," the younger agent interrupted to show they knew something. "She's at the hospital."

"Right. I call the telephone company and get the location of the ass-hole calling her."

"And you didn't tell us because of the ransom," Mitchell said.

Woody looked at him and kept his mouth shut. Mitchell started for the door. The bureau would want to get the computer passwords to the Pentagon as fast as possible.

"I assume there are no charges against my client," Woody's lawyer said.

Mitchell stopped at the door. "Monumentally bad judgment. Monumentally bad attitude."

"Hey, Agent Asshole, Lang went to get his buddy. What'd you do to help?" Woody shouted. "Don't make any trades, pal. You're all field and no hit."

The Castle Restaurant   4 **P.M.** Monday

For this meeting there were no banners waving from tanks, no smug calls waking reporters in the middle of the night. Both sides arrived with scant retinues. Briggs came in by helicopter, wearing brown corduroys, a white Irish-knit sweater and a heavy ski parka. Kostica came by jeep in his rumpled camouflage utilities, heavy boots, oversize army jacket and overlarge cap with a broad visor, the type worn by locomotive engineers in the fifties, with three black stars stitched across the front.

No carefully planned meal this time, only pottery jugs of steaming coffee placed every few feet along a long, rough-hewn table. Aides for the two sides nodded stiffly and waited for the principals to attack.

"We're here because of the missing American," Briggs began, ignoring protocol. "Strategic matters are on hold."

"You've sent murderers into our country," Kostica said. "You've lost your minds."

"Crossing the border in hot pursuit is quite defensible."

"You pursue a phantom," Kostica said. "I told you yesterday, your American was taken by Baba."

"Our intelligence says different." Briggs wasn't sure who was lying more blatantly. Not that it made any difference.

"Is this your so-called information war," Kostica continued, "your team reporting on the Internet to turn the people against our government? Ridiculous. A soap opera, an American game show."

"We want the missing Marine back," Briggs said. "This situation works against your interests. We can't let rogue elements undermine us."

He's offering an out, Kostica thought. *I hand over the American and he'll blame it on "rogues."* He almost laughed out loud at the irony. *I should introduce him to that idiot Saco.*

Kostica took the offensive. "You think your Marines can melt into the woods like Tito's partisans? You have it backward. They are like a lost Nazi patrol. If my soldiers don't find them quickly, the people will cut them into pieces."

Meaning extract them now, Briggs thought, *only we don't know where they are.* "I suggest you return the missing Marine instead."

Kostica waved a hand. "Speak to Baba."

Briggs shook his head, as if disappointed in the truculence of a star pupil. *We have. Baba claims the wrecking machine*—that was how Briggs had come to think of the team—*killed one of his. Wouldn't you like to hear that!*

Kostica tried again. "So you won't call off your killers?"

"Pejorative terms, General, don't change facts. This ends when the missing American is returned." Briggs hoped that would be the case.

"We are not Iraqi Muslims who cower at threats. Every Serb, every last one of us, is dedicated to stopping the killers in our country."

"We have different points of view," Briggs said.

"We certainly do," Kostica said. "And this offering of rewards on the Internet? No Serb takes that seriously." But he was worried. *What if someone sent an e-mail reporting that he spoke to Saco yesterday?* He could control Belgrade's press but not the Web.

Briggs paid attention. *What caused that outburst?*

The meeting ended as testimony to the limits of diplomacy. Kostica couldn't deliver Cosgrove, and Briggs couldn't call off Lang.

The two principals had a few moments to talk privately as they left the castle. "You have my word I don't have your American," Kostica said.

"This incident ruins the withdrawal we talked about," Briggs said.

"Not from me," Kostica replied. Any withdrawal of the Americans was too good a deal. "Your team of Marines is the danger to your own strategy. You don't want to guard Muslims forever."

Briggs called the Razor by secure phone as soon as he left the castle.

"Kostica's in the dark about the missing Marine," he said. "I think someone murdered him. I doubt we'll ever recover the body."

"What about the recon team?" Faxon asked.

"The team infuriates him. Injured national pride," Briggs said. "He thinks we're using the Web to test some new information war, with Serbia as the guinea pig. It has him worried for some reason."

"When this is over, I'm convening a court of inquiry," Faxon said. "Full public disclosure. We'll show the Serbs, NATO, everyone. There's nothing rigged here."

Warning bells went off for Briggs. Faxon knew nothing about the waters into which he was sailing. "Isn't that a bit early?" Briggs said. "Weren't you involved, pulling back that first rescue effort?"

"I don't see how that had much effect. The team disobeyed orders. This may push us into a shooting war. We have our hands full with terrorists. We don't need a distraction."

These were Briggs's lines being played back to him. He hated it when every general and admiral thought he was the new Kissinger. "*The Guns of August* is out of print," Briggs said. "You'll have to be more specific."

"Kostica strikes back out of pride and we're at war."

"Strikes where? With what? He'd be committing suicide. You military types would destroy him."

"Okay, then, he employs terrorism. Bombings in Europe, that sort of thing."

"That takes months of planning, agents, networks," Briggs said. "One betrayal or slipup and we'd have the smoking gun, wouldn't we? He's seen how we'd respond." He sensed that logic was the way to proceed with Faxon. "We'd cripple their economy again," he said. "Do you think the Serbs will risk that because of one recon team?"

"I thought we saw this the same way," Faxon said.

"We do. This is a distraction to be contained. I thought a few days of diplomacy would get your officer back." Briggs wanted to yell *You screwed up! How did that team get loose?* He went on. "We need to put a cork in this bottle of piss. A court of inquiry gives everyone a bad whiff."

"What's your idea?"

"No major inquiry, a bad start for someone who will work with the Europeans in Naples." Briggs softened reprimands with promises of promotion. "First things first. Get them back, then bury them in obscurity. They're not real soldiers, are they? Only reservists."

"The Marines don't make that distinction."

"The press will with a little coaching. I trust you read the editorial in the *Times*? Came out rather well, I must say," Briggs said. "Now we convey to the press that these are a few insubordinates disrupting a settlement affecting nations. Their condottiere is an egomaniac. That's our message. No parades, no welcome-home banners for them when this is over. That would poison a settlement."

Faxon said nothing. He sensed this wasn't the time to let Briggs learn about the medical experiments. He'd leak that the team was drug-crazed.

Northern sector of Koplje Mountain Range   **Monday afternoon**

The team pushed northward at a withering pace. They took turns pulling Harvell, who suffered silently as he absorbed a thousand accidental bumps. They had unrolled the one sleeping bag, and he snuggled in. They held to the scrub along the high pastures and cursed the farmers for clearing so much land and cursed the land for its endless streams and ravines. They were glad their packs were light, though, and they developed a routine on particularly steep slopes for passing Harvell up from one man to the next, with ropes at each corner of the sled. On level ground Harvell held the folded ropes inside his bag, then pulled them out whenever they reached the next ravine.

They set a goal for themselves, three clicks, three kilometer squares on the map, each hour, an astounding two miles over the pitching ter-

rain, up and down, up and down. They called it "the hundred-mile shuffle." It was a pace they practiced once a month, moving from one dawn to
the next. On the flat lands, they aced the hundred miles, and suffered for
a week from aches and blisters. In the mountains, they couldn't make
that distance in one day, but they learned to hold a grueling pace. In the
shelter of the stunted pines and gnarly bushes, they settled into a quick
shuffle, half fast walk, half slow jog. Soon the sweat was coursing and
their breathing was jagged. Each wanted to slow down and settle into an
easier pace. But they were tied to each other, their minds passing back
and forth the energy and the message: Don't be the first to quit. Any one
of them alone would have slowed. Together they shoved back the pain
and silently shared it, each hurting and knowing the others felt the same
way, each determined not to be the first to ask for slack.

Their tactics were deliberately poor, only one man at point, the others
manning the ropes. They were traveling so fast over such twisting terrain
that they dismissed stumbling into an ambush. By cutting horizontally
along the side of the long ridgeline and not following any easy contour
line, they avoided crossing most roads and paths. Safety lay in speed and
concealment among the shrubs and trees.

Every hour, Lang gave them ten minutes, exactly. Feet were tended to
and upper garments wrung out, sweat running like faucets. Then, for a
few precious minutes, they flopped on their backs and placed their feet
on the lower branches or trunks of the fir trees, permitting some blood to
drain from their tired leg muscles. For those few motionless minutes, the
men seemed attached to the trees, as if gaining sustenance from the sap.
They would slowly and steadily sip the frigid water from their collapsible
sacks until their bellies were swollen against their rib cages, and they
would hold their GPS receivers in front of their faces, following Blade's
instructions as he read off the digits for a new rallying point. Then they
would lower their legs, roll onto their stomachs, come to their knees,
gather themselves and push off for another fifty minutes of climbing,
slipping and trudging.

They said practically nothing as they moved north, and their thoughts
were a jumbled mess without pattern or plan, fleeting images chased
away by the next tug on the rope, the next sidestep down and the next
stream to cross. They had consumed the last of their Meals Ready to Eat,

and all had reached the nausea stage of overendurance. They shut out the cold by accepting it. They filled their canteens often, adding iodine, and kept guzzling the cold water, much as they detested the taste. Each knew what he had to do to sustain his body, and each, in his own way, tried to preserve energy on the too-fast rate of march.

Dr. Evans watched the monitors in the Operations Center and checked her logs. The staff had rearranged the desks so that she, the watch officer and Bullard, as the commanding officer, sat side by side at the front of the room. A computer technician had split the huge center screen so that the most recent messages from Pepperdogs.com were displayed above the electronic map.

"They're really moving, almost jogging," Evans said, "hour after hour. They're in a hurry to get somewhere. Their heart rates are over ninety, high for them. Pressures are rising. That's expected."

"How far can they go?" Bullard asked.

"They once crossed seventy miles of desert in fourteen hours. Different terrain, though."

"Watch Officer, what do you think?" Bullard asked.

The burly captain thought for a moment. "They're staying high along the ridge to avoid being seen. Cross-compartment up there's a bitch. Add in the cold and snow—maybe a mile an hour, sir, two if they're insane."

"How long can they hold that pace?" Bullard asked.

"Based on past performance," Evans said, "until tomorrow morning. Depends on their food. They burn five, six thousand calories a day, three times more than we do."

"In another day they'll be halfway to Belgrade. The admiral's not going to be happy," Bullard said. "What if they run out of food?"

"Unlike most of us, they have no fat reserves to burn. None, nada," Evans said. "What happens to a car when it runs out of gas?"

XIV

Near Dadjak District, Serbia

Dragging Harvell took its toll. By midafternoon, after several hours of the hundred-mile shuffle, they were plunging straight ahead, minds empty to shut out the pain, noticing nothing. They stumbled through the bush, sometimes turning around to smash back first through tangles of brambles and dead summer vines, paying no attention to their flanks. Lang called for a respite.

"Rein it in. We'll lose the light soon. No way we make it to an overwatch before then. Let's save something for the night search. Take fifteen mikes."

No one objected. Though exhausted, they were proud they had covered thirty-five kilometers on the map and twice that over the rough ground. They were within range of the sawmill and darkness, their friend, was approaching. Soon they would begin their stalk. Now was the time to recuperate.

Lang signaled a break midafternoon, fifteen mikes. They quickly stripped, wrung the sweat out of the poly and redressed. So what if they'd be sopping again within the hour? For a few minutes there was a delicious, humid, semidry warmth next to their skin. They re-sorted their loads while waiting for water to boil. When the bubbles were popping, they poured cups of steaming coffee, dumped in sugar packs and collapsed in the snow, slurping noisily. Heaven.

"I didn't think we'd ever do real combat, like Nam or War Two," Blade said. "Now look at us! All these white men to hunt." He was high, jacked up, savoring every minute. This was his environment.

"Pension," Roberts said. "We earn bonus points for combat."

Everyone laughed.

"We'll see who's laughing when I'm drawing forty a year from the Corps and sixty from NYFD."

"You'll still eat peanut-butter-and-jelly sandwiches," Blade said. "It's your nature, Staff Sergeant."

"Wait till you have kids," Roberts said. "And girls cost more than boys. Take clothes. They have to have the right look with the right labels, for God's sake. We're guarding these people in Kosovo, right? So why don't they do something useful and knock off designer labels? The recon gunny with the Thirty-first MEU? Two daughters and a wife, same as me. In Hong Kong he got everything for a year—eleven hundred bucks. Eleven hundred'll barely see me through Christmas."

"Tell us how you really feel," Lang said.

"I'm serious, sir. Look at inflation for tuition. It's—"

"Stop, stop!" Lang said. "We believe you."

"Providing for a family is serious shit," Roberts said, and then shut up.

"I'm out when we get back to the city. I don't need any more college aid," Harvell said. "Maybe I'll . . . What about you, sir?"

"I have my love of Corps and country," Lang said.

"And I have my shooting. But we know why you're in, sir," Caulder said. "To go to war."

Lang drank from his water bottle.

"You could enter politics, sir," Harvell said. "Look at who—"

"Shut up, Harvell," Roberts said.

"We're here for Cosgrove," Lang said, "that's all."

"We've put a hurting on some people," Caulder replied.

"Yes," Lang said, "yes, we have."

"We've covered some ground," Blade said. On a map they were forty kilometers north of the observation post they had left a day ago. In between lay a mile-high mountain range and two hundred ridges and gullies.

Caulder stood and stretched, trying to touch his toes, then glanced around. "Not enough ground," he said. "They're behind us."

All afternoon the routine had been the same, slowly pulling Harvell up a hillside covered with scrub fir trees and bush, weaving through the mature stands of trees above the open fields, then down again into gullies and ice-laced streams. Blade had balanced the risk as he led them. Working along the edge of the grazing fields made the progress swift, but they might be in the open at the instant a farmer glanced out a back window. Stay high in the bush, safe from sight, and it could be midnight before they reached the district. They hadn't hit the right balance.

There were three or four of them almost upon the team, heads bobbing up on the back hill before disappearing into the thickets. The snow had quickened, and visibility was less than a football field. Lang dragged Harvell behind a rock outcropping and quickly led the others in a wide loop uphill, so they came out above their own tracks before their pursuers reached the top shoulder. If these men were an advance guard, the team would fire downhill, grab Harvell and begin a run east up the mountain range. They were confident they could outrun any pursuit, but it would end their chances of getting Cosgrove. If there were only a few, as it seemed, the Marines would snuff them and hide the bodies in the shrubs.

The team lay in straight-line ambush, facing downhill, ready to fire on Lang's signal. Their pursuers came ahead quickly, talking excitedly, sometimes whispering. The voices sounded nervous; feminine, young or both. Three figures crashed through the undergrowth, half walking, half trotting in a group, not looking to either side, showing no tactical sense, dragging toboggans, eagerly pointing out the tracks of the Marines. They were bundled in thick coats and hats and mittens, their faces obscured, passing perhaps fifteen meters below. One held a bolt-action rifle and another wore a bright red woolen cap. They giggled as they walked. These weren't soldiers. Lang wondered how to let them pass, how to get back to Harvell and get out of there. One was small and walked with the bubbly bounce of a child, distracted by the icicles on the branches, ignoring the tracks on the ground.

The child solved Lang's problem by looking right at him, stopping, her mouth open, gawking. He hadn't moved. His chin was in the snow.

Still, she had spotted him. *Damn,* Lang thought, *her eyes are better than Caulder's.*

He stood abruptly and yelled, *"Dos tras! Dos tras!"*

He wasn't sure whether that was the right phrase. Anything to freeze them in place. He held up his rifle in one hand and gestured with the other, as if he were Moses. His hope was to paralyze them with fear, keep them from running.

It partly worked. The girl moved not a muscle. Her mouth remained open with no sound. Her companions, two boys, stumbled back a few steps, then the one with the rifle turned and ran through the bushes down the hill. The other one, wearing a black coat that reached his knees, followed. Blade reacted immediately, springing up and running at an angle to get in front. The boys saw they were going to be cut off and reversed direction, running frantically uphill, almost colliding with Roberts, racing around him as though he were a tree, in their panic not seeing his weapon or, if they did, not caring. They tore through the bushes, their hats knocked off, moving with the speed of pure terror.

"Go after them?" Roberts asked Lang.

Lang shook his head. "Not worth the risk of a fall."

"They move faster than deer," Blade said.

They turned to look at the girl. She, too, had bolted, running clumsily downhill, stumbling free of the undergrowth to reach the open pasture, tripping and sprawling full on her face, arms outstretched, not moving after that.

The Marines stood, not knowing what to do, gathering their thoughts.

"We're blown," Roberts said.

Lang laughed. "We've been blown since we started. How could we be more blown?"

"They'll find us now, sir," Roberts said. "Before, they didn't know where we were."

"Staff Sergeant," Blade said, "it's snowing. Give it an hour and we're ghosts."

"They'll have a local pos on us," Roberts said. "Time we move feet."

"Check these sleds," Blade said, pointing to the toboggans. "We'll take two, for Harvell and Cosgrove."

Lang liked that. As long as they assumed they would get to Cosgrove, they would keep moving forward, grab the sleds and di-di. The afternoon light, never strong, was dimming. They looked at the small crumpled figure in the open.

"That little one's not moving," Roberts said.

"Stay in the bush," Lang said, "there's a kid up there with a rifle."

"Scared to death," Roberts said.

"The rifle may not know that," Lang said, looking at the growth where the boys had disappeared.

"Ah, hell," Roberts said, striding downhill, "just like my daughters. Don't know enough to come in out of the rain."

He knelt and picked up the girl and placed her in a sitting position. She looked no older than ten or eleven, shaking and whimpering and hiding her eyes behind her mittens. Blade trotted down with the Translator. He handed it to Roberts, who sat down in the snow next to the trembling girl. "Don't cry," he said.

"*Dush kent,*" the Translator said perfectly.

"I won't hurt you." *Nit ken kujsha te.*

The girl said nothing but stopped crying and peeked out, looking for the voice. Roberts placed the Translator in her lap.

"Say something, please." *Tey bluka fey.*

She giggled a tiny bit, then remembered she was frightened and shook her head and trembled.

"She's wet her pants," Roberts said. "She'd better get home quick." He picked up the Translator and addressed the girl. "Do you know how to go home?"

She shook her head and would not look up. After a moment she lay back in the snow, stomach down, so she wouldn't see them.

"Her brothers will pick her up. Let's go," said Caulder. "Di-di mau."

Blade shifted uneasily. "No, they won't. They're scared shitless. They ran into the ravines. They'll have to move cross-compartment to get home, and their old man will gather some friends with weapons before he comes this way. It'll be four, five hours."

"She'll be hypo before then," Roberts said.

"We can't stay," Lang said.

Roberts slowly stood up. "Shit."

"This sucks," Caulder said. "Why do civilians get in our war?"

They turned away. Caulder and Blade picked up the rope leads to the toboggans and headed toward Harvell's hiding spot.

"I could carry her back, then catch up," Roberts said, lagging behind.

"It's not our mission, Staff Sergeant," Lang said, lowering his voice. "You're feeling a little guilty after our talk about Lolita. You're tired. You're not thinking straight."

"Evette."

"What?"

"Her name is Evette," Roberts said. "We helped that Muslim woman and her kid."

"That was different. She helped Cosgrove."

"So we don't help a little girl?"

Lang didn't want to argue. They had been on the move for a day and a night and now another day, with less than an hour's nap. He wasn't thinking any clearer than Roberts. He felt Grendel crawling inside his head again. Mrs. C. wasn't here. She was in a hospital bed. He tried to ignore the promptings, the soft voice with the clipped European accent enunciating each syllable, the hazel eyes he felt watching him. *How do I tell her I left a kid to freeze to death?*

"All right," Lang said, "put her in the extra sled. We'll drop her near a farm. You haul her, Staff Sergeant, it's your brilliant idea."

This was Roberts's problem, not his. He was just keeping up morale, no sense in having Roberts mope. He would have left the girl, but what the hell. At least Grendel had gone away for a while. Well, not quite. He could see her face a few feet away in the snowflakes, hovering above him, transparent. He could see right through her. Mrs. C. was smiling, approving. He knew he wasn't thinking straight. Okay, he did feel a little better.

Blade said nothing. Caulder was less restrained.

"A nursery," Caulder said, "we're running a goddamn nursery."

Newport, R.I.   **Monday morning**

Sylvia was propped at what seemed an uncomfortable angle, waiting for news of her boys, all notions of time drained from her. She had insisted on sitting up, the discomfort helping her to fight the morphine torpor.

Too fatigued to speak, she looked at Bart through dimming eyes, hoping he could sense she wanted him right beside her.

He had placed his laptop on the windowsill in the corridor outside her room, connected by a long telephone cord. He told himself he had done it to let Sylvia rest. Not really. He didn't want her to see he was still directing the operation. The computer buzzed once softly, signaling an incoming message. He got up and stretched.

"I think I'll stretch my legs," he said. He bent down and kissed her forehead.

"Desertive?" she whispered, her eyes wide in fear.

"It's called deserting," he said, stroking her cheek. "Never. Never. You know that. I'll be right back."

Once in the corridor he pulled up the message.

```
From: Professor Tiliac              10:00 A.M. Mon., Dec. 22
To: Mr. Easton

Over 200 responses to reward. Five are from Transpeca, all reporting
Saco in town in last hour. He and one other, not a Serb, were in the
Stassa bank. Drove off in a tan Toyota pickup. Best news—have
location of sawmill.
If confirmed, recommend $3,000 for each who reported seeing Saco and
$50,000 for the location of sawmill.
```

Bart quickly typed: *Mr. Minister: Agreed. Terrific work. Thank you very much.* He confirmed the location of the sawmill on a topographic map on his computer and sent the information to Lang. He considered calling the regiment, then remembered the admiral said he'd ask Brussels before launching a rescue. For now Easton would leave this to Lang.

He walked back in and was surprised to see Sylvia's eyes shut. He took her hand, which felt clammy and cold. Her ragged breaths sounded like gurgles. In a sudden, cold panic, he thought she might never wake again, never speak to him again, and that their last words would have been about deserting. He forgot about Lang and Tyler and Alex and the admiral and the computer. All he wanted was for her to speak to him. He sat there willing her to awaken, thinking of nothing else.

• • •

Bart's message wasn't received right away. Lang had more urgent tasks. The girl had offered no resistance when Roberts placed her on the toboggan. She was whimpering softly, and her pant legs were sopping wet, cold to the touch. Roberts took the sleeping bag from Harvell and stuffed her in it. When he got a piece of rope so she wouldn't slide off the sled, she buried her face inside the bag, and her body shook. He patted her shoulder and told her through the Translator that it was going to be all right, they would take her to the nearest farm. She gave no sign that she had heard.

"Captain Cosgrove's not going to like how that bag smells," Caulder said.

For the next hour they continued north, staying along the edge of the bush, Caulder setting a hard pace. Blade navigated while Roberts and Lang pulled the toboggans. Going uphill, all pulled on the ropes. At four P.M., they took their pills and picked up the pace a notch. When the thin daylight was gone, the team emerged from the bush and walked along the edge of the pastures.

"We're four clicks from where we picked her up, sir," Blade said. "Almost at the district."

"Use the Translator, Harvell," Lang said, "and put a note in her pocket saying where we picked her up. Warn them to stay away from the mountain to the west."

"Think they'll buy that?" Blade asked.

"A little deception is better than none," Lang said.

Harvell printed the note in Slav on a slip of waterproof paper the size of a credit-card receipt, and Roberts folded it once and put it in the girl's mitten. The little girl had burrowed into the sleeping bag, refusing to talk. The snow had slackened, but in the cold fog they could not see the lights of the farms below them. Caulder turned on his thermal scope, picked up large heat sources and read off the azimuths to several farms.

"I'll go down," Roberts said. "Hold dinner for me. Make it a sirloin, well done."

"No," Lang said. "We go together. You'll knock on some door and be invited in for beef stew by the fire."

"I can take care of myself."

"I know that. We're hungry, too."

The descent was easy, but they took their time. One hasty step and a hole or loose rock would break an ankle. They angled across the pastures until they struck a road, which they followed downhill until they were near the farmhouse. From the rear the lights were dim and the wind was blowing toward them, providing no scent for dogs. Roberts unzipped the bag and pulled the girl out. She lay on the ground, immediately shaking with cold. Roberts tried whispering into the Translator for her to walk to the house, but she didn't move.

With the others set to provide cover, Blade slid up to the house, cut the telephone line and trotted back. "Voices in the kitchen. Be careful," he said.

Roberts slung his rifle over his shoulder, picked up the limp girl and slowly walked into the backyard to leave her near the back door. The others watched through thermal scopes.

How was Roberts to know that the woman threw dishwater off the back porch? How was he to know the yard was slick as a skating rink under the snow? He found out when his feet flew from under him and he lurched forward to catch his balance, his feet churning crazily, trying to hold the girl up so her head wouldn't hit, all dignity, caution and silence gone. He landed noisily on top of her, her head cradled in his elbow. Lying twenty meters away, the Marines laughed.

The rear door flew open, framing a large silhouette that stood looking at the figures sprawled on the ground, caught full in the light from the open door. For a fat woman, she moved fast. The firewood must have been stacked inside the door. She never turned away, just reached back and then was down the two porch stairs, legs far apart so she wouldn't fall, shrieking and whacking at Roberts with the thick piece of wood. After taking the first hit, Roberts rolled off the girl, arms in front of his face. Then the helpless, inert, sniffling little girl was on her feet, clutching the formidable woman, yelling in a thin adolescent voice and kicking at Roberts, who was rolling to get beyond their reach.

The next figure through the door held a rifle in his hands.

"Fire into the steps, don't hit anyone," Lang said.

Caulder snapped off two quick rounds. The sharp crack of bullets through the wood shocked the woman. She dropped her club and pulled the girl up the steps. The man ducked inside behind them. Roberts ran back to the other Marines, and they slid down a gully and ran, Harvell bumping along behind them, until they were several hundred meters from the farmhouse. When they stopped, Caulder sat down, rifle in his lap, head in his hands, shoulders shaking. Blade took a knee next to Caulder, rifle butt in the snow, head down. He, too, was laughing. Lang, standing next to Roberts, was having trouble keeping a straight face.

Caulder came up for air. "Here lies John Roberts," he said, "killed by a farmer's wife."

"I thought you were done for," Blade said, "when the girl piled on."

"I think what you did was right, Staff Sergeant," Harvell offered from his toboggan.

"Stop sucking up," Caulder said.

"No more helping civilians, ever again," Roberts said. "And Harvell— if you put one word of this on the Net, I'll break your other knee."

Harvell took out the Quotron to check for messages. After one glance, he hastily handed the Quotron to Lang. "Two messages, sir. One from Joint Task Force, using Easton's encryption."

"Don't sound betrayed, Harvell. They have to cooperate back there or go to the slammer. We knew this would happen. Let me see that thing," Lang said. He looked at the screen and read aloud. " 'Captain Lang, you are hereby ordered to report in immediately. Commander, Joint Task Force.' Well, that's clear enough. Now for the good news. They didn't shut down Easton fast enough. Look at that."

He passed the Quotron to Roberts and the team gathered close to read the illuminated screen.

```
From: <%x^v                                11:00 A.M. Mon., Dec. 22
To: #@V+

Large man in bear coat (Saco) and man in cammies seen at local bank.
Driving tan Toyota pickup. Gave address as sawmill at 20.473 43.180.
At 1600 your time, received telcon to wire funds tomorrow. I will
pay if package confirmed. Act at your discretion. Not passed to
uncle.
S/F, Bart
```

"All right! We have a firm target location," Blade said. "And if they're paid instead, they'll still release Cosgrove."

"Or next spring some farmer finds a body in a ravine," Lang said. "How far to that sawmill?"

"Ten clicks," Blade said. "Let's push."

At a fast gait, they walked back up the slopes toward the high tree line. No one asked about the direct order from Vice Admiral Faxon.

With her monitors showing no change, Commander Gail Evans dozed sporadically in her straight chair. She thought of calling her husband, Dan, a surgeon at Massachusetts General Hospital. She couldn't wait to tell him about the admiral, who was so much like Dumphy, the chief surgeon, brilliant at his job but notorious for never remembering the name of a patient. Dan would laugh at that.

She didn't dare leave the Ops Center, though. Between them, she and Bullard had worked out what the signs meant—when the dogs were scared, or exhausted, or in a fight. It was Lang she couldn't leave. It was obvious he was stressing—pressure slight rise, heart rate up. He was the patient who needed supervision.

XV

The sawmill   **Evening**

Cosgrove had decided to go home. It wasn't a conscious thought; his head pounded too much to think, and his tongue felt swollen like a balloon. He imagined he looked like Quasimodo, head lolled over to one side, tongue hanging out, incapable of uttering a clear sentence. He accepted that his life was over, that he was deformed, stuttering, a mental cripple. Somewhere deep beneath his dim consciousness, he didn't care if they shot him; maybe he'd welcome it. They could kill him, but they couldn't injure him any worse. He wasn't sure he wanted to live banged up forever. He didn't want them to keep him, though. There was a shame to that. *Move out*, his unconscious was urging him, *move out. One, two, three, four, three, four your left.*

Twice during the day he had staggered outside to relieve himself. When he first wobbled into the main room after Saco left, one of the men had roughly shoved him back into the bedroom. The left side of Cosgrove's face was swollen black and dark purple, and the rags around his head flopped over his unfocused eyes. He had bumped against a chair, barely keeping his balance, then started to urinate against the wall. A woman had angrily pushed him out the door as some of the children giggled. When a man protested, the woman told him to go hold it for him. Everyone laughed, and a few minutes later the American stumbled back inside.

The second time was in the afternoon, after he had asked for water and gratefully drunk some soup. That time, when he put on his jacket, no one paid attention. It was cold, and the snow was falling steadily. Those in the main room ignored him, and he returned after a moment and tottered back to bed.

The third time was at dusk. The lights were on, and the men had settled in for some steady drinking when Cosgrove stumbled by and reeled out the front door. One of the men said he was drunker than they were, and a few laughed in a strained way. They weren't callous or cruel. The American was not a *hadjuk*, and his silent suffering made them uneasy. When Saco sold him back, they would be rich. Why laugh at him?

On the porch Cosgrove steadied himself by leaning against his motorcycle, which had been pushed up the steps to keep the snow off. He tried rocking it off its kickstand but lacked the strength. He bent over and put his hands on his knees to clear the spinning in his head. Then he reached in a pocket, pulled out his gloves, put them on, slowly stumbled down the steps and staggered away.

Inside, the children played and helped prepare the evening meal. The fire was blazing, and in the relaxed predinner atmosphere, the men exchanged desultory small talk about nothing. Over ten minutes passed before anyone mentioned the American, and another five before a man reluctantly pulled on his coat and tramped over to the outhouse. When he rushed back in, saying the American was missing, the others weren't hugely concerned. As they dressed for the search, they reassured one another that he was probably in a shed, somewhere close. He was injured, could hardly walk. He was weak, demented. He had no place to go. *Quick, as long as we find him before Saco comes back, there's no harm done.*

They scurried like ants but with less energy and sense of direction. They took flashlights and looked for his trail, starting at the outhouse, where he hadn't gone. Soon they were following their own footprints around and around the house. The boys and girls dashed through the woods, excited by the new game, while the women shrieked at them not to wander out of sight. Someone brought out torches to save batteries. Two mittens and one hand were quickly burned. They yelled, "Hey, American, is okay, come back!" They ran in circles, stomped and shouted. No answer.

They stopped and thought and concluded the obvious. He was walking down to the highway, where he would ask for a ride to the border. The four men started downhill, allowing the two oldest boys to accompany them. One boy carried a rifle. He yelled at the others to get their weapons. They yelled back that the American was weak, unarmed. Weapons would attract attention on the highway, and people would ask questions. Well, the boy shouted back, what if others found him and wanted to keep him? That was different. They went back for their rifles.

That was how Saco and Luc found them, milling around, nervous and unsure, gesturing awkwardly with their guns. Saco lost no time. He ranted at their stupidity for only a few minutes before agreeing the American was heading for the highway. His plan was simple, to split up. Saco would take a guard in the truck, drive to the highway and block the American if he got that far. Luc and the others would slowly walk down the road, shouting to him, *We are friends!* They had to find him before he froze. They couldn't bring a corpse to the bank.

"What if he went the other direction?" Luc gestured up the mountain beyond the mill. "What's up there?"

"Nothing," Saco said. "An old monastery and some monks. If he went up the trail, he'll die before morning. No, he went down the road."

The map identified three sawmills in the district, and Blade set the GPS for the one farthest from town. If that proved not to be the one, they would move on to the next, and the next after that. The mills were under fourteen kilometers apart, but the GPS satellites calculated distances as a straight line, true for the sea and stars but not for earthbound Serbia with its mountainous eruptions. On the map they were fifty kilometers from the OP they had left a day and a half ago; on the ground they had covered twice that distance.

It had been dark for several hours, and the cold had seeped into their bones and seemed to freeze their brains. They trudged along like zombies, too chilled and fatigued to think, crossing the rolling pastureland, accepting the slight risk that someone with night vision binoculars might scan the upslope scrub growth. They were past the point where any one of them could navigate well by map and compass. The GPS was their guardian, their point star, their insurance. It did the thinking for them. Every few kilometers Lang would halt to share a new rally point on the luminous screens. Then they were off again.

They weren't concerned about an ambush; no Serb knew where they were or where they were going. They drowsed as they walked, the satellites telling them where they were, how far they had to go and how long at their current pace before they arrived. The team measured distance in time—four hours to go, two hours, one . . . fifteen minutes.

As they approached through the crusty snow, the wind died and they could hear shouting. The lights and activity around the sawmill served as their beacon. They hadn't crossed roads recently, so they homed in on the yelling. When close enough to see lights, they were in the tangled undergrowth. They slowed their pace through the wattle, lest the cracking of branches carry to the house. The slope they were on was higher than the house, and from the distance of a football field they stopped to observe, adjusting their night vision goggles and turning on two thermals.

They had to stand and spread out to peer through the bushes, and no one had a clear view. Each picked up different, fleeting images. There was a boy, a man with a rifle, a huge man in a shaggy coat, another armed man, another boy. Some were climbing into a pickup. Others were running back and forth, yelling: "Hey, American! Hey, is okay."

Blade moved forward at a crouch until he had a clearer view. He watched intently while the others sneaked forward and joined him, Harvell remaining in the rear.

"No sign of Cosgrove," Blade whispered in Lang's ear. "Do we take these out?"

The distance for the slaughter was about seventy meters. Lang shook his head and gestured for Roberts and Caulder to pull back, leaving Blade to watch. They crawled for a bit, then trotted bent over until they were down in a small gully.

"They've lost him," Caulder said. "That 'Hey American' shit. No reason they'd fake that. I knew it. He was too smart for them."

"He's hurt," Lang said. "They wouldn't waste their breath yelling if they thought he was long gone. The pricks hurt him, and now they've lost him, and he could freeze to death out here."

"We can waste them," Roberts said, "find him, go home."

"Firing would bring others," Lang said. "And we haven't seen Cosgrove."

"So what's our move?" Roberts asked.

"We do our own search. Use a square pattern. Odds are, he went toward the highway. Roberts and Caulder, search downhill. Blade, search uphill, that's the less likely direction," Lang said. "I watch here with Harvell."

They heard the pickup start to pull away.

"They're going to the highway, too," Roberts said.

"Nothing we can do about that. If they find him, they'll bring him back inside," Lang said. "Trouble is, he'll hide and freeze to death before he'll give it up."

"What if they do find him? We don't know how to bust in," Roberts said. "Shit, look at the mess we made back at that cabin."

"In Juneau, an Eskimo woman used to clean our house, look after me," Lang said. "She told me sometimes a bear would come to an igloo, eat the sled dogs and wait by the ice tunnel. If a person came out without listening first for the dogs, *bam!*, the bear would knock his head off."

"That's our plan?" Roberts said. "Whack them when they come out?"

"Best believe it," Lang said. "This time, Caulder, I'll sign your chit for as many as you want to knock down."

They set their GPS receivers for a square search pattern, walking around the house from a distance of three hundred meters. They might find his track before the loose-falling snow covered it. Each put in the waypoints of the others and a rally point. Every fifteen minutes they would check in by radio with Lang. Blade slowly eased through the bush to the north, and Caulder and Roberts headed south.

"Those Serbs would be better off with that polar bear," Caulder whispered as they left, "the skipper is mightily pissed."

Lang found a stump with enough brush to break up his silhouette and a clear view of the front porch. He dragged Harvell behind the stump and cleared away some snow. Harvell sat upright, warm in the sleeping bag. Lang shifted every few minutes, the cold too biting to endure without some movement. His chest was still warm, but his feet and hands were beginning to ache, especially the feet. The first sign of frostbite. He had to get all of them inside to warm up. He was shaking one leg and then the other, trying to stir up a little circulation, when Harvell poked him. He'd slid out of the sleeping bag.

"You take the bag, sir."

Lang shook his head.

"You'd insist anyone here on watch use the bag. We'll rotate when the others get back. It's your turn. Now take it. I'm not crawling back in. You go down on us, we're all in hurt city."

Harvell was tugging him toward the warmth. Lang pulled the bag over his body, boots and all. He felt like he had entered a warm bath. And immediately felt guilty. Knowing it was the right decision didn't make it easier, so he busied himself planning two moves ahead. If they got Ty, he'd report in, climb high and call for an evac. If they missed Ty, would they walk out or call for a chopper? *What's this "if" business?* Lang thought. *Ty is ours, tonight, tomorrow. We'll find him.*

His mind was cluttered, thoughts drifting in and out, his reactions slower. Too long without sleep. Too cold. Too little food or heat. Too many hours on the hump, too many hills, too many adrenaline rushes. That marathon had taken something out of him. Was that only yesterday? Only forty hours ago? He was fuzzing out, starting to go on instinct. What instinct? He hadn't practiced for this kind of op. He was breaking trail, not following it.

Harvell took the night vision goggles and strapped them on his head, the single lens protruding from his forehead like a cyclops's eye. He peered through the green light at every bush and tree, M-16 at the ready.

"You're catching on, Corporal," Lang said.

Corporal! For once Harvell hadn't heard his surname, only his rank. It didn't matter what his name was; it was what was expected of him as a corporal of Marines. Harvell glared sternly through the goggles, forgetting Lang couldn't see his face. He imagined the enemy skulking behind some nearby fallen trees, suddenly leaping up only to be cut down as Harvell fired short, aimed bursts.

"Only don't forget to monitor the Net," Lang said.

Harvell held his pose, the daydream banished as he tried to remember when he had last checked. *Damn!* He hadn't turned on the screen since they dropped off the little girl. That was five, six hours ago. He handed the goggles back to Lang and turned on the Quotron. *Shit, nuts.* Oh, man, he was glad Staff Sergeant Roberts wasn't here now.

"Sorry I didn't check earlier, sir," Harvell whispered, handing over the Quotron. "Joint Task Force has found us. I don't think the admiral is happy."

From: 4@9*b   1900 Mon., Dec. 22
To: #@V+

Pepperdogs: You are ordered to report in immediately.
Commander, Joint Task Force

Lang wasn't surprised. Sooner or later they had to figure it out, though he'd hoped for more time. This close to Cosgrove, no way he was responding. He turned off the Quotron and handed it back. "We'll deal with it later."

"Good," Dr. Evans said, looking at the monitors. "Lang's pressure is down, heart rate down to fifty. He's stopped moving."

"The others still moving?" Bullard asked. He had been dozing.

"Yes, but their heart rates are down, too, and pressures are up," she said.

Bullard considered. "They're doing a close-in recon," he said, "scoping something out, and Lang's directing it."

"It's time they took a serious break," she said. "In that cold, they're consuming five thousand calories a day and taking in two thousand, if they're lucky. They have to rest and refuel. Soon."

"And if they don't?"

"Someone will vomit until he dry-heaves, then his body will dry up and heat up, and eventually he'll come down with hypothermia," Evans said. "If we're lucky, someone will cramp before that happens. Excruciating pain but not mortal. That would incapacitate the team, prevent them from moving. I'm surprised that communicator hasn't held them up."

"What do you expect next?"

"The harder they work, the faster they wear down. They know that," she said. "Pretty soon we're going to see them shut down for a few hours or they'll go over the edge. Their decision skills will unravel."

"They could tell us where they are and we'd go get them."

"Who is 'we'? NATO? The President? Admiral Briggs? You're pretty low on the food chain, Tim. And speaking of low, these signals are weak and intermittent."

"Meaning they're moving away from the border."

"Correct."

"I'll report that to the admiral. What do I say about their physical condition?"

"Nothing." She shrugged. "For people like us, situation critical. For them, what can I say?"

Newport, R.I.

Sylvia didn't awaken for lunch. Instead she went on dozing, propped up, her head tilted slightly, her breathing measured with long lapses. A few hours later, Dr. Sikorsky came in quietly, listened with his stethoscope and shook his head.

"Soon," he said, "soon."

The sawmill road   **10 P.M.**

Saco drove down slowly from the sawmill, headlights on high. He forced his companion to sit on the right side of the hood and look for tracks. Occasionally he stopped, beeped the horn and yelled, "American, is cold! We have car. Come! We help."

There was no response from the dark woods, and after thirty minutes they arrived at the intersection with the highway. Throughout the afternoon the light, steady snow had persisted. It was now over ankle-deep, light and fluffy. They stood outside the pickup, lights pointed back at the road. They shouted and listened and shouted. A truck occasionally passed at slow speed, and each time Saco's stomach turned over. What if the American had beaten them to the highway and was in some truck, heading for Kosovo? Would his brother Serbs help an American, obviously a soldier, an enemy? It was the Americans who had bombed Belgrade. All Serbs hated Americans. But some were so stupid they had forgotten the bombing. Yes, some would help the American. Perhaps he was gone.

It was almost an hour before Luc and the others finished their search and reached the pickup. Saco heard them shouting to the American several minutes before he saw them. All were glum.

"Maybe he got a ride," Saco said.

Luc shook his head. He refused to think that. "Too weak, I think, to walk all the way down here," he said. "He may have fallen down in the woods."

"He'll freeze."

"Don't you think I know that?" Luc said, unsure what to do. "I'll work back up the road. You stay here. I'll call you from the house."

When they struck the road, Roberts agreed to search to the south while Caulder continued to the north. Roberts could try to confuse the Serbs by crossing the road three or four times, but that would make his track all the more obvious. So he bounded across the road in long strides, almost skipping, leaving as few prints as possible. Back in the bush, he looped to the west, crossed back over his own trail, headed east and returned to his starting point, leaving a trail of butterfly wings to confuse a careless tracker.

Then he walked on north, looking carefully for any tracks of Cosgrove. Only a few flakes were falling, and there was enough reflected light that he could see, by peering intently, any tracks a few feet in front of him. It was slow going, and he walked bent over. Occasionally he would cut another short loop or walk backward and wander off at a random angle before returning to his northern route. He hoped that if the Serbs did come after him, they would trample his tracks and hopelessly entangle all footsteps.

Working in safer terrain, Blade and Caulder took fewer precautions. The GPS receivers ensured that each could plot his gyration. When they linked up in ninety minutes, they would have searched the entire square around the house. If Cosgrove was on the move, one of them would cut his track.

Cosgrove had a plan. They would think he walked down the road. He had seen footprints leading up the road. He'd go that way for a while, find another road down to the highway, then hitch a ride. The pain in his head was throbbing in dull, heavy, repeated blows. If he moved too suddenly, he felt an electric shock encircle his head. He could think, except for the pain. It was that electric current and flashes of white light, like lightning inside his brain, that worried him. He could feel his fingers. That was a good sign.

He tried speaking aloud, timidly, afraid he would hear a slur where there should be none. Simple syllables. No S's.

"I think, there . . . fore I am."

Something wrong. Came out as two words. There. Fore. He tried again.

"Hello, hello . . . I hate this fuck . . . ing . . . coun . . . try." *Better. Speak deeper, from the chest. Sing it out.*

"One, two, three, three, four your left."

Where had that come from? The drill field. He'd save that for last, when there was nothing more.

"Hear the . . . whistle blow . . . one hundred miles."

His mother had taught him a hundred songs, her voice clear and rich. With her slight German accent, she put an edge on each syllable, and the words came out sharp and distinctive, not drowned out by her guitar, words he remembered. He knew all the oldies, Dylan, Springsteen. He could carry a tune and fake his way on the guitar and had been surprised by how much men liked to sing together.

He had the rhythm now, music in his mind, his body responding, his feet shuffling along in the snow, mixing with the other tracks on the road. *Making progress. Keep it up. Walk back to Kosovo.* He hummed "A Hundred Miles" and giggled. Lang would love this shit. Not Katharine, though, she'd freak if she saw him now. *Don't think about her.*

So, what next? Walk up the trail for maybe half an hour. Hit another road. Then downhill to the highway. Someone would pick him up. He could do this. Keep the feet moving. Never stop. Keep talking.

"Enu . . . si . . . ate each word. Speak loud . . . ly."

He worried about his head. His tongue felt thick, like after a needle of novocaine at the dentist.

They were on him while he was thinking of his next silent song. No warning, no sound. He never saw them. Two black figures right in front of him. Another step and he would have walked into them, or had they backed up? A bright white light blinded him, the band of electric pins encircling his head like a crown of thorns. He swayed. Somehow one had his arm, not pinning him, holding him up. The flashlight went out. That was better. He stood with his legs spread apart for balance and breathed deeply, once, twice. He kept his eyes closed until the white spots faded, and then he opened his eyes again and looked at them.

They were dressed in black, all right. Even in the dark, he knew that from their outlines. Robes. Monks. Here in the snow, monks wearing robes. Hoods. Beards, long beards. This was too weird to be a dream. He felt the wiry strength of the one holding him. That was real.

"I know . . . the pope," Cosgrove said. *Uh-oh*, he thought, *I forgot. They don't like the pope.* He giggled again.

The men spoke briefly to each other. Cosgrove knew they were arguing, although they didn't raise their voices. The one who had his arm tugged at him and started to walk up the road. The monk meant to help, but his grip made walking difficult, and Cosgrove shook him off. The pace was slow, very slow, and the other monk lost patience. He said something, walked faster and soon disappeared up ahead. Cosgrove was struggling now, as if at the top of Everest. A step, a pause, a breath, another step. *Not the way to the giant's house*, he thought. That gave him the energy to go on.

He never saw the monastery. His head was down and he was concentrating only on his feet, taking one exhausting step at a time, when the monk took him by the elbow and helped him up the stone steps. The cold stone vestibule was bare of furnishings except a wicker chair into which Cosgrove slumped, exhausted. *Wouldn't have made the highway*, he thought idly, too tired to care. He wanted to lie down on the floor and rest his pounding head on his arm. He flashed back to when he was little and fell asleep in church, bumping his head on the pew. His mother had cradled him in her arms. Comforted, he started to fall into unconsciousness when he remembered that his mother was dying. He lolled his head back and opened his eyes wide to stay awake.

He jerked with a start. A set of eyes, not inches from his own, was peering at him. He must have dozed off. The other man drew back a bit, holding Cosgrove's cheeks in his large hands and looking at him carefully, gently moving his head from side to side.

"I did . . . no wrong," Cosgrove said. Couldn't hurt to try.

"*Das lunk,*" a monk was saying. "I couldn't leave him, Abbot." Cosgrove didn't understand a word.

The abbot was in his late sixties or seventies, his white beard quite long, his deep-set eyes clear and caring. "I heard," he replied.

"I didn't think we should leave the injured," the monk repeated.

"You could have brought him to the sawmill." The abbot was testing him.

"I think they are the ones who hurt him."

"Umm." The abbot didn't like to hear that, but he didn't disagree. "We'll send him back in the morning."

"I can walk down and inform them," said the monk who had gone ahead.

"In the morning," the abbot said. "Bring him inside. He needs food and a bed."

The White House

Many of the President's staff had left for the holidays. Cahill and his family were flying to California the following day. But the news story was building instead of ending. His national security adviser called from Colorado, offering to fly back. No need, the President said, he was leaving this one to the Pentagon.

In midafternoon, the Chief of Staff slipped into the Oval Office between meetings. "Have you seen the financial-news networks? They keep replaying those FBI agents making an arrest on the trading floor," John Mumford said, rubbing his bald spot. "The evening news will have a field day. We have to keep this at arm's length, Mr. President. This is the Pentagon's tar baby."

"You keep telling me that," Cahill said. "And stop rubbing your head. That's why you're losing your hair."

Mumford read the signals and withdrew, leaving an irritated President stewing in the Oval Office. Cahill called the Secretary of Defense twice during the afternoon, though he knew the man was as frustrated as he was. Explanations about doing business through a NATO command weren't reassuring. These were American troops. If this became a real mess, Congress and the press wouldn't fly to Brussels for an explanation.

And the President was bothered by the team's report on the Web that they had killed the crew of a snow trac. It seemed they were always shooting someone, like they were at war. And this Web posting of a reward for the address of a Serb named Saco? The CIA hadn't warned him something like that was possible. The President felt he was watching a little cloud form into a tornado.

His daughter thought Lang was a hero? Ha! That photo reminded him of when he first ran for governor, when he put a hundred thousand miles on that old bus in five months, averaged five hours sleep a night. He had no illusions about Lang, someone that smart, that disciplined, from New York City, at this time in that city's history. He knew a fellow fanatic when he saw one. The next report would have Lang going down the chimney of the presidential palace in Belgrade, with a hearty *ho, ho, ho* and a sackful of grenades.

The Secretary of Defense, of course, called the Chairman of the Joint Chiefs more than a few times. General Scott, in turn, was supposed to have his J-3 call the NATO headquarters in Brussels, which would call the deputy headquarters in Naples, which would call the Joint Task Force headquarters on the *Bon Homme*, which would call the Marine regiment, which would say they didn't know anything. Scott did it the first time by the book. It was like skimming a rock across a pond, hoping for seven skips before the plop. It took ninety minutes to be told there was no news. From then on he had his J-3 go directly to the *Bon Homme* and, a few times, straight to the Marine Combat Ops Center.

Finally, in the late afternoon, Ray Scott ignored channels entirely and called Bart Easton. He had been impressed by the report from the FBI agent who had gone to the hospital. It sure sounded like Easton believed the team could get in and get out. It *was* possible. Scott had carried a wounded South Vietnamese colonel out of Quang Tri in '72, with North Vietnamese battalions all around him.

"Mr. Easton, Ray Scott here from the JCS. My first tour was sixty-eight." Scott was trying to establish old war ties. "Don't think we overlapped. You were on Stingray, huh? I heard about that NVA battalion. Where'd you hit them?"

"West of the Rockpile."

"Track them long?"

"Four days."

"That was a heavy kill. Always wondered what you used. Cluster munitions?"

"A pair of two-thousand-pounders." The voice was dull, dispirited.

Scott kept on. "They were lucky you weren't pissed," he said. "You might've used something heavy."

"Little bastards were back inside a month."

Scott gave up trying to establish the old-boy network. "How's Mrs. Cosgrove?"

"She's slipped into a coma." The voice sounded weary, resigned.

"Ah. I'm sorry her son didn't make it home."

Bart didn't reply. Scott felt he was talking to dead air.

"You know we're tapping the sat phone you have there, and Warburg gave us the passwords to the computer," he said. "Admiral Faxon has ordered the team to report in, and they haven't replied. So I assume you've fed them some info from that reward you posted."

Still no response.

"Look, Easton, I know you're hurting, but you got them into this."

Someone had to be responsible for this mess. It couldn't be the government. They were right when they bombed, and they were right when they negotiated. The press supported both alternatives. And it couldn't be the team. The Web had humanized them, given them faces and life histories. Harvell made it sound like they were off on some adventure. That left Easton.

"I'll ask you what I asked Faxon," Bart said. "Will you send choppers, cleared hot to fire, to bring them out?"

"You know I can't order that. It's a NATO operation." Scott felt a twinge as he spoke, remembering he had cut out four layers of command in his call to the Marine Ops Center that afternoon.

"Right, I had forgotten the Joint Chiefs or White House don't give orders." The flat tone took the sting out of the sarcasm.

"Each President has his own style," General Scott said. "This one doesn't get involved in military ops."

"Apparently neither does Faxon," Easton said. "So who does?"

"Don't try to put this on us. The President was elected. Faxon and I were selected by the system, which works well most of the time," Scott said. "You're the hot dog here."

"Don't pat yourself on the back too hard. The higher up the flagpole you go, the more one part of your anatomy shows." Easton's voice had timber now. "You had the coordinates Sunday, and you choked. You left a Marine on the battlefield. What kind of Corps does that?"

Scott was rocked. No one had talked to him like that since, since . . . *Calm down,* Scott thought. *Wrong tack. Slow this down.*

"Joint Task Forces take a while to work out the kinks," Scott said. "We'll review it later. The important thing is to get that team back. You're wrong to encourage them."

"Tell me, General, when you were in Vietnam, would you have gone into Laos after a missing Marine?"

"We have to keep perspective. You know that," Scott said, wondering why Easton wouldn't let go. "The rules are different now."

That did it. All the frustration and anger Bart had struggled with over the past two days burst forth. "Rules?" He was almost yelling. "We bomb Serbia and occupy Kosovo, yet we don't go after a kidnapped U.S. soldier? This is Kafka-esque. Like I told the admiral, we're on different tracks."

"Which track are you on, rescuing or ransoming?"

"Whatever works."

"You know our policy. We don't ransom."

"Oh? What was Reagan doing with the Iranians? Policy is what the politicians decide, any morning they wake up and feel like it."

"Easton, you're in over your head, and your judgment is clouded."

"So people keep telling me." His voice again sounded weary, winding down. "But I don't see anybody else helping, including you."

"That's a cheap shot, Easton."

Scott hung up the phone and sat still, regaining his composure. He hadn't lost control like that in ten or fifteen years. This damned incident was stressing everyone. Easton had stung him by asking if he would have crossed into Laos to bring a soldier back. Stupid-ass question. He wouldn't have hesitated.

Had the Joint Task Force flinched from hot pursuit Sunday when the chopper was hit? He thought it was a bad judgment call by the admiral. He didn't like the new technologies: too easy to meddle.

. . .

The team closed on the monastery after the evening prayers. Blade had
seen the tracks on the road a few hundred meters up the west slope
above the sawmill. There were several sets. It was the one who couldn't
lift his feet above the ankle-deep snow that caught Blade's attention. He
called Caulder, and together they followed the path higher, becoming
more excited, telling each other this had to be Cosgrove. They brought
up Lang, who was less sure and sent Caulder back to complete the search
of his sector. Blade scouted ahead while Lang retrieved Harvell. When
Caulder met Roberts on the north side of the house, as arranged, neither
had seen any other tracks off the road. They hurried back to where the
others waited.

"This is it. I feel it," Blade said.

Caulder was looking at Lang and rolling his eyes. *Look at Blade, Skipper,* he thought, *and you're always pinging me as the hyper one.* Still, he was
caught up in Blade's enthusiasm. Lang had to force himself not to join in,
to keep level, in case Blade was wrong.

"We don't know that," Lang replied. "If this doesn't work out, I don't
want us losing momentum."

"This person is too tired to lift his feet. He's dragging ass." Blade
pointed to the footprints. "Who else would stumble around in the snow
at night?"

Blade set out at a fast pace, following the tracks. The team practically
jogged to keep up. The bush was too thick to use the night vision goggles,
and Lang feared they would run right up the rear of those they were
tracking. Maybe that was the right tactic: total surprise, coming out of
the dark and the snow. Anyway, there was no holding them back now, not
without taking point away from Blade.

Where the bushes stopped, so did Blade. He froze so abruptly that the
others slipped off their safeties as they joined him. They stood in the
shadows, looking out over a long field at a huge black edifice that towered above them.

"The map shows a monastery," Blade said. "That's a city block."

The monastery had the formidable shape of a castle, with thick walls,
narrow windows set well back in the stone and few entrances. A few dim

lights came from what seemed to be the living quarters at the west end of the complex.

"Not many people live there anymore," Caulder said.

Blade and Roberts swept the flat fields with their night vision goggles.

"No movement," Blade said. "They've got great fields of fire."

"Monks aren't in our business," Roberts said.

"Then you take point going across," Caulder said.

"We cross together," Lang said. "We'll leave by a different route."

They left the cover and, in open formation, crossed the field at a brisk pace, Blade occasionally looking down to assure himself that the tracks led straight ahead. Just short of the building, they crossed a dry drainage ditch and were close enough now to hear the faint, deep tones of men singing. While the others spread out near the walls, Lang walked to an oversize wooden door, large enough for two men to enter abreast. There was no knocker, only a large Orthodox cross in the center of the door, its beam longer than a rifle barrel and its stem twice that length. The center of the cross was thick glass, which Lang assumed was a peephole. He knocked brusquely with the butt of his heavy weapon. So thick was the wood, it was like banging against a vault door.

The symbolism bothered him. "Keep the weapons out of sight," he said.

"How do we do that?" Blade asked.

"What's that singing?" Caulder asked from the shadows.

"Beats me," Roberts answered from the dark. "Too late for compline."

"How do you know?" Caulder asked.

"Two years in a seminary," Roberts said. "And that's all you need to know."

Caulder and Blade laughed. Lang smiled, waiting patiently. He knew the banging had been heard. When the door was opened by a youngish monk whose eyes took instant fright, Lang immediately pressed the button on the Translator.

"We intend no harm." The Translator quickly did its work. "Please, we must talk with your superior."

The monk stood stock-still. He had a lantern in his right hand, and Lang took it from him and placed it on the stones inside the entranceway, so they weren't silhouetted by the light.

"Abbot, sir," Roberts said. "Use the word *abbot*."

Lang repeated the word *abbot*. The Translator squawked, and the monk recovered and exited through an inner door.

"This may take awhile," Lang said. "Let's move inside. Staff Sergeant, take first watch."

They piled into the large foyer, took off their packs and slumped down gratefully. They could scarcely see the steam from their breath. They all noticed the lone straight-backed wicker chair in the corner.

"I think they forgot something," Caulder said.

"Let's not get our hopes up," Lang said, hoping Caulder was right.

They waited a full ten minutes, anxiety mounting that the monks might be calling the local militia. Lang rotated the watch outside every three minutes, so everyone could taste the warmth. Caulder stood by the outside door, rubbing at the thick glass of the cross. At length, the inner door opened and the abbot walked out, followed by another monk with a lantern. Lang signaled his men to stand in respect.

"*Parlez-vous français?*" the old man asked.

"*Non.*" Lang held up the Translator.

The abbot made a fluttering, resigned gesture with his hands, as if saying *I hate these absurd technologies, but if we must, we must.*

"We seek an American. He was kidnapped and injured. He did no wrong."

Silence. *That,* Lang thought, *is good.* "We are his friends. We have come to take him home."

The abbot said nothing. His face betrayed nothing. He seemed about to leave when Caulder spit on his glove and rubbed at the glass.

"There's a dent," he said through the Translator. Lang said nothing. Anything to keep the abbot from leaving.

"Many young monks have done what you are doing." The abbot smiled slightly. "You cannot see through the cross of Saint Demetrius."

"Why not?" Caulder said.

"They used much lead."

"When was that?"

"About eight hundred years ago," the abbot shrugged.

Caulder gently touched the glass. That triggered something in the abbot. Instead of leaving, he looked at Lang.

"You would do damage here?" he asked.

The question startled Caulder, who tried to answer. Lang cut him off.

"Perhaps we destroy the monastery." Lang paused, then added, "And take all the food. Much food."

The abbot showed no fear. He looked Lang full in the face, then turned and left with the other monk.

"That was a new dialect," Blade said. "Ute or Sioux?"

"He needs cover," Lang said. "If he's questioned later, he can say I threatened him. Let's give it a few minutes."

Caulder was stroking the indent in the glass. "Like wearing down a rock," he said. "Hey, Blade, I can see flecks of red, like rubies, deep down inside! This is serious stuff. I mean, your Indians were planting corn when here, right here, they were making colored windows. Heavy."

Caulder lowered his face slightly so that his eyes were level with the center of the cross. He cocked his head at odd angles, trying to catch the glimmers of the colors. "Hey, some bright blues, and orange, you know, like a fire glowing."

"You won't have to go to any more flicks, Caulder," Blade said, "you can look at windows."

Caulder ignored him and appealed to Lang. "Eight hundred years, sir," he said. "We're a blink, a second, and we're gone. Imagine all this cross has seen: knights, witches, marriages, funerals, singing, all that shit."

"It is amazing," Lang said. For once he wasn't putting someone on.

A few moments later two other monks came out, carrying a large pot, several bowls and large, round loaves of black bread.

"*Ses stracs das,*" one said before leaving them. "This is all we can offer."

The Marines drank and munched, savoring each mouthful.

"What is it?"

"A little turnip, a little onion, plenty of warm water."

"Amen to monk's soup," Caulder said. "This where you learned to cook, Skipper?"

After leaving Saco at the highway, Luc and his soldiers had trudged slowly back up the road, dutifully calling out and looking for tracks, more in ritual than in hope. They had been down the road once. What would change now?

When one of the boys did see Roberts's tracks, Luc had already walked by, absorbed in his own bitterness. He had been so close to a ticket out of here, so close! The boy had to call to him twice. He walked glumly back. Boys imagine things.

Not this time. They were definitely fresh footprints, cutting from south to north. Now they could use flashlights, but no, these idiots had burned out the batteries back at the house. Still, by bending over, he could see the tracks well enough to follow. He left the road, the others eagerly jostling around him. Up they went into the bushes. *Careful, don't push, don't step on the tracks. Around a tree, straight on, easy enough to see* here, down this little slope, now up again. *Wait*. The footprints were turned around, now headed back to the road.

"*Merde!* Halt! Halt! *Arrêtez*. Stand still! Do not move," Luc yelled.

Too late. Their own stupid, cloddish tracks were everywhere. "What a mess. All right. Stop. All of you, stay here."

Alone, Luc walked northward. When he estimated he had walked a soccer field, he stopped and turned around. Then slowly, nose almost to the snow, he walked downhill, parallel to the road. How far should he go? Was he going in the right direction? This wasn't his business. He was a sniper, not a two-legged bird dog. *Wrong attitude. Stop. Get out your compass*, he thought, *ten minutes you search west. Ten minutes you search east.*

The others didn't give him enough time. Soon they were somewhere ahead of him, stomping around, softly calling his name, as useful as cows. The only way they'd find the American would be to step on him, and then they'd probably squash his skull. He took out his small radio and alerted Saco to the tracks. The American might yet show up at the highway. Then he yelled to the others to return to the road, and they all walked back to the house to warm up.

Once inside, the men stood by the hearth and passed around a bottle while the boys sat at the kitchen table and excitedly told the women of their adventure. Luc sat alone in a corner, sipping coffee and brooding. In the morning they would try again to find the American. At least they had his tracks. Well, somebody's tracks.

"Hey! Who lives around here? Anyone who goes out in the woods?" he shouted at them.

"Only the monks!" a teen shouted back, and the other boys giggled and poked each other. "Yeah, they go out to do things!" More adolescent laughter until a mother swatted at the boys to shut them up.

Luc stood up and looked at them. "I'm serious. Do monks go out in this weather? And where do they live? Can you call them?"

"They take long walks and collect firewood," a woman answered. "Every day. Weather makes no difference. They live up the mountain, about a kilometer from here. No phone."

"Let's go," Luc said to the men, zipping up his armored vest.

The men looked at the women, who looked away. They missed their Saco. This Frenchman had eyes like those of a hawk, looking only for prey. The men put on their coats and picked up their rifles. The boys had already tumbled out the door, chattering like squirrels about their new adventure.

XVII

The Marines sipped the soup and chewed the bread slowly, savoring it while wondering what would come next. Was Cosgrove here? Or had a gimpy monk left those tracks? They sat by their packs, pinning their hopes on an empty wicker chair where Cosgrove may have sat.

After perhaps twenty minutes, the inner door opened again, and there stood Cosgrove, supported by a monk. He wore his cammies with his jacket buttoned up. His head, bound in a thick white bandage, was down, and he didn't see them at first. They all came to their feet; even Harvell hobbled up. Lang walked forward and took Cosgrove by the shoulders as the monk stepped back and closed the inner door behind him.

Lang bent his knees and ducked down to look at Cosgrove. The bandage was looped down over the left eyebrow, the eye swollen shut, the socket and cheekbone black, blue and yellow. The left side of his face was the size of a grapefruit.

"Hey, bro," Lang said. He put on a slight smile, as if speaking to a shy child. Cosgrove looked at Lang's face, focusing his right eye. Then he slowly reached out a hand to touch Lang's nose.

"Careful, Ty," Lang said. "I don't need it broken again."

Cosgrove started to smile, but tears came instead. "It's my fuck . . . ing head." Each syllable dragged out, slurred. "They filled it with wa . . .

ter." He tried to lift his head by pulling back his shoulders, as if he could raise his head only by falling backward.

"Whoa, partner, is it easier lying down?"

"How . . . you . . . guess?"

"Born bright."

Lang and Blade lowered him to the floor while Caulder brought over the sleeping bag. Soon they had him comfortable and were bending over him.

"Hey . . . Blade . . . Caul . . . der . . . You . . . brought . . . the . . . gang."

"Never leave home without them," Lang said. "Roberts is outside."

Blade went out and Roberts came in. He, too, leaned over Cosgrove, bringing his face close. "Hey, sir."

"Put . . . out . . . an . . . y . . . fires?"

Roberts smiled. "You rest. We'll put out the fires."

"Go . . . home?"

"Soon as we find a cab," Lang said. "Did you vomit?"

"No."

"Snot come out your nose?"

"No . . . Thirs . . . ty."

Lang held up Cosgrove's head while he drank.

"What day is it?" Lang asked.

"Mon . . . day . . . ass . . . hole . . . I just . . . need rest . . . I dream . . . of Kathar . . . ine."

This jolted Lang. He realized again he hadn't thought of Alex.

Blade dragged in the toboggans, and they began to pack Harvell and Cosgrove. The team said little. Caulder smiled a tight grin, clenched a fist and hammered the air once, twice. Other than that, they went about getting ready to leave as if it were Sunday morning back at base forty hours ago. What would the Marines on Iwo Jima or Okinawa or Hue or Quang Tri do? They wouldn't dance or hug or shout. One man rescued, no one lost. No biggie. They had gotten off easy. Marines in other battles, it had been harder for them, much harder. No biggie.

Still, they were happy. Oh, were they happy, all right! *Take one of ours? Think a mountain or a border or some snow or a few days' hump makes a difference? Pfft. Here we are and there we go. Sayonara. Out of here.* They couldn't help smiling. Every time they looked at one another, they smiled. Even Harvell, wacky Harvell, they shared a smile with him.

Cosgrove was embarrassed to be strapped onto a sled. "Big bas . . . tard . . . suck . . . er . . . punch."

"We know," Lang said. "Nothing you could do. Nobody's pissed at you."

"Mom glad . . . you . . . come . . . home . . . too."

The joy rushed out of Lang. *He remembers she's dying.* He took the digital camera from Harvell.

"You look like shit," Lang said, focusing in. "Now, smile for Sylvia and Katharine."

Only a few hundred meters from the sawmill, Luc came across the maze of tracks left by the monks and the Marines. He stood, surrounded by his motley gunmen, and tried to puzzle it out. How many monks might take a walk together? Probably two, sometimes three or four. So who were these others? A Serb patrol? No, none for months. The news on the radio of an ambushed snow trac and those Americans thirty kilometers south? Ridiculous, too far.

They proceeded cautiously, halting when they reached the open fields in front of the monastery. Luc motioned for the others to stay put. He took his rifle from its bag, adjusted the heavy scope and swept the front of the building, picking up some heat from the front door. He continued scanning and caught a figure standing erect at the corner of the building. Luc could see the man's whole body, his head shining in the scope as white and bright as a new winter moon. Luc could shoot him in the head, or back, or legs, wherever.

He lowered the scope and thought. They were behind that door, in some sort of entryway, except for that sentry. There couldn't be more than three or four of them. They couldn't get across the field to him before he dropped them. But what about his American? Was he in there, too? He would wait for them to come out. Then he could tell which one was wounded. That was the one he wouldn't shoot. If he shot the sentry now, they wouldn't come out. He'd let the man live another few minutes.

He told his men to spread out to his right and left. They couldn't see a thing. They were to fire only on his order. In great excitement, they scurried around, bent over the way they had seen it done in the movies. One promptly tripped, a full, sprawling, clanking fall, capped by a low curse and giggles from the excited boys. Luc, furious, glanced quickly through the scope. The sentry—had he heard? Yes, he had dropped out of sight. No, there he was, lying prone, his head pitch-black in the greenish scope. Not a round head, though, only part of a head. *Why? What's he doing?* Of course, he was sighting in, his stone-cold rifle not reflecting any heat, blocking out part of his face.

But not enough, my friend, Luc thought as he formed the sight picture on the black spot and took up the slack in the trigger. It was so easy to kill with a thermal scope. Luc fired, his shoulder rocking back under the heavy recoil.

When he heard someone fall, definitely heard the *clank* of a rifle hitting the ground, Roberts had dived into the drainage ditch. He quickly snapped on his night vision goggles and peered across the field, bringing the Kalashnikov up alongside his cheek, looking for a target. He extended his left hand along the rifle stock and—

Son of a bitch! Son of a bitch! A sledgehammer smashed his hand and slapped away the rifle, the butt hitting him in the mouth and chipping a tooth. Shot! He'd been shot. He rolled back into the ditch, his hand on fire, burning under a searing flame, a torch held to his palm. *Son of a bitch.* The pain, the hand in an open flame. He shoved it into the snow, packed more snow on top. He could feel the vomit coming up, the bile spewing from his mouth. The pain eased enough for him to scream.

"Sniper! Sniper!"

The others already knew. The .300 Magnum fired from 150 meters away on a dead-still night had made an unmistakable *crack!*, like the clap of thunder when lightning flashes directly overhead.

Luc knew right away that he had hit the rifle stock. *Lucky bastard, I'll finish him later. Force them out now,* Luc thought, *don't give them time to plan.* He fired quickly at the door. Inside, the Marines were flat on the stone floor when the second round blew in the eight-hundred-year-old glass and slammed into the inner door.

"He's using a thermal," Roberts yelled. "South from my pos!"

"Got your cape on?" Caulder yelled back.

"That's a neg. Could use a little help." Roberts's voice was strained.

"Two mikes," Lang yelled. He gave orders to the others. "Keep Cosgrove and Harvell on the floor near the door. Capes on."

He, Caulder and Blade hastily unrolled squares of light, white aluminum, pulled them over their heads, raised the hoods and attached thin, clear plastic face shields.

"Caulder, the sniper's yours. Blade and I'll give you cover fire. We'll go left to where Roberts is," Lang said.

"I'll break right," Caulder replied.

"Low crawl."

"Best believe it."

"Roberts," Lang called. "We'll pop a twenty-six, then break to you. Ready?"

"Ready." Roberts sounded strangled, as if he were biting down on his hand to suppress the pain.

"Fire in the hole!"

Lang pulled the pin, opened the door slightly and flipped out a grenade. The hard earth threw the blast and heat of the explosion up in the air. Luc's scope lit too brightly for him to see through, and the three Marines tumbled out and rolled into the ditch, loosing wild bursts. Lang and Blade crawled to where Roberts lay, his right hand a vise grip around his left wrist, trying to cut off the nerves that were bombarding his brain with knife-sharp waves of pain. Blade patted him on the shoulder—"Hang on. We'll be back"—and wriggled up to support Lang.

Each took a turn playing with death, crawling up the side of the ditch to point a rifle vaguely in the direction of the sniper, snap off several rounds and slide back down. They knew the antithermal hoods were about as good as the flimsy rain ponchos they resembled. Eventually the thin plastic shields would heat up, or an uncovered leg or arm would stick out, or a snap would pull loose and a shoulder or hip would glow in the sniper's scope. Twice they heard the boom of the sniper's Magnum and once a great *whang!* as a bullet ricocheted off the monastery wall behind them.

Evans saw it on the monitors, the systolic pressure on Roberts suddenly spurting to 120, the heart rate hitting 110, the other monitors elevating seconds later.

"Attention on deck!" she yelled. "Serious stuff here!"

Bullard rushed over as the noise in the Op Center ceased.

"Roberts is hit," Evans said. "Systolic's down to one hundred. He's in mild shock."

Luc was getting no thermal readings on the Americans. He had heard the wounded one yelling in English. He knew where they were, and if they left the ditch, he would have them. They were firing blindly, short, disciplined bursts, never from the same spot. They had something holding his thermal in check. But they had a bad position in the ditch, nowhere to go.

"Go right! Get on their flank," he yelled at his men. "Shoot down the ditch line. Go, go."

Would these idiots shoot his American by mistake? No, he couldn't have gotten out of the building that fast. They had left him inside. Good. Nothing to do but wait now, wait until the Serbs were firing down the ditch. Then the Americans would try to run to his left, and they would be his. There were only three or four of them. A few rounds until then, so they wouldn't try to move. Not many rounds. He had to conserve. The bullets were sent from Italy, a dollar each. In Colombia, he wouldn't have to worry about trivial expenses. He was tired of this country. Let them kill one another without his help. *I'll get my American,* he thought, *call Saco. Drive to the bank tonight. Sleep in the truck. Finish this thing tomorrow.*

Twenty meters south of where Blade and Lang were firing, Caulder lay still, the plastic mask several inches in front of his face so it wouldn't warm up. His rifle rested on a bipod, and he was scanning with his thermal. Farther to his left, he saw various figures hopping around like rabbits, crouched over absurdly as they noisily broke through the bushes and pushed their way north. He guessed they were working around to a flank, where they could apply enfilade fire against the ditch. That was a problem for ten, fifteen minutes from now.

Right now, where the hell was that sniper? He had some sort of flash suppressor. Two shots and Caulder still didn't have a spot. The sniper knew his trade. *Come on, shoot again. Give me one more clue.* One of the rabbits on the other side of the field was coming back. *Hippity-hop, hippity-hop. Good. Go to Daddy.*

Luc lay prone in a slight depression. He had cleared away some of the snow and set his bipod in firmly. He was shooting at a slight angle to his right, a bit awkward but not a problem at such a short range. He heard the clumsy cows moving off, then one stumbled back, doing his best to bump into every tree and rustle every bush as he approached.

"Luc," the boy was hissing. "Luc?"

The awkward boy stood out plainly, and Caulder wondered as he tracked if he was old enough to shave, then banished the silly thought.

"What?" Luc whispered.

The boy stopped directly in front of him. "They want to know when to shoot."

A reasonable question. "Tell them when they can see down the ditch. Now, get back there."

Luc shifted slightly to his left to get a better angle. *I'll be glad when this is over. Too cold on this damn ground.*

Caulder caught the movement, a faint, slight bulge of black against the pale grays in his scope. *Green light. Good night.*

Luc felt he had been hit with a hammer, a single, hard white jolt of pain. He knew he had been well shot in his left shoulder, the blow driving stars and flashes of light into his eyes. He tried to breathe but could not. He felt a tingle in his fingers.

The 7.62 mm copper-tip bullet had struck his shoulder bone. Another inch higher and it would have missed him. But as life was, it had shattered his collarbone and drove several half-inch shards of bone into his left carotid jugular, which would bleed him to death in three minutes.

What happened? he thought as he dimmed. *What happened?*

Caulder quickly hit him three more times. One round went through the armored vest on Luc's back, losing power as it blew out his left lung and lodged in the chest cavity. The next bullet hit square on his hipbone and fragmented it. The final round passed through his left buttock, gouging out flesh and fat. Had that been the only bullet, he could have crawled away and been carried to the house, where half-drunken men would have laughed at a shot in the ass. The problem was, he had three other, mortal wounds

. . .

Caulder turned and quickly sprinted to his left, ignoring Roberts, who
was tucked in a fetal curl. He flopped down next to Lang and Blade.

"Nailed him," he said. "Five or six headed toward our one o'clock.
The sniper was their only base of fire."

They crawled to the lip of the ditch, facing east. Caulder and Lang
had thermals, Blade a night vision scope. All three saw the Serbs
crouched in a cluster in the bushes, about a hundred meters away, standing or kneeling. None had enough experience to lie prone. They were
milling around like a group of deer by the side of the road, not enough
sense among them to make one good soldier, some craning their necks to
see across the field, all waiting for the next *boom!* from Luc's rifle.

"On three," Lang said, "one, two, three."

The noise was deafening, and none of the Marines had put on earplugs. In the initial fusillade, four Serbs jerked and collapsed. Since the
Marines couldn't hear, they couldn't discuss whether the other two were
hit or, with the sense born of terror, had thrown themselves down. So they
changed magazines and sent more rounds downrange, tearing up the bodies on the ground. After the third magazine, Lang signaled to cease fire.

The Marines eased back down into the ditch and crawled to new firing
positions several meters away from where their muzzles had been flashing. They scanned all directions for movement or sound before Lang and
Blade left Caulder on watch and crawled down the ditch to Roberts. The
staff sergeant lay on his stomach, his face in the crook of his right arm,
his left arm outstretched in the snow.

"Not so bad now," he said. "Kinda numb."

Lang looked at the mangled hand. The bullet had struck between the
knuckles and passed right through. Lang gently wrapped the wound and
fixed a sling. Roberts rolled onto his back, propped up by the bank of the
ditch, head back, resting.

"I'm starting to get it together," he said. "Felt like I'd been hit with a
sledgehammer. Son of a bitch."

From across the field they could hear crying and groaning.

"Sounds like cats," Caulder said. "Have to break that sniper's scope
before we go."

"You stay with Roberts," Lang said. "Blade and I'll see to it."

"If he's one of the groaners, pop him again," Caulder said. "Bastard
shot out the glass in the window."

They approached the sniper from the rear, Lang covering while Blade removed the rifle from Luc's arms.

"Great thermal scope," Blade said.

"Too heavy for us to carry," Lang said.

They destroyed the rifle and scope, keeping the bolt for Caulder and stripping the fleece jacket from the corpse. They didn't bother to search Luc, too tired to have any interest in his history. Had Luc been sipping a bitter demitasse in some ramshackle Kosovo bistro, as he liked to do, when the team ran by on a conditioning run, he would have scorned them as pretend soldiers, American jocks. What did they know about killing?

Lang and Blade walked cautiously back across the field to join the others.

"Caulder was pissed about that window," Blade said, "tore that guy up."

"Caulder disapproves of theodicy," Lang said.

"He speaks well of you, sir."

"He has an overdeveloped sense of right and wrong. Hates the wrong. Good shot, though."

"He *is* a little nuts," Blade said.

"Yes, yes he is. And you admire dead Indians who take long walks."

"I'm on that walk to Canada. They're here or I'm there."

"No wonder you and Caulder get along."

"No, no. Don't you ever feel you're standing on the other side of a one-way mirror, watching yourself? You're you, but you've gone and you're looking back?"

"That's Grendel talking," Lang said.

"No, Grendel is spinning out from exhaustion. This is different. The Nez Perce are walking with me. They're here, helping me. Haven't you ever felt someone out there with you?"

"Maybe. Maybe we're all dream walkers. But we'd better stay awake now. Time to head home."

"We've done it, haven't we?" Blade said. "You're the man now, sir, and that's no dream. Caulder's always saying you should run for senator or something."

"We all did it. And hold the rain dance till later," Lang said. "We're still in the middle of nowhere."

But Blade's enthusiasm was catching, and Lang had to admit he was feeling good, very good. When they reached the ditch and slid in beside the others, he had to stop himself from pumping his fist in the air.

"Can I post it, sir?" Harvell asked, holding up the Quotron.

"Absolutely, let them know," Lang said. "Let them all know. Send a pic, too."

Harvell already had the message typed. He hit send.

---

www.pepperdogs.com   0100, Dec. 23

After heavy fight, we did it! Captain Cosgrove recovered.
SSgt Roberts took a round in the hand, but he's good to go.
Yes!
Posted by: J. Kirwin

The groaning brought the team back to where they were. It was louder now that they were lying in the ditch: the whimpering of young voices, the cries of the badly wounded, frightened and cold, shivering and weeping, no longer playing at being soldiers, wanting their mothers, sensing death creeping toward them. Blade waited for Lang's signal to help them. It didn't come.

"One hard-core with a grenade," Lang said, shaking his head. "Too much risk. Leave them."

They placed Harvell and Cosgrove on the toboggans and rigged light cloths over their faces to keep off the snow.

"Smells . . . like . . . piss," Cosgrove said from the sleeping bag.

"Staff Sergeant was using your bag, sir. He couldn't hold it," Caulder said.

Harvell lay bundled in Luc's coat, the blood from the dead sniper sticking like glue to his own jacket. The wind was up again from the west, sharp and bitter, flurries of snow stinging their faces.

"We can push east up the mountain or circle back south the way we came," Lang said.

"Let's go upslope and call for choppers," Harvell said.

"Shut up, Harvell," Roberts said. He was standing with his left arm tied across his upper chest, the maimed hand numb and iced in a wrapping of snow, the morphine giving him a warm, tingly feeling. They had taken his pack, but he held on to his AK. He felt light-headed but confident he could stay ahead of the toboggans.

"We could get trapped up there if this snow picks up and the choppers can't get in," Blade said.

"That's affirm," Lang said. "They'll be coming after us, following these toboggan tracks."

"If we hole up, they'll mortar our ass," Caulder said.

"They can't catch us if we run," Blade said. "The Nez Perce walked fourteen hundred miles, the army behind them all the way."

Lang laughed. "Harvell, tell Ops we're stepping. We call for extract once we're clear."

When Harvell's message to Pepperdogs.com arrived in the unclassified admin section, a dozen officers began yelling, drowning one another out. A few minutes later his message to Ops Center came across the screens. More cheers. Now they had a fix on the team.

To: Ops Center Admin   0103, Dec. 23
From: Pepperdogs

Have secured Capt. Cosgrove. Oscar Mike south.
20.48 43.18.
Will request TRAP when in secure area.
Two wounded ambulatory.
Posted by: J. Kirwin

The harried watch officer let the grins and backslapping go on for a few seconds. Then he roared out orders to prepare an extract, and they broke into teams. The TRAP determination team joked about using a CH-46 for the pickup. The intell team fretted about so many Serb forces on the move. The admiral would fry them if a second chopper went down, but they couldn't find a landing zone that wasn't near Serbs. The rifle platoon assigned to land urged intell to pick quickly; they were praying to encounter Serbs.

Bullard called Vice Admiral Faxon.

"The dogs have him, sir," Bullard said. "Your staff has a copy of what we received. Incredible. It looks like we've pulled this one off."

"Fine, Colonel. You execute the rescue. I'll ensure all the pieces fit." Faxon was jotting down notes. "I'll keep higher headquarters informed."

Blade had plotted their route and was anxious to be off. Roberts stood next to him, fidgeting with the shoulder sling of his AK-47. Lang and Caulder each clutched a toboggan rope.

Caulder glanced down at Cosgrove and turned to Lang. "Something's not firing right, Skipper, some synapse is out of whack," he whispered. "You know, like a car engine running rough on a cold morning. He'll smooth out."

"Thank you, Doctor," Lang said. Actually, Caulder's remark made him feel better. They were both hoping the head injury was temporary.

"Sir, I'm going to beat your ass," Caulder whispered, hoping Roberts wasn't paying attention. "You can't cheat this time."

"The Fabergé collection is on exhibit at the Met," Lang whispered back.

Caulder's eyes widened. His favorite collection, never seen. He'd read three books about the design. The screensaver on his home computer monitor displayed a different egg each week. Before he recovered, Lang was four steps in front of him. Caulder ran to catch up.

"Your psych job isn't going to work this time, Skipper . . . It's that Mayer stuff, the Gorbachev egg, isn't it? Copies, that's all. You're bull-shitting me, aren't you?"

Lang said nothing. Six steps in front.

"The original eggs from before the revolution," Caulder said. "You sure?"

Lang was too far ahead to answer. Caulder cursed and ran harder. The race was on, but distinct over the scraping rustle of the toboggans, they could hear the cries and groans of the wounded Serbs. Lang stomped hard through the snow to shut the voices out.

With his head cushioned, Cosgrove was comfortable in the down sleeping bag. Roberts walked in front of the sleds, rifle over his shoulder, his gait a bit wobbly. If he folded, Lang thought, they would flop him on top of Harvell and pull as hard and long as they could. *Bad thought.* Roberts fell behind once he could no longer hear the cries of the wounded and Lang eased off. It would be a slow walk.

The Serb women in the large house next to the sawmill heard the screaming of the hysterical boy long before they could see him. Ever since the dull, distant firing had stopped, they had fretted and paced, opening the front door every few seconds. Now they could hear his cries, more like bleatings and his mother rushed out without a coat and half dragged, half carried the teenager into the house and laid him on a bed. His side was soaked with blood and his face was ashen with fear and pain.

"They're dead," the boy kept screaming, "all dead."

"Who? Where is Zita? Andrei? Lats?" No use asking. The boy was in shock. Somehow this was related to the wounded American who wandered away, that much they agreed. Now other Americans had come. They would attack the house.

Some rushed around, waking and bundling the little ones, anxious to run out into the snow and get away, somewhere. Others stood numb, sensing what the boy said was true. No one else had come back. Five were missing, not counting the Frenchman. The wailing began.

Such was the scene that greeted Saco when he walked in, having tired of waiting for a call from Luc. He didn't hesitate. No one had ever questioned his courage. He took his two men and rushed up the trail. The wounded boy had been incoherent. Of course the others were alive. Some sort of firefight, and his brother and cousins scattered, that was all. Run away a little bit. And why not? They weren't soldiers. Luc had brought boys with him. Damn that Luc if any of his family had been hurt. Who was doing the shooting? The American was too hurt to shoot, wasn't he?

Saco could see lights moving in the bushes, more lights farther away at the monastery. *No firing. See? They probably got a little scared in the dark and cranked off a few rounds. That foolish boy, getting everyone upset about nothing.* Okay, being shot in the side wasn't nothing, but it was over now. *They must be beating the bushes looking for the American. He'd better be alive.*

The monks had carried the first body back and realized their mistake when they reached the doorway and saw the blood all over their robes.

After that they used wheelbarrows, one pushing and two others balancing each body. It was hard work, moving six bodies across the field, and
they still had two to go when the giant arrived and stared and walked in a
small circle, yelling and shaking his rifle and then weeping with grief and
rage. His brother, cousins, nephews . . .

"Four?" he yelled at the monks. "You saw only four Americans? There
must have been more, hiding. There must have been." Had they heard a
helicopter, or a truck? No. Any engine sound? No. Saco calmed down
quickly, drawing his anger inside him. The bodies were laid in the entrance hall where the Americans had eaten—no monk mentioned
that—and the women would come for them in the morning, perhaps before.

Saco looked at Luc's torn-up body, feeling only anger. *You caused this,*
you prick, with your schemes. Where's your big rifle now, eh? You couldn't protect
crap.

The last wheelbarrow came up balanced by only two monks, its load
small and light. Saco was ranting, swearing, bellowing foul curses the
monks had never heard. They stopped, astonished, lost their grip on the
handles and the barrow tipped over, spilling a boy to the ground, faceup,
eyes wide and unseeing. Saco ran over, looked down at his nephew and
swung his arm, rifle and all, at the clumsy, fumbling monks. The blow
caught a young, skinny monk full on the side of his head. He fell without
a sound, his skull split open. The other monks rushed to the body, yelling
and gesturing, their hands fluttering and flapping, helpless.

Saco turned and went back to the house. While his companions dealt
with the hysterical women, he called regional headquarters. He told only
a few lies. He had found an American with a head wound, he said, and
was taking him to a hospital. His pickup had trouble with the snow, so he
had stopped for a while at his house at the sawmill. The American had
wandered off to his neighbors, the monks. The murderers had attacked
the monastery, slaughtered his family, killed a monk, taken the American. Who? A band of Americans, of course. No, not by helicopter. They
were walking. Yes, *walking.* No, no, I'm not waiting. You can catch up to
me. Bring some bags. For the American bodies, of course.

XVIII

The e-mail announcing the rescue hit the Internet shortly before seven P.M. on the East Coast, and within minutes millions of Americans saw Cosgrove's battered face. For once the four major news networks didn't split three-to-one based on their politics. The story came too late to reach a consensus on how to present it. One network devoted a minute to the story, featuring the Secretary of Defense.

"It's always good to recover a missing serviceman," Nettles said with his clenched-jaw smile. "How this happened in the first place, I leave to the military to sort out. I don't have the facts, and I won't speculate."

That was the administration's line. Get it off the news, don't hype what you don't control. The rescue was an obscure oddity, thankfully close to finished.

Two networks devoted three minutes to the human-interest angle: how a tough team had gone after their friend and succeeded. The reporters repeated the phrase "elite commandos," and General Scott, watching in his quarters at Fort McNair, winced. Marines were the one service that opposed a special-operations branch. Now they were being praised for what they believed injured the esprit of the Corps. Still, the old general liked the basic story line.

General Scott clicked to the fourth network. *The News Wrap-Up* fea-

tured Veljko Nego, the Serbian president, a slender man in an ill-tailored
suit who spoke in a strained voice through an interpreter.

"American terrorists have molested a ten-year-old girl and attacked a
monastery. A boy and a monk are among the dead. I have ordered our
military to apprehend these terrorists. We have cooperated with the
United States and NATO. Now they should cooperate with us."

The News Wrap-Up then cut to its anchorman, renowned as the new
Walter Cronkite, whose calm voice of reason could be trusted. Sure
enough, he didn't take sides.

"Clearly, Serbian officials feel strongly that they have been wronged.
We have no facts to confirm who is telling the truth, the Serbian government or this tiny team with access to the Internet," he said. "As they say,
this story is to be continued."

Scott sat back and sipped his bourbon. How could saying nothing
pass for wisdom? he wondered. Well, at least he had a fix on how this was
playing. To the press, the team was a curiosity; to the Joint Task Force, a
disciplinary problem; to the Serbs, a symbol of criminal America; to the
administration, a closed incident. Trouble was, it wasn't closed yet. Oh,
their battalion was ready to extract them, all right, but would NATO give
the go-ahead? Bureaucracies tied themselves in knots and called them
bows. Easton might be right in saying the dogs were on their own.

General Scott would soon find out. The President wanted his national
security advisers to "drop by."

The Situation Room, three steps down from the National Security Adviser's small office, was cramped and sometimes conversations spilled
over from the military communicators jammed on the other side of the
wall. But Patrick Cahill felt the shirtsleeves atmosphere fitted his presidential style better than the formal Roosevelt Room. So the principals
squeezed together at a small rectangular table. If they pushed back their
chairs, they squashed their senior aides wedged along the wall. No one
complained. Cramped quarters bid up the competition for admission.

It wasn't a formal national security meeting; those invited were the
advisers the President most trusted. Except for Scott, the principals at the
table were middle-class millionaires, with sufficient wealth to be comfortable, in the ten- to twenty-million range. Not for them the obscene

sums lusted after by Enron and Worldcom types, whom they regarded as porcine swindlers. Nor did they aspire to the meretricious exclusivity that animated the New York set—white-fenced farms and spacious apartments, costing per month what an ordinary worker earned in a lifetime. These men believed in a deity, attended church—Episcopal preferred—and sensed a postlife reckoning unfavorable for those who frittered away their lives accumulating and consuming material wealth. Wealth was a means to an end, and the end was to serve. These men assumed it was their celestial duty to steer the ship of state. Overweening pride did surface occasionally, but by and large they were serious men who assumed lesser matters like the Pepperdogs would be attended to by lesser men.

Secretary of Defense Nettles was exasperated, a sentiment shared by most at the table.

"Isn't the Internet a marvel?" he said, breaking the ice before the meeting began. "Five young men send a few messages, and half the world's atwitter. Ah, for the days of Teddy Roosevelt, wooden ships and no telegraphs. My predecessors had whole fleets sailing for months without hearing a word; I have a lost squad which wouldn't obey if I could talk to them."

"I believe the Marines call it a fire team, considerably smaller than a squad," the Director of Central Intelligence said. "You exaggerate your influence."

Everyone chuckled at the camaraderie and the SecDef flashed his smile, as bright as stainless steel. "They'll feel my influence soon enough."

The President came in, a bounce in his step, followed by his Chief of Staff.

"Hands off, John, that's what you advised," Cahill said as he sat down. "We played it that way and it worked." Grinning, he tapped his knuckles lightly against Mumford's shoulder, and the Chief of Staff smiled brightly.

"It knocks that stupid story from the trading floor off the news," Mumford agreed.

With no new information to share, the situation briefing was quickly over. Not given to affectations, Cahill made no effort to hide his excitement.

"This is great! 'Tis the season of good cheer. I wasn't feeling that way a few hours ago, I don't mind telling you. Now let's wrap this up. How do we do that?"

"We get them out of Serbia," the Secretary of State said. "Ambassador Briggs and Vice Admiral Faxon are meeting with the Serbs to bamboozle a safe passage." A professional diplomat for most of his career, James Rodney had served in so many senior posts that he could give the brief for the other departments. With his innate courtesy, he addressed only the diplomatic track.

" 'Bamboozle'? I'll use that in my next press conference," the President said.

"Getting them back may not be easy," the Director of Central Intelligence said. "The president of Serbia thinks he's telling the truth." Andrew Marsh was a slight, bald septuagenarian with a reticent manner and inquiring mind. He was never casual or long-winded in his comments, and Cahill valued his unusual methods and insights. Now the President looked at him quizzically.

"In his TV speech, our eye scanner and voice fractals revealed high stress but no deception," Marsh continued. "He's convinced those Marines are psychopaths and sex fiends." He giggled as though he had told a joke.

"Who's feeding him that garbage?" the President asked.

"Our phone intercepts at his residence fell apart after some Chinese contractors installed land lines," Marsh said. "But Serb radio stations and the Internet are full of wild stories. The farmers over there use VHF radios, same as we have on our pleasure boats. Their conversations sound like the telephone party lines we had in the thirties, when every farmer was convinced Dillinger was about to rob the local bank."

"Dillinger was a genuinely bad guy," Cahill said. He fell silent for a moment before adding, "Oh, I get your drift. The Marines are their Public Enemy Number One."

"Exactly. Next they'll be eating babies," Marsh said. "This will boost President Nego's political fortunes. He faces a tight reelection race. He's been too pro-American."

"Meaning?"

"When the Marines are caught, he'll parade them through downtown Belgrade."

"Whoa, whoa, we all saw the pic of that kidnapped soldier. His eye's a mess," the President said. "Nego is out of touch."

It was the Secretary of Defense's turn to speak, and as usual, he was detached and self-assured. "I haven't seen any fat lady," Nettles said, "so it ain't over. Until it is, Mr. President, this is a NATO operation, and I recommend we leave it like that. Excepting the fine diplomatic offices of our distinguished Secretary of State, of course."

Nettles exchanged a practiced smile with Rodney, then nodded toward the Chairman of the Joint Chiefs. Scott kept his message direct. "We have two packages turning on the deck, Mr. President. We can lift the team out in an hour if it's done administratively."

"Why am I always the last to get it?" The President's good humor was fading. "What are you telling me?"

"As Secretary Nettles said, sir, this is a NATO command. The Europeans won't authorize shooting to get our team back."

"Shooting? Who's talking about shooting?" the President said. "This is over, isn't it?"

"Only if the Serbs agree," Secretary of State Rodney said. "We'll know when Briggs calls."

"Um. Well, how's the mother doing?" the President asked of the table. "We have to get that captain back here as soon as possible."

"I understand," Mumford started to say.

"She's failing," General Scott cut him off. "She's slipped into a coma."

The President leaned forward, surprised. How would the old general know that? Scott was retiring in June and had kept his distance from the White House, letting his theater commanders take the lead in the strikes against the terrorists.

General Scott caught the question in the President's glance and answered, "I talked to Easton, the man who was trying to ransom Cosgrove. He's with her."

There was silence.

"We were all praying she'd see her son," Cahill said. "My wife's going to be shocked. I told her we had the captain back."

"It's tragic, Mr. President," the Secretary of State said. "As for our people, let's hope Briggs delivers us good news."

"Can we talk with him?"

"We can videoconference anytime, sir."

"Can we contact the team, General? Where are they?"

Scott walked to a large electronic map at the rear of the room and used a laser pointer to place a red dot on a blue triangle inside a knurled skein of black lines that looked like a web woven by a drunken spider.

"Here's where they were forty minutes ago, Mr. President," Scott said. "We can send them a digital message. If they're not too busy staying alive, they might respond." He paused. "If we spot any movement, you'll be able to see it. Anything we have at the Pentagon, we'll show here. It's snowing over there now, and that's a problem."

The President noticed that Scott looked grim. "Something else, General?"

"That team's running hard, sir, but they can't outrun radios. Either they come out damn quick, or they're going to be ripped up."

"Then get them out of there!" the President said. "Only don't go in with guns blazing."

"That's Vice Admiral Faxon's call, sir," General Scott said. "This new Russian surface-to-air missile? He has to be careful how he extracts them. He could lose a chopper and fifteen, twenty people."

"Five minutes ago I was in a good mood," the President said. "What's next?"

"If we're lucky, Briggs will wrap it up," Secretary of State Rodney said. "He should call soon."

In midafternoon the nurses called Dr. Sikorsky back to the bedside. He spoke to Sylvia and received no response, squeezed the pale skin of her forearm, shone a beam of light into her eyes and looked at the morphine drip, which read eleven.

"She's in a coma," he said. "She won't awaken. I'll be back."

Father Tom Easton, Order of Friars Minor and Bart's younger brother, had flown in from the monastery in Santa Barbara for the final vigil. Tom was slim, and his face was open and soft with a glint of merriment in his eyes. He was the sort of person you would chat with on an airplane or cast in the role of a monk. He had tended the dying for eight years, and two months earlier he had flown back from the monastery to prepare

Sylvia, who was fond of him, for the path to death. He anointed her and retired to a corner. Bart spent the afternoon arranging financial transfers to those who had provided the information on Saco. Katharine and Alexandra monitored the Pepperdogs.com home page, Alex refusing to speak to Bart. Once an hour a nurse came in to check on Sylvia. There seemed no change.

They were surrounded by signs of Christmas, small strings of colored lights taped along the sides of the corridor, poinsettias in every room, a small fir tree in the corner hung with Sylvia's favorite German ornaments, passed down in the family for three generations. On a portable stereo they played her favorites, Brahms, Chopin, Schubert. Bart omitted Bach. She wanted that played at her memorial service.

It was full dark, before seven, and no one wanted to eat supper. The room lights were on—the nurses said they wouldn't bother her—when the rescue message came in. Bart read it and beckoned to Father Tom, who looked at the laptop and nodded back as if to say *I never expected less.* Bart showed Katharine and patted her back as she read. She and Alex hugged each other and went out into the corridor so they wouldn't disturb Sylvia. Or perhaps they felt their joy was unseemly in the room.

A nurse came in and checked Sylvia's heartbeat. "We're at the end," she said. She called Dr. Sikorsky again.

Bart sat by Sylvia, stroking her hand, thinking how Tyler had almost made it back in time. One by one the others drew close, Katharine, Alex, Father Tom, Dr. Sikorsky, three of Sylvia's favorite nurses.

What the hell, Bart thought, *why not tell her, even if she can't hear?* "Sweetheart," he said, stroking the top of her hand, "Mark found Tyler. Tyler's coming home."

Her fingers closed tightly around his thumb. He almost jumped. He peered into her eyes. The lids were half closed, and he could see only the whites, no iris. No difference from the previous hours. He jerked his eyes up at Sikorsky, jaw set in anger. "She squeezed my hand."

"I assure you, she feels no pain. She's in a deep coma."

"She's squeezing my hand."

"I see that," the doctor said. "She wants to communicate with you. Morphine, something, can't be explained. As a doctor, I promise you she's resting comfortably. No pain."

Gradually her fingers let go of Bart's thumb. The large nurse who had brushed her hair that morning leaned past Bart with a stethoscope and listened to her heart. Sylvia's jaw was open slightly, and Bart thought he heard her sigh. Sikorsky listened with the stethoscope. He straightened and patted Bart on the shoulder. "She's left us."

The doctor and nurses backed out of the room. Alex and Katharine held hands, ignoring the tears running down their cheeks, as Father Tom recited the Our Father. Bart looked away, neck cords straining as he fought back his own tears. He tried to close her jaw, but it was locked. He knelt by the bed and held her hand and cried noiselessly. The others left and his brother stayed. The silence lasted and the time passed.

"She's a donor, Bart," Tom said. "They have to take her."

"She worked so hard," Bart said, slowly standing. "I wanted her to see Ty, to know she had done something with her life. I feel like shit."

"Bart, remember the *Pietà*? The Son is carved from the shoulder of the mother. That's why His head looks so natural resting there," Tom said. "Sylvia died with her son resting on her shoulder."

"That's priest's talk."

"Most people die alone at four in the morning. She hung on, waiting. She heard Ty was safe. She knew what you did."

"I didn't do a damn thing. It was Mark, all Mark."

"That's not true."

Bart stood up and walked over to the laptop on the hospital tray. The women had come back in, and Alex plucked at his elbow.

"You're not going to tell them," she said, "not even you could be that cold."

"They have to know," Bart said. "They're not clear yet."

"This seems so cruel," Katharine said. "You'll depress them, Bart. Wait until they're back."

Bart shook his head.

"You are one son of a bitch," Alex said. She walked out, followed by Katharine. Father Tom waited.

"They don't understand, Tom," Bart said. "The team will risk too much if they think she's still alive. They have to be told."

Bart finished typing and hit send. He stroked Sylvia's still hand one more time and left the room.

XIX

South of the monastery   **2 A.M. Tuesday**

Blade was veering lower and lower toward the flat pastures, knowing that trudging up and down every ravine, every creek bed, every stand of trees, was sapping the energy from Roberts. The wind was freshening, biting into the right side of their faces. They tried to shut out the cold by not thinking about it. They would keep moving until the choppers were inbound, or they would walk until they dropped. No more stops. Homeward bound.

"Hey, listen to this." Harvell was checking the Quotron. "Joint Task Force says stand by for orders and don't cause any more confrontations."

"Why do we pay staffs to be stupid?" Caulder asked.

"When you're a sergeant major," Lang replied, "someone will ask that about you."

The team was now down off the shoulder of the mountain, close to the backyards of the farms, the angle of the wind keeping their scent from dogs. Had they gone far enough, opened up enough distance from the monastery and local troops to call for the evac? Lang checked the GPS. Three kilometers in the past hour. Slow going cross-compartment, now that they had to raise and lower two toboggans. Too slow. Lang was becoming concerned. Blade was shaving it too close to the houses. Time to turn back uphill and squirt a message for a pickup. Have the choppers come in over the mountains to the east where the SAMs wouldn't expect them.

"Lang!"

Harvell's voice was a bark, a sharp yip, so close and high-pitched it startled them. Not "sir," not "Skipper," just "Lang!"

"Shut up, Harvell!" Caulder whispered, knowing whatever would follow was not good.

"Lights behind us!" Harvell said.

They looked back toward the north. The slopes were fairly steep and clear of trees except for the gullies, and the lights stood out clearly, five or six pastures behind and higher, about where they had been a half hour ago. The lights seemed to be handheld, bobbing and dipping and waving as the men holding them scrambled along.

"Not too tactical," Roberts said.

"Remember that flick, *Butch Cassidy and the Sundance Kid*," Blade asked, "where the posse keeps coming and coming, and finally Newman says to Redford, 'Who *are* those guys?' "

"The gi . . . ant came . . . home . . . and Jack . . . was . . . gone," Cosgrove said.

They looked at him.

"The gi . . . ant," he repeated.

"Don't worry, sir. Once he's inside six hundred meters, I'll introduce him to David," Caulder said, patting the strap of his .308.

"If they get that near," Lang said, "we'll be pinned and miss our ride home."

"They're closing, sir," Blade said.

Lang let the air out of his cheeks, and the steam whipped across his cheek. "Take three twenty-sixes. Wire one here. Put the other two fifty meters farther along our track, one on each flank. They trip the first, clean up the mess, spread out, and hit the next one. That'll slow them down."

"All right!" Caulder said.

"No, no, it's not all right," Lang said. "We booby-trap three grenades. They trip one, maybe two. Guess who finds the third."

Silence.

"They'll be on us in an hour," Roberts said.

"Set them," Lang said.

They wired the grenades, scuffed snow over them and continued on. Harvell sent their position to the Ops Center and a quick message to the home page.

---

www.pepperdogs.com   0230, Dec. 22

Homeward bound. Posse behind us. Not smart. Set trip grenades. This is over. Don't they get it?
Posted by: J. Kirwin

Soon they came to another gully and unslung the ropes to lower the toboggans. They struggled down and up, lengthening their strides when they reached the next pasture. After a few moments Lang called a halt.

"This takes too long. We don't have the speed," he said. "Let's shift tactics. We get to the highway, take any car and drive as far as we can."

"They'll have roadblocks," Blade said.

"We drive without lights, thermals to the front, and bail when there's trouble."

Without another word, they tugged the toboggans out of the ravine and followed the natural folds in the fields down to the highway. As they descended, the thickets and trees fell away, replaced by low stone walls and barbed-wire fences. They passed a farmhouse with no lights and struck a road with several tire tracks covered by a few inches of snow. They stayed on that road, which led them across railroad tracks and onto the two-lane macadam highway. They seemed to be over a kilometer from the nearest heavy tree line.

"Great cover," Blade said, looking at the open country, "we'll hide as fence posts."

"Who's going to be out at two in the morning, with a security alert?" Caulder asked, looking up and down the empty stretch of road.

"I'm betting on drunks," Lang said. "There are always pubs that don't get the word."

"Do I stick out my thumb or throw myself under the wheels?" Caulder asked.

"I'll show you," Lang said, pointing to headlights to the north. "Get in the ditch. Alert me if it's military. Otherwise I'll flag him down."

"What if he runs over you?" Caulder asked.

"Then shoot the son of a bitch."

The headlights grew brighter, and the Marines lying in the ditch hid their faces. Lang stood calmly in the middle of the road, eyes lowered so he wouldn't be blinded, rifle casually held in his right hand with the muzzle down. He raised his left arm commandingly at the lights, as if he were a school crossing guard shepherding unseen students.

The car slowed abruptly, then went into a right-hand skid, bearing down sideways on Lang, who leaped for the ditch. The car swept by sideways, then the front eased ahead of the rear as the driver got lucky or remembered to turn the wheel in the direction of the skid. In a moment the car was gone, the rear lights a blur of red down the road.

Caulder clapped his gloves together, and Blade did the same.

"That was great, sir," Caulder said. "Years of training?"

They walked south until they hit a stretch of road where the incline was fairly steep, with a bend that limited a driver's vision as he reached the top of the curve. There they piled bushes and scrub growth across the road, and waited. They had planned a withdrawal route and a rally point. Caulder and Blade lay prone on either end of the bend. Blade saw another set of lights to the south. "Truck," he yelled. "No passengers."

The truck slowed and almost stopped at the debris. That was all Lang needed. In three quick strides, he was at the driver's window, jerking open the door and screaming, "Halt!"

The startled driver hit the brakes but not the clutch. The tires locked as the truck stalled out and slid to a halt. In seconds the frightened, drunken farmer was tied and placed in the open truck bed along with the Marines on the toboggans. The scrub growth on the road was thrown in the ditch. Blade drove, with Roberts beside him.

"In an hour we'll be back where we started a day ago," Blade said to a dazed Roberts soaking in the heat. "The Nez Perce didn't use trucks."

Caulder propped his rifle on the roof of the cab to scan ahead with the thermal scope while Lang sat between the toboggans facing to the rear. He reached over and took the Quotron out of Harvell's pocket and fumbled with it. With headlights out, they headed south at thirty-five kilometers an hour. Harvell watched the road disappear behind the truck. He couldn't talk to Cosgrove with Lang sitting between them. Nothing to do but look out into the black.

He felt uneasy. The team didn't seem as tough or as focused. Roberts was trying to stay off the morphine and was obviously hurting so much he couldn't concentrate, shuffling around like a big child. Blade had started talking about Indians again. Caulder was raving about old glass. And the skipper, standing out in the road to nearly get run over. What was that all about? *They're making mistakes.* The thought surprised Harvell. *They're so worn down, they're acting giddy.*

They had let him sleep, had carried him, kept him warm, while they had gone almost forty-eight hours without real sleep, with few breaks, going, going, in the snow and cold, no food left. They were running on empty.

"Hey, Skipper, let me do that," he said, reaching for the Quotron.

This was his job. Lang handed it to him without a word and slumped forward, resting his head on his knees.

At his comfortable headquarters in Kraljevo, General Kostica was studying the map and wondering where the Americans had gone when Ambassador Briggs called, demanding an immediate meeting.

"What's so important, Mr. Ambassador, that we have to meet at this absurd time?" Kostica asked.

"We have to finish this, General," Briggs said. "The kidnapped American was found in Serbia."

"You mean that digital picture you drew in Washington," Kostica said, looking at his computer monitor. "This is one of your infantile war games."

"Horse shit. I'm not debating with you. We meet now and settle this."

Kostica needed time to get this under control, to erase his connection to Saco. But what if something happened while he was at the meeting? "If you feel so strongly, you are welcome to come here."

"And be jerked around for a day? Stop playing. The Castle Restaurant in one hour."

"I can be there about four A.M. Full sovereign privileges. Neutral ground rules. My staff has sovereignty in one half, you Americans in the other."

"Oh, for God's sakes, Ilian. This isn't Versailles. But agreed, agreed. Now, will you please get your ass in gear?"

Before leaving, Kostica sat down to sort things out. Briggs must be feeling heat from his president. Now that the kidnapped American has been found, what was Briggs going to say, *Let's call it even? No hard feelings, I hope, about the trail of dead. Americans sometimes litter, old boy, bad habit. We simply want our own back.*

That was it. The Americans had only one advantage: those damned aircraft, up so high you just saw their white tails and the noise when they cracked the sound barrier to remind you how mighty they were, knocking down bridges and buildings, terrifying women and children. What had they accomplished by bombing his troops in Kosovo? Nothing. Sure, he took dead in thirty days of American and NATO bombing. And so what? It didn't change anything in Kosovo. Then the Americans hit the cities, blasting Belgrade. Television stations, bridges, trolley cars, buses, gas stations, anything. Bombing civilians. The Americans lacked guts.

Look at it. The Vietnamese, the Lebanese, the Somalis all used the same tactic. Americans didn't have the stomach to bleed. He had the border covered. Kill these few Americans and they'd pull all their troops out of Kosovo. Sure, he'd promise to pull back in return. What difference did a piece of paper make? The North Vietnamese had shown that. The Americans wanted cover once they decided to get out. They wouldn't care what he did later on.

It was only seventy kilometers from Kraljevo to the castle, but the highway had many twists and turns. It usually took Kostica three hours, because he would inspect units as he went. Rarely would he stop for more than a few minutes. That was enough for morale and information gathering. He wasn't too tough on them, poor bastards. How alert would he be for eighty Euros a month? Two years of sitting on their asses while that weasel Baba and his vermin gnawed away at the border, a mine one month and a mortar attack the next, protected by the worthless Americans in their ridiculous suits of armor, waddling when they walked, like medieval knights at a jousting tournament.

As he approached Zurice, headquarters for the regional company, he had his aide radio ahead for Saco to meet him at Raska, on the highway. He wanted a firsthand report of the fighting at the monastery.

Saco wasn't hard to find. They drove until they saw the flashing blue lights. Bulky figures in dark brown were fumbling to pass two stretchers across a drainage ditch and onto the highway. One of the wounded was screaming, a boyish voice shrilling an aria of terror, knowing his legs would soon be sawed off. The steam of the men's breath mingled with the exhaust from the vehicles and swirled around like stygian fog. In the center of the Dante-esque scene towered a robed figure so wide he seemed twice the width and a full head taller than the others, roaring un-intelligibly, shaking a rifle skyward as though it were a sword with which he would behead those who had done this to his legion.

Kostica considered driving on. He'd heard the story of the coat many times. A berserk Saco would butcher any captured Americans. *Well, first we have to capture them.* He sensed many of his men wouldn't stand up to those Marines, would look the other way and let them pass. Too many stories swirling of how tough these Americans were. Damn the Web! Damn the stupid rumors.

Kostica admitted he, too, feared this team of Americans. The dis-tances they had walked, the speed with which they struck and disap-peared. *Like they've put one of their aircraft here on the ground.* He pushed the thought from his mind.

Saco. The bull, the bear. No brains, no fear. He wouldn't back away.

The driver opened Kostica's door. His bodyguards had already spread out on the macadam. The others respectfully abandoned the complaining wounded and stood dumbly, waiting for someone to tell them what to do with a general in their midst. Saco lumbered forward and saluted uncer-tainly, absorbed by his anger yet knowing he had disobeyed about the American. Kostica gestured for him to walk to the far side of the road.

"Bastards left grenades, sir," Saco said. "Two more down."

"How many Americans?"

"A platoon, maybe a company." Saco had no link to the Internet.

"Five or ten, plus the American you captured two days ago."

"He was hurt, General. We were bringing him to a hospital."

How stupid, Kostica thought, *I tell him there are only a few Americans. He doesn't hear that, he's so busy telling his lie.*

"Sergeant, no more cow shit. Those Americans were coming after you. It's on the computers and the television. If those Americans get back, I can't protect you. The Hague . . ." Kostica shrugged. Saco was about to become a famous war criminal.

"There have to be more," Saco said almost to himself. "They kill Isvec, with me four years, Istan, Luc the sniper, little Icvic, he used to light my farts . . ." He flopped his rifle toward the wounded. "These . . . what for? What for they leave booby traps?"

He's about to cry. I'm losing even Saco? "Sergeant, I have the passes sealed. They can't get across the ridges at night. I want you as my reserve. When we locate them, you stop them. Can you do that?"

"It's not over?" Saco asked. "The American Black Hawks don't pluck them out?"

"Thirty kilometers to the border," Kostica said. "Small area. I've set SAM teams. It's snowing. Who knows? The Americans may try it, they may not. The question is, are you ready to finish it if I can get you close?"

"I will break each neck."

Saco seemed to swell. So much for his self-pity, or had it been genuine loss?

"No! If they surrender, the president wants them put on trial."

"Yes, General." Saco suppressed a grin.

Ask the lynx not to kill the watchdog when it is held by its chain, Kostica thought. Saco could implicate him in this foolishness. Best to get this mess over with. "All right," he said. "Get in the rear vehicle."

"I have my own." Saco gestured to the Toyota. "And thank you, General. I will not let down our homeland."

He meant it, every word. Kostica climbed back into his high-back jeep, feeling better. Why wouldn't this work out? The Americans left Somalia after one fight with a warlord who couldn't write. Once they lost these men, they'd leave Kosovo.

Saco walked to the two wounded and promised to kill the Americans for them. The older one nodded and tried to grin. The teenager was sobbing too hard to hear.

As the truck rolled along, Harvell balanced the Quotron on his chest and checked messages. He read the first and stopped. The skipper seemed to be dozing, his back against Caulder's legs, his eyes closed. *Let him sleep,* Harvell thought. *Hide this.* But Lang said, "What have you got, Harvell?"

The captain's tongue seemed thick. Harvell had no answer. The antenna was receiving no interference, and the black type showed clearly on the backlit screen. All he had to do was read it aloud. He couldn't. He handed the Quotron to Lang.

From: <%x^v   9:00 P.M., Dec. 22
To: #@V+

Sylvia died ten minutes ago. She knew you had Ty. Come home safe.
S/F, Bart

After a long minute, Lang poked Caulder in the calf and handed back the Quotron, the message screen open. Then he leaned over and nudged Cosgrove.

"I'm awake," Cosgrove said.

"How's the head?"

"Hurts, man . . . But I'm speaking . . . better, huh?"

"Yeah, good to go."

Cosgrove caught the tone, flat, strained. "What . . . is it?"

"Your mother's gone," Lang said. "Bart, ah, says it was peaceful."

Cosgrove didn't move or say anything. His arms were inside the sleeping bag. Lang reached over and patted the bag. Then he stood up next to Caulder. There was scarcely enough room for them to stand shoulder by shoulder. He took the Quotron from Caulder, rapped on the roof and passed it in through the window for Blade to read.

Caulder wore his face mask and kept a hand cupped over the forward lens of the scope, shielding it from the snow, uncovering it every few seconds for a quick glance. Lang let the frozen air knife into his face as the truck drove on. The snow stung like shotgun pellets, and he had a hard time seeing. He wasn't aware of any tears until he felt Caulder's hand brushing at his eyes and cheeks.

"You're icing up, Skipper. Wind'll do that," Caulder said, taking off his face mask. "I need some fresh air. Put this on."

Caulder kept his eyes to the front while he handed over the wool mask. Lang put it on and the tears continued to flow. *This is stupid,* he thought. *I can't do this in front of the men. Focus on something.*

"You snipers keep count, Caulder. How many have we put down?"

"About thirty, sir. So far, that is."

"That many?"

"We've been out a while, so the number keeps growing. We had two batches, whacking the SAM and that drill at the monastery. Rest were road kill."

"Road kill," Lang repeated.

Lang's voice sounded low and dispirited, worn out. *He's slipping.* Caulder thought, *carrying too heavy a load. He shouldn't be thinking about that damn message. Have to get him off that.*

"We don't want you meeting Grendel, Skipper," he said. "Blade and I can take it from here, if you want. Blade navigates to the nearest LZ. I shoot anything that moves. I would have won the nationals at Pendleton. Sea breeze, hell, it was blowing twenty knots on the thousand-yard line. West Coast Marines didn't give us any warning. I overcorrected on my first two shots."

"You've told us that story six times," Lang said.

"Making sure you're still with us, sir," Caulder said. "I'm serious, though, Blade and I can take the next leg. I got your back. But you have to tell the staff sergeant to let me fire earlier."

Harvell was sitting below them, listening. "You can't just shoot, sergeant," he said. "They might be civilians or Muslim freedom fighters or something."

"Shut up, Harvell," Caulder said. "We're the only freedom fighters out here. The rest are targets."

There was a rapping on the roof, and Lang leaned around to take back the Quotron. He scrolled to the next message.

From: Combat Operations Center   0200 Zulu 23 Dec
To: #@V+

Send us spotrep and pos. Will send choppers. Bravo Zulu.
Semper Fi: Bullard

"Time for our chopper ride?" Caulder said.

"I don't know," Lang said. "Think there are SAM-fifteens around?"

Caulder laughed. "Are there cows on those farms?"

"How long to the border?" Lang asked.

Caulder took out his GPS and clicked on a waypoint. "Fifteen mikes to that cabin where we stashed the bodies. From there uphill, another nine clicks."

"What do you think?"

"If there's not too much snow, we could push it. They're out there somewhere, though, waiting for us to make our move."

Lang leaned down. "What do you think, Corporal?"

Harvell almost jumped. He was being consulted?

"I, I'm with Sergeant Caulder, sir. Push while we can."

Lang felt like he was carrying lead on his shoulders. He had a sharp pain in his forehead, behind his sinuses, so sharp it was hard to see. Maybe he shouldn't have stood in the wind so long. He remembered he hadn't had anything to drink since before the firefight. Amateur mistake. He reached for a canteen. Frozen. Another mistake. Harvell handed up a bottle he had stored inside his jacket. Lang drank thirstily.

"Thanks. Harvell, send a spotrep. Caulder, got any aspirin?"

"No, sir, I got white heat." He rapped on the roof for the truck to stop. "Three engines off the road six hundred meters ahead."

"I knew it was too easy," Harvell said.

"You know shit," Caulder said. "Which way, sir?"

"Mountain to the east is six thousand feet, to the west three thousand."

The truck backed up to the western nearest track and turned off.

XX

The castle   4 A.M. Tuesday

Three Marine amtracs—large steel boxes with treads and cramped space inside—were guarding the landing site next to the Castle Restaurant, one equipped with a satellite dish and televideo display for the admiral's use. When the CH-53 helicopter lumbered in, only a few passengers walked down the ramp. Ambassador Briggs led the way, dressed in Gucci working clothes, high-top waterproof leather boots, double-stitched pants guaranteed not to rip under the claws of a polar bear, an L. L. Bean red-and-black-checked wool shirt and a down ski parka with eight pockets and ten zippers. This was serious business, and his clothes indicated he was ready to lead the rescue operation himself.

The cold was sharp, and even walking the few dozen meters to the castle, Briggs felt its bite and dug his face deeper into the collar of his parka. He thought of the team. *This is their third day out in this. How do they do it?* He shivered and strode on.

Vice Admiral Faxon didn't seem to notice the cold. His camouflage utilities had enough starch to stand by themselves in the stiffest wind. His whippet frame, clipped hair and purposeful gait signaled a man with pressing business elsewhere. He wanted to be back at his Combat Information Center on the *Bon Homme,* collecting information and piecing together the tableau. In that search he now had three unmanned aerial vehicles with thermal cameras, a four-engine P-3 aircraft with optical scopes that could see a man at twelve miles, two EC-130 electronic intelligence aircraft that could record up to twenty telephone conversations at once, the Tall Pine and Sherlock imagery satellites from the National Reconnaissance Office, twenty collectors and analysts per shift onboard the *Bon Homme* and thirty more per shift in the U.S. He called the latter his "virtual" staff: they were so tied in by computers, multimegabit data pipes, voice-over-data circuitry and televideo that they were "virtually" on the carrier. So far, for the price of $4 million an hour, this wizardry had yielded a 90-percent probability that the missing Marines were somewhere in Serbia.

They got out of the wind and stood in the vestibule, watching the approaching lights of Kostica's party of Serbian military.

"The Secretary of State didn't give me much wiggle room," Briggs told Faxon. "James Rodney said to get passage out for the Marines. That's it. I'll dangle a U.S. withdrawal anyway. Might help."

"You don't have permission to do that."

"Nothing gets done in government if you wait for permission."

"What was that stuff Sunday about being close to a full deal, provided I kept the Marines in check?"

"My literal instructions were to keep Kostica from attacking the guerrillas. I knew he'd go for the larger package, a mutual withdrawal," Briggs said. "I can read him like a book. I gain his concurrence, then persuade the Secretary. That's called initiative, Admiral."

" 'Exceeding your authority' is another way of putting it."

"It's negotiating," Briggs said. "We have to work this as a team. Don't be surprised how we bullshit each other. It's only talk."

"Like your earlier talk with me about the CinC South job."

"Don't take things personally."

"Do you even know the Secretary of Defense?"

"Oh yes. Nettles loathes me. Doesn't mean we don't do business, though."

The NATO checkpoint separating Kosovo from Serbia was a bunkered guard shack only a few meters from the restaurant, giving the guards easy access to coffee and meals. In defiance, the Serbs had set up their own crossing point a few hundred meters north, next to a small bridge. Since NATO held control, this was a token gesture, a shack where two guards, miserable in the cold, stumbled out uncomprehending when General Kostica's vehicles clattered over the bridge.

Kostica came with few vehicles, although he included a lumbering flatbed carrying the newest Russian SAM, with its tiny radar dish and a battery of six small missiles that looked like drawn daggers. The implication was clear: more like this waited in Serbia for any American helicopter on a rescue mission. The SAM in turn was guarded by a Soviet-era truck brandishing the twin barrels of the ZSU .37-millimeter antiaircraft gun. A truck with bodyguards brought up the rear.

They drove into the courtyard and parked along the east side of the building, the drivers hurriedly stringing a line of yellow tape around the parking area, as if marking off a crime scene. This was temporarily Serb territory, off-limits to NATO troops. General Kostica waited in the cold until they were finished, then demanded to see the rooms for his delegation before agreeing to proceed to the main hall, where the Americans were waiting.

As on Monday, there were no formalities or pleasantries. The two sides sat stiffly at the table near the fireplace, well stocked with logs. Steam rose from the clay pitchers holding hot coffee, but no one joked about the costs of heating a stone castle. The hotelier, in a tasteless pursuit of modernity, had installed fluorescent lights that dangled absurdly from the thirty-foot ceiling and cast such a harsh light that the negotiators had to shield their eyes. Briggs impatiently gestured to an aide to turn them off, and they sat in the light of the side lamps and the bright fire, adequate but throwing off strange shadows, suggestive that the two rows of men were locked in some dark struggle.

"General, you are to stand down your air defenses so we can pull our people out," Admiral Faxon said without preamble.

"Ah, I understand now," General Kostica said. "Those who destroyed the SAM, killed the crew of a snow trac, raped a little girl, attacked a monastery, killed a monk—those terrorists are to go free. You rig a photo on the Web and all is forgiven. Santa Claus comes early."

Briggs spoke quickly to reassert control over Faxon. "Rigged? All right, let's go together and see whether this kidnap victim exists. Bring as many of the press as you want."

"I'm not playing your games. You can visit your murderers in jail."

Faxon spoke again. "We want our people back."

Briggs could have kicked him. Ultimatums never worked.

"And we will defend our homeland," Kostica said, looking directly at Faxon. "This is no joke to us."

"Do you have any positive suggestions for ending this?" Briggs asked, ever the diplomat.

"Of course. Defend them in court," Kostica said. "They can hire Johnnie Cochran."

"Let's be serious," Briggs said.

"I'd be relieved of command if I let murderers go." Kostica looked at his watch. "A fair trial, that's what we're offering. By now, President Nego has called Brussels. This is a NATO command, isn't it?"

The White House   **10 P.M. Monday**

Secretary of State James Rodney had taken the call in another room. Now he returned solemn-faced.

"That was the NATO Secretary General, Mr. President. At least four NATO countries want the Marines to surrender. Belgrade's charges have rattled them—rape, multiple murders. The Secretary General proposes a compromise—turn the team over to the International Criminal Court at The Hague."

"These are Americans, and so is that admiral, Faxon," Cahill said, looking toward his Secretary of Defense. "Isn't NATO overstepping?"

"In judicial matters, yes," Nettles said. "But not operationally. Faxon's commanding for NATO, not just for us, Mr. President."

The President was rubbing his forehead, the wrinkles standing out in rows. "Can we get them out without starting a war?" he asked. "Ordinarily we'd leave this to our staffs, but this'll be over before we can regroup. Any ideas?"

The President was looking at the Director of Central Intelligence. Andrew Marsh was the administration's proof that imagination did not fade with age. The President had been impressed by how Marsh had penetrated the hierarchy in Beijing. "We have a black program, hologram stuff. We call it Charlie McCarthy, after the ventriloquist's dummy," Marsh said. "We can beam up Nego better than Belgrade can."

"You mean, play back a video?"

"Better than that. We project his own image, with his own words, re-arranged by us. It'd be like you appearing on *Saturday Night Live*, only you're not there and the writers have you say anything they want."

"Might help my reelection," Cahill said, "but how does it help now?"

"This is a huge story in Europe. Belgrade television is still broadcasting, and the local Serb units are watching," Marsh said. "If Nego ordered his military to stand down, that would take the pressure off the team, let them slip across the border."

John Mumford started to rub his bald spot. As Chief of Staff, he stayed clear of national security, but this was politics. "The European press will shrick, Mr. President. Think of yourself enshrined somewhere between Attila and Mussolini. Our media will see this as the Big Lie, like printing our own version of the *Times*."

"I'm liking this better and better," the President said.

Everyone smiled or chuckled a little bit.

"Seriously, how nasty could this get, Rodney?" the President asked. "More cracks that we're acting like Hitler?"

"It could spill over into commerce, sir. Our support in Europe is slim. We used up our chips on Iraq," the Secretary of State said. "Italy has already protested our radar aircraft interfering with their TV broadcasts. This does raise the stakes. The Europeans may retaliate by grabbing more frequency spectrum."

The President looked at his Director of Central Intelligence.

"I can't disagree," the DCI said. "We've superseded the Europeans. So they carp. It's a pathology. Would they cancel a commercial deal out of resentment? They might."

"That would cost American companies billions, Mr. President," the Secretary of State said. "Perhaps there's another way."

Rodney hoped to slow down the momentum. Marsh liked his toys more than he liked the independent Europeans.

"The Europeans need our trade as much as we need theirs. We're in Kosovo because they wouldn't go in without us," the Secretary of Defense said. "Information war is like the Stealth aircraft. Everyone knows we have it; it's only a question of when we use it."

"They were helpful in Iraq and Afghanistan," Rodney said. "We need them against terrorism."

"We need each other," Nettles replied. "The Eiffel Tower was on the hit list before the Twin Towers. Bali was even farther away."

"True, but make no mistake," Rodney said, "if we deceive their television networks, it'll be years before their press trusts us again."

"So, State and my Chief of Staff oppose, and Defense and CIA support," the President said. "General Scott, where do the Chiefs come down?"

"They think this information-war stuff has taken a lot out of their budgets, sir, but I can't speak for them. As your military adviser, I'm in favor because I believe it will confuse the Serbs."

The President nodded but did not respond.

"Where's the hardware?" the Secretary of Defense asked.

"Onboard the *Lincoln,* sir," a navy commander sitting along the wall answered. "A thousand-watt transmitter in the belly of an antisubmarine aircraft, ready to orbit near Belgrade."

"What about the words we want to put in Nego's mouth?" Cahill said.

"At Langley, I, ah, had the programmers work up some language," Marsh said. "With nonlinear editing, it's done in minutes. They can send it to the *Lincoln* anytime."

"If we can make Nego sing another song, let's do it. Caveat emptor," the President said. "I'll tell you who'll understand this—the American public."

XXI

Blade drove slowly, peering through his night vision goggles at the greenish landscape. The snow was only a few inches deep here in the valley, where the wind whipped across the bare fields, and he was following the outline of a farm road unmarked by any tire tracks. The military map gave no hint of these paths worn into the slopes by tractors and hay wagons. For the first kilometer the track had headed roughly westward, and Blade held hope of an easy passage, knowing he was deluding himself. Roads always led to buildings. Too soon he turned one more curve, and there stood a farmhouse on a knoll a soccer field away. Worse, there were lights in several windows. He slowly reversed back around the curve and stopped.

Blade and Lang climbed down and walked to the crest of a hill. The snow shower had stopped, and the stiff westerly breeze had blown most of the clouds out of the valley. They could clearly see the dark edge of the long ridge to the southwest. They stood in the dark studying the topography, noting the gentle crests of farmlands, the occasional clusters of lights, some near, some far.

"Doesn't anyone sleep in this country?" Blade asked, looking at headlights on other roads as obscure as the one they were traveling. Tractors with farmers and Kalashnikovs? Trucks with infantry and machine guns? Mobile SAMs repositioning to ambush helicopters?

"They're on full alert," Lang said. "We're the most fun they've had since they herded their neighbors into barns and burned them."

They went back to the truck and shrugged into their packs. Harvell turned on the Quotron and sent their position and direction of march to the Ops Center. With Blade in front, they struck out to the southwest, heading across the open slopes for the mountain range. Fifteen minutes later Harvell checked the Quotron.

"How long will the batteries last, Harvell?" Lang asked. He had been drinking more water, and his headache had subsided.

"We're set, sir. I keep it switched off mostly. Hey! Good news! From Combat Ops Center: 'Have you on thermal imagery,' " Harvell read. " 'Three vehicles southwest at nine hundred meters. Turn to one eight five magnetic. Air Force Night Hawks standing by to pick you up. Signed Bullard.' "

Over the wind they couldn't hear the soft sound of the unmanned aerial vehicle engines, but it heartened them to know a thermal camera was tracking them. They were not alone anymore. Other cameras were probing their flanks, looking for the black smudges of engine heat. Individuals under trees were hard to detect, but vehicles stood out clearly.

"Reply 'Thanks for the steer,' " Lang said. " 'We'll call for choppers when we find a safe LZ.' Keep the Quotron on."

It would be full dark for another hour, and despite the usual slow-downs in crossing the inevitable gullies and small creeks, and cutting the wire on some fences, and detouring a few times to stay far from the occasional farm, they were confident they would be in the trees and climbing the ridge before dawn seeped into the valley. They were approaching forty-eight hours on the move, in the cold, with no food, and they were dizzy, light-headed. It seemed they could float along. They knew this was when you tripped and fell into a ravine or broke an ankle.

Roberts walked like a zombie, his mind in a semi-hypnotic state outside his body, suspended from thinking by the morphine, the pain and the exhaustion. He knew the others would think for him and guide him. It was his job not to stop. He didn't have to walk fast, he didn't have to talk, he didn't have to keep alert. Put one foot after another. Never stop. Never stop.

Caulder did his best to ignore the drag of Harvell on the sled, pulling him roughly over the bumps, concentrating on holding to a straight line behind Blade, far to the front. He forced his eyes to rove from spot to spot, ahead, to the right, to the rear, ahead again. He had to scan close and far at the same time, and night vision goggles took away depth perception, so he wasn't using them. Occasionally he glanced to his left at Lang, who was lagging a little. No play race now. Caulder hadn't the energy left to spur Lang on. It was all he could do to keep a steady pace and not be the one to fall behind.

Caulder was vomiting every few minutes. His stomach would spurt out some bile, and he'd lean forward and scoop up some snow and swish it around his mouth to get rid of the acrid taste, then drink some water and trudge on until he vomited and began the procedure all over again. He seemed to feel the cold more than the others. He wasn't shivering now, he was shaking, his bones rattling inside his skin. So much for telling the skipper he could take over. He worried whether he could hold a sight picture. Maybe he'd have to let the Serbs get closer before he fired the next time. That offended his sniper's instincts.

Lang had the left flank, and his eyes moved in the same pattern as Caulder's. For Cosgrove's sake, he tried to avoid the sudden little dips in the field and let Caulder stay a little ahead, so he could see when Harvell jounced. He was trying to think of the team's next move and, at the same time, stay alert to what was happening around him. How to pick a landing zone and not call a helicopter into a missile trap? He couldn't get a handle on that. The headache had subsided, but it still hammered enough to be a distraction. His mind kept darting around, wouldn't settle down. *I feel like shit. She's dead. Don't think about her. That's Grendel sneaking up on you. Cos has Katharine—he'll be okay. Roberts has taken a bullet and he's still trekking. We can do this.*

Blade paid attention to following the heading Colonel Bullard had sent, checking it against the GPS receiver. It kept his mind active. He thought of the unmanned aerial vehicle somewhere over his head and had to smile. He wasn't much of an Indian when he had an airplane to guide him. He tried to read where the slopes dropped off without steep pitch, to make it easier for the toboggans. Every few minutes he would take a look through his thermal scope. To be doubly safe, he stopped the team for a break while he walked to the top of a hillock to check the terrain.

That was how the Serbs found them. It wasn't because Blade was silhouetted on the skyline. That made no difference since the Serb outpost was above him on a distant ridgeline, where they too were scoping the valley with a heavy thermal sight. Through the Internet, General Kostica had purchased modern surveillance gear for the key posts along the border. The men in the outpost were dozing in the predawn dark and a young teenager had the thermal scope all to himself, sweeping slowly back and forth according to the book.

The boy excitedly shook the shoulder of his drowsing father. By now the rest of the American team had appeared in his night vision binoculars. "Yes, yes," he insisted over the radio, "they're moving south, across Vakik's lower pasture, where he keeps the bull in the summer. About a dozen of them, hauling heavy weapons behind them. They are walking toward the mountain. Hurry, hurry!"

Blade walked down from the knoll to the team, who stood leaning on their rifles. They dared not sit down. They would tighten up, and it would take fifteen minutes to reach stride again. They waited for Lang to direct them.

"We call in the choppers as soon as we find a safe zone," he said.

They looked at the ground, at the sky, avoiding him.

"Something to say?" Lang knew but wanted to hear it.

"They walked out at Chosin," Roberts said.

Morphine talk, Lang thought. *That was half a century ago.*

"I'm with Roberts," Cosgrove said from his toboggan.

"No one asked you," Lang said. He had to quash this now. "You're a passenger."

"I'm . . . the . . . Two . . . your . . . intell officer." He had reverted to diaeresis, each word spaced out. "I . . . assign . . . your missions . . . We walk . . . out."

The others smiled.

"We've never quit a race," Caulder said.

"This isn't a race," Lang said. *Roberts and Caulder agreeing?*

"We've knocked out one SAM," Blade said. "There are others out here. It would suck to lose a chopper and fifteen Marines."

"Ten clicks to go, one pissant ridgeline," Caulder said, looking south. "Easy hump."

Three thousand feet up in snow, Lang thought, *carrying two. Roberts with one arm. Bad choice.* "We'll let the task force decide about SAMs," he said. "When we find a secure LZ, we ride out."

Caulder was looking up at the slope to the north. Lang followed his glance and saw several lights flickering. Vehicles moving. He looked to the west. Here and there, more lights bouncing. They resumed their walk south toward the base of the ridge, trying to move faster.

Can't pull the plug now, no place to hide, Lang thought. *There goes our night pickup. It'll be light before we reach real cover.*

"Blade, rig two more twenty-sixes," he said. "They'll have to dismount to follow us across these fields."

With no electronic jamming, no incoming fire and no interference, organizing the pursuit had been easy for the Serbs. Burgage alone did not explain the energy of the local militia. Few shirked the call at five in the morning. Many brought along sons and even a few daughters. The work wasn't difficult. Drive around and check areas where the Americans might hide. Stay together. Report in, do not engage. Repeat, do not engage. The army was on the highway and along the ridge. They would do the fighting.

Rumors about Americans had circulated in the valley for a full day. They were raping, slaughtering families, burning farms, new crimes reported every few hours. Where were they? Close, lingering in the valley, like rabid wolves, too crazed to know when to run away. Weren't they on the east side, where those bodies were discovered in the *hadjuk* cabin? Muslims helped them attack a monastery. Now a sighting here in the west end of the valley. Forty-dollar VHF radios spread the alert in minutes.

Saco was on the highway, waiting for news. He had a platoon of regulars in three high-wheeled personnel carriers. They seemed tough troops. Still, he was concerned. Anyone who rode concerned him. They became too comfortable. He had briefed them twice, stressing that they stay under cover if they spotted the Americans. "Don't rush at them," he told them. "Work up on their flanks, box them in, trap them. Then we call in mortars."

He had his four-wheel-drive Toyota and his nephew and three others from the sawmill. These were the only males left from the big house. The women had begged him to leave them, but without saying a word, the men had climbed in the truck and shut the doors and waited for him to drive off.

After the general gave Saco the platoon and permission to kill the Americans, he had lectured the others as he drove. "Remember, stay with me. I'll send those soldiers first. You've done enough. It's their turn. No matter what, don't leave cover."

How many times had he said that before a battle? *Idiots saying, Hey, Saco, you're so big, you're lucky not to be hit. Then they stand up when the shit starts flying, or leave the trench, or step out from the trees.* Why were so many so stupid? He was alive for the same reason bears survived. He knew how to hide.

These Americans also understood how to hide. But no longer. A corporal from the district knew Vakik's farm, even knew the bull pasture where the Americans had been seen. Saco placed the corporal in the lead personnel carrier, and the convoy started out. They bounced along for several minutes, lights on bright. At one point Saco slowed his Toyota and motioned another vehicle in front. Whoever had killed Luc knew his business. No sense making a target out of a fine Toyota.

Eventually they ran out of ways around the low spots and bogged down in a marshy field where the slush reached over the axles of the lead vehicle. The corporal was certain the bull pasture was the next hill over. They dismounted, took their weapons and lights and followed the excited soldier like young dogs on a fresh scent, yipping to one another, jostling to be at the head of the pack. After several minutes they found the toboggan tracks. The platoon sergeant radioed the news and set out on the chase, lights to the front. Saco walked at the rear, twice striking his nephew for trying to push his way to the front.

The eager corporal, a local resident who played practical jokes, insisted on going first and so was the first to die in the western end of the valley. Two others also went down, screaming more from fear than the pain of the burning shrapnel. Until the grenade went off, they didn't know the corporal had tripped it. Stepping in the footprints of others, Saco walked up cautiously to the platoon sergeant who was tending to one of the wounded.

"I warned you," Saco said. "I warned you about trip wires."

The platoon sergeant looked up, his hand on his Kalashnikov, and Saco thought he might shoot. Saco turned away. What had he done? He'd warned them.

With the wind stiff from the west, the team was too far away to hear the dull explosion of the grenade. Lang had set the booby trap at the top of the field so that they would see lights bobbing and fluttering. When they did, they confirmed the location by shooting a compass back azimuth. Harvell sent a message to the Combat Operations Center. He almost signed it, then thought better. Perhaps the ops chief—Gunnery Sergeant Twigs Twitchell—wouldn't understand. Marine gunnery sergeants weren't known for their tolerance. He left the message unsigned.

```
To: Combat Operations Center Admin              0545, Dec. 23
From: #@V+

Pursued by a platoon. Trip grenades slowed them for a while. Our pos
is 67 54 38 98. OM 230 degrees.
```

Next Harvell sent a message to the Internet. This, of course, he did sign.

```
www.pepperdogs.com                              0547, Dec. 23

Still on the move. Our pursuers never learn. More down from
trip wire. They seem to be everywhere, but we're soon home.
Posted by: J. Kirwin
```

They were so tired their minds shuttered on and off, like a camera taking pictures, with no concept of how much time passed between. They measured time only in distance. They were almost to the trees at the foot of the ridge; then they would gain the top of the ridge; then they would cross the border. Three tasks. Concentrate on one at a time.

There were occasional flutters of snow, not the heavy fluffs that block roads and break tree limbs, but light, thin flakes that caught in the updrafts and seemed not to fall to earth. While waiting for Harvell to set up the Quotron, Caulder dropped the toboggan rope and walked over to Blade, who was holding his fingers close to his face.

"Frostbite?" Caulder asked.

"Tiny feathers," Blade said, softly blowing the snow on his gloves, "dancing."

"No more of that Indian shit," Caulder said. His shivering was more pronounced now that they had stopped.

"I wonder if snowflakes have happy lives."

Here Caulder was, concerned about holding a sight picture, and his crazy friend had gone off into his private world again. "Not once the sun comes out. I like stuff that lasts, like the glass cross that asshole shot out."

"You miss a lot of beauty with that attitude, Caulder. You capped him."

"Didn't bring back the glass." Caulder glanced back at Cosgrove's toboggan. "We didn't get Captain Cosgrove back home in time, either."

In good order, the team reached the foot of the ridge. It had been six hours since the monks had given them food, and the team knew they were on the edge of running out of fuel. Thirty-five hundred feet to climb, in the snow, pulling two. They stopped at the edge of the bush to boil snow. No one sat for fear of cramping up.

Harvell slowly read numbers from the Quotron to Blade, who walked over to Lang and repeated them. They now had two GPS receivers with the locations of Serb units seen by the unmanned aerial vehicles. Lang and Blade studied the scattered black marks on their screens. No helicopter could safely land among those dots. Time for a final nonstop climb before Serb reinforcements poured in with the light.

"Fewer units along the ridge to the east," Lang said.

"Steeper over to the west," Blade said. "Bitch of a haul for you and Caulder."

Caulder looked up at the black mass. "I'll cut Harvell loose if I get tired."

They picked up the ropes and began to climb at an angle. The toboggans slid to their right, gravity pulling them perpendicular to the slope. They shortened the ropes and pulled harder. In the dark, every root and sapling seemed to snag the sleds in a tug-of-war. Soon both Lang and Caulder had slung their rifles and were walking backward up the slope, both hands on the ropes. Roberts tried to help, but they shook him off, concerned he would tear his hand further.

"No job for cripples, Staff Sergeant," Caulder said.

Blade walked beside them, staring at his GPS. "Two hours to the border." Too slow.

"Let's leave Harvell as rear guard," Caulder said.

"I'll do it to help, sir," Harvell replied, his voice muffled.

"Oh, shut up, Harvell," Roberts said. "Set more grenades?"

"If they get a firm track, they'll radio our direction and cut us off," Lang said. "How many back there, Blade?"

Blade looked back at the lights, now coming on again. "Shitpotful. Platoon, maybe."

It never stops, Lang thought, then laughed aloud at his self-pity. It's their country!

Blade looked at him quizzically.

"All right, set two more grenades," Lang said. "That should stop them."

The Serbs came on cautiously, following the scrape marks of the toboggans. In the dim predawn light, they had no chance of seeing wires. Saco was trailing well back when the dull *crump!* again carried to the rear of the column. Two more down. This time he stayed away from the platoon sergeant. Five more for the litter party, cursing and swearing revenge, shouting, "Don't finish the Americans before we get back!" Saco wondered if they would be enthusiastic after they had carried the wounded for an hour.

The platoon sergeant halted them temporarily but didn't give up. He waited for the smudge of first light and then resumed the chase, now able to watch for any tracks that veered off to set trip wires. Soon they left behind the fields and hit the scrub at the bottom of the ridge. A kilometer in height, the ridge was a rough slab of shale rock and stunted fir trees, too short to be called a mountain but with real pitch and steep sides, a climb one made with the hands as well as the feet. All his life Saco had avoided these steep ridges, useless for timber, barren of game, too sharply angled for vehicles.

As the first edges of light crept into the valley, enough to limn the blackness of the ridge, Saco pulled his men even farther back. He didn't want to climb the damn thing, not with the Americans looking down. They had shot Luc after he was dead, messed him up. He knew there was a scope playing over them now, falling on first one, then another. Would they hit him in the stomach and laugh as he rolled around screaming? He wanted the battle fully joined by others before he engaged these Americans.

The platoon started up the slope, not caring about the noise they made as they slipped and stumbled through the thickets, many slinging their rifles so they could grab hold of the branches and pull themselves up. Already another platoon was working its way in. The trail of the Americans at first angled up the ridge to the west. But soon their trail led south, straight up the slope toward the pass where the highway crossed into Kosovo. The platoon scrambled forward, anxious for revenge, worried another unit might reach the Americans first and finish them.

XXII

The negotiators had haggled through the predawn hours. Finally, as light crept into the hall, General Kostica played his key concession.

"Very well, a trial at The Hague, not in Serbia," he said. "That Canadian woman judge, any judge, we don't care, you pick."

"We're not agreeing to a farce," Briggs replied. The suggestion was too reasonable. He had to move it quickly off the table. If Belgrade was consulting with European capitals, the Americans could be boxed in diplomatically. Kostica was about to reply when an aide walked up briskly and whispered to him.

"I suggest a break," Kostica said, "while you consider my offer." As they rose from the table, he addressed Faxon. "You're running out of time, Admiral. I don't want more of my men dying, and yours surely will die."

Faxon and Briggs headed to the amtrac with the satellite dish. Inside, two Marines operated the computers. A small electronic map showed the location of Serb units near the border and another screen showed thermal images from an unmanned aerial vehicle called *Predator*, three hundred feet above the ridge. Each time the operator spotted the heat from bodies, the UAV turned in a dizzying circle, giving the location in bright white numbers. Once the location was stamped on the electronic map, *Predator* resumed its lazy circles, like a buzzard looking for carrion.

The diplomat and the admiral squeezed past the operations officer to look at the displays.

"We're getting solid hits on the dogs, sirs. They're on the move, heading west. I make them four clicks from the border, about here," a small corporal with coffee breath said, pointing at the center of the monitor. "*Predator* dropped its load on a couple of vehicles a click to their south. It's Whiskey, but we're holding it on station to track the team."

"Who authorized *Predator* to shoot?" Admiral Faxon asked.

The corporal stiffened in his cramped seat. Should he have kept his mouth shut?

"The task force did, sir," the ops officer said. "We monitor here. We don't control the birds."

"It was a good call. Any more coming on station?"

The corporal relaxed.

"Two more, sir, now that we have a fix on the team," the ops officer said. "They're about twenty mikes out. Each carries two Hellfire missiles. Plenty of targets. The large black blobs are vehicles. You have to look real close to see individual soldiers. They give off less heat."

Ambassador Briggs peered at the monitor. To his untrained eye, it looked like a checkerboard. Every other square was a black blob.

General Kostica had retired to a back room where his communicators had set up radios, two Russian military FM/VHF models and a German commercial high-frequency receiver, all with long wire antennas strung to one of the castle's minarets. The World War II technology worked quite well to contact the units on the ridgelines five kilometers to the north. A Hewlett-Packard seven-hundred-megahertz laptop was plugged into the restaurant's telephone line, the modem connected at fifty-six kilobits per second, antiquated but adequate to monitor the Pepperdog home page.

"We've captured them, General," a radio operator said, "congratulations."

Kostica smiled. "Who? Where?" He tried to act gruff and self-contained. Already he was thinking of his return to Belgrade, of the television cameras and the press, the stream of interviews, the ambassadors and the formal meetings, each televised around the world. A slight tug, a nagging worry about Saco. He'd send him to a unit far from the cities.

What to do with the captured Americans. A trial? Or hand them over? Briggs had mentioned a loan. *Don't ask for too much.* A billion? Two?

"We don't know the details, sir. The president announced it ten minutes ago."

Kostica looked at the tape of President Nego. The sentences seemed a little awkward, but the man had been up all night.

"Citizens of the Republic of Yugoslavia, the American terrorists have been captured. Our military has defended our fatherland, and we all thank them. The militia may return to their homes. I will say more later."

Kostica's anger was immediate. What was the president doing issuing orders? Who had taken the credit away from him? "Who reported to the president without my permission?"

His aides and the radio operators avoided his gaze. None knew. None ventured to speak.

"Have you called Belgrade?" he asked.

"We've tried, General," an old major said. "It's confusing. The Americans are jamming."

"Get me President Nego on a land line."

It took half an hour for Kostica and Belgrade to confirm positively that the television report was a hoax, and in the meantime the rumors swirled. Various regional companies and platoons, tired and cold, drifted down from their posts, some having watched their president on television, others called by their families. Some units stayed, but most decamped, leaving large gaps. The line of troops along the ridge crumbled.

News of the captured Americans would have surprised Saco's platoon. They were closing the gap, only a matter of physical strength and time, those in the lead with enough light now to see the toboggan tracks. They were scrambling uphill, tramping noisily through the brush and scrambling over rocks and around trees. Eventually they broke free of the thick bush, Saco still trailing behind. An open patch of ground, as wide as a beginner's ski slope, led up toward another tree line.

Into the third hour of the chase, the men were sloppy with fatigue, the shock of the trip wires having worn off. The platoon sergeant repeatedly warned them to stay in the tracks of the toboggans, not to wander off to the sides where more grenades could be hidden. "Walk in trace," he yelled, "walk in someone's footsteps." Which they did, clustering together in a double file, almost tripping over one another's boots.

No one tripped another grenade. The blow that killed them came from a Claymore mine directly to their front, the blast as sharp-sounding as an artillery shell. Snow, rocks and dirt got scooped up in the detonation, and the air was laced with hundreds of aluminum shards hurled at a thousand miles an hour, slicing through the packed column, slitting open the two front scouts, decapitating the radioman, eviscerating the conscientious platoon sergeant and the three soldiers trotting a few meters behind him.

The remaining column froze in shock, dazed by the ferocity of the blow, not realizing that the sound blotted out the automatic weapons scything their ranks. The firing from in front and to their left was so loud, so cacophonous, that there was no sound. The dead couldn't hear, and the ears of those who lived a few beats longer were reverberating from the Claymore, like an echo chamber filled with drums. They didn't know enough to get down. In seconds, twenty bodies lay crumpled in the field, like a tangle of broken trees on a riverbank after a flash flood.

Lang's problem was stopping the firing. "Cease fire! Cease fire!" he yelled over and over again. None of the Marines had earplugs, and each went through two magazines before heeding his yells. The barrels were smoking before the first magazines were emptied, and toward the end they were firing blind through the ice fog created by the steam rising from their weapons. Caulder, the designated marksman, leaped up and took a stand behind a tree to see downslope. He hit three more men stumbling downhill. The other Marines, still prone, got off no more shots. Despite the chill wind, the sulfurous stench of the cordite and the heat from the weapons hung over them for several seconds, and they enjoyed the illusion of warmth. In a tree line downhill Caulder picked up a hot spot—a whitish round face, big as a pumpkin in his scope—and splattered it with one round. There was no return fire, and no one else peeked out of the trees.

General Scott came out of his chair in the Situation Room with no sound or warning, bumping against one of the undersecretaries perched against the wall, scrambling around the President to gaze intently at the un-manned aerial vehicle screen. For an hour the screen had shown blurry black-and-white terrain, looking like images from a handheld camcorder in a small plane flown in dizzying circles. In fact, the UAV was operated by a navy chief in a four-engine P-3 circling fourteen thousand feet above the ridgeline. She, too, had seen something and was directing the plane in a tight circle, zooming in the camera. The Chairman pointed his finger at black dots clearly visible in the center of a white slope.

"I make it fifteen, maybe more," he said. "Anyone else have a count?"

An Air Force sergeant opened the door from the control room at the rear. "Twenty-two, sir."

"For a moment I thought we'd lost them," Scott said, returning to his seat. "That's a real recent ambush. Bodies haven't cooled off. Too many down to be our people, though."

"Those people are dying," the President asked, "as we're watching?"

Caulder scoped the killing field and zoomed in on the downed radioman in the detritus of the platoon.

"Third one in. See the one twitching, holding his knee in the air? Just to the right of him. The guy's not moving, but he's got a square box on his back."

They knew it had to be done. It made no sense to let those on the south ridge build an intelligence picture, and no one was going to walk out into the kill zone and disable that radio. Still, throwing the grenade was like hitting a child with a hammer. They waited for the captain to tell them what to do.

Lang straightened the ends of the pin and cupped the grenade in his mitten. It fitted comfortably in his palm, like a heavy baseball. He tried not to listen to the groans and sobs only a few meters in front of him. He had learned that the screams and pleading were still a few minutes away, after the shock wore off and the pain burrowed into the nerves. He let the spoon flip free before he lobbed the grenade. *If I'm going to tear them up for a stupid radio*, he thought, *I'm going to make sure I nail it.*

"Fire in the hole!"

It wasn't a long throw, and Lang wasn't under fire. Little chance of missing. The grenade struck the radio operator on the arm and exploded before it hit the ground. If the radio wasn't out of commission before the blast, it was after. Two wounded joined the dead.

At the Combat Operations Center, they knew the fight had ended. Ten minutes earlier Dr. Evans had seen the blood pressures and heart rates peak at the same time.

"Attention in the Ops Center!" she had yelled.

"Overexerted?" Bullard asked, looking at the monitors.

"No, it happened all at once."

"Blade's soaring," Evans said, "he's labile. His pressure takes off more than the others."

There was silence in the COC.

"Look!" Evans pointed at the other monitors, where every rate and pressure had spiked even higher.

"They're into it," Bullard said, "they're firing, I know they're firing."

They watched without speaking. After a minute, not more, the pulse rates abruptly plummeted.

"That's finished," Bullard said. "Had to have been an ambush."

"The heart rates dropped fifty beats in less than a minute. Unbelievable," Evans said. "What an article I can write. We're taping this, right?"

The corpsmen assured her they had it recorded.

"Those are my boys," she said, looking at the monitors.

"Did we call that, huh? Telepathy." Bullard grinned. "Damn, we're good."

It was another few minutes before the messages came in.

From: Pepperdogs   0605 Tues., Dec. 23
To: Combat Operations Center Admin

Firefight. No friendly casualties. Twenty enemy down. Prelim Whiskey Alert. OM south.

"Not good. Make sure the Joint Task Force understands they're low on ammo," Bullard said, turning to the watch officer. "Dragon Fire displaced forward?"

"Yes, sir, six tubes at the castle."

"Keep pushing ammo up the road. All it costs us is sweat and fuel. Bald Eagle ready to go?"

"Two platoons in the first stick, sir. Company standing by."

The 25th Marines were ready to go to war whenever NATO said go.

---

www.pepperdogs.com   0607, Dec. 23

Heavy fight. More of them down, a whole lot. Why don't they stay away from us? We don't want to do this. We're going home.
Posted by: J. Kirwin

The watch officer looked at the screen. "Harvell's a whiner, sir. I'd give anything to be in his place. Shit, the whole regiment would like to be out there."

"We haven't killed anyone yet," Bullard said. "Cut him some slack."

While Caulder swept for more targets, the others headed uphill. The crying and sobbing amid the cluster of bodies was constant, and Caulder could see heat from several life sources in his scope, twitching or crawling feebly. He ignored them.

The far tree line held his interest. There were confused shouts toward the wounded, names hollered without hope of a reply, subdued words of encouragement. No one ventured onto the open slope. Someone was organizing them, holding them back. Someone knew what not to do. When his shivering became shaking, Caulder knew it was time to leave. Checking his GPS for the rally point, he walked away, throwing one final round downrange to show he knew someone was organizing the survivors.

XXIII

The adrenaline from the ambush carried the team west at a fast pace for the first several minutes. Their pulse rates were up, the slope seemed less steep, the toboggans felt less like anchors. They weren't trying to gain altitude, only to put distance between them and the crippled platoon that had pursued them so foolishly.

In their fatigue and excitement, they underestimated the Serb technology. They walked in the open as though the semidark were a curtain behind which they could move unseen, a conceit for which they mocked their enemies. Three or four times they were picked up by small mounted patrols in the valley, each with unobstructed views of the slopes to the south. The Pepperdogs had done the same in their own exercises for years, settled into a position with a view of a clearing and waited for hours until some tired squad or platoon cut across the open to save a few minutes. The team would take a picture, call a mock fire mission and present the embarrassing evidence at the debrief. Now they were the unwary.

Once they could plainly see one another's silhouettes in the gray, they avoided the open spots. They might have made it, clinging to the tree lines and angling their way up, heading across the ridge to some thick place where patrols wouldn't notice. But they hit a clearing with no easy way around. A rock slide centuries earlier had sent boulders tumbling down hundreds of feet, splintering trees and ripping out the undergrowth. Decades of spring rains had sluiced through the thin layer of topsoil, exposing strata of shale on which the roots of new trees could not gain a purchase. Some of the largest boulders had come to rest halfway down the slope, forming a small fortress with deep crevices that had given refuge to hibernating bears.

The open cut was too long to bypass, and the dawn light was now strong enough to read a map without a light. Blade, towing Harvell until Caulder caught up, looked at Lang, who nodded. They started across, Roberts in front. The open area wasn't much wider than a parking lot at a suburban mall, a three- or four-minute walk from one side to the other. They were almost at the island of boulders when they realized their mistake. The ground was more uneven as they reached the center. Years of rains had plowed long furrows and filled them with loose rocks, like walking over the crushed stone foundation of a new highway. Under the pressure of their boots, the snow settled between the sharp points of the rocks, and the toboggans scraped to a quick halt.

The team assessed the problem. If they continued dragging the sleds, the slats would rip out. They hoisted the wounded on their backs, cinched the tow ropes around their waists and continued, hoping the empty toboggans wouldn't come apart. The shards of the rock bed extended only a few dozen meters.

Caulder hadn't yet caught up. The swift pace of the team had surprised him. Now he stood at the edge of the clearing and saw them struggling across. *What the hell are they doing so exposed?* he thought. If he could see them, so could others. No time to tarry. He started across at a trot, for the first time in days forcing his stiff legs up in a high pumping action above the ankle-deep snow. In the initial strides, he felt relief from the constant shivering. Perhaps by the time he reached them, his body heat would raise his core temperature and he could be warm in his own sweat.

He caught the first cramp high in the back of his right thigh. The hamstring knotted in midstride and he fell heavily, thrusting out his arm to protect his rifle. That instinct cost him his left leg. As he went down, it folded, too, and the cramp snapped shut like a trap. He was facedown in the snow, both heels pointing skyward, the giant femur muscles pulling like cables, trying to winch his Achilles tendons up through his knees and into his hips. The pain wracked him. Even worse, he felt helpless, unable to free himself from the vise of his own tendons. He didn't want to cry out. He was embarrassed, enraged. The pain had brought tears, knotted his neck muscles. He was clenching his teeth, not hearing the guttural hoarseness of his breath as he spat out the snow.

The sound carried faintly, enough to cause the others to look back. They turned and retraced their steps, looking a bit absurd, grown men playing piggyback. Lang and Blade left Cosgrove and Harvell among the boulders and walked quickly to where Caulder lay.

"Son of a bitch," said Caulder, "son of a bitch."

Lang and Blade each grabbed an ankle and pulled. It was like drawing back a heavy bowstring. They held his feet to the ground. "Don't let go," he said, knowing both legs would snap back like elastic bands.

They rolled him onto his back, and Blade pushed down on Caulder's knees to keep the legs rigid while Lang lifted him under the armpits. Then Blade pushed down with a rifle barrel across the thighs while Lang pulled Caulder backward, his heels dragging on the ground. It took several minutes before they had him propped in the shelter of a boulder.

They had been in the open for at least four minutes, long enough for the patrols in the valley to make them out. The Serbs didn't hesitate. They drove pell-mell toward the slope with not the slightest vestige of caution, as if oblivious to the firing that had echoed not minutes before. The first troops to arrive ran up the slope, scrambling eagerly, bursting out of the trees but unsure of the clearing. Roberts lay prone, his Kalashnikov propped against a rock, and knocked two back before they had a chance to get their bearings. A third soldier stumbled and sprawled headlong, not hit but disoriented. Two men darted out, grabbed their comrade by the arms and tugged him back. Roberts watched but held his fire.

Lang glanced around. The team was halfway across an open slope dotted by a few sere trees and scrabbly shrubs, tucked among a half-dozen boulders, each the size of a garage door. The team held the higher ground, and flanking them would take time. The ridge south ran like a long finger toward the border. The Serbs couldn't get around to cut them off without crossing the border. They could only come straight up from the north, and they hadn't yet built up a base of fire to cover an assault. If the team could climb another half kilometer, they would reach the border. All they had to do was cross a hundred meters of open ground, as flat and white as a shroud. Then they would be back in a tree line.

Commander Evans was watching the monitors. Caulder was spiking hard.

"Caulder's down!" she yelled.

Pulse 100, systolic 100. Couldn't be, Caulder was never a hundred. Now coming down. Still too high but steady. A glance at the others. All high readings. *They're back in it,* she thought, *only they didn't spring an ambush this time.*

"Caulder's stabilized, hurting. I don't think it's internal. He's out of play," she said to forty silent Marines. "That leaves only Blade and Lang able-bodied. The team's in trouble."

After the last solitary round had snapped through the branches, Saco lay flat, head behind a tree, hissing orders at the shaking survivors and at his own confused men. His nephew lay next to him, where he had dragged him, the back of his head torn off. Saco had hit the corpse once or twice, heavy blows of frustration to the legs and buttocks. Who stands up in a firefight to see what's going on? They all do at first. He hit the corpse again. What would he say to his sister?

Fucking Americans. They were like Luc, seeing in the dark. Striking like snakes. The platoon was destroyed. Still, everyone had heard this fight. The Americans couldn't get over the border. They'd block them up top somewhere. What to do? Get back to the vehicles, send help, get some more troops, wait for the next report.

He grabbed his three men and one of the regular soldiers. He wouldn't leave his nephew here. They'd carry him back. It was all downhill anyway. The soldier would lead others back to help with the wounded. He looked around. About a half dozen left. "It's safe to go out now," he told them. "Do what you can do. I'll send help back, but it'll be an hour before it arrives." Saco didn't want to tell them it would be closer to three hours. That was why he didn't want to look at the wounded. *If you can't do anything, don't make it worse on yourself. Save it for the Americans.*

As he walked away, he glanced back. Not one soldier had moved. They were in shock. He shrugged. Nothing he could do.

A half hour later, before his small band reached their vehicles in the farmland, Saco heard more firing, a few bursts, some isolated shots, then more uneven bursts. More militia from the valley were moving up and engaging. He waited for the Americans to spring another trap, for the sudden, murderous roar, for the sustained volume of fire followed by the silence of the dead. Instead the ragged firing continued, alternately swelling and subsiding, sounding no more threatening than firecrackers, yet always persisting.

He reached the vehicles and was surprised to see a line of men where there had been only a few an hour ago. Troops stood in a long column in the early light, ready to move out but obviously waiting, with a short colonel at the lead. Saco vaguely remembered him.

"Where's Sergeant Basdra?" the colonel asked.

"Ambushed," Saco said. "They need help up there."

"Who's in charge of the platoon?"

"Dead. Most are dead."

The colonel eyed Saco's men, carrying the body of the foolish nephew. "So you and your men left?" he said. "We've been on the radio with a survivor up there for the last fifteen minutes. He's out of his mind with fright. Says you left them."

Saco's anger came as easily as spit. "Colonel, I came for troops, to go after the Americans, get around their flank, up above them."

"You led a platoon into an ambush, abandoned them, and you want more?"

Saco stood stunned. This colonel didn't come up to his chest. He was from Belgrade, the new political crowd. He hadn't been in the trenches at Prista, or at the bridge at Hecta, or under the artillery at Vaja. "General Kostica ordered—"

"General Kostica ordered me to give you one platoon, which you deserted. I just reported to him that we can still hear firing, that . . ." The man trailed off. "Get out of my sight. You sicken me."

"Colonel, the Americans—"

"I don't want to hear about the Americans from someone who left a fight."

"I haven't left!" Saco shouted.

"Then what is this I hear, eh? Open your ears. They betray your mouth."

A soldier came running up to say General Kostica was on the radio. As the colonel turned away, Saco called after him, "Sir, may I speak with the general?"

"Not over my radio. I'll tell him the fight goes on without you," the colonel said. "He's at the castle. Tell him yourself why you came back without the platoon. I won't lie for you."

Saco ran over to the Toyota. "You three sit in back," he yelled. "Put him in front."

They strapped the corpse in the passenger seat, crawled in back and sat dumbly while Saco clashed gears and spun away.

Lang looked at the tree line a hundred meters higher up the steep slope. If the team could get up there, they could resume their climb to the top under cover, and it would be the Serbs exposed if they followed. One hundred meters. A football field. The team's chances were about as good as those of a football player running a hundred yards for a touchdown. It sometimes happened, but it wasn't the way to bet.

Caulder was sitting upright, the small of his spine braced against a boulder, legs straight out, chest and arms jackknifed forward, fingers hooked like talons over the tops of his boots, hanging on to prevent the tendons from snapping back, stretching, stretching.

"Staff Sergeant, ammo count," Lang said.

"Three are red. Harvell and I have two full mags."

"In the Old Corps," Lang was shaking his head, "it was one bullet, one kill."

"We've reduced friendly fire since then," Caulder replied.

Blade came around a boulder. "Two vehicles down there," he said, glancing at Lang's square rifle.

The rifle had two barrels, the upper long and sleek, the lower short, thick, heavy. From a vest pocket Lang took a magazine that held three cartridges as thick as cigars, tips painted red. Next he screwed on a telescopic sight and followed Blade around the boulder. At the foot of the ridge were two trucks parked side by side. Troops were clustered around them, gesturing. Blade adjusted his binoculars and clicked on the laser sight. "Five six five meters," he said.

Lang extended the bipod, twisted the dials on the scope and sighted in on the first truck. The boulder provided a fine rest point. Soldiers jumped and scattered as a headlight shattered. The second armor-piercing round struck the center of the hood, and a puff of steam spurted out. The third shot disabled the second truck.

"They weren't going to drive up here," Blade said. "Seems unfair."

"People shouldn't ride, not natural," Lang said, detaching the short, thick barrel from the underside of his rifle. "It'll shake them."

Roberts came around the rock and cautiously peeked downslope. "So what's the plan?" he asked. "Wait until we're cut off?"

They had an ideal defense down in the rocks, in a crevice between two boulders, safe from all small arms.

"I'm hoping for a United Nations cease-fire," Lang said, "like between the Palestinians and Israelis."

"So . . ." Roberts wanted an answer, not Lang's wise-ass.

"So it's time to test the Joint Task Force," Lang replied. "Harvell, send this message: 'Pinned in rocks. Request fire mission. Target: platoon in tree line. Polar. From our pos, one hundred meters. One five magnetic. Danger close. One VT on the deck. On my command. Will adjust. Stand by for multiple closed sheaths. Give us a box and walk us out.' "

Lang was requesting fire support, artillery to be laid down on the platoon shooting at them. He was asking the NATO command to join the fight. The written request gave the Joint Task Force all the information needed to fire. For almost two days the team had cut off communications. Now they were asking Admiral Faxon for help.

"That's a joke, right?" Roberts asked. "We're in Serbia, sir, fucking Serbia. The admiral doesn't allow us to spit toward the red line. You think he's going to tear this place up for our sorry asses?"

"Long way up that slope," Lang said, looking at the open space uphill.

Roberts's hand was throbbing again. *This is no time to jerk around. Lang must have a plan; he always has a plan.*

The incoming fire was steady now from downhill as soldiers spread out and fired randomly. Each time a rock was hit, there would be a sharp crack and high-pitched whine as the bullet ricocheted at a crazy angle.

The team was too low to hit, but the zings and whines set off sharp echoes, and the Serb soldiers liked to hear that they were hitting something.

The team had a text reply in less than a minute.

"Message back, sir," Harvell said. "It reads, 'Wait. Out.' "

"That's your decoy, Skipper," Roberts said. "Now, what's your real plan?"

At the castle, Ambassador Briggs and General Kostica were debating the same points for the twentieth time when Admiral Faxon prodded Briggs to look at his PalmPilot. Briggs read the entry while Kostica sipped coffee.

```
From: Combat Operations Center               0650 Tues., Dec. 23
To: Commander, Joint Task Force

At 0646 Pepperdog requested fire support. They are cut off near
border, four kilometers north of castle. We are prepared to fire on
your command.
V/R, Bullard
```

Briggs suggested a break and Kostica readily agreed, anxious to hear his own radio reports. Once the Americans were alone, Faxon wasted no time. "Bullard's on his way here," he said. "I'll authorize the fire mission."

"Admiral, let's think this through. First, NATO won't give you permission to fire. I was the ambassador there for three years. I know how they think," Briggs said. "Second, escalating to a major battle gets the U.S. in, but it doesn't get the team out. It would be senseless to open fire. How many other commands have seen this request?"

"Operational messages stop with me," Faxon said. "That's not the point. The team needs help."

"Good. Let's get Kostica to agree to a cease-fire."

"I thought your instructions—"

Briggs cut him off. "My instructions assume common sense: Movement. Movement is essential to success. First we get the cease-fire. That helps the team, doesn't it? The rest will take care of itself."

"No, first we consult with Brussels and Washington," Faxon said. "We're not—"

"Admiral," Briggs interrupted, seizing the admiral's forearm, "we have to work together to stop this *now. Then* we consult. Otherwise there won't be any team to consult about."

Once he had someone listening, Briggs relied on fervent energy and close contact, his agile mind supplying the arguments, sliding off objections, intent on winning. On the seventh floor at State, he was called "Blowtorch Ambrose."

"I'm not going to leave them dangling while we—"

"Precisely my point," Briggs said. "We, you and I, have to persuade Kostica to put a quick stop to this. He holds the cards, so we have to outmaneuver him. The team loses if this escalates. You know I'm right about that. Ten minutes of intense diplomacy, that's all I ask. Back me on this, for the team. Let's get him in here."

Kostica came back to the table, his face calm, perhaps smug. His colonel had assured him the Americans were trapped and under fire, with reinforcements moving up; the colonel understood how he was to end it. The report about Saco running away was disturbing, out of character. Well, if Saco showed up, Kostica would keep him separated in the Serb sector of the compound and deal with him later. He sat down, spread out his hands palms up, eyes exaggerated wide. "You have something for me?" he asked.

"Playtime's over. Our bombers have left Aviano," Briggs said. "Your economy's going back to the seventeenth century."

Kostica hadn't expected this. He looked at each of them as though he wanted to strike them. "I didn't think you had it in you. What do you want?"

"It's not what we want; it's what you're going to do to avoid a manmade earthquake in Belgrade. Our people are under fire," Briggs said. "You're going to order an immediate cease-fire, followed by safe passage out."

"Hah! They're murderers. They'll start shooting again."

"Nonsense. We'll have them put down their arms," Briggs said, looking at his wristwatch.

"All right, I agree in principle. A cease-fire and no arms. In return, you call off the bombers, now."

"Ilian, Ilian, always manipulating," Briggs said. "There is no principle here, only the practical. Those bombers continue until there's a cease-fire. I mean it."

"I must confer with Belgrade."

"Ten minutes. Remember, Admiral Faxon needs time to turn those bombers off—after the cease-fire. And we, not you, will bring those American soldiers back here."

"No. We'll do it together. As soon as it's safe, we take a helicopter out there. My helicopter."

"Russian junk falls out of the sky," Briggs said. "We'll go first-class, an American Black Hawk with padded seats and a steward serving coffee."

"Always with the jokes, Mr. Ambassador," Kostica said. "All right. We take one of your choppers—if Belgrade agrees."

Faxon was stunned. Hours, days, of obstacles, recriminations, refusals—all overturned in a minute by the threat of bombing? If it was that easy, why hadn't the Serbs agreed a lot sooner? What was missing here?

XXIV

In the Situation Room at the White House, it was almost one in the morning, but no one was tired. They sat riveted by the video feed from the thermal camera. The image turned constantly as the unmanned aircraft circled in a tight spiral. Though the circular motion was disconcerting, the images were clear, showing a slope of white with a cluster of boulders in the foreground and dark lines of trees farther off. Rows of white digits in the upper left corner of the picture shifted as the plane banked and turned. General Scott, holding a laser pointer, squinted at the image and placed the red dot on a dab of black among the rocks.

"Look, on the side of the rock, see that darker spot? Heat from someone's head, one of the team," he said. He moved the red dot an inch to the right. "And another. And another, right in there, between the two big rocks. That's their wounded."

He waited as the plane flew a wider circle and passed over the trees.

"There, there," he said too loudly, "in that clearing, see the Serbs? Clustered together, talking, safe from small arms. Along the edge of the trees . . ." Scott's voice trailed off as he searched the picture. "One!" He clicked on the red dot. "He won't last long if he doesn't duck back. There, he's gone, back in the woods, safe."

"Are they shooting?" the President asked.

"Every chance they get," Scott said. "The dogs have a sniper, won the East Coast championship. He's probably put down four, five of them, and the others are hanging back."

Scott forgot to say "sir." He paused as the plane passed to the south of the team.

"There, see those two faint black spots? Dead. That's body heat still leaking out," he said. "Wait, here's a better image. See these two bright black spots at the bottom of the picture? Vehicles. Engines lose heat slower than bodies. No people around them. They're disabled, abandoned. Wonder how the team took them out. That was good work."

Glances all around. The general sounded like a football coach critiquing the video of a recent game.

"Now what happens?" Cahill asked.

"Nothing until the Serbs bring up mortars, sir," Scott said. "Then they'll grind those rocks to powder."

"How long?" the Secretary of Defense asked.

"About an hour. They have to haul the tubes and shells up that slope," Scott said. "Maybe longer if our sniper taps a couple more."

The President reached for a keyboard and began typing: *Hang in there.*

The words showed on the room's center screen.

Harvell was crouching behind a boulder, watching the Quotron screen for any response to the request for support. He typed back: *Where's our fire mission?*

We're trying, the President typed, shrugging at the cabinet members. *What fire mission? What's he talking about?* he wondered.

Bullshit. The words stood out clear on the White House screen.

Whoa. Remember chain of command.

Mine's Lang.

Good leader?

Fucking best.

Hang in there.

You said that once. You don't talk Marine.

I'm the President.

I'm Bill Gates.

The President took his hands off the keyboard. *Good for you,* he thought, *give it back!*

Scott had an angry look. The others looked amused.

"Young troop, sir," Scott apologized.

"I wanted to reassure them. Didn't do it the right way, did I?" the President said. "What's this about a fire mission, General?" No such message showed on any White House screen.

"I don't know, sir," Scott asked. "May I talk with Admiral Faxon on this televideo? I'd like to find out."

The team tried not to move in the rocks. When someone did, he crawled or scrambled on his knees, offering no target to the Serbs downhill. They had been here for over twenty minutes, and their sweat had cooled, clinging to their undergarments. Under a biting west wind, they were starting to shiver as their muscles contracted. They were pinned, with open ground on all sides, and their morale was dropping with their body temperature. Only Roberts, who had taken a second shot of morphine, was feeling pretty good.

"Harvell, stop poking at that thing," he said. "Keep the channel clear."

"I was only blowing off some asshole, Staff Sergeant."

"Probably a superior officer."

"Nah, a civilian," Harvell replied. "Said he was the President."

Roberts noted that Lang's fresh mouth had rubbed off on Harvell. *President, my ass.* He'd scrub away that salty talk when they got back.

"Where's our damn mission?" Roberts said.

"We'll hear *shot out* soon. Bullard will pull the lanyard," Blade said.

"A lieutenant colonel against three stars?" Caulder laughed. "He'll pull a toilet chain."

A bullet whanged between two rocks, almost ricocheting into the enclosure where they huddled. They all flinched. Caulder, who had the downhill watch, scanned from his prone position, puzzled by the angle of the bullet.

"Up above us, two o'clock," he said, sighting in, "the idiot has climbed a tree."

"Hit the tree," Lang said.

"What?" Caulder asked. Even for Lang, this was strange humor.

"He'll be so scared, he'll drop a load and stink them out of there," Lang replied. "Go ahead, hit the tree."

Blade hit the trunk a foot above the soldier's head. The soldier slid quickly down.

"They mean to kill us," Caulder said, "and we play tag?"

A white flag fluttered at the edge of a tree line, about three hundred meters downhill. No soldier could be seen.

"We're supposed to surrender," Caulder said. "That's how this ends, isn't it? So don't piss them off by snuffing more of them, right?"

"Seems so," Lang answered. *Cos, now Roberts and his girls,* he thought. *They have to get home. I fucked this one up big-time.* He felt like vomiting; his body couldn't support him anymore. He knew that, just as he knew how much his mind had slowed down. His nerve endings felt like a giant toothache, blotting out thinking. He wanted to curl up and close down, let someone else take over. *Why did they believe I could work this out?*

"We surrender and get put on trial, we look like assholes," Caulder said. "What'd we do this for?"

Lang glanced at Harvell and Cosgrove tucked under an overhang.

"Don't look . . . at me," Cosgrove said. "Give me . . . a rifle . . . Fuck them."

No one asked who "them" was.

"I can shoot, too," Harvell said.

"Shut up, Harvell," Roberts said. "Tell me you're not serious, sir."

"What else, Staff Sergeant?" Lang said. He was beyond offering an out. His body had beaten down his brain; the Sunday marathon had come to call. "Without fire support, you think we can carry Cos and Harvell out of here? That slope's as open as a rifle range."

"The mission was getting Captain Cosgrove back, not dying out here," Roberts said. "We've chewed them up good. If we surrender, they'll waste us for payback. Hell, I'd waste us. You're the tricky one, sir. You think us out of this."

Lang couldn't think. It was beyond him. He missed her now. *She'd fight,* he thought, *she'd be as angry as Roberts.* He had to smile. He pictured her lecturing that three-star admiral for not taking care of six Marines, as if the team were her students and the admiral a college dean too busy with administrative matters. *She wouldn't take no for an answer, why should I?*

He was still smiling when he looked at Harvell. Roberts and the others looked relieved. *All right! Here comes the skipper with another wild-ass idea. Good to go!*

"Harvell, we're requesting mast," Lang said. "Send the fire mission to Pepperdogs.com. Let's find out who's listening. Post it on the Net."

The fire mission came up instantly on the left-hand screen in the Situation Room, the same request sent three minutes earlier to the Marine Ops Center.

"In thirty-seven years of service, I thought I'd seen everything," General Scott said. "He's forcing our hand before the whole damn world."

"What does it mean?" Nettles asked.

"That captain wants us to wipe out the Serbs, Mr. Secretary," Scott said. "And everyone's reading it."

"So we were not getting all the messages from that team?" the Secretary of Defense said. His face was taut and Scott thought he looked like a dog about to snap.

"It appears not, sir," Scott said.

As they and millions of others around the world read the request, a technician interrupted to say the teleconference link to the Joint Task Force was up and the NATO commander in Brussels, General Stevens, was listening in. The U.S. four-star admiral in Naples was airborne and would join the conference as soon as he could. Ambassador Briggs and Admiral Faxon came on the screen.

"Mr. President," Briggs said, taking the initiative, "I'm pleased to say we have a cease-fire, effective in a few minutes. General Kostica's talking with Belgrade right now."

The President gestured slightly, inviting the Secretary of State to talk.

"General Scott," James Rodney said, "do you have any technical military considerations?"

"That ridge is a heavy fire zone," Scott said. "It'll have to be secure before a chopper can get in."

"So we're talking a two-step process—first a cease-fire and then a pickup?" Rodney said.

"Yes, sir, if they don't break for it instead," Scott said.

"I assume this time they'll follow orders," Briggs said.

"Why wouldn't they?" Rodney said.

"That team's been capping Serbs for two days," Scott said. "We're asking them to surrender to the people they've been killing. They're scared and exhausted, and their brains may not be working too good, but they know what that means."

"Doesn't that solve it if they run?" the President asked. "I mean, they're so close to the border and all."

"They have that open field above them, sir. They'll take grazing fire. Without supporting fire, at least one of them will go down, and the rest will stay with him," Scott said, looking at the video screen. "The Serbs will mortar them till their eyeballs bleed. Then troops will get on line, two shooters on each Marine. They'll shoot them in the feet, the legs, the buttocks, back, head. Then they'll roll them over and plug them a few times in the face, so all the hits aren't in the back."

The others looked at him, as though he had belched loudly.

"That's how you fight when you've been on the receiving end too long," Scott said.

"That's why we need this cease-fire," Briggs said. "It'll work."

"We don't need martyrs," Mumford said, agreeing with Briggs. "New York City will riot if we lose them."

"My point exactly," Briggs said. "This needs a positive ending."

"The networks are staying with the story. Worldwide, twenty, thirty million people are tuned in," Mumford said. "Problem is, that J. Kirwin character may get the last word."

"He's not a character," Scott said.

"He's out of control with that website of his," the Chief of Staff continued. "Suppose the President agrees to the cease-fire and he comes back with something like 'Nuts'?"

"Oh no," the President replied, "we all know what he's really apt to say."

They smiled a little, even Scott.

"What happens is on them, not us," the Chief of Staff said. "This is a NATO matter, something for the admiral to handle. We've done everything we could to be helpful, but it's not our responsibility. They disobeyed. If they won't accept a cease-fire, there's nothing we can do. That's how we present it."

"Got a bowl for me to wash my hands when I tell the American people that?" the President said.

"I wonder why they posted that fire mission to the world," Scott said, looking at the televideo screen. "Was there a previous request, Admiral?"

The others looked at the seven or eight screens in front of them. Of course they had seen all messages from the team. What was General Scott talking about?

"The call for fire came into the admin section of the Ops Center a few minutes ago," Faxon said. "It seemed premature to bring it to this level, given the state of negotiations."

"In other words, you didn't give them fire support because you were negotiating their surrender?" Scott asked.

"I didn't think the White House was the locus for operational decisions," Faxon said. "And I object, General, to the term 'surrender.' We're working on a cease-fire."

"How do they get out *after* the cease-fire?" Scott asked.

"That's my next move, General," Briggs said. "Now, if you'll excuse us, Mr. President, we have to get back to Kostica—"

"Hold on, Mr. Ambassador, I want to be clear on what's about to happen," the President said. "At the end of this, I don't want to see yellow ribbons all across Middle America."

"And I have to know for the press briefing," the Chief of Staff said, "where does this operational chain of command stop?"

"With me," Cahill said.

James Rodney looked down at his hands. *No, it doesn't. This is a NATO decision.* But he said nothing. This was the time for silent diplomacy.

"Mr. President," a voice came over the rear speakers, "this is Hank Stevens in Brussels. I'm not up on the screen, but the audio's fine, sir. The NATO military committee meets in two hours. I, ah, promised the Secretary General that in the meantime I wouldn't change NATO standing rules."

"Meaning you won't authorize this fire mission?" the Secretary of Defense said.

"As the NATO commander, it's . . . very awkward. I don't have an execute order from the Secretary General. This is hot news over here, it's all the radios and televisions are playing right now."

"It's receiving a bit of attention over here, too," Nettles said.

"I mean the European capitals insist on being included, given the charges, murder and the like. It's not obvious this is a military operation."

"Who says it's not obvious?" the President asked.

"Spain, Germany and several others see it as a matter for the courts. There'll be a hell of a row if I ignore the Secretary General and unleash artillery now. A cease-fire'd be much better."

"Thank you, General," the President said, then turned back to the table. "I'm still not getting this. Is Faxon commanding American forces or NATO forces?"

"Both," Secretary of State Rodney said. "We agreed the Kosovo operation would be joint with our allies under NATO. General Stevens is correct. They'll be furious if we pull the rug out from under them."

"We're up to—what—twenty-five or twenty-six nations wanting to be in Nato? I've lost count," Nettles said. "Some of them are disruptive. Two dozen nations cannot make a military decision."

Briggs forced his way back into the conversation. "I have a slightly different perspective, Mr. President. We've had a solid alliance for over fifty years. We can't act unilaterally because a few soldiers disobeyed orders. The cost versus the gains doesn't make sense. The fracture would run too deep."

The President turned to his Secretary of State. "You're the world thinker. Sum this up for us. How do we get out of this mess?" No "please" in his request, no collegiality in his tone.

"After the cease-fire, the Serbs may not let them go," Rodney said. "A European judge could find them guilty of some crimes. However, we've been through worse."

"A black eye looks bad but goes away," the President said.

"It's worse if we order them to lay down their arms and they fight or the Serbs kill them. Their deaths might remain with your presidency, like Waco."

The President winced.

"This is between the Pentagon and its soldiers," the Chief of Staff said. "The President's not in that loop."

The President shook his head and waved his hand back and forth, as though erasing an imaginary blackboard. "It's too late to shut that barn door. We've read the request for the fire mission. Hell, the whole world has read it."

"It's inappropriate to drag you into operational details, Mr. President," Nettles said. "And I sure don't want to end up a caricature like Robert McNamara, using a magnifying glass to pick out bridges to bomb. The question is whether our use of force will end this or extend it. I've heard nothing that convinces me further shooting does us any good. That e-mail message is emotional blackmail."

General Scott considered the Secretary of Defense to be a bully, but a fair bully, intolerant rather than narrow-minded. Nettles pushed, but if you pushed back and knew something he didn't, he'd listen. So Scott decided to tell them what they didn't know.

"Directing fire missions is what this team does for a living," Scott said. "If we deliver what they're asking for, they may walk out of there."

Anyone at the center table could slap Scott down for speaking out of turn. No one did. He had entered a world of tactical fighting only he understood. He was taking control from the Commander, Joint Task Force, ignoring protocol, bypassing General Stevens in Brussels and all the NATO nations, talking out of turn.

"You place your high explosives like this," Scott used the laser pointer to trace a red square on the screen showing the thermal images, "then walk the barrage south. The team moves as the artillery shifts."

"That sounds like World War I, where the casualties were horrific," Briggs broke in, risking a rebuke to undercut this politically clumsy general before he upset an alliance and ruined an honorable withdrawal.

"Those casualties occurred after the barrage was lifted and the soldiers continued to advance," Scott said. "In this case, we're going away from the enemy, and the barrage is going to shift with them, not lift."

Admiral Faxon was paying careful attention. He had shoved his ego out of the way and was approaching this as an engineering problem. He didn't resent Scott now. If someone had a sound idea and offered data, he listened. The latitude and longitude of those tree lines were data, the applications of fires were data. At last, Faxon was in his element; these were tangible, physical things he could work with.

"Will this work?" the President asked.

"One short round and we lose the team," Scott replied "But it worked for a company raid at Khe Sanh, sir. We laid down five thousand rounds in six hours. We never let up."

"The leader of that team, Mr. President, has placed us on the verge of war." Briggs's florid face was distinct on the screen. "Serbs are hysterical, irrational, about their homeland. Firing like the general suggests gets us in big-time, not out. NATO will disown what we're doing. This invites disaster."

"I disagree, Mr. President," Scott said. "The Serbs have only two, three platoons up there, not dug in. We hit them hard enough to cross their eyes, they won't come back for more. I'm not talking about a fair fight. I'm talking about massacring them, wiping them out. Smash them. Grind them into the slopes. Hit them so hard the crows won't find body parts."

Once more uneasy glances around the room. Why couldn't this general be diplomatic? A euphemism like "suppressing them" or "neutralizing them" would do nicely. On the screen, Briggs was shaking his head, his hand theatrically clasping his forehead. Faxon sat with his forefinger tapping his lips, oblivious of the camera.

"This is a NATO command decision," the Secretary of State said. "We can't decide this alone. We have three heads of state wanting to speak with you, Mr. President."

"Someone should order that team to obey a cease-fire, and that's it," the Chief of Staff said. "And whoever that someone is, it's not the President."

Scott concluded his lesson in tact and diplomacy: "The battlefield's going to decide this damn quick."

Faxon understood, although he wasn't sure the others did. He prided himself on being detached under pressure, or standing outside of himself and seeing if the pieces fitted together. The President couldn't order General Stevens to ignore NATO and fire the mission, and most in the Situation Room seemed to favor the cease-fire.

So it came down to him, didn't it? Scott was talking to him, coaching him, reassuring him, prodding him. Scott was telling him the fire mission might work, but Faxon had to give the order without asking Stevens or anyone else for permission. Scott was inviting him to disobey, to ignore General Stevens and the NATO Military Committee, *just like the team had ignored him when they entered Serbia.*

"Mr. President," Faxon said, "I have some urgent coordinating to do here . . ."

"Yes, yes, of course, you're excused, Admiral," the President said.

The guy wasn't contributing anyway, the President thought.

XXV

Faxon fumbled his way out of the amtrac and breathed in the cold air. He felt demeaned. With two Navy Crosses, Scott knew battle. Still, he didn't have to rub everyone's nose in it with his country-boy bullying ways.

He was direct, though. You didn't have to strain to see any hidden face in the picture. Faxon's instinct was to fight the ship, to train a crew to bring the data together for the captain to make the right decision. That was the only way a submarine survived. That wasn't going to happen here. He'd never get these Marines to think that way. He didn't know their battles.

Providing fires to infantry seemed simple to Scott, who had called hundreds of fire missions. Who was in charge of the Supporting Arms Coordinating Center onboard the *Bon Homme*? Oh yes, that bright Navy captain who knew all about cruise missiles. Maybe he'd already come to the same conclusion as Scott and was preparing an artillery barrage. And would Faxon have listened to a Navy captain?

Briggs had him going for a while with that cease-fire jazz, talking and talking until it seemed to make sense. Kostica had seemed to go along; in the meantime, his troops were closing on the team. Why hadn't Faxon seen it earlier? How would the team get out after a cease-fire? They wouldn't. A cease-fire inside Serbia was a surrender of the team, or worse. Kostica had outfoxed Briggs all along. It came down to a choice: support them or surrender them.

The Razor looked at the bulky Marine waiting a respectful distance from the command amtrac. The admiral walked over to the lieutenant colonel. "If I order this mission, Bullard, are you set to fire it?"

"Yes, sir, up and ready."

Faxon went right on as if he hadn't heard him. "We can't employ attack choppers. Too many SAMs. Your Fire Support Center can use anything else in our arsenal—laser bombs, cruise missiles, F-Sixteens, GPS bombs, F-Eighteens, whatever."

For an instant the Razor thought he sounded like a used-car salesman. He smiled at the absurd image.

"No fixed wing in close, sir," Bullard said. "This is real danger close."

"All that investment," Faxon said, "and we've nothing precise enough for you?"

"The new stuff does a terrific job," Bullard said, "but it's hard to lase a tree line when you're on the move. I discussed this with Major General Zines, sir, and told him we'll use Dragon Fire. My one-twenty mortars should do this job."

Bullard spoke with command force, yet to Faxon the mention of mortars seemed trivial, anachronistic. This was the twenty-first century, the high-tech military, strategic standoff weapons, ready for prime time. Why, there were more combat aircraft than squads in the Joint Task Force. Faxon vaguely knew mortars existed in his command. Each tube cost less than one high-tech bomb. Hardly had seemed worth noticing.

Scattered across the wide field behind the castle were eight amtracs with open backs. Each held a large 120mm mortar on a swivel plate. Once fed the coordinates of the target, each new Dragon Fire mortar adjusted its fires with an inertial gyro and GPS computer chip. No more handheld twists of dials to level bubbles. Fifty percent of the rounds fired by Dragon Fire would fall within ten meters of the target, the other 50 percent within twenty meters.

To front-line troops closing on Americans, air and missiles were not the feared killers. Those weapons, subject to small vagaries that resulted in fifty- or hundred-meter errors, were employed far in front of the troops. What enemy infantry in close combat feared was American artillery, especially the mortar, creeping in with its controlled blast area, its short time of flight, its vertical drop into any fighting hole, any trench, any depression. Now, with the Dragon Fire, the Marines had increased accuracy and explosive power.

Near each trac was a trailer filled with powder bags and shells, each weighing forty pounds. At close range they fell almost straight down, hissing like a newspaper being ripped, the sound arriving too late to provide warning. For the past ten minutes, the Combat Ops Center and the artillery Fire Direction Center had been plotting not just one mission but a series of them. *Fire mission? We'll give you fire missions, a pluperfect plural of fire missions.*

"It's your show," Admiral Faxon said.

"Good to go, sir?" Bullard asked.

"I'll let you know." Faxon walked to the communications amtrac, intent on calling Zines and demanding to know why mortars were being used.

Bullard turned to his sergeant major. "Assemble the crews. Final brief."

It took only a few shrill whistles and yells to gather the men from their tracs. They trotted up and formed ranks, standing silent, large and imposing in their winter jackets. Bullard stood before them and projected his voice.

"This is your warning order. You know the Pepperdogs. You've trained with them. Now they're out there, cold, wet and in big trouble. On order, you will provide the support to bring them home. You have the firing data. That is all."

Any further words were lost among the cheers, hoorahs and *aaarghs!* of the ninety assembled artillerymen. The assistant director of athletics at Villanova nodded at his sergeant major, an insurance salesman from Philadelphia, who sent them running to their tubes.

"I didn't mean it that way," Caulder said. "Well, maybe I did. We're hanging tough, aren't we, sir? No white hankies."

Lang didn't answer. He couldn't believe the task force wouldn't fire. They had to. It was just taking longer than normal to get through the system. *No,* he told himself, *this one's too hot. No one will step up to this. End of the road. What do I do now?*

"Movement east side," Caulder said.

"Caulder, slide over and cover north downslope. That's where they'll put their base of fire," Lang said. "Blade and I will take the east. That's where the attack will come from."

"I got a guy humping a base plate," Caulder said. "Do I take him out?"

"Not worth it. He's a mule," Roberts said, looking sideways at Lang. "We'd better get the captain under that shelter, sir."

"No," Cosgrove said.

"He can spot for me," Caulder said.

Lang tried to remember. Was it Hemingway who had written about a band of Spanish guerrillas who dug in on a friable hilltop? They hadn't lasted an afternoon. The other side sat back and lobbed in mortar after mortar. In Basic School at Quantico, the instructors had hammered into the new lieutenants never to defend on any open slope. Yet here they were on a bare escarpment, with four knives as digging tools and layers of slate under the snow. They couldn't burrow into the scree and they couldn't move out. *Nice job, Lang,* he thought.

The others seemed to know what he was thinking.

"Not going . . . back to them," Cosgrove said.

"Fifty," Caulder said. "That's my new goal. They'll remember this."

Sprawled prone among the rocks, the team waited for a reply to their request for fire. They were spread out, yet close enough to talk back and forth without yelling. At first they didn't look at one another, instead peering intently at the not-so-distant tree lines, each watching his assigned sector. Occasional rounds zinged off the scree, each with a different pitch. They let several targets go unscathed as Serb troops unused to fire occasionally stood and ran to another position, as if they could outrun a bullet traveling fifteen hundred feet in a second. As the minutes passed without an incoming message, the team began to exchange glances. Blade was the first to break the silence.

"It was a good idea, sir," he said. "One of your best."

"Right up there with getting us out of that swamp in Colombia," Caulder pitched in. "Not your fault they won't fire the mission, Skipper. Can I get back to work? Haven't zapped anyone in fifteen mikes. The natives are getting uppity, working in closer. I have one of their honchos in my scope."

"Ammo count is two forty," Roberts said. "It'll disrupt them, sir."

"One shot, one head," Caulder said. "Harvell signs my chits."

Lang nodded. Caulder sighted in, all his energy focused on his sight picture, the rifle an extension of his body. The shot had a heavy, authoritative sound, like a sledgehammer hitting a metal spike. Caulder absorbed the recoil and peered through his scope.

"Damn, I'm good," he said. "Harvell, record that. How many does that make?"

"Twenty-three," Harvell said, checking his notebook.

"Sixty. I bet I nail sixty before this is over," Caulder said.

No one responded.

"It was a bodacious walk, sir, outrageous," Blade said, smiling.

Roberts said nothing, busy piling rocks around his AK-47 so he could fire with one arm.

"Send a message, sir?" Harvell asked, imitating Roberts and pushing together loose rocks.

"Yeah, tell the task force thanks for all the help," Caulder said.

"No, we have nothing more to say," Lang said. "I got us into this. No one else."

"So what's the plan?" Roberts said. He knew they couldn't fight their way unassisted off the slope, but they were a team and each would finish in his role. Lang did the thinking; Roberts supervised the men.

"We wait for the attack," Lang said. "Then we counterattack into their lines and cut north for the border."

"Short bursts, people," Roberts said, relieved to add something practical.

Only they won't attack, Lang thought. *They'll stand off and mortar the hell out of us. I really screwed this one up, Mrs. C.*

Onboard the *Bon Homme*, Major General Zines sat in the commander's chair in Flag Plot. He had studied every message from the team, though there wasn't much for him to do. A typical role for Admiral Faxon's deputy. Colonel Bullard insisted his regiment was planning a mortar barrage, and his fire support coordinator—a grad student on Christmas break from Columbia—was sending the instructions to a corporal with a Quotron, a bad knee and a bad attitude.

What about the Supporting Arms Coordinating Center on the *Bon Homme Richard*, with all those high-tech strike weapons, the cruise missiles and tacair? Bullard had waved them off, saying this mission had to be shot out, splash, adjust fire, shot out, splash . . . on and on. Close-in stuff like World War I, World War II, Korea, Vietnam.

"High tech has its uses, General, but we can't wait ten minutes between adjustments for the next hit. This has to be hit, hit, hit. Don't let the Serbs get their heads up," Bullard had said.

After Bullard had signed off, Zines remained unconvinced. *I'm not a potted plant,* he thought. He looked around the room. Everyone was busy except for an old colonel standing in back, staying out of the lights. Davis. Zines had forgotten about him. Poor bastard. First he loses command of the regiment and now he's shoved into a back corner. Zines walked down a narrow aisle between the computer stations and firmly shook the man's hand.

"Tom! Thank you for getting here so quickly!" Major General Zines said, half believing it. Possibly the Razor was right in relieving the colonel after the helicopter was shot down on the mountain, but there was no reason to humiliate him. "God, do I need your help."

"Must be some mistake, General," Colonel Davis said. "I was ordered to report for reassignment."

He looked shrunken, face wan and cammies mussed after the chopper flight.

"That's for the admiral to sort out later. Right now I need you as my strong right arm," Zines said. "The admiral has all these missiles and aircraft standing by, and Bullard wants to use only his mortars. I'm stuck. This is out of my league. You do this combined-arms stuff all the time."

"What do you want from me?" Davis asked.

"Command judgment, Colonel."

Davis looked at him. Zines returned the stare without blinking.

"Mortars are the right weapon in close," Davis said. "But the team needs more help isolating the battlefield—interdicting roads, taking down comm nets. I'd throw an outside shield around them, if I had command."

"They're still your people, Tom," Zines said. "Thank you."

He called the Supporting Arms Coordinating Center, one deck below.

"The Marines have set an artillery box, right?" he said. "Well, can you lay down an outer ring beyond the danger-close line?"

After a night of tracking dozens of targets—and being told all were off-limits—the intelligence and targeting sections did not hold back, once given the green light. The Supporting Arms Coordinating Center divided the cruise-missile targets among the cruisers and destroyers steaming with the carrier, each ship anxious to be included.

"Ah, *Bon Homme*, this is Kincaid, if you'll give us targeting data, we'll get started and you can fill in the rest later."

"*Bon Homme*, this is Stethem, we monitored Kincaid's request and we'd like to do the same."

"*Bon Homme*, this is the *Elliott*, request targeting data."

Within four minutes seven guided-missile destroyers and cruisers received fire missions over the classified SIPR net.

Zines was on a ship with a large landing deck for helicopters and VSTOL jets. The clatter of rotor blades and the whine of jet engines, twenty-four hours a day, reminded the one thousand embarked sailors and Marines—and the one National Guard general—of airpower. It seemed to Zines that every other officer dropping off something for him to check or to sign was a naval aviator, Marine or Navy, made no difference. All had the same message: *We're holding station right above their heads, ready to roll in.*

On the horizon was the carrier *Lincoln*, with dozens of attack aircraft and new bombs. Metastable munitions—voices dropped to whispers for Zines's ears only—this stuff was *hot*. The little molecules in those bombs rolled around and snuggled up to one another and got little hard-ons, and when they were about to do it, well, the scientists jerked them apart and they got real hot and frustrated, then they let them zip back together and presto—super heat! *Blammo!* A metastable had three, maybe four times the power of regular high explosives, like a mini nuc.

Aviano was on the phone. How had the Air Force in Italy gotten the word? The Joint Task Force had a close hold on all operational matters. Admiral Faxon would have a kitten. What happened to operational security? Right, as if the electronic intelligence boys aloft in the KC-130 hadn't figured it out from listening to the Serbs or looking at the radar tracks of the vehicles on that ridgeline. For that matter, anyone listening to the chatter among the F-18 pilots on station would know a strike was being planned. *Pilots*, Zines thought, *have their own worldview, and it begins with "if it exists, we can hit it."*

The Air Force commando unit, the Night Hawks, earlier had reminded him every ten minutes that it was dark in the valley, so they could swoop in and pluck the team out. The surface-to-air missiles? "Hell, send a few fast movers along, an F-15, to pop any radar that lights off." And what about Tor, the infrared no-warning SAM-15 Kostica was bragging about? "Hey, we'll be in and out before they blink. With all due respect, General, once daylight comes, the Marines will shoot the shit out of the place and depress real-estate prices. We're a scalpel; they're a sledgehammer."

Roger, but it was after seven in the morning, Marine time now.

In their barracks Serb soldiers joked about Vietnam; they, too, could beat Americans on the ground. The foolishness of ignorance, not understanding that the Americans had left five years before Saigon fell. Had they read about battles like Meade River, Hue City or Dewey Canyon, they would have feared what was coming. The Marines knew their business. The Joint Task Force knew its business. They might stumble in peacekeeping and nation building, but they knew how to do war.

The Razor was on the line from the amtrac. "Are you ready to fire, General?"

"On your command, Admiral."

"Stand by. I'll be back shortly."

Faxon walked over to the other amtrac with the satellite dish, ducked inside and sat next to Ambassador Briggs.

"You've missed little," Briggs whispered. "POTUS has been speaking with the NATO Secretary General. Our cease-fire's looking good."

The President was returning to the televideo conference, lips compressed. His frown left dark creases across his forehead. He looked tired.

"The consensus is for an immediate cease-fire," he said, letting his breath drain out. "Soo, unless there's something else—"

"There is, Mr. President," Faxon said.

In the White House, glances of surprise and irritation at the televideo screen. A three-star in Kosovo did not interrupt the President.

"Those Marines are under fire. As their commander, I am providing them immediate fire support. By your leave, sir."

The President was caught off guard. It was so abrupt, without warning or preliminaries. Faxon had seemed to dither, a passive man following Briggs's lead. Now he had swung to Scott's side. For a moment the silence was complete. No chair squeaked, no one coughed or cleared a throat. It was as if the sound had been cut off.

If the President overruled Faxon, he was making the decision. The Serbs would deliver the team in orange jumpsuits and shackles, if at all. If he let Faxon run with it, the decision stayed in the military chain of command, whatever the outcome. The President nodded, then realized that on televideo a nod was not enough.

"Yes, yes. Go ahead, Admiral. Good luck."

Faxon ducked out before General Stevens, both his NATO and his U.S. commander, could recover and weigh in.

The Razor swiftly walked over to the amtrac where Bullard was huddled with his fire support coordinator. It was too crowded for Faxon to crawl in, so he stuck his head in the hatch. "All set?" he asked, startling those inside.

"Uh, yes, sir," replied the captain. "A CRITIC just came in for you to call General Stevens. You can use our switch."

"I don't want to tie up your comms," Faxon said. "Inform Brussels that I'll get back to General Stevens as soon as possible."

Calculated disobedience, Faxon thought. *Now I'm doing it, too.*

"Yes, sir," the captain said, turning to a small corporal hunched over a computer. "Tell SACEUR to Wait, Out."

Marines have a way with words, Faxon thought, picturing the reaction of the Supreme Allied Commander, Europe, to the voice of a reserve corporal from Puerto Rico who normally answered the phone in a Madison Square travel agency.

"Colonel, this is your execute order," Faxon said, looking directly at Bullard. "Execute."

"Yes, sir. I'll inform the team and commence fire."

Faxon next called Zines. "Execute, General."

"Aye-aye, sir."

The Razor hung up. It took a second to register. Then he smiled; Army generals did not say aye-aye. Zines had style. Faxon turned to leave, but the regimental commander stopped him.

"By your leave, Admiral," Bullard said, "I'd like to move troops close to the border, inside the red zone, to pick up the team if they cross over."

Faxon had no hesitation. He didn't give a damn now about his career. That team was coming home. "Approved. If you determine hostile intent, engage."

Faxon backed out of the hatch, careful not to bang his head and ruin his exit. He stood erect and breathed deeply, grateful for a break to take stock. At last, by God, he had done something. He had taken command and it felt good. Someone was standing behind him, crowding him. He turned around, knowing it had to be Briggs. So much for feeling smug.

"You kicked over the lantern in there," the ambassador said. "Remember that line from *The Bridge on the River Kwai*? 'Madness, sheer madness!' Isn't that how William Holden summed it up? Are you mad?"

"They're my crew."

"So that's it. Scott got to you, did he? And who gets thrown away when this is over? Not Scott—Old Scarface is retiring. And not the Prez, no, no. His keepers will keep him clear of this." Briggs sounded both scornful and pitying. "It's your posterior at the top of the flagpole, Admiral. You can forget about that delightful villa in Naples."

Faxon wasn't angry with Briggs, only a bit surprised to hear him speak the truth. "If you'll excuse me, Mr. Ambassador, I'm going to be busy for a few hours."

"Don't condescend, Faxon. You're not starring in a replay of *Glory* or *Sands of Iwo Jima*." Briggs stood close, biting off each word. "A few hours? I spent two years hammering these venomous idiots into a cease-fire. We had the Serbs on the right track and we were working well with our European cousins. You've made a hash of that, thrashing about, unable to find one pack of, of—well, never mind what they are. You military types have put the President in an impossible position. He has to back you, but he'll be scorned as a cowboy. So go on, fetch your recalcitrants home. But don't act bloody superior about it, not after I asked you to keep those Marines on a short leash. Tell me, is that one soldier worth the backlash we're all going to feel?"

"I'm not changing my mind," Faxon said. "And I'm not going to waste time debating with you."

Briggs paused, then switched tactics. "All right," he said, throwing up his hands, "but before you start your pyrotechnics, tell Kostica straight out. He might still go for my mutual withdrawal once you've shoved his nose in it, like a puppy."

Briggs was indefatigable, Faxon had to give him that. A rubber ball of energy. They walked into the castle, Faxon tense and unsmiling, Briggs unruffled and relaxed, with no idea what a barrage meant. He grasped and dreaded the political fallout, but a few bombs? They were out-of-season Fourth of July fireworks, a few sparklers, some big bangs, a few bodies rolled in old rugs later, the detritus of geopolitics.

Kostica strode confidently back to the negotiating table. His latest report couldn't sound better. A platoon was hauling mortars up to the district guard who had the Americans trapped. This would be over in an hour. Kostica sat down and nodded at the Americans.

"Ilian," Briggs said, "something a bit nasty has come up. I'll let Admiral Faxon explain."

Kostica waved a hand. Why not indulge them?

"We open fire in one minute, General," Faxon said.

Kostica sat without moving, thinking it through. It was stupid, changing nothing. More dead, more sobbing and wailing, same result. "A few shells won't get back your trapped Marines. What is this, war by remote control?" He started to rise. "We direct our troops while we talk to each other? This is a game for children."

"Don't protest so much, Ilian," Briggs said. "You met all the time with Croats and Muslims during battles. You leave here now, and some Air Force pilot will fry your ass. We'll have to haul your burned-out Mercedes to the dump and ID your skeleton. Be sensible and stick around. We need to talk."

Kostica had no intention of being burned alive. He'd wait at the castle until the American artillery fizzled out and the team died. He got up and walked back to his makeshift command center, refusing to speak.

XXVI

The border   **8 A.M. Tuesday**

The aviators started the show. Four F-18Es came in from the east to strike at the edge of the valley floor, cutting off the Serb troops from reinforcements. The pilots centered their first drop on the two disabled vehicles, easily marked by photos from the UAVs that had been circling for the past hour. A pair of two-thousand-pound metastable bombs guided in from twelve thousand feet.

There was no warning; no sound of approaching aircraft, no spurt of flame from an antiair missile, no chatter of antiaircraft guns. The Serbs back in the tree lines felt the earth jump, throwing them off balance, some falling down. The shock wave came next, before any noise, a fist of air, hard like a powerful wave, smacking them and sucking at their ears, blowing out some eardrums. Then the sound hit, as if someone held a pot next to the ear and hit it mightily with a hammer, the head ringing, the eyes seeing stars. Boulders and dirt pelted down. No one remained standing.

Those at the tree line firing at the Americans were already prone. When the bombs released their high-energy states, the shock waves sped out, hitting the side of the ridge and bouncing off like enormous tidal waves. Under the blow, the ridge lurched a few feet sideways. The Serbs were lifted up and fell back down, suffering bloody noses, chipped teeth and bruised jaws. The thunderclap split the air, and rocks and tree limbs fell among and on them. All the fight went out of them. What weapon did the Americans have that moved a mountain? No noise of any aircraft pulling out, all bombs falling from ten thousand feet, the attack as implacable and impersonal as a wrecking ball. A ripple of concussions shook the ground before the low, growling, rolling *cruump, cruump*—body blows that could shake down tall buildings.

Then the personal killers smashed in, the heavy 120mm shells that whispered like ripped paper for two or three seconds before exploding in quick, bright flashes with great thunderclaps, clouds of dust and smoke flaring in the trees, flash after flash, crump after crump. The blows rolled on and on without surcease, the smoke thickest on the northern downslope, visibility scrubbed out everywhere.

No organized unit could communicate, no leader could rally his troops. There was little chance a Serb soldier would be wandering in the maelstrom, an arpeggio of dull, pounding crumps that trembled the ground and left a filthy gray cloud to conceal for a few seconds the charred earth. And in case there was a singular, selfless hero, hidden somewhere with a field of fire and an iron will, determined to confront the team as it moved in the center of the hurricane, smoke rounds were laid upwind to the west and, like a thick fog, rolled over the exposed field.

Alerted through the Quotron, the team had lain behind the boulders with their hands over their ears while the bombs exploded. Now, as the mortars impacted, they cautiously raised their heads. Roberts adjusted to the east, Lang to the north and Caulder to the west. Harvell handled the Quotron keyboard. From Roberts—drop five zero. From Lang— repeat fire. From Caulder—add five zero. The team waited for two more salvos to smash in before being satisfied that the tubes had the range and weren't going to veer. Then they stood and walked uphill, not running, two carried on the backs of their comrades, only Caulder with arms free, ready to shoot.

The Fire Direction Center mixed the shells. Some burst on the ground, shaking the earth and showering the tree lines with dirt and rocks, pummeling those who lay cringing, blowing out more eardrums, emitting a sulfurous stench that lingered in dry mouths. Those that had variable timing fuses blew apart above a man's head, hurling burning metal slivers at the speed of sound. The most deadly—the individual combat munitions bomblets—opened high above with little pops and scattered gray Ping-Pong balls, each packed with enough explosive to blow off a foot, shoulder or head. The pounding was unremitting, deep, smashing blow after blow after blow.

At a steady pace, the team moved uphill across the open strip. After the initial volleys, they knew there was no need for speed. On both sides and behind them the fury went on and on, wracking and scouring the landscape. Thirty explosions, sixty, one hundred, two hundred, three hundred, five hundred. Tree lines disintegrated. The snow disappeared, only blackened earth left in the wake of the explosions. Riven trees shattered into a thousand pieces, like glass dropped from a great height.

For two days the Marines at regiment had read and reread every message from Pepperdogs, and everyone seemed to know someone on the team. The guns didn't cease in three minutes, or five, or ten. They banged on and on and on, and trucks rolled in with more shells and they were expended, and more shells arrived and they were expended. Every thirty seconds there was an update of the team's position. Simple adjustments were made, verified, reverified. Fire, again and again and again. The admiral said to knock the shit out of them. So they did.

After the rear-echelon colonel had accused him of desertion, Saco drove fast in second gear back to the highway, grinding his teeth as much as the gears. He spun a hard right onto the main road, the dead boy slumping against his shoulder. Saco pushed the corpse the other way.

"That's all I need," he yelled out loud, "bringing this thing back to my sister. She'll bawl for a week, shrieking and crying. No food prepared. What I work so hard for, huh? Those fucking Americans, those fucking Americans."

He increased his speed. General Kostica had sent some armor ahead to seal off the pass, and the new snow was laced with gravel. The Toyota in four-wheel drive had no trouble gaining a grip and speeding to the summit.

"You know what that colonel's doing, don't you?" Saco roared at his cringing passengers. "He's lying to the general right now. He's never been out of Belgrade. Never been in battle. Lying prick. Damn right, I'll tell the general. To get those bastards, I need a company on the ridge, right now."

The bombardment began as they passed the Serb roadblock at the top of the mountain, the shells ripping down several kilometers to their west. Saco briefly pulled over on a high shoulder to watch. The explosions sounded muffled and deep, reverberating as they rolled across the slopes, slapping like waves at the Toyota's windows. Dirty black puffs appeared singly, then drifted slowly together like a smog-filled fog to smother the ridge. Dust blossomed and hung over the mountain, thick as the smoke from a forest fire.

"Heavy shit," Saco said. "I hope that bastard colonel is in the thick of it."

He glanced up uneasily through the windshield, despite knowing that if he was in a pilot's crosshairs, he would never see the aircraft that finished him. He had to get to the general to undo the colonel's lies. He said nothing more about hunting the Americans. He had lost that chance. He slammed his fists against the steering wheel and drove recklessly down toward the castle. The three soldiers in back hung on grimly and said nothing, knowing Saco wanted to knock out some teeth, anyone's teeth.

The team's unchallenged passage up the white slope was recorded by two unmanned aircraft flying in tight circles as the shells fell. It was a big sky and little aircraft, worth the risk of a shell hitting a forty-thousand-dollar plane for the video, which was spectacular, the thermal images unaffected by the smoke. Against the white surface, each explosion showed as a dark black puff that flared briefly and silently mushroomed before disappearing, replaced by the next blast. It was like watching the burst and bloom of black-and-white fireworks arrayed in a horseshoe. In the center of the video screens, a small cluster of tiny black dots moved slowly upslope. People watched the live feeds at the White House, at the Pentagon, in Brussels, onboard the *Bon Homme*, at the regimental Operations Center and at fifty bases worldwide. Later the major networks would play excerpts from the videotape.

The Joint Task Force delivered a quantity that brought a quality all its own. In twenty minutes seven hundred shells, eighty bombs and forty cruise missiles exploded. When the bombardment began, there were sixty-seven Serb soldiers in the tree lines near the team. When it was over, nine walked down the slopes unaided.

The White House atmosphere was restrained as they watched the successive puffs of black smoke. In the Pentagon the smiles were open and the comments enthusiastic. There were cheers on the *Bon Homme*, with the aviators claiming their explosions were much bigger. In the Combat Operations Center onshore, the Marines set up a chant: *"More! More! More!"* In Brussels, the European NATO officers initially nodded and smiled at the precise pattern, then exchanged discomfited glances as the bombardment persisted in its immoderation. It might be better, they concluded, if their ministers didn't see the whole video; it was rather long.

General Kostica sat with his radio operators as the Dragon Fire mortars banged away nearby. At first he affected indifference, his shrug reassuring his staff. *We've seen this sort of thing before. We've fought in the trenches, and Serb soldiers are used to artillery. So what if the Americans fire a few rounds? They'll see soon enough what happens to their trapped team.*

Kostica waited for the guns to fall silent. The firing went on. The windows shook from the vibrations. The radio operators and his staff exchanged increasingly nervous glances. Radio calls came in. The slope was being torn apart. No communication with the platoons that had the Americans in contact. Kostica's anger grew as he sensed that something had gone terribly wrong.

He had moved forward three Tors, the new Russian surface-to-air missiles. He told the battery commander to get ready. The Americans would send helicopters to pick up the team somewhere along the ridge. The SAM crews were anxious. Hadn't that team killed all members of a SAM unit only a few days earlier? "Don't worry about it," he told them. "This isn't a suicide mission. Yes, the Americans will counterattack after you launch your missiles. So abandon your equipment immediately. Get one helicopter, that's the order. That's all you need to do."

Five minutes later an electronic intercept aircraft sent to the Marine command amtrac a verbatim translation of his order, as Kostica knew would happen. There was nothing he could do to prevent their artillery, and there was nothing the Americans could do to prevent his surface-to-air missiles. He would play this out. In Belgrade they would know he hadn't quit. Americans would die yet.

As the team walked off the ridge, Kostica's SAM battery commanders nervously waited to shoot down the Anerican helicopters that never came.

XXVII

The President sucked in a sloppy slice of cheese and pepperoni, and the Secretary of Defense matched him. Both were excited, and why not? Few officials had watched troops maneuver in battle. General Lee, sick on the third day of Gettysburg, didn't see Pickett's charge. In Desert Storm General Schwarzkopf stopped the firing without knowing his units hadn't sealed the Iraqi escape route. Now, in the White House, they were watching live feeds from a battlefield, while a four-star general provided comments like an announcer at a football game.

The video screens were momentarily blank, the team somewhere in the tree lines. In the Situation Room, they were waiting for the team to make contact with an American unit.

"Thank God we have such men," the President said in a low voice. "They're so damn capable. They've set one hell of an example."

"Capable? Yes, sir. Example? We have to be careful of that," Nettles said. "My staff says there's talk of insubordination because they tuned out the task force. No way I'm offering a public judgment. If pressed, I'll say the admiral was conducting an orchestra and they were improvising jazz. That's it. The military has to handle this."

"They disobeyed because they're reserves?"

"Well, they sure aren't careerists. Once they decided to go after their buddy, they knew they were finished. What do they care about a fitness report? They're the backbone of the nation—our individualism, our Minute Men." The Secretary of Defense laughed shortly. "Mr. President, I don't know how a regular unit would have reacted. But I do know joint task forces mix up organizations too much. Why have a Marine Corps if every operation is joint? Why have an Army or Navy or Air Force? Something like this was going to happen sooner or later. I just want it to end well, minimize the damage and prevent a recurrence. I need my sleep at night."

The team walked out, safe and unscathed inside the cocoon of coordinates sent by a twenty-four-year-old fire support coordinator orchestrating the fury. The guns fired and fired, and the earth shook under explosion after explosion, and the thick smoke of smoldering trees mingled with the acrid stench of gunpowder. When the team reached the edge of the uphill tree line, Harvell sent a one-word signal, and the guns shifted downhill.

Once across the open area, the team disappeared from the thermal video screens into the narrow slot in the uphill tree line left untouched for their passage. Harvell and Cosgrove were again strapped into the toboggans, and the team was Oscar Mike—on the move. Stands of twisted timber hid them from the observation posts in the valley. With luck, the artillery barrage looked like covering fires for a helicopter rescue, and the Serbs' attention would remain on the rocks, now set off on three sides by hundreds of twisted, smoldering stumps.

The team didn't pay much attention to the soot smell and the gray grime staining their faces. The finish was near. They could feel it, like sailors smelling land after months at sea. Another hour, perhaps. Their GPS receivers needed a fairly clear line of sight to the satellites, as did the Quotron for sending digital text. By hiding among the thickest trees, they were out of communications, but they weren't concerned. Any pursuers would be cautious and lag far behind, fearful of another hellish barrage.

The gaps in the Serb lines, where militia units had gone home, were apparent on the radar and thermal screens of the airborne intelligence collectors. It was too cold to shut off the vehicle engines, and the location of each Serb unit shone brightly in the scopes. It was simple enough to direct the team toward the areas where there were no emissions, no troops. There were those on the *Bon Homme* who favored expending cruise missiles against every bunker and every lonely truck, but they were overruled. The ridgeline had so many gaps that it would be difficult to direct the team *toward* an intact Serb force.

The final climb was anticlimactic. No soldiers fired at them, no Marine caught a cramp or twisted a knee. They trudged slowly and said little until they felt that the downward slope they were plodding might not be just another small saddle. They waited while Blade angled off to take a reading. He walked back, smiling slightly.

"Bingo. We're one hundred meters into the red zone. There's a road half a click to the west. It cuts down toward the castle. We are headed home."

"Do they have bunks in the brig?" Caulder asked.

"We get to the road or a clearing, we medevac," Lang said. *If I say we all need a medevac,* he thought, *it'll go down easier for Roberts.*

No one said anything. They followed Blade single file at a slow pace. Lang noticed that Roberts walked between Blade and Caulder, talking to each of them. *They'll all bitch a little,* Lang thought, *but I'll ignore them. We're beat. We'll ride out.*

They reached the logging road, and Lang was surprised at the heavy tire tracks and the mess of footprints heading south.

"Arty flushed them," Blade said, pleased that he had figured it out before Lang. "Every refugee or smuggler within ten miles must have been scared shitless."

Lang glanced around. The road was little wider than a car. "Harvell, request a medevac, lead bird fifteen mikes ahead with C-4 packets and a cable. We'll blow some trees to make room."

"Three clicks to the castle, sir," Blade said.

Lang looked at the beaten snow. *Here it comes,* he thought, *what's the matter with these guys?* He was close to sick each time he thought about Roberts's hand, how smashed it was, pierced through dead center. No way he'd grow those nerves back. Double muster out from the Marines and the New York fire department. *There go his pensions.* Why had he left Roberts outside at the monastery?

"We've done it," he said. "No gestures."

"Hand's numb," Roberts said. "Another hour makes no difference to it."

Lang looked toward Cosgrove's toboggan.

"I'm with . . . the team," Cosgrove said.

What could he do when Cos went stone dumb? Lang recognized the boneheaded truculence, like the time that jerk wrestler mocked him and he insisted Lang stay behind and came back with a broken nose. Mrs. C. was really frosted about that. And then Cos tried out for football at 150 pounds and got two ribs broken. At least Mrs. C. had seen the absurdity in that.

Roberts worked him, Lang thought. *I'll ignore him.*

Blade scuffed at the snow. "We've gone only a hundred miles. The Nez Perce went from Oregon through Montana to get to Canada."

Lang looked at Blade. "You think we're competing against dead Indians?"

Blade nodded. "Knew you'd get it, sir."

"You can't call an evac this close, Mark," Roberts said. "You owe Cos and me. We want to finish this. You're not our father."

Never, never, did Lang expect Roberts to use his first name, to refer to Cosgrove as Cos, to put this on a personal basis. *Father? What the hell is that all about?*

Harvell was typing away. *To his adoring public,* Lang thought, *not asking for a medevac.*

"Caulder, let's pick the trees to cut out a landing zone."

"It'll take an hour to blow the trees, sir," Caulder said. "My hands are numb."

"That's it," Lang said, "when Caulder becomes subtle, I give up. If you're all determined to walk in, we'll walk in, like those Indians."

"Oh no, sir, they didn't make it," Blade said. "The army stopped them at the border."

"It's a good thing you didn't tell me that on Sunday," Lang said.

One more hour. Finish strong.

"One last thing," he said. "Once we're back, we may be separated and asked to give statements. Fault on me. I ordered you on the mission."

"You say what you want, Skipper," Roberts replied. "We say what we want."

The others nodded.

"All right, if you're going to be hard-asses, then don't talk or sign anything. We'll wait for the lawyers. Now, let's di-di."

Dr. Evans stood in the Combat Operations Center looking at the monitors.

"Colonel Bullard wanted a log. Well, here it is," she shouted to a grinning audience of fifty Marines. "In two days the dogs walked a hundred miles in the snow, no fire, no heat, temps below freezing. According to message traffic, they fought eight engagements. The monitors show Blade's condition as green, Caulder, Roberts and Lang are borderline red. All ambulatory. For you jarheads, that means they're walking out!"

A round of cheers, whistles and hoorahs.

"Blade beat Lang!" a stocky corporal yelled.

"Blade's in better condition than Lang?" a major with thick glasses said. "No way."

"Lang was under more stress," Evans said, "he did all the thinking."

Boos from the Blade faction, cheers from the Lang faction.

They walked down the narrow trail in single file, Blade and Caulder leading, with Harvell in tow.

"One hundred miles," Caulder said, checking the log on his GPS, "not up to Indian standards."

"They'll be proud of me," Blade said. "On their walk, they lost their war chief."

"Now you tell me," Lang said.

Roberts walked alongside Lang, who was pulling Cosgrove.

"Didn't mean to overstep any bounds, sir," Roberts said when the others couldn't hear. "I had to finish this."

"Yeah, yeah. Inciting a mutiny, disrespect of a superior officer, willful intransigence, transgression of military parameters."

"You have to clean up your language, sir. An officer shouldn't talk dirty."

They walked on. The toboggans slid easily over the packed snow. The logging road zigzagged at a gentle drop, hugging the contours of the hill.

"Blade and Caulder will avoid a court," Lang said. "Harvell too. And he's coming out of this with his shit together."

"Captain, you know a lot and you have a big vocabulary, but you're dead wrong. Harvell's a con job. He'll never amount to anything."

"You're still pissed about Penelope."

"Evette, sir, Evette. She's nice. She'll attend your court-martial."

Lang hesitated, wondering if he should go on. Why not? The operation was over, and Roberts was the closest confidant he had.

"We lit up a lot of people," Lang said. "Caulder called them roadkill."

"They chose this business. Nobody put a gun to their heads." Roberts paused. "Well, we did, but you get what I mean."

They laughed. Their tongues were as loopy as their thoughts.

"Know what sucks?" Lang said. "The ones who took Cos are still out there. The bad guys got off."

Roberts was thinking how to answer that when Blade froze them with an arm signal. They all dodged off the track on the upslope side. From down the path, voices traveled clearly to them, some high-pitched and nervous, some bass and throaty, shouts and curses exchanged back and forth.

"Sounds like Americans learning Albanian," Blade said, "and locals telling them to stuff it. Can I practice my Nez Perce?"

The team pulled back deeper into the brush, left Cosgrove and Harvell sitting up with their rifles at the ready and crept forward.

"*Das trua! Das trua!*" Below them somewhere Marines were screaming for weapons to be put down.

"Our land. You leave! You leave!" Muslim guerrillas or Serbs were yelling back.

The trees were thick here, and the team wasn't going to push forward into a confused firefight. Blade and Lang took out their intrasquad radios and searched the channels. The FM sets were bought commercially for seventy dollars and had no encryption, but they were handy for communicating inside a platoon.

"Got 'em," Lang said. "Channel fourteen."

A strained voice was giving orders. "Enders, push the SAW more out to the left! Enders, goddamn it, answer up!"

Grinning at Blade, Lang came up on the net, squeezing the push-to-talk button. "Sullo, what are you doing here in the bush? You're a watch officer pogue."

There was silence on the radio net—whoever Enders was, he knew this wasn't the time for him to speak—then Sullo demanded, "Lang, where the hell have you been?"

"Nice recovery, Sullo, nice. We're up above you. You're due south from us about two hundred meters."

"You crazy bastard. You okay?"

"Functioning."

"All right! But we got a problem, a face-off with some assholes in Serb uniforms who say they're guerrillas."

"How many?"

"About a platoon. Cobras inbound. I may have to smoke them, so you pull back."

Lang could hear the excitement in Sullo's voice. After eight years in the infantry, he was on the verge of his first firefight. He was deploying his weapons, marking his lines, setting up for gunship runs. Soon he'd pop smoke to mark the run. This was no time to be a Serb or a guerrilla. Either was a target as far as Sullo was concerned.

"Negative," Lang said. "We're beat. We're not, repeat not, going back up that ridge. Don't you have a Translator?"

"Not on this op. We were looking for you. Now you're screwing us up. Come on, move out of there."

Caulder had crawled to a fallen log to scope the front. Now he crawled over to Lang. "It's that German dude," he said. "Remember? I popped his driver the other day and you got pissed."

Lang turned back to the radio. "Sullo, have any cold-weather rations?"

Sullo didn't respond, determined not to play one of Lang's games with Cobras inbound.

Lang pressed to talk again. "We'll settle for MREs. We're not proud."

"Stop screwing around, Lang. This is serious."

"So's starving, man. Look, his name's Baba, and he's not into suicide. We'll back him off and you provide us MREs. Agreed?"

"I'm not agreeing to shit."

"Then work those Cobras around us."

"I don't know where you are, you mother!" A pause. "Okay, I'll hold the Cobras on station for five mikes."

"Good. Give me a minute to get his attention. Don't shoot uphill!"

"Lang, you're a pain in the ass when you get like this. Out here."

Lang crawled forward with Caulder while Blade and Roberts covered the flanks. They were cautious and nervous. None wanted to be shot so near the finish line by some scared rifleman, Serb, Muslim or Marine.

Lang grabbed Caulder by the arm. "If this goes hot," he said, "don't let them close on Roberts. He can't shoot with one hand."

"No shit, sir," Caulder said, opening his eyes wide.

"I mean it, Caulder."

"Okay, Skipper, I read you six by. I'll cover his ass," Caulder said, grabbing Lang's arm. "You'll sign my chit this time?"

"Only if it's a head shot," Lang said, "clean."

As he crawled away, Lang had a nagging thought. *Caulder wouldn't . . . would he?*

Caulder wiggled forward, stopping now and then to squint through his scope. When he had the sight picture he wanted, he attached the bipod and swept his scope over several troops in Serb uniforms, all looking downhill toward Sullo's Marines. When Caulder picked up a gray peak-billed cap, he gestured for Lang to crawl forward. Lang looked through the scope at the strained, hawkish features of Baba's face. He was at the far edge of shouting distance.

Lang and Caulder wiggled back a few feet into defilade and together shouted, "Baba! Baba!" No shots came their way. Good. They shouted again from cover, knowing the guerrillas were now very nervous, cut off from behind.

"Recon, recon!" Lang shouted.

"Yes, recon! Yes, yes!" Baba's clipped voice reached them.

"He's standing up, coming this way," Blade said.

Baba strode up the road, a German gray overcoat over his tight-fitting uniform. Lang stood up and slowly walked to the bushes at the edge of the road.

"No one point a weapon at anyone," Lang said when they were a few feet apart. "No accidents."

Baba yelled something, and soon his men filed out onto the road, weapons slung or pointed at the ground.

"You are famous!" Baba said, smiling, as the team came forward. "The world knows about you." He was beaming like a proud father at his firstborn. And why not? Now he was part of a tale that would be on TV. This wasn't a Marine captain anymore. This was a *celebrity*.

Sullo and the Marines emerged as the Cobras circled for a look, pilots and door gunners alike taking pictures with their personal cameras. Captain Ben Sullo was shorter than Lang and much cleaner. He wanted to embrace Lang, but neither was into hugging. Sullo settled for warmly welcoming the team. "You look like shit," he said.

"Someone put a pea under my mattress," Lang said.

Marines pried apart a Claymore and cut off large hunks of C-4, and soon the team was sipping coffee and wolfing down MREs. The men didn't ask the team many questions, simply kept offering them food, along with repetitions of "How's it going?," "Looking good, man," and "Way to go, recon."

Sullo was nervous about Baba's men, who clustered around as though they deserved to be part of the reunion.

"How do I disarm them?" he asked Lang.

"You can't without a fight," Lang replied. "They'll leave. You've blown them. Nice work."

"You make fools of Serbs," Baba said to Lang. "That's good."

"We have to collect your weapons," Sullo said.

It wasn't quite true, but he was thinking about it. Baba studied him, then shouted some orders. His troops started to line up, and from back in the trees, an engine sputtered to life. A large tractor with enormous back wheels trundled out, towing a wagon with high wooden sides and no top. It was jammed with at least a dozen old people, women and children. Baba waved for it to drive down the track leading to the border. The adults wore gloomy, stoic expressions. Standing among them was the Muslim woman from the cabin. She smiled at Lang and Roberts.

The children were looking back wide-eyed, talking and clutching one another. A small boy bundled in so many layers he could scarcely stand tugged at the sleeve of the next boy. He pointed to Lang and waved. Lang returned the wave with a small grin, and all the children began to wave. The tractor and wagon tottered out of sight.

"What'd he hold them for?" Caulder asked.

"A Serb general's down at the castle," Sullo said. "I'll bet that tractor came along and he was holding them so they wouldn't blow his ambush."

Sullo spoke to Baba. "Only we came instead, right?"

Baba shrugged. "The Serbs are careless on their radios."

Some Marines were continuing to give the guerrillas hard stares. Why not disarm them? So what if they fought? All the better. The Cobras buzzed back and forth overhead.

"Good-bye, recon," Baba said, leading his men up the road. "We see you on CNN, huh?"

Sullo watched them go, then turned to Lang. "I'll call tracs to pick you up."

"I told the team we'd walk in, finish it on our own. It's what, only two clicks?"

"I don't know, Mark," Sullo said. "You're in a world of crap. The admiral's at the castle. So's Bullard."

"Tell them we're Oscar Mike. What's another forty minutes?"

"Nothing much to you. For me? An ass chewing, relief of command, unsat fitrep, end of a promising career. But why bother you with little details?"

"Good. I knew I could count on you."

They repositioned the toboggans, Harvell sheepish under the jibes several Marines threw at him for malingering, Cosgrove grinning, his face now a healthy black and blue, less pus yellow. Blade led off, Caulder and Lang picking up the tow ropes, Roberts at the rear. Charlie Company moved off the road to let the team pass. As they did, one hundred and thirty Marines saluted.

XXVIII

It was after one in the morning on the East Coast. Thanks to Harvell's website, the press staffs had stayed with the story through the night, broadcasting the rescue, the chase, the prodigious fire mission. Reporters were in the briefing rooms at the White House and the Pentagon, anxious to wrap it up. This was the lead for the morning news.

At Sylvia Cosgrove's house, friends who had gathered to commiserate stayed to watch the team complete its journey. Sylvia's death had been sudden, but her illness had been known for months. Her passing seemed eased by news of her son's rescue. Alex and Katharine alternated between watching television and talking with friends. Father Tom became chief coffeemaker and greeter at the door.

Woody's apartment in New York City was jammed with beer-drinking traders planning a raucous homecoming for Tyler and Mark. Every half hour they called the Cosgroves' about one disconnected subject or another. Each time Tom handed the phone to Bart, a link to normal living.

In the Situation Room, the President was in a jocular mood.

"I haven't been up this late since the campaign," he said. "Fantastic job! I can't wait to congratulate that team."

His advisers looked at one another. The Chief of Staff took the lead.

"It's time we let all our fine assistants and undersecretaries get to bed, Mr. President," Mumford said. "Great job, guys. No need to get to work before six."

After the expected chuckles and congratulations subsided, the cabinet members waited for the next act, the President setting the tone.

"What's on your mind, John?" the President asked when the room had emptied.

"Keeping distance from these Marines, Mr. President," the Chief of Staff said. "There was a lot of killing."

"The Serb president turned Milosevic over to The Hague," Secretary of State Rodney said. "He'll demand we do the same with this team, or he's finished with his electorate."

"We're occupying part of Serbia. We'll ignore him," Nettles said. "Admiral Faxon will handle this."

The President looked at the Chairman. "General Scott?"

"Admiral Faxon may bring charges, sir. It's clear he thinks the team jumped ship. In their view they did it to save a buddy from being eaten by sharks. At the least, there'll be a full-fledged hearing."

The Secretary of Defense looked up sharply in disbelief. "If you're suggesting Faxon is so rigid he'd award them medals *and* courts-martial," Nettles said, "you'd best talk with him before he hears from me. Whatever happened to common sense?"

"I trust you'll find a way of conveying that, General," the President said.

"Inside the U.S. command, yes, sir. We'll have to invoke the status of forces agreement, though, to keep this from The Hague. We can't let peacetime rules apply. A court will give Lang a bucket, a twenty-watt bulb and a bare wall for the next thirty years. That team killed because they thought it was war."

"That's my point," the Chief of Staff said. "No matter what happened out there—which we may never fully know—this is sticky. The Pentagon should handle any homecoming, Mr. President. Please stay away from this."

The President hesitated. He felt fond of those Marines. He almost smiled, thinking of Harvell telling him to go to hell. He'd love to see the corporal's expression as he shook his hand. And Lang—he wanted to look that man in the eye. He knew what he'd see there, a twinkle and a hint of craziness.

"Sounds right. This was a military affair, after all," Cahill said. "General Scott, you'll see the homecoming is done with restraint?"

"Yes, sir," Scott said, sitting at attention.

The President looked at Scott, who looked straight back. The Twin Blues.

"Excuse us a moment," Cahill said. "General, step into my corridor office for a sec."

He didn't speak until he and Scott were alone. "You want me to give them a hug or a pat on the ass, don't you? You think I'm letting them down."

"Not my place, sir."

"No, no, it is your place. They're your people. I want to hear what you're thinking. That team stirred up a hornet's nest, General. I'm a politician, and that means balancing things. I have an agenda, a health bill to get through. The important thing is that we got them out."

Scott knew he was expected to agree. "With all due respect, sir, I believe they got themselves out. The rest of us complicated a simple loyalty."

The President's eyes narrowed into the "I'm in command" squint his children said made him look like Lang.

"You want me to endorse them, General. Well, it's too complicated for that. I'm not going to antagonize Europe and risk finding out later they had feet of clay. You heard my advisers. If your colleagues should have helped sooner, that's up to you to straighten out. Don't bring it across the Potomac."

The squint was replaced by a quick smile as he patted Scott on the arm and herded him back inside the Situation Room. "I'll have them over—after you've looked into it. My kids won't speak to me if I don't. Now let's enjoy watching them come home."

The switchback trail down to the castle was packed smooth by decades of logging trucks; the descent required little effort. As the team neared the valley floor, the road stopped following the contour lines and ran straight downhill, the flat ground below providing a runoff for any vehicle or wagon going too fast. Lang retied his rope to the rear of the toboggan and let Cosgrove slide down in front of him.

"First thing . . . I call . . . Katharine," Cosgrove said.

Lang nodded. Good for Cos. Less pause between his words. Lang planned to call Bart. *Did Sylvia really know about Ty before she died?* What he wanted to ask was, *Did she say anything about me?* But he'd never ask it.

"Doc Evans . . . med . . . priority," Cos continued, "we . . . go home."

Lang said nothing. His friend was going home alone. There would be no "we." He idly tried and failed to remember the name of the three-star admiral. He'd never seen him. Colonel Bullard would probably present the charges.

He felt numb, light-headed. Thoughts flickered like the snow driven by the wind. *Out with five, back with six. Proud of team. Mrs. C. gone. The Corps probably gone. That kid at the snow trac, the cries in the bush at the monastery, that grenade I threw at the wounded in the field . . . why didn't they stay out of it?*

Saco drove back to the castle, where he had been on Sunday. With every turn and counterturn, his anger built. The four-wheel drive saved them twice from going over, the soldiers in back hanging on with white knuckles and clenched teeth while Saco cursed the vehicle, the snow, the mountain, the road, the *hadjuks,* the Americans, Luc, the stupid dead nephew, the Americans. Always he returned to the Americans.

He couldn't escape his fear. Luc had been tough. Luc had dropped three *hadjuks* at eight hundred meters—they had paced it off from the posts where they had tied the prisoners—and those Americans had smashed him up like he was target practice. And the others at the monastery, all riddled. Then the ambush on the ridge, the platoon chopped up, the fields of fire so precise, so continuous. Saco had run. So what? What was once in three years? The colonel had never been out there. He didn't see what those Americans could do.

At last they were at the bottom and the soldiers breathed again. Saco drove west in the growing light. Up ahead was the intersection with the highway. A quick left turn and they felt the macadam under the snow, accelerating now, the castle straight ahead to the south, the American artillery pieces and tracs clearly visible, along with the Serb antiaircraft vehicles Kostica had brought with him.

Saco felt a little better. He could explain things to the general. First he had to cross the checkpoint at the bridge. No problem. He was chief of the bodyguard. He was Saco.

There was a tractor on the bridge, surrounded by *hadjuks* waiting while the driver argued with the two guards. Saco skidded the Toyota to a halt behind the towed wagon and got out. The refugees turned to see a huge man in a bear coat lumbering toward them, his face red with rage, cursing unintelligibly. They crowded against the flimsy bridge railings to let him pass. The stream, not a stone's throw in width, had a film of ice reaching out from each bank, not quite joining at the center.

The driver took one look at the enraged giant and got back into the tractor's high seat, frantically pushed it into reverse, not looking back, forgetting the attached wagon. The trailer jackknifed to the left. The driver tried to go forward to straighten out. The guards and the giant were yelling at him. He stalled the motor and hopped down, not knowing what to do next.

The giant was now standing a few meters from the open wagon, roaring at the hapless farmer to get the tractor and its load off the bridge. The refugees cowered and clung to one another. Litjie in her bright blue coat shrank back, trying to hide in the center of the pack. Had the giant found his dead soldiers, their eyes pecked out by the birds? She let go of her son's hand and crawled over the back of the wagon, squeezing against the guardrail of the bridge and dropping low, out of sight.

Saco's face had turned from red to crimson. The more he screamed, the more he worked himself into a rage. Listen to the *hadjuks*, bleating and whimpering.

"Shut up!" he screamed. "Shut the fuck up!"

Should have exterminated them when Milosevic had power, he thought, *before the Americans came.* It wasn't natural, how those Americans had killed his nephews, and those soldiers on the ridge, and Luc. They had some secret superweapon, probably cost a billion Euros, maybe a nuclear rifle. How could he fight alone against those Americans?

And why had the Americans come? For this scum, this vermin who carried diseases, maybe the plague. Saco had heard about terrier dogs dropped into betting pits to kill hundreds of rats. His small, bearlike eyes glinted at the thought. With a straight-arm shove, he sent the farmer sprawling.

"When I tell you to move, you move!" Saco shouted.

He grasped the hook fastening the wagon to the tractor and jerked it out. The tongue of the trailer pitched forward and the wagon tilted, the refugees gasping and clutching the low sideboards as if clinging to a lifeboat in a pitching sea. Behind the wagon, Litjie squeezed herself smaller. The terrier glowered at his prey. The refugees shrank backward, the wagon teetering like a seesaw. The quicker ones began hopping out onto the sturdy bridge.

Saco laughed and grasped the thick pole that connected the wagon to the trailer. A quick run would drop them all into the freezing waters. He tried to shove, but there was too much weight and he couldn't gain traction. The other refugees were now tumbling out of the wagon, banging elbows, knees and heads, not feeling the pain in their frantic escape. Saco could see someone pinned between the wagon and the guardrail. Good, he'd send at least one off the bridge and then be on his way. He set his legs and began to push.

At the castle no one paid attention to the small traffic jam at the flimsy checkpoint up the hill. The angle was such that the Marines could see only part of the bridge and the crowd gathered there. They didn't care anyway. All eyes were on the slope farther back, where first one armed figure, then another, emerged from the tree line.

"That's Blade!" yelled a large sergeant. "He carries his rifle in the crook of his arm."

A lieutenant with binoculars said, "Looks like Caulder behind him. I can't tell who he's dragging."

In their excitement, they looked only at their fellow Marines, ignoring the refugees at the bridge. Lieutenant Colonel Bullard stood near the road with his men. Vice Admiral Faxon stood back at the amtracs. This moment belonged to the Marines. Ambassador Briggs was inside soothing General Kostica, who refused to come out.

The team was strung out on a steep downhill stretch leading to the highway. Blade was the first to see the tan Toyota drive up to the bridge and stop behind a tractor. He was relaxed, looking at the castle, his mind slow to process what he was seeing. *Is that the same pickup? What's it doing here?* Part of him was screaming, *Code red! Code red!* But he was too close to the end to believe it. There was the castle, and some troops waving. Someone probably waiting to press charges, too. He knew his mind was drifting. Time to get a second opinion.

"Captain up," he yelled, projecting no sound of danger in his voice.

Caulder halted and stepped on the tow rope to keep Harvell from sliding. Lang parked Cosgrove at an angle and walked forward to Blade, who pulled out his binoculars. Lang did the same.

They saw the huge man flailing his arms, unhooking the trailer, the refugees edging back, jostling one another. The farmer was driving his tractor off the bridge, leaving behind the wagon, which blocked the bridge. The giant grasped the tongue of the trailer and shoved with sudden power, smashing the rear of the trailer into the flimsy wooden guardrail. The wheels left the bridge, and the trailer tipped forward and fell with a large splash into the water, breaking off some pieces of ice. The woman seemed to fly for an instant, the blow knocking her into space beyond the trailer, a bright blue bundle suspended above the stream. Then she, too, dropped straight into the water, unseen by the Marines at the castle.

Lang watched this, a frenzy of action over in less than half a minute. "Shit!" he said as he saw Litjie splash into the water.

He dropped his binoculars and ran downhill, dropping his rifle, his long legs churning and picking up speed as his exhausted, knotted muscles loosened. Blade was watching Saco stride back to his pickup before he grasped that Lang had gone. He dropped his binoculars and ran downhill, carrying his rifle. Lang was over ten meters in front of him, in full stride.

"Caulder, shoot, shoot!" Blade yelled.

Caulder snapped out of his daze, fumbled to detach the rope to Harvell and ran forward. He looked for a target. He saw Lang running and Blade scrambling to catch up. *What? Where?* He saw the tan Toyota lurching off the south end of the bridge, wheels spinning, refugees hugging the sides of the bridge as it passed. *What? Shoot the Toyota?* Too late, the angle blocked by the refugees.

Harvell was yelling, "It's that bastard! It's the bastard!"

Roberts was at his side, in one sweeping glance taking it in. "Cover! You cover. I'm going with the skipper." He ran clumsily downhill.

Harvell was struggling to get out of the toboggan, shouting, "I saw her go in. I'm going down." He limped downhill, hobbling in a straight line, his knee holding as long as he didn't move sideways.

"Ah, shit, shit," Caulder said.

He had no target, no sense of what was going on. Cosgrove crawled forward and picked up Lang's binoculars, wiping them clean.

"I'll spot. Bridge is twelve o'clock."

That relieved Caulder. He could concentrate on taking someone down if Cosgrove figured out who that someone was. Caulder lay down in the snow, attached the bipod stand and focused the scope. But on what? The bridge? The guards? In the binoculars, Cosgrove had Lang in zoom. Lang had reached the bank, was shedding his jacket.

No! Cosgrove thought. Lang had launched himself. He was in the water, arms and legs churning. The woman was underwater by a foot or two, a blue spot clear in the frigid waters. Lang was splashing with a powerful, awkward overhead stroke, head above water, boots on. He grabbed her blue coat and tugged for the bank at a furious rate.

Blade plunged into the water up to his hips. He felt like he had been shot with a giant stun gun. His testicles crawled into his stomach, his stomach drew into a hundred knots. He couldn't breathe. How could Lang be out there? He held out the butt of his rifle, dragged Lang in, grabbed the blue coat and hauled the woman ashore.

Lang was shaking convulsively, trembling so badly it looked like he was having an epileptic fit.

Blade, too, was gasping and shaking, scarcely able to hold on to the woman. He jammed his thumb deep into the side of her neck. No pulse. He placed his ear next to her mouth. No breath. He lightly touched her jaw, and the head flopped to one side.

"Broken neck," he said.

• • •

At the Combat Operations Center, they were all smiles, listening to the radio reports, the team in sight. A few more minutes and it would be all over. Dr. Evans had her medical kit packed, three corpsmen and two choppers waiting. About time to leave. Another glance at the monitors.

What? Lang's pulse going from 70 to 130, staying there for twenty, now thirty seconds.

"Lang's over the line, far over!" she shouted. "Somebody get on the net. Get me a report. Talk to me, somebody! Get that slick airborne! Lang's in trouble, big trouble! Move! Move!"

Now Blade was up to 120. What was going on?

Saco drove straight ahead, the castle not a hundred meters up the road, a large group of Americans off to his right, looking at something behind him. He turned off the road into a field, driving around them. Before him, stretched across the far end of the field, was a line of yellow tape. Two Marines manning a machine gun behind a few sandbags next to a gap in the tape motioned him to halt. The old Serb major who had been Kostica's aide for three years hurried forward. "Okay, okay," he said to the Marines, "they're with us. General's bodyguards. Is okay."

"They got a wounded guy," a sentry said.

The sentries looked at one another. The Serb major was the liaison for the Serb general's party.

One Marine shrugged. "All right, sir. But we're not giving aid to that injured man. This vehicle goes into your sector and stays there. NATO rules."

Saco drove past them and parked near the castle, next to the truck with the antiaircraft gun. He got out and gestured to his men to drag out the dead nephew.

"What are you doing?" The major's voice was sharp, high-pitched. "Put that thing back inside. You, Saco, stay by the truck. I'll inform the general."

Saco drew himself up. *If I puff hard, I can blow him away, the little shit.* "I must see the general right away. The Americans—"

"The Americans are marching down the road as we speak. What's the matter with your eyes? And you don't demand to see anyone. The general has ordered you held. Desertion. Wait here."

The major went inside. Saco walked to the door, lounged next to it and looked around. The other Serbs were avoiding his glances. He didn't care. He would speak to the general the instant he came out. One of his soldiers hovered nearby, trying to act relaxed, frightened by the major, clinging close to Saco. The other soldier, less aware, wandered over to admire the antiaircraft guns, climbing into the seat and poking at the controls.

Saco was bewildered. *Desertion? Charges?* They wouldn't dare. Yet no Serb came near him, no smiles, no pats on the shoulder. Those fucking Americans. He was Saco, he had killed eighteen *hadjuks* in ten minutes— the record. *Desertion? Desertion!* One chance, name it, anything. He'd put it right.

XXIX

Blade was down on one knee, his cold hand on the icy face of the woman. No one could be as cold as he felt, no one.

Roberts had come up, breathing hard. One glance told him Lang was in shock. "She's dead, sir," he yelled at the captain.

Lang reached down and grabbed the sopping blue coat, easily lifting the limp body, throwing her over his right shoulder, her head lolling against his neck. He was shaking, and he clasped his arms together under her buttocks, shifting the weight as he walked up the bank.

Roberts ran alongside him. "Not our mission, sir. Remember we said no more civilians? Skipper, let her go! She's not our mission!"

"Whhhoooo tthhheen?" Lang shuffled along, his eyes fixed on the pickup behind the yellow tape.

The refugees stood back, and the Serb guards had the sense not to move. Lang gained momentum and moved at a fast clip toward the castle, walking stiff-legged, hugging the woman to him and leaning slightly backward as he shuffled along. Roberts and Blade trotted after him.

Lang's mind was blank. He flexed his arm muscles to arrest their quivering. He locked on the Toyota. For him nothing else existed. He could do this. His body was shaking. He hugged her more tightly.

He didn't see Colonel Bullard next to him, didn't hear him yelling, "We'll take her, Captain. We'll take her. Mark, put her down!" Bullard turned to give orders to the Marines who stood gawking.

Roberts had spotted the big man in the bear coat on the far side of the yellow tape. The Marine sergeant veered to his left off the road, crossed a drainage ditch and walked in a field parallel to Lang. From there he had an open shot. No time to stop and explain to the colonel. He was holding the AK in his right hand, barrel down. He slipped off the safety.

"Blade, spread starboard!" he yelled. "Get tactical!"

Blade scrambled to his right, looking every which way. Harvell was limping up the road behind Lang as fast as he could, holding the Quotron in his right hand like a talisman to ward off evil spirits.

Lang walked past the two startled Marine sentries at the yellow tape. Roberts, on Lang's left, and Blade, slightly uphill to the right, ducked under the tape, not even noticing it. The sentries looked at Colonel Bullard, who halted at the tape as if it were an electric fence. This was diplomatic territory. Bullard was tempted to barge through. But what would he do then, tackle Lang? Behind him, his Marines were as puzzled as the Serb soldiers, both sides staring at a drama they didn't understand.

"Where's the admiral?" Bullard said to the bewildered sentries.

"In the command amtrac, sir," the sentry replied, pointing to the trac with the satellite dish, a stone's throw to the left of the tape, slightly up-slope. As Bullard trotted toward it, the admiral emerged from its hatch, bent over, not seeing what was going on.

Lang stumbled against the tan Toyota and leaned against the roof, the lightness of the woman not affecting him, breathing hoarsely, the shakes almost convulsing him, trying to remember what he was doing. He saw the bear coat a few meters away. He had lost all feeling in his legs, and his arms were shaking as if firing a .50-caliber without any base mount. His brain, his consciousness, had shrunk down to one thought. *The big man killed this woman. Not over yet.*

As Lang lurched forward from the pickup, Saco moved away from the stone wall, and both his companions came alert. He sensed this wet, quivering American with a dead *hadjuk* on his shoulder was one of them, the killers of Luc and his nephew and the others. Saco was frightened. He could feel the blood leave his face. Bile rushed up from his stomach like a sudden flame. He swallowed back the vomit.

He reached his right hand deep into the folds of his left sleeve and grasped the knife hilt. He wouldn't break, wouldn't run again. That had been a mistake. He wasn't a fool, like that Milosevic. No rotting in a prison cell for him. He was Saco. The Muslims were animals. The Americans were animals. Saco told himself that, knowing he feared the shaking man in front of him, refusing to give up, refusing to admit it was finished. They would see, all of them. He was Saco.

As Caulder's spotter, Cosgrove was no help. He could see Lang and the man in the bear coat coming closer and closer together, but he didn't know what he was supposed to do. He didn't know he was the judgment man, designating the target to be killed.

"Mark going . . . up to . . . the giant," Cosgrove said.

Caulder was taut behind the scope. Three hundred meters was warm-up range. He was shaking from the cold, trying to hold steady.

"Give me green, sir. I'll put his lights out." *Come on, get this over with.* No answer from Cosgrove.

"Sir, Lang had my ass when I shot without permission. Tell me to light him up. That's all I need."

Cosgrove understood. He tried to speak and no words came out. His head wouldn't process the air coming from his lungs. He shut his eyes and blocked out everything except speaking, tried to force the words out. What was wrong with his head?

"Sir, tell me to pop him. Cosgrove, goddamn it! That fucker's dangerous. Nod or do fucking something. Let me light him up—*now!*"

Cosgrove's tongue would not find voice. He lay there hearing Caulder, agreeing with him, wanting the giant dead. He couldn't speak. His head was splitting. He pounded his fists and vigorously nodded his head up and down. *Yes! Yes!* He banged his forehead against the frozen earth. Not smart. He kept banging his head.

"Okay, okay, I got it. Good to go," Caulder said, his tone changing to the sniper's prayer. "Green light, good night."

Caulder had Lang in the center of the reticle, the bear coat a little to the left. He shifted the barrel left and tightened on the trigger. *Damn!* Harvell was hobbling up, his fat head in the way. *Dumb-ass.* "Get out of there, Harvell," he muttered, "get out of there."

Now directly in front of Saco, Lang could smell the huge man's breath, fetid like a carrion eater's.

"You left something," Lang said, and moved to hand the dead woman to Saco.

Quick as a blink, Saco's hand leaped out of the sleeve. The long, thin blade thrust forward. A wrist flick and it was back in the sleeve.

Lang felt the stab, deep, a burning nail that took his breath away. *Son of a bitch,* he thought. *Doc Evans is not going to like this.* He stood paralyzed. For an instant he saw Sylvia, with that half-smile of hers, welcoming him. Then there was blinding white, like a light turned on without warning in the bedroom at night, only brighter, a corridor of light. All was white.

Evans was watching the monitor, disbelieving. Lang's heart rate a few minutes ago had come down to one hundred. Good. Now the rate was sixty, fifty, thirty. Thirty! Diastolic eighty, seventy . . .

"Code red! Code red!" she screamed. "It's Lang. Someone get to him! Now! All radios, call, for God's sake. Call for the nearest corpsman to stabilize him! Get to him now. He's going under! Anyone near him, help him! Call, call! Help him! Don't stand there! Call! Call! Someone, anyone, get to him. Now! Now! What's the matter with you all? Are you blind?"

In the Combat Operations Center, the network crew tried not to breathe, knowing if one Marine took notice of them, they were out in the snow. The cameraman kept the focus on the thin blond woman in front of the screens. Every few seconds he zoomed in on the monitors above her head, then dropped back to her, keeping the lens tight.

The President watched the television screen, tightening his grip on the arms of his chair.

"Come on, Lang, come on," he said.

General Scott stared straight ahead, his elbows on the table, hands clasped under his chin, fingers white with strain. His radio operator in Quang Tri had taken some shrapnel in the elbow, a minor wound. His heart had stopped while Scott was joking with him. Shock hit each person differently.

At Sylvia's house Alex had dropped her cup of coffee on the Persian rug, in front of the TV, where the stain spread unnoticed.

The woman slipped off Lang's shoulder. He stood still, lost in the dazzling white light, beyond pain, thinking he didn't want to fall, not in front of his men. He bent his knees and knelt, his buttocks resting on his heels. He tried to draw a breath.

Roberts had seen a glint, nothing more, as if it hadn't happened. The captain was standing, arms at his sides, now sliding down onto his knees. It took another second for Roberts to think, *Knife!*

"Nooo!" he screamed, raising the AK full-length above his head, then jerking his arm down as if pulling hard on a chain.

Harvell bent over to see what was wrong with the skipper. Caulder fired, the bullet slamming Saco back against the wall. Stunned, Saco brought his hand up to his chest, feeling the armored vest under his bear coat. It had slowed the bullet, but that made no difference. The next round hit him under the nose, shattering his front teeth and smashing out the back of his skull. Before he could fall, Caulder hit him once more, this time low in the neck, the force spinning the body to the right.

The soldier next to Saco was experienced. He knew Roberts had sent the signal that finished Saco. He brought his rifle up a second late. Roberts was holding out his Kalashnikov, firing with one arm, only a few meters separating them. The first burst hit the man in the crotch, and he screamed as he fell. Rounds chipped the stone wall and zinged away. Roberts stood flat-footed, legs wide apart, AK extended, firing burst after burst until the clip was empty.

The second soldier with Saco had turned toward Lang, perhaps to do him further harm, perhaps curious to see the knife wound. Whatever the reason, the result was the same. Harvell was tentatively touching Lang, trying to understand what was wrong, when the soldier moved forward. Shots followed immediately, and Harvell cringed, biting his tongue. He had only the Quotron. He swung it wildly at the soldier, who jerked back and tripped. Harvell scrambled forward, swinging, swinging.

The soldier on the antiaircraft gun saw Saco's head blow apart. He grasped a small wheel and frantically spun it, desperate to depress the muzzles. Bullard and the admiral were standing outside the command trac. The Marines in Bullard's battalion were frozen in place, some prone, some crouching, all confused, not knowing who to fire at or why, waiting for someone to tell them.

Blade had no such doubts. He shot the man in the antiaircraft-gun seat. At the first burst, the soldier jerked back but remained seated. A second burst and he slumped sideways. The third burst knocked him to the ground.

In five seconds it was over, three Serbs down, one Marine on his knees. Vice Admiral Faxon was striding forward, shouting, "Cease firing! Cease firing!" Tense, frightened, adrenaline pumping, Bullard's Marines and Kostica's bodyguards were eyeing one another, weapons semi-pointed.

"Move forward and disarm them," Bullard yelled at his Marines. "Keep open fire lanes. Shoot any Serb who raises a weapon."

The Marines moved forward in a line, rifles up to their shoulders, sighting down the barrels, screaming at the Serbs to drop their weapons, slapping their rifle stocks to drive the point home. The Serbs, moved by survival instinct, had no problem understanding. They placed their weapons on the ground and raised their arms.

The shouting stopped, and the only noise was a squealing, sobbing sound from Harvell, who was pounding the soldier, holding the shattered Quotron like a brick. The man's head was split open and he was thoroughly dead.

Faxon stood over Harvell. "That's enough, soldier, that's enough!"

Harvell, face strained and tear-stained, looked up at the admiral. "I'm a Marine, sir," he said, "a fucking Marine!"

He whacked the corpse one more time and dropped the bloodied Quotron. He half crawled the few feet to where Roberts and Blade stood, one on either side of the kneeling team leader. Blade had taken off his gloves and had his thumb on Lang's neck, feeling for a pulse. Roberts reached down his good hand for Harvell to hold.

"Corpsman up! Corpsman up!" Roberts was shouting.

Blade was holding Lang, almost rocking him, softly saying, "Goddamn it, goddamn it, goddamn it."

"Hurts like fire, Blade," Lang whispered, "can't move."

"We got you, sir, we got you," Blade said.

In less than a minute two corpsmen had cut open Lang's jacket and were peering at the wound. There was a finger-length slash high on the left chest, the blood oozing dark red, almost black, the white of bone glistening through the gash.

"Ugly wound," a corpsman said. "Let's get you out of here."

The corpsmen grabbed Lang under his shoulders for the short run to the waiting helicopter.

"Don't, don't. Can't breathe." Lang's voice sounded like a gasping ten-year-old's.

Roberts shoved the corpsmen back. Caulder strode up behind Roberts and pushed his way in, dropping the toboggan rope, forgetting about Cosgrove. The team members hovered on either side of Lang.

Lang was wheezing rapid, short breaths, little white puffs of steam hanging in the air as if from an invisible cigarette.

"All present or accounted for?" he whispered.

That snapped Caulder out of his shock. He turned around, lifted Cosgrove out of the toboggan and held him up by the back of his jacket. Cosgrove bent over and put his face close to Lang's eyes. "All present, bro," he said. Lang's lips were parted. Hanging over him like a puppet, Cosgrove waited for him to reply. It was a moment before he realized no steam was coming from Lang's open mouth.

ABOUT THE AUTHOR

F. J. Bing West, a Marine captain in Vietnam, was a member of the reconnaissance patrol that initiated Operation Stingray, attacks behind North Vietnamese lines. He rose to be Assistant Secretary of Defense for International Security Affairs in the Reagan administration. His company—*www.gamacorp.com*—trains Marines in combat decision-making. A graduate of Georgetown and Princeton Universities, he is the author of numerous articles on foreign policy as well as two books of nonfiction. He lives in Newport, Rhode Island, and Washington, D.C., and can be contacted at *www.westwrite.com*.